Readers' Comments:

The O'Connell Boy: Educating "The Wolf Child"
An Irish-American Memoir (1932-1950) by Tom O'Connell
(Sanctuary Unlimited)

"**Tom O'Connell connects with readers soul to soul.** He writes of personal challenges and achievements **in a way that inspires readers.**" "**Thanks for a terrific interview the other night.** I had no idea of your background or writing accomplishments until we agreed to talk on my show. **I am most impressed. Best of luck with this memoir.**"
—*Jordan Rich, WBZ News Radio 1030,*
Boston, Massachusetts

"**I read the manuscript in one day. I couldn't put it down.** It brought back old memories, some of which **I cried** and some **I laughed.** I felt like I was still in the time period of 1932-1950. **Your talent for writing is beyond anything I have read and I read 3 to 5 books a week.** Congratulations to you, Sir, for **I certainly enjoyed it.** Thank you."
—*Ethel Mace Thompson, Dedham, Massachusetts*

"**He provides lively impressions of his 'wolf child' life in homes run by Irish immigrants** . . . experiences in a **Catholic Charities group foster home** in Norwood and **with his grandmother** in East Dedham are **vividly highlighted** . . . memories are provided in **earthy dialogue sprinkled with wit, candor and affection.**"
—*The Dedham Times, Dedham, Massachusetts*

"It's like a stroll down memory lane and the memories are of a simpler and quieter time we were so lucky to be able to share. I really enjoyed the book. In fact, I'm reading it over."

—*Jean Barry, Norwood, Massachusetts*

"To put it mildly, former Norwood and Dedham resident Tom O'Connell didn't live a typical childhood . . . . experienced more trauma than most. The memoir is meant to touch on an orphan's feelings, quest for freedom, and struggle to find a place in the world through both the Great Depression and world War II."

—*Brian Falla, Daily News Transcript,*
Needham, Massachusetts

The O'Connell Boy:
Educating "The Wolf Child"

An Irish-American Memoir (1932-1950)

Tom O'Connell

Sanctuary Unlimited

The O'Connell Boy:
Educating "The Wolf Child"
An Irish-American Memoir (1932-1950)

Published in the United States by
Sanctuary Unlimited
P.O. Box 25, Dennisport, MA 02639

Library of Congress Control Number: 2002096026
ISBN :   Softcover   1-4134-6916-7

1. O'Connell, Tom 1932-   2. Journalists-United States-Biography.
3. History 4. Family Life 5. Rites of passage 6. Inspiration
7. Spiritual life. I. Title.

This book was printed in the United States of America.

To order additional copies of this book, contact:
Xlibris Corporation
1-888-795-4274
www.Xlibris.com
Orders@Xlibris.com
26727

Prologue

Once, very long ago, there was a boy who was separated from his family. From infancy he lived in a cave in the forest with wolves. When he was found, they tried to "civilize" him and taught him language. But if someone asked him his name, he simply responded, "The wolf."

Although I was not raised in a cave, when I heard this true story I identified with the wolf child because I have always felt so "different" from people raised in more traditional families.

This memoir takes a look across more than half a century at the "wolf child" experience that shaped my early years. The impressions I offer here were engraved on my mind during the years from birth to age eighteen (1932-1950).

Some three decades ago I began writing about the traumatic dislocations I experienced in my youth. Therefore, as I wrote this memoir in recent years, the wealth of impressions in my archive greatly helped me. Those impressions came in very handy when I revisited the lone wolf I was developing into as a boy and when I reflected on the people who populated my life.

As I review the story now, the sentimental passages bring tears and the outrageous passages bring laughter. Also, I need to note here that I view this adventure of "life" as an ever-changing saga that we illustrate with images comprised of thoughts and emotions that can at times be contradictory. But I think that goes with the complexity of the human condition.

This is a story about real people who could be open and honest, passionate and intense, eccentric and odd. I remember well what they were like, and despite any flaws that I may have revealed here, I have loved each and every one of them. They did the best they could to cope with life, in their own way. Each of them made a lasting impression on me, and they enriched my life during those very sensitive early years.

1

Some people seem to arrive on this planet during very good times, and others are fated to arrive during difficult periods. It was February 11, 1932, when I came screaming into the Greater Boston area after an unusually long struggle to make my escape from my mother's womb. It also happened to be the time of the Great Depression, an economic collapse that had plunged America into daily fiscal disaster and enormous stress.

My father, who was known as Fred O'Connell even though his first name was Thomas, was one of the unemployed. All I know about those early years is based on a series of very disconnected impressions, and a jigsaw puzzle of fragments of conversation dropped into my ears by my father during random conversations many years later.

It seems that my mother, Margaret Henderson, was employed as cashier at Children's Hospital in Boston when my father met her. He told me that they soon fell in love, and nearly five years before I was born they married secretly because of family biases about religion.

My mother's family had a Scottish and Protestant background, while my father was an Irish-American Roman Catholic. In those days the two faiths were incompatible, so even though Margaret and Fred were married, they pretended to be single and stayed for a while in their respective homes.

After their marriage came out in the open, they remarried in the Catholic Church, formed their own home, and tried for years to have a child. But they were unsuccessful. Then the family doctor told them, "You're trying too hard." It seems that by being more relaxed, they were able to conceive me.

Apparently, the pregnancy went smoothly, but the birth process in a rented house on Curve Street in Dedham did not. The labor was prolonged, and according to my father, the moment I was born "everything deteriorated."

At the time when I made my entrance into this journey we call life, there were many home births like mine. The idea of being hospitalized had not yet taken hold. And there's no way of knowing whether a hospital environment would have helped my mother's severe postpartum depression.

In 1932, effective antidepressant medications had not yet been invented. Unfortunately, her depressed state of mind worsened, steadily moved her away from reality, and eventually led her into a state insane asylum where she was considered to be "terminally insane."

In the meantime, I became a difficult child. Being highly sensitive and stubborn, I cried loudly and often. Then, to complicate matters, when I was six months old one of my lungs collapsed and I lost half my body weight, which brought me to the brink of death. According to my father, I was restored to health at Children's Hospital in Boston.

When I was about a year old, my brother Jackie was born, and my mother was no longer able to care for us. To solve the problem, we were placed in separate temporary care situations somewhere in the Boston area. According to stories my father told, I lived with relatives and strangers, sometimes in very acceptable neighborhoods, and also in Boston area slums.

Jackie, I learned, was a friendly and calm child. As my opposite, he was easy, not difficult like me. But he suffered from neglect in the home where he was located, contracted pneumonia, and he died in my father's arms en route to the hospital in Boston. In an eerie coincidence, the date of his death at age one was February 11, my second birthday.

The earliest memory that stayed with me later on was the stiff, unreal image of Jackie in his casket during the wake that was held in the living room of Granny O'Connell's house. It was common then to hold wakes in homes, not in funeral parlors.

As for my mother, if she was already in a deep depression before my brother's untimely death, this tragedy certainly intensified her condition. It seems that when I was not yet three years old, she went back to live with her parents, who locked her in their attic, according to my father. He told me that when he finally got expert psychiatric care for her it was too late. She was committed to a state asylum where she was described as "incurably insane."

My father told me that the last time he and I saw my mother was during a visit in which she took my body in her arms and then heaved me into the air across the insane asylum lobby in an attempt to kill me. But he said I landed in a potted plant. I have no memory of that episode, nor do I have any other clear memories of my earliest years except for that still picture of my only brother lying in a casket.

From what I was told later by my father, I was bounced around in those early years like a piece of baggage with a confused destination label. I have no idea how many foster homes I lived in. But I know that from about age four to five I was living with my father and Granny O'Connell in her old duplex at 22 Walnut Place in East Dedham, next to the railroad station. I assumed that this would be my permanent home, but that was an erroneous assumption. Fate had other plans.

2

It was a humid summer day in 1937, and I was very quiet as my father's shiny new Plymouth sedan passed the "Entering Norwood" sign.

"It's a nice town, Tommy," I heard my father say, as if through some kind of echo chamber. "It's only a few miles from Dedham, and you'll like it at Mrs. White's. There are boys your own age to play with. It'll be better for you there."

I said nothing, but my mind was whirling with thoughts of going to live in a strange town with a woman I had never seen. My thoughts were not cheerful thoughts. Instead, they were angry thoughts. And they were aimed at the man who was supposed to be my father.

Not that I questioned the reality of my father's relationship to me, but I wondered how a father could leave me behind, over and over, in homes where I didn't want to be, and then take me back to Granny's where I really felt at home, and then once again take me away to another place where I didn't want to be.

During that ride from East Dedham to Norwood, I told myself I would never call Fred O'Connell "Dad" again. And when I made up my mind to do something I could be unusually resolute about it.

"The Bureau says Mrs. White's is one of their best homes," explained my father as we drove along Washington Street across the Westwood-Norwood town line. He pushed several strands of windblown hair into place over the growing bald area on his forehead. "You know your grandmother isn't well. She's found it hard keeping up with you. So there's no other choice right now. It'll work out for the best, Tommy. You'll see."

I said nothing as my five-and-a-half-year-old mind rejected my father's explanation. I was furious about being uprooted from Granny's old duplex near the railroad tracks. On the previous day, after I had heard the news about my impending departure, I had screamed and shouted ferociously, but the screaming and shouting had not stopped the packing of bags.

Additional screaming and shouting before we had left had not stopped the trip in my father's new Plymouth on this overcast August Sunday. So now I had switched from boisterous outrage to stubborn silence. My dark brown eyes were rimmed with an irritated redness and were watery now, and my chest and stomach were aching, but I held back the tears.

I'm not gonna stay there, I thought as we left the cobblestone main street and took a left turn near Clark's Pharmacy at the corner of Washington Street and Railroad Avenue. I'm just gonna run away from there first chance I get.

As we drove by a cluster of factories, I took in an exotic smell. Then we bounced over some railroad tracks, made a left turn, and a couple of minutes later we stopped in front of a large dark brown house with white trim and a small front porch.

I hate this place, I thought as my father said, "It's a nice house, Tommy. It's much better than your grandmother's." I stared straight ahead. I didn't share my father's opinions on my new location. There was only one place where I wanted to be, and it made no difference to me that Granny's place was old and small. I loved it there.

My father's large-veined hand reached out and touched the back of my head and rubbed it. "I guess we'd better go in now. It's time." I felt like I needed to vomit, and I also felt like pushing my father's hand away, but instead I just sat quietly staring through the windshield with blurred vision, looking at nothing in particular.

My father's hand paused softly on the nape of my neck. "I love you, Tommy. I'll be up to see you as often as I can." The tears began to push their way from my eyes as I thought, If you say you love me why are you putting me in this stupid place? You're sick of me, or else you'd keep me. But I'm not gonna stay here. Nope. I don't know where I'll go, but I won't stay here in this stinkin' place.

"I'll get your things from the back seat and we'll go in." My father's voice seemed to be coming at me like part of a bad dream. But it was no dream. And the reality of it almost paralyzed me. The reality of it was very present in my mind as I balked at leaving the Plymouth. The reality was there when I started screaming in outrage as my father pulled me up the front walk. And the reality was there as I continued to scream in outrage for the better part of five days.

3

At the end of the fifth day though, when my tear ducts were just about bone dry and my throat was aching and my chest muscles were constricted, I knew that my rage was not going to return me to Granny O'Connell's. I knew the world wasn't going to adjust to my wishes. And I knew that everybody else was fed up with my crying.

"Hey, I want to tell ya somethin', Tommy." It was the friendly voice of the dark-haired boy my own size, but I held my head in its face-down position against the tear-soaked pillow, and I kept my body in its prone position on the large double bed.

For nearly five days I had stubbornly maintained that posture, and I was not planning to give it up without a struggle. "Aw, come on, Tommy. I want to tell ya somethin'."

For five days I had refused to communicate, had answered no questions, and had asked no questions. I had ignored the presence of all the other boys, including the two in my bedroom. And I had refused to acknowledge the existence of my new guardian, Mrs. White.

Well, I thought, maybe I ought to listen to this kid. Maybe I should stop cryin' now. I'm gettin' sick o' cryin' anyhow. Moving my head a little, I opened my eyes and looked up at the dark-haired boy. But I still said nothing, holding my tears in check, figuring the other boy would understand that I was willing to listen.

"I don't want to scare ya, Tommy, but in Boston there's a place worse than this where they send kids like us. It's The House of the Angel Guardian, and it sounds nice, but it's wicked there. They beat up kids, and whip 'em and everything. Bobby Resker says there's a boy named Chocolates that just left here, and he came from there and he had scars all over his back from the whippings. So you ought to stop cryin'. Anyhow, when people leave kids in this place, they don't come back even if ya cry your head off."

"But I don't want to live here."

"You have to. Anyhow, we can be pals. I'm gonna be in the first grade same as you."

I pulled myself to a sitting position. "I guess I'll try and stop cryin'." I looked around the room next to the attic on the third floor and I thought, I hate this stupid room way up in the air. I hate the way the ceilin' prackly comes right down on top of us. I don't want to live here. But I guess I won't be goin' to East Dedham to Granny's house. My father won't take me back. He doesn't want me anymore.

"I'm Dave Rothwell." The dark-haired boy held out his hand and smiled. "We just came here too, me and my brother Joe." For the first time in five days I smiled, because I was feeling a hint of something other than horror and unhappiness. Dave's friendly message had reached me.

We shook hands and I said, "My name's Thomas O'Connell Frederick Junior." I gave him my version of what I thought was my full name. Dave laughed and asked me what my "reg'lar name" was. Then I said, "Tommy." And Dave told me, "We were all wonderin' when you was gonna stop bawlin'."

Up the stairwell came Mrs. White's voice. "'Tis time for supper, David."

"Okay, Mom. Be right down." He nudged me and whispered, "Everybody here calls her Mom, so you better too."

I nodded and said nothing. I questioned the idea of calling this woman "Mom" as the others did. As far as I was concerned, she was not my mother and I had not asked to be housed with her, and I didn't care what the others did. I was only concerned with my own predicament. No "Mom" White for me.

"Has the O'Connell boy stopped his blatherin' yet?" It was Mrs. White's voice again.

Dave shouted, "He just stopped."

"Well, 'tis grand to hear that. Thanks be to God for small favors. Bring him down with ye to supper."

"Okay, Mom." Dave turned to me. "We better get goin'. If you don't do things quick around here you get the switch on your behind."

Although I didn't know what the switch was, I didn't like the sound of it, so I decided not to resist the supper invitation, and as I went down the stairs I wiped the remaining tears from my swollen eyelids. ". . . five boys would be plenty, Margaret." I could hear a man talking as we neared the kitchen. "You've got your hands full already."

Into the large kitchen went Dave, with me close behind. At her gleaming white Glenwood gas stove, the Irish widow, Mrs. White, was there energetically stirring the steaming contents of an oversized blue enamelware pot. "Sure they were the farthest away and praise be to God they're first to the table."

"They look like two stray ponies," said the man with the gray-black hair. "But they'll fill out soon. Maggie White's stew and dumplin's will stick to your ribs, boys." I wondered what he meant by food sticking to my ribs. How could it do that?

My head was tilted downward, with my eyes fixed on the geometric pattern of the white and green inlaid linoleum. When the man's feet came toward me I didn't look up. "I'm Mister Vincent, the boarder." As I looked up, I saw the man Mrs. White called "Charless" peering down at me through steel-rimmed spectacles. "It's good to have you here with us now, Master O'Connell." Charles Vincent's gentle hand took mine, shook it lightly, then released it. I didn't understand the use of the word "Master," but I didn't ask about it either.

"He's a quiet one, Margaret."

Her voice resounded through the kitchen, "Sure it hasn't been quiet since he set foot on the front piazza, Charless. In all my born days I never heard the like o' his cryin' and blatherin'. Jesus, Mary, and Joseph, 'twas enough to drive a person daft."

I slowly raised my eyes and carefully examined the heavy woman who was to be my guardian. She had large fleshy arms, powder-white skin, blue-white hair, a round ruddy face, and rimless glasses perched on her small nose. In her large right hand she wielded an oversized spoon that she was using to stir the concoction brewing on the range. Her free hand shot out then, and tapped the side of my head.

"Faith and your eyes will be red for a month o' Sundays, Tommy O'Connell."

"Here come the rest of the Indians," announced the boarder as the other boys crowded into the kitchen and pulled me along with them toward the white enameled-steel table surrounded by wooden chairs that were painted a shiny white. "Take that chair near the wall, Thomas," ordered Mom White. "That's your place from now on. And mind ye, don't ye forget it." I took my seat as commanded.

Mister Vincent introduced me to the other boys and explained that Dave Rothwell was going into the first grade as I was, his brother Joe was going into the second, Bobby Resker into the fourth, Richard Roy into the ninth, and John Desmond had already graduated from Norwood High School.

As the introductions were made, each boy nodded politely at me, and I nodded shyly at each of them. I wondered why they were so quiet. At this point I had not learned Mrs. White's commandment: "There'll be no blatherin' at the table, and ye'll speak only when spoken to."

After the food was served, Mrs. White sat in the chair nearest the stove. Then there was a sudden burst of action. When Joe Rothwell's hand reached toward the dish full of bread, Mrs. White's large arm flashed through the air and her chubby fist whacked the back of the outstretched hand. Joe withdrew it, breadless, and massaged it to ease the pain. "There'll be no boardin' house reachin' in the White house," she warned. "I told ye that yesterday, Joseph. When I say a thing I say it once and that's that." Mrs. White took the large plate of bread, passed it first to Mister

Vincent, then to the older boys across the table, then to Dave and Joe, and finally to me.

I was learning about seniority, along with the other clear message that it was self-destructive to reach out for items on the White table. As I thought about her strictness, I heard Joe noisily slurping his stew. "We don't eat like pigs here, Joseph," she warned. "We eat like human bein's. If the stew's hot for ye, let it cool off a mite."

I leaned over to watch Joe's reaction. "What are ye lookin' at, Thomas?" Her brow was furrowed as her electric blue eyes drilled into my brown ones.

"Nothin'," I mumbled, with my face reddening as she focused her attention on me. "What is it ye said? We don't mumble here. We mind our own bee's wax and when we eat we keep our eyes on our own plate and ye speak when spoken to. And we say please when we ask for somethin' and we say thank you when we get it. And when I land on one of ye if another one gets too nosy he gets the back o' me hand in his puss."

I paid close attention to her lecture, with deep fear building up inside of me. I did not want the back of her strong hand. As I continued to eat, I thought about the difference between Granny's house and this new place. I could talk at Granny's and grab things if I felt like it, but Mrs. White was much stricter.

At age five-and-a-half I was learning fast that I was under Mrs. White's jurisdiction, like it or not, and there was no questioning her authority. In the house at 42 Mountain Avenue in Norwood it was extremely clear that she was undisputed monarch.

4

Later that evening, as I was getting ready for bed with Dave and Joe, Dave said, "What a crier you are, Tommy. I never heard anyone cry so much."

"Didn't you cry when they took ya here?"

"A little, but I never saw anybody bawl like you."

"Well, I'm not bawlin' now."

Joe took off his undershirt. "We thought you was never gonna stop cryin'. We could hardly sleep or anythin'."

I shrugged my shoulders and slipped into my pajama bottoms. Then I noticed a massive scar on Joe's chest. "What's that?"

"Where I was burnt when I was little. My sister spilled a pot o' hot coffee on me and I almost died."

Dave explained, "He's okay now though."

Joe added, "Except the skin's tight where the scar is." His chest seemed sunken, as if the taut skin were pulling him inward.

We all became quiet. Then I thought about Joe's infringement of the supper table rules. "Joe, did she hurt ya when she hit your hand?"

"Yuh, she can really hurt a kid." I looked toward the stairwell, then whispered, "I hate it here."

"Me too," said Joe. "She's a pain in the behind."

"She better not hear ya talkin'," warned Dave.

"Who cares?" Joe shrugged his round shoulders. "She ain't my mother."

"Ya gotta do what she says," said Dave, "or else you'll get licked or switched."

"How come she licks everybody?" I asked.

"I dunno," said Joe. "She just does."

Dave fired a question at me. "When's your Pop gonna take you back? After the elementary school's all done? Like our Pop's gonna do?"

As I tried to reply, tears filled my eyes. "I dunno. He . . . didn't . . . say . . ."

"Oh brother," said Joe, "I hope he ain't gonna go and cry five more days."

I wiped the new tears from my eyes and said, "I won't cry anymore."

"You got any brothers 'n sisters?" asked Joe.

"Nope." I shook my head. "I had a little brother once but he got sick and died."

"We got five sisters and five brothers," said Joe proudly. "There's twelve of us . . . and Pop."

"Our Mom died," added Dave, "so we had to come here." Dave's eyes became watery.

"Some of our older brothers and sisters are stayin' with Pop," Joe explained. "But us little kids had to go, so me and Dave came here a couple o' weeks ago and some of our sisters went to a convent."

"What's a convent?" I asked.

Joe shrugged his shoulders. "Some kind of a holy place, I guess."

Dave sniffled, wiped his nose, and asked, "You got a mother, Tommy?"

I shook my head.

"Is she dead?"

"I dunno."

"How come ya don't know?" asked Joe.

"I never saw her and nobody said she's dead either."

"If you never saw her she's dead," said Joe with authority.

I responded, "They said my brother was dead but nobody said that about my mother."

"She's prob'ly dead," said Joe.

"Yuh, she's dead," said Dave. "Like our Mom."

"Maybe," I said.

I hated their questions and their comments and wished they would mind their own business. But the questioning continued and I didn't know how to answer the two of them. "Who did ya stay with?" asked Joe.

"My father and Granny." The tears came pouring down.

Then Dave's hand squeezed my shoulder. "It's okay. Even if it's wicked here we can be pals and have fun and stuff."

Mrs. White's voice came up the stairwell. "It's off to sleep with ye or I'm up to ye with the switch. It's early to bed and early to rise."

"Okay, Mom," replied Dave.

"Okay, Mom," said Joe.

I said nothing because I had decided to maintain silence instead of using her name.

When Joe was asleep on the other side of the double bed, and Dave was dozing in the middle position near his brother, I lay wide awake, gazing at the shadows on the sloped ceiling. There were tears in my eyes as I conjured up grotesque figures in the shadows. The night was not my favorite time. I had often cried myself to sleep in East Dedham after hearing my father's car drive off, and Granny, who was partially deaf, had seldom climbed the stairs to comfort me.

I don't want to be here in this place, I thought as the tears began to flow down my cheeks. I want to be back on Walnut Place in East Dedham. I really hate Norwood and I hate this house. He said The Bureau picked out Mrs. White special. What do I care about the stupid Bureau? I thought a bureau was a thing with drawers. But I guess it's a place where they take kids from their houses and put 'em in other people's houses. He was callin' them on the phone and Granny and him were talkin' about The Bureau and I didn't even know what they were talkin' about. I hate The Bureau for puttin' me here. I wish I was back at Granny's so I could play with my pals. He said Granny wasn't feelin' good and she couldn't keep up with me so I had to go to

Mrs. White's house and he said I'd like it here. But I hate this stinkin' place.

I didn't even talk to him in the car, I recalled as I lay there crying. I didn't want to talk to him. I knew he was takin' me away and leavin' me some other place and I knew him and Granny must have been sick o' me. Else they would have kept me. I thought he'd come get me if I cried a lot. But he didn't come. Nope. He just left me here and went away and he won't come back 'cause he doesn't even like me anymore.

I began sobbing in a muffled way as I tried to sleep in the third floor finished room next to the attic in Margaret White's house at 42 Mountain Avenue in Norwood. I was in a room I did not wish to be in, with people I did not want to be with, in a town I did not want to live in. And in this very busy house I felt completely alone.

5

Mrs. White had ordered Bobby Resker to take us to the end of Mountain Avenue to "the woods" and act as our guide. He seemed to be enjoying his role. "That's Sled Tree. See way up where the sled is? Some day I'll double dare you kids to climb up there. But you gotta have old clothes on. She'll kill you if you wreck your good ones. There's lots of shinnyin' to do around here, lots of good trees. When you go up Sled Tree you can see prackly all over Norwood."

"This ain't bad," said Joe, "havin' our own woods at the end of Mountain Avenue."

"We'll come down here a lot," said Dave.

"Yuh," I said with minimum enthusiasm. I was slower than the Rothwell brothers in adjusting to my new neighborhood.

"Follow me," said the fair-haired Bob, who was going into the fourth grade at the Cornelius M. Callahan School. "I'll show you Hangman's Tree." He explained how a man had once fixed a noose around his own neck and leaped from a high branch of the tree and committed suicide at that very spot.

Then we found a large smooth flat rock and sat cross-legged on it while Bobby filled us in on life at the White house. "If you don't do what she says, you get the switch. That's a long stick from a bush in case you've never seen one. She makes us get 'em ourselves, and if they aren't big enough or long enough she makes you go out and get the kind that really hurts when you get it across the legs or on your rear end."

"Does it hurt awful?" asked Dave.

24

"You'll find out soon enough. Oh yuh, there's one thing she does that's worse than switchin' if she catches you lyin' or stealin' stuff. She hates liars and thieves worse than anything. So she takes you down cellar by the ear and she shoves your head in that old toilet down there and she flushes it all around your head till you promise you're not gonna lie or steal again." I could feel my stomach turning.

"She's real fussy about things. She hates it if you answer her back or talk at the table before you're spoken to, and if she finds any dirt on your knuckles at supper 'cause you didn't brush 'em hard enough with the stiff brush, she has a fit. You better not mumble when she talks to you either, or squeal on anybody. She hates squealers."

"How come she hates so many things?" asked Joe.

"She just does, that's all."

"It's wicked livin' here," I said.

"Sometimes it's wicked," said Bobby, "and other times it isn't so bad. We get to go to the movies and her desserts are really something and she makes fresh bread on Saturdays. All kinds. Raisin and bran and white, and sometimes she makes bread puddin'. That's everybody's favorite. And we get to go to Neponset Valley Farm for ice cream cones sometimes, too. They give big ones down there. Especially if you know a guy that works there. Let's see, what else? Oh yuh, sometimes after she makes cakes she lets us lick the frostin' bowl. Uh-oh, I almost forgot. She said I could take you guys down to Furlong's for some penny bags."

"Yum. Let's go now." "Yuh, let's go." "Yuh."

Bobby took us along Mountain Avenue to a rocky path that led to Hill Street next to the railroad tracks. Then we walked by the place with the exotic smell that came from tanned leather, and soon we were strolling along Central Street by a tavern that Bobby described as "The Irish Heaven." It was a nearly windowless structure with its front door wide open.

Bobby explained, "The old guys drink whiskey and play cards in there. Listen to 'em." Their gruff whiskey-soaked voices were uttering exaggerations as we carefully edged our way past that dimly lit saloon where large men's silhouettes hovered over board games and they tilted their glasses high.

The next thing we saw up ahead was the Police Station, and across the street we saw the large red fire trucks at the Fire Station. Behind the Municipal Building was the compact one-story building with white bars. "That's the jail," Bobby explained. "It's always filled up with drunks on Monday mornings." In those days public intoxication was a crime.

As we neared our most important destination, Furlong's candy and ice cream store, Bobby pointed toward the Norwood Theatre, another very important location in Norwood. It was the place where boys let out very loud burps during love scenes and threw popcorn over the balcony railing onto the innocent people down below.

Bobby explained that this was the place where we would be entertained every Saturday afternoon, and sometimes on Sundays. "They show newsreels called the March of Time, and they've got serials between movies too, like Tarzan." The serials only lasted a few minutes, and always ended with a brave hero or heroine being threatened by a crocodile, a fiendish villain, or a long drop over a waterfall as high as the Empire State Building, which in those days was the world's tallest building. But in the next episode the brave ones always survived, and went on to conquer.

There was another place to see movies too, Bobby explained. "It's the Guild Theater, but it's crummy. The movies they show there aren't so hot, and the projector's always breakin' down." He pronounced its name as "Guy-elled" and said it was located further along Washington Street at the end of the shopping area. "They don't have a balcony like they do here."

In the late 1930s, movies added to the sense of community. Everybody went to see the same films and would discuss them for days. Also, having the movies run continuously allowed a viewer to arrive late and pick up the missing opening of the story later. This behavior led to the expression, "This is where I came in," a comment I still use in situations that have no relationship to movies.

When we finally reached Furlong's, which was right next to the movies, Bobby Resker gave each of us a penny. Then we went inside this kids' paradise and stood in the penny bag line.

A minute later, a thin gray-haired man in a green apron leaned over the counter and gave each of us a waxed-paper envelope that was overflowing with bits of fudge, broken candies, and deformed chocolates. "You boys were just in time," he said with a grin. "That's all the penny bags for today." His comment made the desirable contents of the elusive penny bags seem all the more delicious.

Before we returned to Mountain Avenue, Bobby led us down the street a bit and then pointed toward the Sport Center on Cottage Street and said, "That's where people go bowlin' and play pool and stuff. When you guys get older maybe you can go there. They hire pinboys there too, and I know some kids that do that, but they have to duck when the pins go flyin' and sometimes the bowlers start rollin' the balls before the kids have a chance to leap up to the special platform where they can be sort of safe. Next I'm gonna show you guys where we get haircuts."

Back to Nahatan Street we went, and up a small hill to Washington Street, where Bobby showed us the barbershop where we would get haircuts before going to school in September. "Nick's pretty good, but sometimes he pulls your hair too much with the clippers."

A few doorways past the barber shop we passed a store with a large amount of empty floor space in it. "That's the Waiting Room. Bonica owns it. It's where the Boston bus stops every half hour, and people can go in there and wait. They've got great licorice in there too, the red kind and the black. Next week we'll prob'ly go to Bonica's to get the bus to Boston when we go to Kennedy's. That's a big store in the middle of the city where she gets all our clothes for school.

"On the way to Kennedy's we get to go up the escalator at Forest Hills and we ride on the Elevated. It's like a train, but it's way up in the air. We'll get all kinds of clothes at Kennedy's. Knickers for best and for school. Regular shirts, polo shirts, jerseys, overalls, knee sox, underwear, pajamas, mackinaws, mittens. Everything. We get a lot of stuff in there."

Bobby led us back toward Nahatan Street, and as we left Washington Street to go toward Mountain Avenue, he said, "Some people call where we live Cork City. I think Mrs. White lived sort of near there in Ireland, in a little town named Rathmore. The other side of Washington Street over there they call Dublin. Those are Irish names, and I guess almost everybody in Norwood's Irish. Mom says there's only two kinds of people in the world, the ones who are Irish Catholics and the people who wish they were. I'm German and Catholic. At White's everyone's a Catholic, and almost everybody's Irish around here."

"I think we're mostly Irish," said Joe Rothwell.

"Me too," I said, remembering Granny describing herself as "Irish born and bred."

Bobby deftly changed the subject. "That's Saint Catherine's Church where we go." He pointed to a large Gothic structure with a sign out front that said, "St. Catherine of Siena." Then he seemed to fix his attention on me. "Everybody at our house goes to Mass there every Sunday." I didn't know what Mass was, but Granny had talked about it often.

Soon we left Nahatan Street and went up Central Street to Railroad Avenue, where we walked between two low-slung buildings that made the street seem like a deep canyon. Then Bobby said, "This is the Winslow Brothers and Smith tannery. They tan sheepskin in there. We get hunks of it to polish our shoes. Wait till you see the shine it makes."

On we went, across the tracks, past the small railroad station, and up the rocky path that led to Mountain Avenue. As we walked, Bobby kept telling us the rules of the house. "Boy, is she fussy about our clothes. She has a fit if we get them dirty or rip 'em. She says you're judged by the way you look, and she wants us to be the neatest kids in Norwood."

"How come?" asked Joe, kicking a rock with his right shoe and scuffing it in the process.

"She just does. And you better not wreck your shoes or you'll get the switch."

"Who cares?" said Joe.

Bobby responded, "You'll care if she makes you do twice as much stuff when we clean the house on Saturday morning. She'll probably make you get tons of vegetables in the cellar, and run a million errands. And if you complain about doin' stuff she'll give you ten times as much to do, so if you're smart you'll keep your trap shut."

"I don't care," said Joe with a shrug.

"You'll care," said Bobby. "I really hate gettin' vegetables in the cellar. It's dark and spooky down there with cobwebs and everything. I don't mind goin' down there to the bathroom in that old toilet, but I hate it when I have to go in that room where she keeps all the piccalilli and carrots and potatoes and stuff."

"Who's scared of that?" said Joe. "That cellar's nothin'. What I hate is that stupid attic."

Bobby said, "But we don't even have to go in the attic very much, except when she puts us in there for punishment."

"I hate sleepin' next to it," said Joe.

As for me, I hated both the thought of the dark attic and the dark room off the cellar where I knew I'd be sent to get vegetables and preserves. I had an intense fear of darkness. It meant nightmare time.

That evening, after having a supper of frankfurters and beans, we took our Saturday night bath in shifts. I shared the tub with Dave Rothwell in water left after Joe and Bobby had taken their baths. And we had to use stiff brushes to get any trace of dirt out of the little creases on our knees, elbows and knuckles.

Upstairs, in the third floor finished room, as we were putting on our pajamas, I shook myself out of my silence and asked Joe, "What's Depression?"

"Our Dad always talks about jobs when he says Depression. I think it's when lots of people ain't got work."

"Oh," I said, "I was just wonderin'. And I was wonderin' about somethin' else Mrs. White said too. What's a lukewarm Catholic?"

Joe replied, "I think she means people that don't go to Church every Sunday. She's from Ireland and she thinks Church is swell and hates people that don't go all the time."

"Where's Ireland?" asked Dave. "Near Canada?"

"Naw," said Joe. "It's far off and all the people that come from there talk sort of funny like Mom White and those people across the street near . . ."

Her voice came booming up the stairwell, "It's off to sleep up there, or I'll be up with the switch to the lot of ye."

The talking ceased, and I was alone with my thoughts of the differences between this new place and the familiar old house on Walnut Place. The dull black iron Magee stove at Granny O'Connell's. The shiny white Glenwood at Mrs. White's. Granny's old ice box. And "The Frigidaire" at Mrs. White's.

Everything's different here, I thought as I lay looking at the shadows on the sloped ceiling above the double bed where the three of us slept. My mind swirled with thoughts of Sled Tree and Hangman's Tree and penny bags and having to go to Mass at St. Catherine's Church the next day, and I trembled as I considered how I might get switched or have my head shoved down the toilet if I messed up my good clothes. Then, as I had been taught to do by Granny, I made the Sign of the Cross and whispered sleepily to myself, "Angel of God, my guardian dear, to whom his love commits me here, ever this day be at my side . . . ever this day . . . ever this . . ."

6

Time passed slowly for me during that first year at Mrs. White's house because I was always in a state of tension. Fear was the underlying emotion for me in that home, no matter how good things were at times. How can I explain my feelings? How does an innocent prisoner with an indefinite sentence feel? How can I explain feeling like a lone wolf even though I was surrounded by people? But it was my reality.

Except in flights of fancy, I couldn't hope for a future with Granny O'Connell and my father at 22 Walnut Place in Dedham. I was definitely stuck at Mrs. White's in Norwood, where I didn't want to be. So, in a very determined way, I resisted any internal resignation to life under her control. Yet I outwardly conformed to her wishes to avoid being the victim of her terrifying punishments.

As for the lives we had lived before arriving at Mrs. White's, we boys spent very little time talking about that. And we avoided complaining publicly. In those days if you complained about anything at all you were called a "crybaby," so we learned to keep our most painful frustrations to ourselves. But in an unspoken way, we certainly shared a common bond of horrendous inner pain which brought us very close to each other.

On another level, when we were with each other away from the house we were very open in private discussions of current events in the household. Out of earshot of Mrs. White we could talk about our guardian fearlessly because we had a "no squealing" code of honor. Looking back, I realize that the other boys, especially Dave and Joe Rothwell, provided a mutual support group for me that helped ease the pain of my life as an exile.

With time, we shared group memories that gave us an endless supply of stories to recall. One such memory was the ferocious hurricane of '38, which caught us by surprise during our playtime in "the woods" at the end of the street. By the time we got back to the house we were crawling on all fours, and holding onto small bushes and trees to keep from getting blown away. But we all made it back safely.

That legendary storm removed large numbers of ancient trees and changed the face of our woods. For years to come we would be clambering over toppled trees and using them for games of all kinds. And the huge tree stumps eventually became giant anthills.

"Ye can go down the woods now, but be back in time for supper," was one of Mrs. White's standard lines. "The woods" at the end of Mountain Avenue ran along the length of Roosevelt Avenue toward the Callahan School. Those woods were a kids' domain and we engaged in some tribal rituals there that are better left undescribed here. And when I think back on it, I am amazed at how primitive we could get when we were away from Mountain Avenue and operating in our own little wilderness where the rules of civilization were suspended.

Being out in the elements was part of our daily adventure, during which we shared rituals designed to test each other's courage, like shooting uncooked peas at each other with our peashooters, and later aiming BB guns at each other's rear ends. We had a life of youthful adventures together as we chased each other and raced with strapped-on roller skates, or skated on thin ice, or rode too fast down steep hills on our tricycles, and later on bicycles. Most of all, we had each other during the howling winds, hailstones, snow, pelting rain, or scorching sun. It's no exaggeration to say we were together through thick and thin. For brief periods of time, in our own little world of close friendships, we could distract ourselves from the reality of our severed connections with home and family.

However, regardless of distractions, I was always haunted by my father's unpredictable behavior. On the one hand I longed for his visits, and on the other his long absences kept me in frustrating suspense. His infrequent visits flung me into a frustrating cycle of hope and deep disappointment, so at the end of each visit I felt wrung out emotionally. When he would say, "See you soon," I knew I might not see him again for months. And I was never able to adjust myself to his unpredictability.

Deep down, I'm sure I wanted my father to find a way to make up for my mother's loss. But he had his life to live, and he arranged to keep me from getting in his way. Maintaining his remoteness, he kept me on the outer fringes of his life, and the slim connection between us was very fragile. Never knowing where I stood with him, the very thought of him left me confused. Paradoxically, that confusion triggered a curiously strong emotional attachment to this mostly missing parent who was my only link to my family of origin and my life at Granny's place.

On reflection, there's a good chance that my habit of silence in my father's presence contributed to his long absences. But my gut reactions had a powerful life of their own. My inner fury about what he had done to me remained constant, and knowing that my fits of rage upon my arrival at Mrs. White's hadn't worked, I saw no other way to respond to him than through silence.

When we were together I was the exact opposite of an enthusiastic companion. Then, to make matters worse, when he picked me up in the shiny 1937 Plymouth I would usually get carsick. This was partly from the cigars he smoked and partly from the murky feelings his presence would stir up in me. Even when I was not carsick, when I was with him I would shrink deeply within myself, hiding in some sacred sanctuary way down inside, retreating to a silent place where I was safe from outside harm.

Shyness in the presence of adults was one of my most outstanding character traits in those days. In any group of people I was painfully self-conscious. I didn't want people's eyes aimed at me. But in school, even though it made me very anxious, I would raise my hand when I had the right answer. I was proud of being known as the smartest boy. And perhaps that achievement helped offset the deeper sense of alienation that I carried with me.

Alienation? Well, I certainly developed the mindscape of an exile at 42 Mountain Avenue, and my father's random visits served only to expand the defenses I erected to protect my overly sensitive psyche from destruction by terrifying outside forces. His visits were the only ones I recall receiving from any of the O'Connell relatives during my years at Mrs. White's. And no words are sufficient to describe the gnawing sense of loneliness and rejection I felt there.

Although it was a busy household where good times happened, there was nothing on the face of the earth during those years that could convince me to be happy for more than a few minutes. Actually, I distrusted the word "happy" and omitted it from my vocabulary. Nor was it a part of my inner reality during my time at Mrs. White's. Instead, my usual state was one of underlying apprehension and anxiety.

When Christmas eve of 1938 arrived, it was my second one at 42 Mountain Avenue, and I wondered if my father would come. I was in the big old bed with Dave Rothwell, in the third floor bedroom next to the attic. His older brother Joe had graduated to a private cot across the room. And it felt good not to have three of us sprawled all over each other, often farting in each other's faces and not admitting it, and sometimes one of us pissing the bed and in the process wetting the others, also without ever admitting it.

When you wet the bed at Mrs. White's you were publicly humiliated. "Shame on you!" That loud, clear voice came at you like a Celtic heroine's spear as she responded to the unacceptable behavior, and she knew exactly how to trigger shame in us. We had to take the sheets and underwear with the large yellow stains and hang them on the clothesline to air out before they were laundered, and this sent a visual message to all of our neighbors.

But on this Christmas Eve our bed was dry, and we were having a talk session when we heard Mom White's voice rush up the stairwell at us. "To sleep with the lot of ye now," she commanded.

"Okay," Joe shouted out. Dave said "Okay" too. And in my own private act of rebellion I said nothing.

Dave whispered to me, "Do you believe that stuff about gettin' the coal in your Christmas stockin' if we weren't good this year?"

"I dunno. But I know if we don't keep quiet we're gonna get it."

"Yuh, we better go to sleep. Merry Christmas, Tommy."

"Merry Christmas, Dave."

From across the room, in his cot under the dormer window, Joe said, "Merry Christmas, you guys." We returned his greetings.

Dave turned on his left side with his back facing me, and I turned on my right side. Then we crossed ourselves and silently said our evening prayers.

When the Rothwell brothers had drifted off to sleep, I stayed awake. I was usually the last to fall asleep because my mind was always racing, doing a review of the past, present, and future.

As I examined the shadows cast on the sloped ceiling by the street light outside, I thought, Maybe my father won't even come this Christmas. He hardly ever comes see me anymore. I wonder if he's gonna bring the Flexible Flyer sled I asked for. I hope so.

Christmas isn't too bad here. The tree touches the dining room ceilin' and we get some pretty good presents. She's wicked strict, but at least holidays are okay. I'm sort of getting a little used to it here now.

I wonder if Jimmy Dervan's gonna come over tomorrow. It's funny how he lives on the next street and always comes over here to talk to Mom White. I guess she tells him what to do when he gets mixed up. She's pretty good at tellin' people what to do. Jimmy's so tall. I wonder if I'll ever be as tall as him. My head's only up to his belt now.

I'm sort of glad Tom White's living back here now. I like him. He's very kind. I wonder why he didn't become a pilot like everyone thought he was gonna. It's funny with John Desmond gone. But he's lucky. At least he's livin' with his own uncle now. Some day I'll go back and live with Granny and my father. Then I won't get switched anymore. God, do I hate gettin' switched.

Brother, she gives ya the switch for everything, like when I ripped my overalls shinnyin' up Sled Tree, and when I whispered she was a pain in the behind for telling us off so much. Boy, she hated it when she was lickin' Joe that time and I said, "You don't have to hit him so hard." She gave it to me twice as hard as she gave it to him. I can still hear her yellin', "That'll learn ye to mind your own beeswax!"

When I mumbled at her under my breath while I was combin' the fringe on the parlor rug, that day I got it real good. If there's one thing I hate it's gettin' switched. Brother, she knows how to punish kids. She makes us go in and out and close the door quiet twenty times if she catches us slammin' it, and we have to stand in the corner for hours if we don't do somethin' right away.

But at least I have some fun with the Rothwells when we're outside. Like all the things we did last summer. Makin' tarpaper huts in the woods. Takin' ice chunks off the back of the ice truck. Buyin' all day suckers at Bonica's. Swimmin' over at Ballicky Pond. Pickin' blueberries. Sellin' them to Gertrude's Pastry Shoppe. Yuh, we had some good fun last summer. But I didn't mind goin' back to school. I guess that's 'cause I sort of like school and I like bein' the smartest kid in my class.

I hate these teeth though, I thought as I placed the fingers of my right hand against my two front teeth and pushed hard. Why'd I have to get these big teeth and all the freckles? I really wish there was no such thing. I wonder if he'll come tonight. He doesn't come see me much anymore. Ah, if he doesn't come, who cares? I'll have a good Christmas anyways. But I hope he comes.

Hearing a noise from below that sounded like a car, I slipped from my bed and peered out the window under the eaves. My heart raced when I saw my father walking toward the front door with a long package. It must be the sled, I thought. Yuh, that's what it is. Now I won't have to use cardboards to slide down Cemetery Hill and I won't have to beg for other kids' sleds anymore.

In a moment I heard voices down below as my father and Mom White began talking. I wondered what they were saying, and I decided to go down near the bathroom on the second floor to eavesdrop. I slipped out of my bed and quietly descended the flights of winding stairs, tiptoed along the second floor hallway, and stopped at the head of the stairs leading to the first level. Then I heard my father's voice clearly. ". . . and he was just a baby then."

"It was too bad." Mom White was talking. "That boy could have used a mother. There's a lot going on in that curly head but he keeps it mostly to himself."

"He doesn't have much to say anymore when I take him for rides."

"Sure an' he keeps it all inside him. How's his mother doin' now?"

"Not well. She's still at the insane asylum. I'm afraid she's there for good."

Insane asylum? I wonder what kind of place that is. It doesn't sound nice.

"There's no hope?" asked Mom White.

"None at all," replied my father. "They tried everything, but nothing could bring her back. It was hopeless."

Hopeless, I thought. That's what Mom White says when we slam doors. I guess it's like givin' up.

My train of thought was interrupted by Tom White's voice. "Why, hello, Tommy, what are you doing up?"

Big Tom, as he was called, had surprised me. "I was . . . uh . . . just gonna go to the bathroom."

"I see." He nodded and headed downstairs.

When I had finished doing nothing in the bathroom I stepped out to the hallway and almost walked into Mom White. I was startled by her unexpected presence. "I . . . uh . . ."

"Tommy, sure I didn't know ye were still awake. Your father's down in the parlor. Why don't ye run down and say hello to him."

"Okay."

I went downstairs, shook hands with my father, and sat with him for a while as he talked about the winter weather and what was going on with Granny. Then he told me that in the morning I would find gifts from the O'Connells under the tree, but as he talked I was not listening closely. Instead, I was wondering about my absent mother. Insane asylum? Hopeless? I'll have to look up those words.

After a while, my father said "Merry Christmas" and goodbye. And I was left with the desolate, empty feeling that always accompanied a visit from him.

The next day, after all the presents had been opened, and I had examined my new Flexible Flyer sled, thumbed through my new books, sampled the jar of candy from Granny, and opened gifts from people in the White household, I asked Big Tom if I could use his large dictionary.

My request was granted, and as I entered his room his framed Boston College diploma caught my eye. There was something special to me about the drawing of the eagle on that parchment document.

Opening the gigantic old Webster's International Dictionary, I leafed through pages while sounding the word "insane." Indigo. Intern. Oops. Too far. Inroad. Here it is. I-n-s-a-n-e. I don't know these words. Unsound. Not sane. Mad. Then my eyes took in these words: "Syn. Insane, mad, crazy."

I reflected on the word "crazy." I know what that is. Us kids say it to each other all the time. I guess my mother's really crazy.

Looking for the word "asylum," I started with the E's. No, it's not E-S. Maybe it's A. Here's "aside." What else sounds like an I? Y does. Astro. Asur. A-S-Y-L-U-M. Inviolable sanctuary. Place of retreat. Institution for the insane. Brother, I'll be here all day lookin' up words. This is really somethin', tryin' to find out where she is.

I looked up "institution" and found that it could be a "building," and I looked up "hopeless" and found some words like "despairing" and "desperate." I could not obtain a clear idea in my seven-year-old mind of the exact meaning of "hopeless" but I believed it was when a person could not wish for something or ever expect it.

As I left the dictionary, I was horrified by my mother's condition. I did not want to think of my mother as a crazy person, in a building with other crazy people, in a hopeless condition. And I certainly didn't want to discuss it. So I never told anybody I had overheard the conversation, and I tried not to think about my mother's condition.

However, reminders of her insane status were frequent. "Crazy" was a common word in the vocabulary of boys and girls and adults. So the word "crazy," and the other words I had looked up in the dictionary, always reminded me of the hopelessly insane woman that was my mother. The missing mother that had been torn away from me. The missing mother my soul yearned to connect with. The missing mother I couldn't quite picture anymore.

But life in the White household was a busy life with school to attend, projects around the house to work on, games to play, and books to read. And I tried not to think about my mother.

7

Life at Mrs. White's house was a very structured life. She was obsessed with the idea of running a perfect household, and usually achieved her goal. She had a day for everything she did. Wash day. Ironing day. Baking day. Cleaning day.

We all had tasks to perform, based on our age, and if those tasks were not completed there would be a relevant consequence. In addition to fierce physical punishment, we could lose privileges such as our trips to "the woods" or to the movies.

In the militaristic environment that Mrs. White created, dust was a bitter enemy. Under her direction we attacked it on Saturdays with varying degrees of energy, using feather dusters and lint-free scraps of old bed sheets. We would also apply a mysterious substance known as "elbow grease" to her silverware, kept in a special velvet-lined case in the dining room cupboard, where it was not allowed to tarnish.

It's important to note that our guardian did not just give orders and then sit around twiddling her thumbs. She worked extremely hard herself, without any rest that anyone could observe. "We'll get our reward in heaven," she would say, and she expected her example to rub off on us. But I was never a high physical energy type. Except for using my mind with ease and facility, I was the slow one. I had two physical speeds: slow and stop.

Her standard of perfection was evident in every room. The furniture in the parlor and the dining room was mahogany. The rugs were oriental. And the curtains were made of lace that you could see through from indoors, but not vice-versa. Those two rooms were off-limits for us except on Sundays. And even then we had to sit on the rug, not on the sofa or chairs. Only on special occasions were we allowed to play Monopoly at the dining room table. Otherwise, our board games were played at the kitchen table.

On a typical Saturday all the boys would line up, go down on our knees, and work on the fringes of the two oriental rugs with large combs, eliminating all snarls and making sure that each strand ran parallel to the next one. Perfection was the rule, not the exception.

Another team effort was hanging the old wooden storm windows in the winter time. I remember those heavy windows with their thick layers of paint, and how we polished each large pane before installing them, rubbing them with ammonia and pieces of old bed sheets until they were spotless. Mrs. White used to call our labor "elbow grease," and no matter how often she used those words the expression mystified me because I knew of no grease supply in my elbows. It made no more sense to me than "This stew will stick to your ribs."

Another one of Mrs. White's pet slogans was, "A place for everything, and everything in its place." There was no such thing in that house as flinging clothes around and expecting someone else to pick them up. Regardless of your age, you organized them neatly in your bureau, or deposited them in the appropriate hamper . . . or else you were punished.

The only time we achieved some relief from the rigid structure of life at Mrs. White's was when we were sent outside, either to run errands or to play. And it was while doing errands that I became more familiar with the names of the streets on Presidential Hill, which was our neighborhood.

It was obvious who the town planners had in mind when they named Garfield Avenue, Monroe Street, and Cleveland Street. But I never figured out whether Adams Street, the next street over from Mountain Avenue, was named after John or John Quincy. Yet I am pretty sure Roosevelt Avenue was named after Teddy, not Franklin. And Grant Avenue was definitely named after Ulysses.

Railroad Avenue set a boundary for the hill, and so did Hill Street, near the railroad tracks. There was no President named Hill, so the name probably indicated topography. Also, I think they named the street I lived on Mountain Avenue because there was a huge rock formation at the end of the street near Railroad Avenue, and our neighborhood was also the high point of the area between the nearby railroad tracks and Route One, which ran from Fort Kent, Maine, all the way to Florida.

President George Washington wasn't honored on Presidential Hill, but a walk along Railroad Avenue over the tracks and up to the center of town led to Washington Street, Norwood's main street, which was named after "the father of our country." It ran not only through our town but out toward Walpole, and all the way back into the heart of Boston.

The only institutional building in our area was on Garfield Avenue near Pleasant Street. The Cornelius M. Callahan School was where I spent the first six grades in a learning atmosphere that was precious and intimate because of a team of nurturing teachers including Miss McManus, Miss McIntyre, and Miss Grant. Why did the "Miss" come before their names? Marriage was not allowed for women teachers then. Female teachers were educated in "normal" schools, and it was "Miss" or no job.

At the Callahan School we marched our way to assemblies in single file while martial music played on an old hand-cranked Victrola, to the sound of a piece of classical music to which we children silently added these words: "The monkey wrapped his tail around the flagpole . . . around the flagpole . . ."

Also, while I was at the Callahan School we had many spelling bees which I inevitably won, despite my high level of performance anxiety. I had a competitive spirit when it came to achievements of the mind, and that helped me to risk the pains of self-consciousness.

During holiday seasons we did skits, with each child memorizing a line or two. When I was on stage dressed as a mouse nibbling the Christmas stocking, the costume helped me to be much less shy. On the other hand, in class recitations with no mask my heart would pound very hard. Instead of being a born extrovert, I was the other extreme. An introvert from the core. Yet I would still accomplish things that brought me attention.

At any rate, life at Mrs. White's was a busy life, with school and play and work around the house. And when we got back there to number 42 after a foray into the outside world, the structured lifestyle there was always immediately apparent.

Inside the back door, which was the one we had to use, there was a little entryway where we hung our coats, lined up our rubbers and overshoes in their assigned places, and hung up our mittens if it was during the winter.

Even in the good weather we still had to get every last speck of dirt off the soles of our shoes or sneakers by kicking them back and forth on the special bristly rug she put before the entrance to the kitchen. If you ever looked straight down at the kitchen linoleum you could just about see your face in it, and she was determined to keep it that way.

She was fussy about her appliances too, and very conscious of brand names. Any name other than the ones she used herself was considered to be inferior. Her Electrolux was the best vacuum cleaner. The Glenwood was the only gas range one should own. And we didn't call the refrigerator by its generic name, nor was it called a "fridge." It was simply the Frigidaire. When it came to canned goods, there was only one acceptable brand too, and it was Monarch.

Even the dishes we used were part of her perfect household. They were color coded. We each had a set of dishes, including our own private egg cup for hard boiled eggs. The reason for our own special color was that we were expected to take care of those dishes, and put them neatly into the pantry sink for washing after each meal.

Perfectionism was the prescribed way of life at 42 Mountain Avenue in the reign of Margaret Monahan White. There was no questioning it, just as there was no questioning the accuracy of the U.S. Constitution or the Bill of Rights, and her way of life pertained not only to the outer self but to the inner self as well.

I was fidgety as I sat in St. Catherine's dressed in white, waiting to receive my First Holy Communion on a very sunny Sunday during May 1939. I was seven years old, and had arrived at what they described in that era as "the age of reason." So I was finally in the proper state of mind to receive the Sacrament of Holy Eucharist.

I tapped my fingers on my knees as I waited for the Bishop to ask the question Sister Teresa had rehearsed with me. I hoped I had memorized it well enough to recite it before the entire congregation.

"Now that we have thoughtfully discussed what Holy Eucharist is," said the short, pudgy, florid-faced Bishop, "I would like to see if perhaps one of you children can answer my first question. When did Christ institute the Holy Eucharist?"

My heart pounded rapidly and my face reddened as I quickly raised my hand. I had been told to do this by the Sister, and the other children had been warned not to raise theirs.

"What is your name, young man?" the Bishop asked. "Thomas O'Connell." "Thomas, can you tell us when Christ instituted the Holy Eucharist?" I paused for a moment to catch my breath. "Christ instituted the Holy Eucharist at the Last Supper . . . ."

The reality of the situation suddenly struck me as I stood there with the eyes of the whole congregation on me. I faltered and my face got red. ". . . on the night before he died." "Thank you, Thomas. Your answer was fine." The Bishop waved his hands, indicating that I could be seated. Brother, I thought as I took my seat, I'm glad that's over with. I almost forgot the answer and I thought I had it memorized perfect.

"Children in Christ," said the Bishop, "you have learned that Christ gave his priests the power to change bread and wine into his precious Body and Blood. As Thomas has told us, this was done at the Last Supper on the night before Jesus died. Then, my children in Christ, he said to his apostles, 'Do this in remembrance of me.' Never forget that, children. When you approach the altar, remember those words of Christ."

All the people assembled there in St. Catherine's nodded their heads in reverence at the mention of Christ's name. "The Holy Eucharist is a form of giving thanks," the Bishop continued. "It is an offering in which we all join together to give thanks to the Lord Our God. The Sacred Host looks and tastes like bread, my children, but in the Sacred Host you are partaking of the Body and Blood of Our Holy Savior, Jesus Christ."

I nodded my head in reverence along with the rest of the parishioners, although I couldn't imagine how bread and wine could be somebody's body and blood. "Now we will have our next question," said the Bishop. "What is necessary to receive Holy Communion worthily?"

A girl said, "To receive Holy Communion worthily it is necessary to be free from mortal sin, to have a right intention, and to obey the Church's laws on fasting before Holy Communion."

Her answer to the question reminded me that my stomach was empty and growling after fasting from midnight, which was the requirement.

When the Bishop's questions had been answered, the congregation went back to the Mass. Then came the long procession of white-clad boys and girls. Boys were segregated on the left side of the church, girls on the right. Day students at St. Catherine's school up front. Sunday School students toward the rear.

I went to the altar rail, bowed my head in prayer, and awaited my turn. The Bishop reached me, made a Sign of the Cross, muttered in Latin, and lifted the unleavened bread wafer toward my open mouth. I saw my distorted reflection in the gold chalice while taking the round wafer on my tongue, which was now dry and felt swollen. When I tried to swallow it, it stuck to the roof of my mouth.

Shuffling down the aisle on my way back to my seat I raised my eyes and scanned the crowd to look for my father. But in the large throng gathered in St. Catherine's I saw neither my father nor Mrs. White. So I continued to follow the line of communicants back to my assigned seat, and solemnly bowed my head in prayer.

Once again I tried to swallow the stuck wafer, but it again refused to be dislodged from the roof of my mouth. Then my hand moved involuntarily toward my mouth, but I remembered the sister's warning that we shouldn't touch the wafer with our fingers. So I returned my hand to its resting place on the back of the pew in front of me because, for a brief moment, I had visualized a bolt of lightning from Heaven entering the church and striking me dead on the spot.

Soon the wafer began to dissolve slowly in my mouth as I wiggled my tongue against it. Finally, when it partially curled under my tongue, I pushed it toward the rear of my throat, gulped, and swallowed. A sigh of relief followed when I realized I had made my First Communion.

As the sacrifice of the Mass proceeded, I followed along in my new white St. Joseph's Children's Missal, a First Communion gift from Mrs. White. I knew that now I was even more of a Catholic than before, having received three Sacraments: Baptism, Holy Eucharist, and Penance.

The day before, in the dark chapel to the rear of St. Catherine's, I had pushed aside a heavy maroon curtain, entered a pitch black confessional booth, and after the slide had been drawn back by the priest inside, there had been nothing between us but a black screen, and I had whispered "Bless me, Father, for I have sinned."

I had confessed to the priest that I had been "disobedient" and "angry." And he had absolved me of my sins and told me to say three Our Fathers and three Hail Mary's for my penance. Then I was ready for my First Communion.

After the First Communion service was over, we white-suited boys rose and made a procession which brought us to the crowded vestibule at the rear of the church where proud parents awaited their freshly blessed children.

Soon I saw Dave Rothwell coming toward me. He had received his own First Communion with the parochial school boys who were seated preferentially in the front rows of the church.

Special preference was part of the way of life at St. Catherine's Parish. For example, it was obvious that members of Dr. O'Toole's family had a mystical aura around them. Their impressive brick home, which included his offices, was opposite the Guild Theater, and this respected physician was known as the largest contributor to the famous Annual Collection at St. Catherine's.

The results of that collection were publicized in a printed list of all contributors that served as both a motivational device and a sign of appreciation. The whole town knew who gave the most and who gave the least, and who wasn't even listed. It was one of the most treasured annual publications ever printed in the town of Norwood.

St. Catherine's was not bashful when it came to raising funds. It was an active parish where enthusiastic parishioners helped organize a virtually endless succession of fund-raising activities. One special event was the annual carnival, which was held in a large schoolyard behind the Parochial School, near the convent where teaching nuns, the Sisters of St. Joseph, resided.

The carnival attracted many volunteers and took in much money, not just from people attending but from the sales of books of "chances" that were good for prizes of 50 gallons of heating oil and other lures. To help with that effort, Mrs. White had us boys canvassing the town, street by street, selling chances. The whole parish seemed to be involved in that carnival and other functions, which brought a real sense of community to the parishioners.

For reasons never explained to me, the Rothwell brothers had been sent to St. Catherine's Parochial School and I had gone to the public. I wished they had come to the public with me. But I definitely had no wish to accompany them to St. Catherine's where nuns inflicted torturous memorizing on the students, as well as cruel physical punishment.

When Dave and I got together after the service, he took my arm and pointed. "Mom's over there." "Yuh, I see her." As we moved through the crowd toward where she stood, I scanned the faces to see if my father might be among them. Not seeing him, I wondered if he might be outside because it was too crowded for him in the church.

Mom White's bluish-white hair stood out in the crowd, and so did her flower-covered hat. Her round ruddy face beamed as she laid one heavy hand on my shoulder and the other on Dave's.

"I was proud of ye today. Thomas, you answered the Bishop's question very good. David, your father's near the door on the rectory side of the church." As Dave left, she said, "Thomas, your father couldn't come, but he sent ye this silver dollar."

"Oh." I took the new silver dollar and held it in the palm of my hand, and as I examined it I was impressed by it, but a mist came over my eyes and a sinking feeling settled into my lower body. I was deeply disappointed that my father hadn't come.

"I'm takin' ye down to Furlong's for a banana split," said Mom White. "Sure, ye make your First Communion only once. Ye might as well celebrate."

As she led me out of the church and through the crowd on the wide granite steps where children stood with their parents and families, I was thinking about how my father didn't show up. Then, as we walked across Washington Street toward Furlong's to get the banana split, I said to myself, Who cares anyhow? Not me. And if he doesn't care about me, then I'm not gonna care about him either. Why should I care about him? I wonder why I even think about him. He hardly ever does what he says he'll do, so I never can tell when I'll see him next. I don't even know why I want to see him. I'm really sick of thinkin' about him. Why bother?

8

The summer of '41 was drawing to a close and I was not disappointed that it would soon be time to start the fifth grade. There had been fun, but I had done enough blueberry picking, building huts, and playing games.

Also, there had been many errands to run. At Mrs. White's the number of errands seemed to reach infinity, and we were expected to carry them out with no mistakes. Aborted or poorly handled errands led to great embarrassment. Like the mishap I had on a hardware store errand.

There was a certain amount of confusion that went with the name "hardware." Which one was it? The Town Square Hardware or Norwood Hardware? They were both on Washington Street. And one day it was my solitary duty to fetch a quart of white paint to renew the luster of the kitchen chairs and table.

I went to the right store, but as I stepped off a curb to cross Railroad Avenue, the bag broke, the can fell to the pavement and got dented, and it began leaking one small drop at a time. It leaked for about half a mile, along Railroad Avenue, up Hill Street, and along Mountain Avenue right up to the house which I entered with tears of apprehension in my eyes. I was amazed that Mrs. White didn't punish me, and simply called it an accident. However, the need for perfection was so deeply ingrained in me that for many months I felt shame each time I saw those droplets of dried white paint that marked my clumsy path. Finally, to my great relief, the telltale trail was covered when the road received a new layer of gravel and tar. My karma was cleansed.

That summer we did our share of playing sandlot baseball games in the field next to the Callahan School. These unofficial games were played with school pals and other boys from Mrs. White's. And there was no adult supervision. The adults had their own lives to live, Little League didn't exist, and we had no uniforms. Who needed them? Even if there had been a Little League I doubt if we'd have joined it. We enjoyed doing our own thing, with no adults involved.

Also, we spent considerable time in "the woods" that served as a kids' domain because nobody seemed to know who might own that undeveloped area. For us it was a place to return to nature and engage in tribal rituals of our own making. That was where we had tree climbing contests and constructed bows and arrows that we used to shoot at each other from a distance. Also, we had very dangerous rock fights. When we went out beyond the end of Mountain Avenue and were no longer in Mrs. White's line of vision we were "beyond the pale" and her rules no longer held sway.

In Mrs. White's domain at 42 Mountain Avenue, however, one of the civilized rituals that prevailed each summer was when we boys went out picking blueberries, which we would sell to eager customers, after setting aside a supply for her own baking. We had to turn in the money.

In search of the best blueberries, we would plan special expeditions all the way to the sandpits on the other side of Route One near the Islington section of neighboring Westwood, which was quite a trek. But the large size of the low bush berries on those hills was worth the effort, and sliding down the sandy slopes owned by the sand and gravel company was exciting. We never gave a thought to the possibility of getting buried in one of the sand slides we created.

Before calling it a day for picking blueberries, we would go behind the old "pumping station" to the fairly stagnant small pond we called Ballicky Pond. We swam naked there, leaping from a concrete wall into that place of dark water and snapping turtles, and as we jumped we cupped our hands over our genitals to protect them. But although our genitals remained intact, we often emerged with the shape of a turtle's mouth on an arm or leg.

It wasn't hard to sell our berries to Gertrude's Pastry Shoppe or Lewis' restaurant, which welcomed our fresh-from-the-woods offerings. But by the time we got to our customers, the berries had settled in the quart milk bottles. And we had to shake them to make the level rise to the top again. I wondered if this was cheating. But I didn't wonder about it much.

Gertrude's was our consistent blueberry customer, and that was where Mrs. White bought pastry when she didn't make the delicacies herself. Most of the time she made her own luscious pies and cakes that nobody in the world could match. But she didn't do the fine pastries, nor the jelly doughnuts that would call out to you in your daydreams.

When the early "supermarkets" began to sell mushy squeezy white bread, Mrs. White condescendingly described those loaves as "store bread." Gertrude's bread, in a pinch, was considered acceptable, but supermarket bread was unacceptable. She must have been ahead of her time with her awareness that there were unhealthy additives in that mushy bread.

Mrs. White's own bread, which she made every Saturday afternoon, had real substance to it and her white bread, wheat bread, and raisin bread were beyond criticism. What a treat it was to butter that bread with its tantalizing aroma while it was still warm from the oven, and sprinkle sugar on it.

Periodically, she provided a special delicacy known as "bread pudding." This was my favorite dessert, especially when it was the white bread pudding with the plump raisins. Not that I didn't like the chocolate bread pudding, but to me the vanilla with the raisins was the ultimate.

Obviously, all was not misery at Mrs. White's house. For example, the food from the C&W Food Mart was delicious and healthy. Some of her relatives owned Curran & Wall's, and although their building was very unpretentious they operated a quality business, with their prime cuts of meat, the special Monarch brand of canned goods, and fresh produce that came straight from Boston. They also took the weekly order by phone and delivered it to the house. Mrs. White was one of their largest customers, and one of their fussiest. Often she would call them about a cut of meat that wasn't just so, or complain about produce that didn't meet her standards.

Not only were the food staples good, her cooking and baking were superb. And we were clothed better than most boys in town. Our basic hygiene was excellent, and the house at 42 Mountain Avenue was comfortable. So in many ways we were not deprived children. It was more of a "lace curtain Irish" environment.

But her ferocious reign of terror always had us on edge, and no matter how comfortable it was or how many good things happened, I was constantly preoccupied with fantasies of leaving Mrs. White's perfect place at 42 Mountain Avenue in Norwood and rejoining my own family at 22 Walnut Place, an unfashionable address in Dedham, stigmatized by its location next to the railroad station "on the other side of the tracks." My inner mindscape was that of an exile, and a long list of benefits available at Mrs. White's could not cancel that out. I was living as an exile, with other exiles, and felt like a prisoner with an indefinite sentence. That was the way it was.

It was warm that Friday afternoon, and Joe Rothwell and I had just completed an errand for Mom White. We were lingering in Norwood Center in spite of her warning that we were not to hang around the Square, and we were feeling the intensity of the sweltering summer heat.

"Let's grab a cold drink o' water at the Greasy Spoon," said Joe. I replied, "You said it," and soon we were in the luncheonette next to Gertrude's Pastry Shoppe. The townspeople had caustically labeled it "The Greasy Spoon," and if it had another name, nobody knew it. I think the only edible food product they sold was Jello.

The main appeal the place had for us was its water dispenser that you pressed an empty glass against, and out came a fountain of water that was comfortably cool and especially welcome on hot days. But the manager of the establishment didn't appreciate our uninvited incursions into his oasis, and chased us out with a flying fist each time we showed up. I recall how we called him a cheapskate, shouting at him, "It's only water! And water's free!" We had no idea that people paid for water, and I'm still surprised that we have to.

On this occasion, after checking to be sure the manager wasn't nearby, we walked casually toward the source of cold water where, as if by magic, the spigot would produce a delightful supply of clear, cold, thirst-quenching water.

We each took a clean glass from the rack next to the water fountain, and Joe poured himself some water. I followed suit. When I had gulped down half of mine I paused to say, "Ah, that's so good."

"So you brats are here again." Turning toward the door to the kitchen, I saw the gaunt, bald-headed manager with the weeping cold sore on his lip. "You little shits better get the hell out of here or I'll call the cops on ya."

I put down my half-full glass of water and edged toward the exit. But Joe wasn't so easily motivated. Confidently, he said, "This place is public." The manager came toward us. "You bastards! I'll kick your fresh little asses but good." Joe ducked his curly head, grabbed me by the arm, and whispered, "Let's scram!" We scooted out the swinging door.

"I better not catch you God damned brats in here again!" shouted the manager of the Greasy Spoon, standing at the swinging door of the cut-rate eating establishment waving his fist in anger at us.

"Aw, who cares?" Joe shouted defiantly over his shoulder. "You're just a cheapskate. Water don't cost nothin' and you won't even let us have a sip. Anyhow, you don't even own the Greasy Spoon."

The manager started after us and Joe shouted, "Cheese it!" We fled across the street toward the "Five-and-Ten." We never called it

Woolworth's. It was our favorite place for getting cheap supplies for school, Halloween masks, water pistols, and candy. Oh yes, and chewing gum too. Doublemint. Maybe once in a while Beechnut, or Dentyne, but mostly Doublemint. That was our brand.

When I had caught my breath, I said, "Hey, Joe, he really got mad when you said he didn't even own the Greasy Spoon."

Joe grinned a yellow-toothed grin and wiped the sweat from his forehead. "He's a horse's ass." We stopped to stare at the display window of the Five-and-Ten, and Joe said, "Shit, did ya ever see so many toys and stuff? I'm gonna go in and get a water pistol and some candy."

"How much money you got on ya?"

"Nothin'," replied Joe.

"Me neither. So how you gonna buy the water pistol and the candy?"

"I'll hawk 'em. You know, clip 'em."

"But that's stealin'. It's a sin, Joe."

"If you don't take much, it's only a venial sin."

"I dunno about that."

"Well," said Joe, "if you were a crook and ya robbed a bank or a gas station or somethin' and took a lot of money that'd probly be a mortal sin. But hawkin' apples or clippin' stuff from the Five-and-Ten ain't hardly a sin at all."

"I dunno."

"Well, I know," he said. "I'm two years older than you and I know all about stuff like that."

I visualized the counter in the Five-and-Ten that had always fascinated me. The one stocked with small pads of paper, pens, pencils of all shapes and colors and sizes, and erasers. And I thought, If it's not that much of a sin I ought to get some of that stuff. "But what if we get caught?"

"We won't get caught. All you have to do is tuck your shirt in your pants and leave one of your shirt buttons open and make like you're just lookin' at things. Then ya shove the stuff in your shirt real fast and ya walk out o' the store real slow and ya don't even look to see if anybody's watching."

"I'd be scared to do that. We could go to jail or something if we got caught."

Joe laughed. "Are you kiddin'? They don't send little kids like us to jail. They just bawl you out and call your house and tell on ya."

"Mom'd kill us. She'd prob'ly shove our heads in the cruddy toilet." I had not yet received that dreaded punishment, and the very thought of it terrified me.

"Even if we get caught," said Joe, "we don't have to say we live with her. We can say we live with the Maguires. You say you're Bobby Maguire and I'll say I'm Dick."

"Then we'd be lyin' too and get really killed."

"Those'd be just white lies," said Joe, blinking his blue eyes rapidly.

"White lies?" My own eyes widened.

"Yuh, those are lies that ain't so bad. They'd only be venial sins, not mortal. Hey, come on, Tommy. Everybody hawks stuff. Didn't you ever hawk stuff?" I shook my head. "Hawkin' stuff's fun, Tommy. I been doin' it since I was as old as you, and never been caught yet."

"I never knew you did that."

He laughed. "Well, I wasn't gonna tell everybody. Somebody might squeal. But you won't squeal, huh Tommy? We're blood brothers, remember?" Years before, we had pricked our fingers with pins and I had mingled my blood with the Rothwells' and we had sworn, "We are now blood brothers and we're never gonna squeal on each other."

"I won't squeal, Joe."

"Okay. Come on, Tommy." He squeezed my arm. "Let's hawk some stuff now."

I was silent for a moment, wondering about the whole idea. Then I said, "Okay, Joe. I'll hawk some stuff with ya."

When we went in the Five-and-Ten, Joe headed toward the candy counter and I went to my favorite place where school supplies were located. And as I set out to complete my first theft my heart pounded heavily in my chest. Although I tried to appear outwardly calm and honest, my hands and knees trembled and I felt like Public Enemy Number One. I was terrified.

Despite my anxiety, I followed Joe's instructions carefully. I would first hold an object in my left hand as if examining it before buying, and then with my right hand I would take the item and rapidly shove it into my shirt. And when my shirt held all it could hold I began inserting things into my pants pockets.

When I had taken all the loot I could reasonably conceal on my person, I began to move through the Saturday afternoon crowd in the aisles of the Five-and-Ten with my heart beating wildly as I stepped toward the exit, feeling as if my whole body was paralyzed. When I passed Joe, who stood at a counter which displayed water pistols, he looked my way and winked. I winked back and kept moving. The only place I wanted to be was out of that store.

Joe looks so calm, I thought. I guess he's used to hawkin' stuff. But I'm not. I hate this. I bet my face looks just like a crook's face, and before I get to the door I'll prob'ly get caught 'cause everyone in the whole store can tell from lookin' at me that I'm a real live crook.

I got to the door without difficulty, although time seemed frozen, and I soon found myself on the wide sidewalk in front of the Five-and-Ten. Trying to act casual, I strolled away from the store, and while I walked I felt that the eyes of all pedestrians were fixed on my guilty face.

A few doorways down the street, near Cottage Street, I stepped into the same doorway where we sometimes ducked through to take short cuts on rainy days. A long flight of stairs led up to an office area with a wide corridor, which led to a down flight of stairs at the end of the long block.

Huddling in the doorway like a wanted criminal, I waited there for Joe and wondered if he had gotten caught. Brother, if he gets caught I'm in trouble too. I guess he'll have to tell on me even though we're blood brothers. Mom White would kill him if she caught him lyin'. "A liar's worse than a thief," she always says. "Ye can reform a thief but ye can't reform a liar." Boy, does she hate liars. If we get caught we better tell the truth and maybe she won't punish us so much.

"Hey, Tommy, how'd ya do?" Joe was there in front of me grinning. Although his teeth were yellow and he was short for his age, I envied him his straight, small teeth. I would rather have been short like Joe with even yellowed teeth than to be tall and thin, with large uneven white front teeth. I despised the crookedness of my teeth and thought the whole world was noticing them and thinking less of me because of them. I wanted to be perfect, and wasn't.

"Wait till ya see the stuff I hawked, Tommy." Joe looked around furtively. "Let's go down near Dunn's Pond. Nobody'll see us there. And there's a place where we can hide the stuff."

We left Norwood Center, went down Nahatan Street by the Armory, and walked under the granite railroad bridge. In a moment we were near Hollingsworth and Vose Company with its glue smell, and the Plimpton Press with its smell of ink. "We better not go by where Mister Vincent works," I warned Joe as we neared the press where many books were printed, including those published by the Christian Science Church.

To avoid being seen by Mrs. White's boarder, who worked as a printer at Plimpton's, we crossed to the far side of the street and soon reached the small shallow pond where we went ice skating in the winter. At the edge of the water, behind a cluster of bushes, we found the culvert where we often played. It was about three feet in diameter and water flowed through it only during the spring months.

In the summer when the culvert was bone dry we would hide within its long, shadowy emptiness and bounce echoes around. During the grape season we would crawl through it to a back yard near Lenox Street where we "borrowed" grapes. We called our secret culvert "Piper Town" and half-believed that after dark it was inhabited by tiny elfin creatures like leprechauns who disappeared into the earth when the sun rose in the morning.

"This is a swell place to hide our stuff," said Joe as we sat cross-legged at the entrance to the concrete culvert. I was in a trance as I watched Joe remove his loot from his shirt front. He took out three water pistols, and a vast assortment of several different types of candy. Then he lined everything up on the grass. "Well, what did ya get, Tommy?"

I emptied my treasure trove from inside my shirt and on the ground I lined up several pens, a few colored pencils, some lead pencils, small pads of writing paper, a couple of large erasers, and a small pencil sharpener.

Joe gave me a quizzical look. "Why'd ya hawk stuff like that?"

I shrugged. "I like this kind o' stuff."

Joe looked at his own loot and smiled. "Hey, how about these terrific water pistols and all this candy?"

Not a word did I say. I was deep in thought as I sat cross-legged on the heavily matted swamp grass, tapping my forehead with my index finger.

"What's the matter with you, Tommy? You don't like hawkin' stuff?"

"Nope. I think it's a sin, and I think we ought to take this stuff back to the store and sneak it back on the counter."

"I don't get you, Tommy. I thought everybody liked hawkin' stuff. Anyways, it's only a venial sin."

"But isn't a sin mortal if ya think it is?"

"I guess that's what the stupid catechism says, but I don't think hawkin' stuff's mortal."

"Well, I do." As I had entered the store I had thought of myself as an evil master criminal and I had thought of myself that way as I had tucked the stolen items into my shirt front. The hawkin' expedition had been no lark for me, as it had been for Joe.

"Here." Joe shoved a large piece of red-and-white striped candy into my hand, "Taste this. It's terrific." Joe thoroughly enjoyed his first piece of stolen candy. He was a completely satisfied and guiltless remover of items from the Five-and-Ten.

Slowly I removed the cellophane wrapping and inserted the red-and-white candy into my mouth. "Ach!" I spat the piece of candy onto the ground. "It tastes lousy!"

"Are you shittin' me or somethin? This here's the best candy I ever tasted."

"Nah. It tastes lousy to me." I could find nothing good about the candy.

Joe swallowed the rest of his first piece of candy and put a second piece in his eager mouth. As he sucked on the candy he mumbled to me, "You're funny. You really don't like hawkin' stuff, huh?"

"Nope. I hate it. I don't even feel like usin' the stuff I hawked."

"Listen," said Joe, "we'll hide the stuff here in Piper Town and come back for it tomorrow. Then I bet you'll feel like usin' it and you won't feel so bad about hawkin' it."

"Maybe." I unenthusiastically complied with Joe's suggestion. Then we went back to Mrs. White's house where I had a difficult time appearing calm and unruffled.

Haunted by my dishonesty, when I went to bed that night I lay there for a long time staring at the shadows cast by the street light on the sloped ceiling of the third-floor finished room. As I reflected on the "hawkin'" expedition, I thought, I shouldn't have done it, and I shouldn't have let Joe do it either. But he said, "Aw, come on," and I went and did it. I must be crazy or something. No, I shouldn't use that word. It reminds me of my mother. I wonder what it's like to be crazy. It must be wicked. I wonder what she looks like.

Even if she's crazy I bet she doesn't look like the crazy people you see in the movies sometimes. Anyhow, "crazy" is just a word. That's what one of the kids said the other day when somebody called him crazy. Well, I'm not crazy, but I must be stupid or somethin' to let Joe talk me into doin' stuff I don't even want to do.

I'm the smartest kid in my class in school, but if I'm so smart why did I take that stuff? Well, I guess I'm smart in some ways and stupid in others. I knew stealin' stuff was a sin, and I wish I never let him talk me into doin' it. Why did I do that? What's the matter with me?

I hope God doesn't strike me dead before I go to Confession tomorrow. Thou Shalt Not Steal. It's one of the Ten Commandments and I broke it. If you break a commandment and ya know you're breakin' it, it's a mortal sin. If God struck me dead tonight I'd go straight to hell and stay there forever. Burnin' and burnin' and burnin' without end.

Please God, I prayed, don't strike me dead. I didn't mean to commit a mortal sin. I'm sorry I broke one of your Ten Commandments. I never stole stuff before. I "borrowed" apples and grapes and stuff but I never really stole anything.

I'm really sorry about it, God, and I promise I'll go right up to Confession tomorrow and I'll go to Communion Sunday and I won't clip any more stuff from Five-and-Tens or any other place. Please don't strike me dead tonight and send me straight to hell. I don't want to go to hell.

Angel of God my guardian dear, I prayed, to whom His love commits me here, ever this day . . . and night . . . be at my side . . . to light and guard . . . or is it guide . . . to light and guide . . . to rule and guide . . . I mean guard . . . Amen.

I guess I should make an Act of Contrition too. O my God I'm heartily sorry for having offended Thee, and I detest all my sins 'cause I dread the loss of heaven and the pains of hell, but most of all 'cause I offend Thee my God who art all good and deserving of all my love. I firmly resolve with the help of Thy Grace to confess my sins . . . tomorrow . . . to do penance . . . and amend my life . . . Amen. Please, God, hear my Act of Contrition.

9

"It's gone, Tommy. All our stuff's gone!" Joe's voice echoed through the culvert we called Piper Town. ". . . gone . . . gone . . . gone . . ." Joe came out of the culvert rubbing dust and grit from the knees of his dungarees. "Boy, are my knees sore from goin' in there. Some dirty no good sneaky rats took it all. Cripes. I never in my life owned three water pistols before. And all that candy. Jeez. There was enough there to last me a month. The dirty stinkin' rats."

"Well, I'm sort of glad the stuff's gone, Joe. Last night I decided I was gonna bring it back to the store today and sneak it back on the counter anyhow."

"Sneak it back? You're crazy, Tommy."

"Crazy's just a word, Joe. Hey, we better get to Confession before it's over. If we don't and she finds out about it we'll get killed."

"If she finds out we clipped that stuff from the Five-and-Ten we'll get killed anyhow." He laughed, showing his yellowed teeth, as we stepped onto the sidewalk which would take us toward St. Catherine's chapel.

"Boy, I hope she never finds out, Joe. She'd shove our heads in the toilet."

"Ain't she done that to you yet?"

"Nope."

"She's shoved my head down the hopper a lot," said Joe, a chronic infringer of Mom White's rules. "I don't even cry anymore when she does it. I just hold my breath."

"Don't ya mind it?"

"Sure I mind it. It feels lousy when she pushes your head down the hopper and flushes the chain and that stupid water splashes all over your head and makes noises in your ears and everything. But I ain't gonna let her make me cry anymore no matter what she does."

"Mm." I tried to appear calm, but my mind was filled with a vivid picture of my head being shoved down the cellar toilet, and the thought terrified me.

As we neared St. Catherine's I took Joe by the arm and looked around to make sure nobody was listening. Then I asked in a low voice, "Are you gonna tell the priest about hawkin' the stuff at the Five-and-Ten?"

"Nope. Why should I? Anyways, it was only a venial sin."

"Even so, they're still sins."

"So what? Who cares? I only tell what I feel like tellin', like I might tell him I got mad, or I swore, or somethin' like that."

"But that won't be a good confession."

Joe laughed. "It'll be good enough for me."

As we entered the chapel behind St. Catherine's and were about to dip our fingers in the Holy Water font at the entrance, I paused and whispered to Joe, "Which priest are you goin' to?"

Joe shrugged. "What's the difference? I'm only gonna tell what I feel like tellin' anyhow."

I wet the tips of my fingers with Holy Water, crossed myself, and told Joe, "There's a long line outside Father Williams' Confessional but that's who I'm gonna see. I wouldn't go to Father Griffin again for a million bucks. He talks so loud everybody in the chapel knows your sins."

Surveying the situation, I saw a small group of people waiting outside the small dark cubicle where the lenient priest was hearing the sins of the faithful. Another group waited in the Confessional pew. I tiptoed to the other side of the chapel and filed into position at the far end of the pew.

Meanwhile, Joe nonchalantly went to a pew where a mere handful of people waited for the strict Father Griffin. A few moments later, Joe exited from the Confessional booth smiling, went to the altar rail at the front of the chapel, crossed himself, mumbled his easy Penance quickly, crossed himself again, and headed toward the exit at the rear of the chapel. As he went up the aisle, he caught my attention and whispered loudly, "See ya outside, sucker."

"Go jump in a lake," I whispered back to him. Then I saw the people around me focusing their attention on Joe and me, and I blushed.

Joe left the chapel. A man came out of Father Williams' Confessional. Then a woman standing in the waiting line pushed aside the heavy maroon drapery and entered. The man kneeling in the pew in the aisle position crossed himself and moved to the rear of the standing line. Everyone seated in the pew, including me, slid sideways one position to the right.

Finally, I found myself in the kneeling position at the end of the pew, and I examined my conscience, considering the sins I would tell and in what order I would tell them. I decided to save the worst sin for last, then I stood in the waiting line, and after what seemed a long time it was my turn to enter the Confessional.

I pushed aside the heavy maroon drape at the entrance to the penitents' part of the Confessional, kneeled on the hard oak kneeling bench, made the Sign of the Cross, kissed the feet of Christ on the Crucifix, heard the mumbling of the penitent in the opposite side of the Confessional, and while I was waiting for the slide to open I nervously rehearsed the content of my confession.

Finally, the slide opened and I was separated from Father Williams only by a dark screen through which I could see the hazy outline of the priest. Then his shadowy form leaned in my direction, the gray-white hand within made the Sign of the Cross, he muttered several Latin words I did not understand, and I began, "Bless me, Father, for I have sinned." I started with my venial sins. "I was angry a couple of times. I was disobedient a few times . . ." When I was done with my venial sins, I hesitated and then stammered quickly, "I . . . uh . . . I took some things that didn't belong to me."

The priest leaned toward me and then whispered softly, "What things did you take, young man, and where did you take them from?"

"Some paper and pens and erasers, Father, and I took 'em from the Five-and-Ten. It was the first time I ever really stole anything."

"Do you realize it's a sin against our good Lord and against our fellow man to steal what belongs to another?" "Yes, Father." "Are you sorry for what you've done?" "Yes, Father." "Will you try not to do such a thing again?" "I'll try, Father."

"And will you make restitution, my son?"

"Restitution, Father?"

"Now you must return the stolen property to its rightful owner, the Five-and-Ten."

I replied softly, "Well, Father, I was gonna return the stuff, but today when I went to where I hid it, it was gone."

"I see." The priest paused and my heart pounded rapidly as I awaited his next comment.

"Could you perhaps pay for the stolen items?"

"I hardly ever have any money, Father."

Father Williams was silent for a moment. "Are you truly sorry for what you've done?"

"Yes I am, Father."

"I will absolve you of your sins, young man, and I urge you to make restitution if at all possible, and now go to the altar and say ten Our Fathers and ten Hail Mary's very slowly, and say them again before you go to sleep at night, and during the next week I would like you to pray to the Blessed Virgin Mary every day to assist you against further temptations."

"Yes, Father."

"Now I want you to say a very good Act of Contrition."

"Oh my God, I am heartily sorry for having offended Thee . . ." When I had completed my Act of Contrition and said my Penance at the altar rail, I left the chapel and found Joe waiting.

"Boy, you took prackly all day." He was bouncing a small red rubber ball on the sidewalk. "What did ya do, kill somebody or somethin'?"

"I did the same thing you did, that's all, Joe."

"You mean hawkin' stuff from the Five-and-Ten? How many Our Father's and Hail Mary's did he give ya?"

"Ten-and-ten."

"Hah. That's really something ain't it? Ten Our Father's and Ten Hail Mary's just for hawkin' stuff. I got three-and-three from Griffin, but if I told him about the Five-and-Ten he would have given me fifty-and-fifty."

"Yup. He prob'ly would have, Joe." I grinned and shook my head in wonder at his lack of religious fear and fervor.

We walked down the sidewalk out of the business section of Norwood past St. Catherine's, across Washington Street by the front of the Town Hall, past the Fire Station, and off toward Mrs. White's house in the "Cork City" part of the community.

All seemed normal in the White household as we ate our frankfurters-and-beans supper. But when we were in our third floor finished room about to undress for our Saturday night bath, and looking forward to listening to a crime program on the radio afterward, we heard the heavy footsteps of Mom White on the stairs leading to our room.

"Uh-oh," grunted Joe. We both knew that when she climbed those stairs in the evening there was usually big trouble in the air.

She entered our room carrying a large brown paper bag, and she ordered Joe's brother Dave out of the room. "You go down and take yere bath now."

"Isn't Tommy gonna take it with me?"

"No, Thomas and Joseph are staying here with me. Go to yere bath, David, and don't let me hear another word out of ye. Shush now."

There was no other word from Dave as he went down to the second floor for his solitary bath, a rare ritual for any of us at Mrs. White's.

"Stand over near the windows," she ordered as her face flushed redder than usual and her thin lips pressed together tightly in anger.

We obeyed with haste, stumbling over each other in the process. "We didn't do nothin'," said Joe, blinking his blue eyes fast.

"I'll be the judge o' that," she growled. "Speak when ye're spoken to, Joseph Rothwell. I'll tell ye soon enough what ye did. Yesterday when I asked the two of ye to run up the square for me, did ye come right back?"

"Yup, we did," lied Joe quickly.

"Oh, ye did, did ye? Well, 'tis funny but it didn't seem to me ye came right back at all. It seemed to me ye took your time."

"Well, we . . ."

"Ye what, Joseph?" I sensed what was coming and trembled in fear as Joe blurted, "We had a glass of water in the Greasy Spoon, that's all."

"Oh, so you did, did ye?" she replied in forced restraint. "That's what took ye so long?"

"Yup," said Joe without a pause as I remained silent.

"Well, if that's what ye did," said Mom White, "then what in the name of almighty God is all this?" She took the brown paper bag, opened it, tipped it upside down, and dumped the contents onto Joe's cot. There before our astonished eyes were the water pistols, the supply of candy, the pens, the pencils, the paper pads, and the erasers.

"But . . ." said Joe.

Then Mom White's round face shone red against her silver blue hair as she reached out, took Joe by the ear, and shouted, "No buts! Ye're a thief and a liar, Joseph, and don't ye think I don't know it."

Next she took me by the ear, gave it a painful twist, and said, "And you, Thomas O'Connell, I thought ye knew better than to steal. I thought ye had a good head on yere shoulders."

"It's not his fault," yelled Joe. "I told him to hawk the stuff."

"Do ye do all his thinking for him?" she retorted. "I'll be the judge o' whose fault it is and not the likes o' you, Joseph Rothwell."

She said no more as she angrily and silently held a firm grasp on our ears and pulled us down the flights of stairs from the third floor all the way to the cellar. The firmness of her grip on my right ear did not lessen as we descended, and I could not feel my feet touching the steps beneath me. I could feel only the pain in my right ear, and I was afraid she would pull it completely away from my head.

The tears were flowing in a steady torrent down my cheeks by the time we reached the small cellar toilet, elevated on a wooden platform one step higher than the cement cellar floor, and enclosed by rough boarding. The toilet had its flush box overhead and a long chain hung down so the occupant of the throne could pull on it when the job was done.

Mrs. White's hand released its grip on my ear and she ordered, "You stay right there, Thomas, and while ye wait ye can watch what happens to Joseph. Many's the time I've warned the lot of ye about lying and stealing. Sure and I have. Now ye'll get what's coming to ye."

She led Joe into the torture chamber and gave his ear an extra twist. "Take yere shirt and undershirt off," she commanded as she let go of his ear.

Joe slowly followed her instructions, revealing his burn-scarred chest. Although the massive scar was beginning to fade, the skin was as taut as ever.

"Now in with ye," she shouted. "On yere knees." Joe kneeled and held one side of the toilet with each hand, placing his head in the toilet bowl in much the same way he had done on previous occasions. It reminded me of movie scenes in which people were facing death by the guillotine.

Holding his sandy hair in her left hand, Mrs. White pushed his head down as far as it would go into the bowl, and then she reached up with her right hand to activate the flush box. She pulled the wood handle, yanked the chain, and the water poured down with a roar and swirled around Joe's head.

"Yah . . ." He coughed and then clamped his mouth shut to keep the swirling flush water from gagging him. As I watched I trembled in fearful anticipation. When the punishment was done, Mrs. White lifted the dripping Joe from his head-down position and carried him bodily to the dark soapstone set tubs beside the toilet cubicle. There she propped his chin on the edge of the sink so the water on his head would drip into the sink and not onto the floor. "Take a towel now and dry off," she ordered, and I noticed that Joe was very quiet and didn't seem to be crying.

Then her large, fleshy arm reached out and as her strong hand grabbed my left ear I let out a pain-induced scream. "Take off yere shirt and undershirt, Thomas. I'll give ye cause o' crying in a minute." My hand trembled as I undid the buttons of my shirt, hung it on a hook, and removed my undershirt.

"Kneel down in front of the toilet," she ordered. My bony knees shook as I placed them on the hard pine floor. Then, feeling like a prisoner with a death sentence, I braced myself as I had seen Joe do, with one hand on each side of the toilet bowl.

"Now ye'll find out what I do to thieves and liars, Thomas O'Connell," she shouted. "Now ye'll find out by gorry, and get the fear of God into ye." Her left hand grasped my curly brown hair. "Ow!" She lifted my head and plunged it fast downward into the watery darkness of the toilet below, and my eyes closed tightly as my forehead touched the cold water in the bowl.

Then I heard the gurgling of the flush box above as she activated the pull chain, and my heart beat fast. Holding onto the slippery enamel sides of the toilet, I caught my breath as a whirlpool of water engulfed my head, causing ringing sensations in my ears. "Yah . . ." I shouted.

Then I coughed and clamped my mouth shut, but the flush water entered my mouth and nose and began to gag me. So I spat the water out, closed my mouth tightly again, and held my breath. Then, after what seemed to be an interminable time, I felt myself lifted bodily from the toilet and placed on the cement cellar floor near the set of soapstone tubs and the wringer washer. My body was a mass of tremors as I took the towel from Mrs. White. A torrent of tears poured down my face and mingled with the water dripping from my hair.

Now, after more than four years at 42 Mountain Avenue, I had finally been subjected to the toilet punishment I had feared for so long, and as I sat there shaking I was filled with hate for her, to the core of my being.

I hate her, I thought as I began to wipe my hair and face dry. My thin arms trembled so much as I tried to rub the towel against my head that I could hardly make any progress. And all the while I was sobbing uncontrollably.

I hate her for doin' what she did to me. Who does she think she is, punishin' me like that? I hope when she dies she goes right straight to hell and they put her head in a toilet that's on fire and drown her and burn her at the same time, forever and ever.

After managing to dry myself off, I put on my undershirt and shirt, and then, from somewhere in my infuriated head, I heard her voice saying, "Now the two of ye will go up to yere room and get ready for yere bath. But first I want both of ye to promise ye won't steal again."

"I promise," said Joe quickly.

I sobbed. "I pro . . . mise."

"And ye're to confess it in Confession," she said.

"We already did," said Joe.

"We . . . did." I sobbed, trembling all over.

"And ye'll have to bring the stolen goods back to the Five-and-Ten," she said.

"We will," said Joe calmly.

"We . . . will." I sobbed.

"And Joseph," she said, "ye'd better say a special prayer to the Virgin Mary to help ye stop lying. A liar's worse than a thief and harder to reform. Oh, 'tis a terrible thing to be a liar. Liars can't be trusted in the least."

"I'll say the prayer," agreed Joe who was not overly concerned about Mom White's opinions, but knew how to pacify her.

"And you, Thomas, you say a special prayer to the Blessed Virgin Mary that she'll help ye not to steal again. I thought ye knew better than to steal."

"I'll pray . . . to . . . her." The tears would not stop.

"Now it's up with ye to get ready for yere bath," she said, "and there'll be no radio for ye tonight, and no Laurel 'n Hardy movie for ye tomorrow at the Norwood Theatre. I'll learn ye not to lie and steal. In all my born days I've never seen a liar or a thief that amounted to anything, so there will be no liars and thieves at 42 Mountain Avenue, sure as the good Lord made apples."

As we headed up the cellar stairs, she asked, "Do ye think I've picked on ye?"

"Nope," said Joe. "Except Tommy wouldn't of done it if I didn't tell him to. He didn't even want to hawk the stuff."

"It's generous of ye to stick up for him, Joseph, but Tommy O'Connell will have to learn to do his own thinking." Again she asked me her question. "Do ye think ye've been picked on?"

I remained silent and sobbing, looking up at her through my tears as I shrugged my shoulders. I was furious with her and had no intention of saying a word more than was absolutely required.

"Ye must think I've picked on ye. I've said it many's the time before and I'll say it again. Ye're all the same in my eyes and in the eyes of the Lord. I've got no favorites at the supper table and I show no partiality for those who've done wrong. One of ye could rub my feet and cater to me day and night and it wouldn't do ye a lick o' good." Obviously, she was referring to Joe's foot massages. "Mom White's boys are all equals. Sure, if I punish ye it's as hard on me as it is on the lot of ye, but if ye do wrong ye get punished for yere own good."

She looked at me with my spasm-racked body and tear-covered face. "Ye did steal at the Five and Ten, didn't ye, Tommy?" I nodded. "Ye knew it was a sin, didn't ye?" I nodded again. "Did I show any favoritism?" I shook my head. "Go up with Joe and get ready for yere bath, and don't let me catch ye stealing again."

Half numb, I followed Joe up the cellar stairs to the hallway leading to the kitchen, a dark hallway where I had often stood after small infringements of the rules. I had stood in the darkness of that hallway, and in the darkness of the cellar, and in the darkness of the attic. Also, I had been painfully switched with branches of bushes, but having my head shoved into the cellar toilet was in my eyes the ultimate unforgivable punishment.

That evening, after we had taken our baths, and after both Joe and Dave had tried unsuccessfully to comfort me, I lay in my bed staring through my tears at the shadows on the sloped ceiling of the third floor finished bedroom. Thinking, thinking, thinking.

I know I did wrong, but I was sorry and I even confessed it this after. If the stuff we took was still there, I was even gonna take it back to the Five-and-Ten. She shouldn't stuff a kid's head down a toilet. The other kids around Mountain Avenue hardly even get punished when they do somethin' wrong. Their parents just yell at 'em a little. And once in a while they get spanked, but they don't get switched and they don't get their heads shoved down toilets.

She's a pain in the behind, that's what she is. She thinks she's always right about everything, like tellin' us to stay away from the Haddad twins just 'cause they're State kids and 'cause they aren't from the Bureau like us kids and 'cause they aren't Irish. I don't care what she thinks about 'em. I'm gonna see 'em anyhow and play with 'em whenever I feel like it. It's no sin if I don't obey her. She's not my mother. She's only my guardian. I won't even have to tell it in Confession if I don't obey her.

She says stupid things sometimes, I thought as I lay there furious with her. Like after Joe kneels down and rubs her feet she says he's "a good slob." She won't catch me rubbin' her feet. I wouldn't rub anybody's feet. And she ought to mind her own business, like when my father came the last time and she said, "Here comes your father with his redheaded lady friend."

I don't care what she thinks about Susie. I like goin' for rides with her and my father. I don't even get carsick when she's in the car. I wonder if he'll marry her. Nope. He's still married to my mother. In Sunday School the sister said if a man divorced his wife, he'd get kicked out of the Church. I don't think he'll divorce her. But I don't think he ever sees her in that asylum she's in. I've never seen her either except when I was a baby, but I don't remember that far back. I don't think I'd want to see her in that place with all those crazy people. I don't even like thinking about her bein' in that place. I wish she wasn't crazy.

Well, even if she's crazy at least she's my mother. Not Mrs. White. My mother wouldn't swat me across the mouth with a wet face cloth for mumbling and she wouldn't make me stay down in the dark cellar after supper for talkin' back. I hate that dark cellar. It's like a nightmare bein' there in the dark. Like that nightmare I had the other night with everything spinnin' and flyin' and smotherin' me and scarin' me. I hate those nightmares and I hate that cellar.

She's mean as anything to us kids. I know I shouldn't hate anybody but I hate her for doin' that and I hate this place. I wish I was still livin' with my father and Granny. I wouldn't get my head shoved down the toilet there. And when people asked me about my parents I wouldn't have to tell 'em, "I live with Mrs. White." I could say, "I live with my father and Granny O'Connell." I'm sick o' tellin' people I live with Mom White. I'm not a real orphan, but she has to sign my report cards where it says parent or guardian. I'm sick o' bein' almost an orphan and havin' a guardian and bein' switched and havin' my head shoved down the toilet.

Maybe I'll run away. But if I go to Granny O'Connell's they'll just send me back here, and if I run away to someplace else they'll find out who I am and bring me back here again. So what's the use of runnin' away? Joe tried it once but the police got him and brought him back. But maybe he wasn't smart enough. Maybe they won't catch me. The only thing is, where will I go?

10

There was no escape, so I remained a prisoner at 42 Mountain Avenue on Presidential Hill. At the Callahan School I held onto my status as "the smartest boy" in my grade, and since I enjoyed writing much more than speaking, I was very proud when I won an essay contest describing how the students at the Callahan School had helped the war effort by raising money to buy a military Jeep. My story was published in the *Norwood Messenger*, the primary local newspaper, and it set the tone for my life-long interest in the written word.

After school in the good weather we often played unorganized baseball on the huge playground. In the winter on snowy days we would ski down the steep hill behind the school on short wooden skis that were knee twisters and ankle sprainers, loosely fitted to our feet. But I don't recall any broken bones. Just the thrill of the speed. And bruises.

When we were away from school we played mainly at "the woods" or in a vacant lot on the next street. It was owned by Mrs. White, and everyone called it "White's Field." It was just large enough for a small baseball diamond. Also, it was close enough to the house to hear Mrs. White call us for meals.

When World War II broke out we were at White's Field playing. "The Japs bombed us at Pearl Harbor," someone yelled at us. "We're gonna have a war! President Roosevelt's gonna talk about it on the radio tomorrow."

As the war began to change many lives, I was caught between two worlds at 42 Mountain Avenue. I always dreamed of escaping our guardian's rigid discipline, yet it was a house of close friendships, cleanliness, fine food, a welcome refuge from the elements, and a way of life based on solid values that would stand me in good stead later.

Looking back, I am keenly aware of how much I treasured the camaraderie with my newfound pals who shared the destiny of being "orphans" like me. But we never used that label on ourselves. Nor did we call ourselves "foster kids." When asked, we just said, "I live with Mrs. White." In those days, that was enough. People may have been curious, but they avoided prying into other people's lives. There was a definite code of honor in those days, and its general slogan was "Mind your own business."

The summer of '42 was nearly over. And Dave and I were on the way to Mrs. White's after a day at Norfolk Golf Course. That summer the Rothwells and I had our first experience of caddying at Norfolk Golf Course, located several miles away near the Islington section of Westwood. That day we were only assigned golfers with light bags because we were so young. Later, our extended thumbs had gotten us a ride back to Norwood, and instead of going straight home we decided to take a slight detour for Dave to replenish his supply of cigarettes. "I'm goin' in the Drug Store and get some butts in the cigarette machine," he said.

"I'll wait out here." Looking at myself in the store window, I adjusted the Army overseas cap my uncle Joe had presented to me when he was home on Army leave during one of my brief vacations at Granny O'Connell's. Whenever I saw my own reflection, my head appeared to me like a Neanderthal man's. So I had taken to wearing caps to conceal its long oval shape, which I hated.

I wonder if I look like a soldier, I thought as I gazed at myself in the military cap. Nope. All I look like is a kid with a head that sticks way out in the back and has big crooked front teeth and freckles. I could kill that Bobby Resker for sayin' I look like Stan

Laurel when I smile. So what if I smile with my mouth closed? I don't like showin' my crooked teeth.

"I got my butts," said Dave as he came out of the store. "Didn't need a note from an adult either."

"She'd never give you a note, and she'll kill you if she catches ya smokin'."

"She won't catch me." He laughed. "C'mon. Let's go up the old cemetery and have a smoke."

"I'll go with ya, but I'm not gonna smoke."

"What are ya scared of?" asked Dave.

"Nothin'. I just don't feel like smokin'."

As we walked across the street to the cemetery entrance, Dave said, "So you don't feel like smokin', huh? Well, what the hell do I care? No skin off my ass. You know what, Tommy? I wish school wasn't starting again next week."

"I'm glad it's startin' again. I think I'm gonna like the sixth grade."

"I'd just as soon caddy."

"I'm sick o' caddyin' and I'm sick o' listenin' to dirty talk."

During that summer of 1942, in the dirt-floored, lattice-walled caddie shack at Norfolk Golf Course I had learned some of the lurid facts of life and a few of the outrageous fantasies. Along with Dave and Joe Rothwell I had been initiated into the caddie ranks at a unique ceremony involving the complete removal of our clothes and the nude retrieval of them from the middle of the fifth fairway. The older boys had purposely scheduled the event for the precise time when a foursome was teeing off, so we would be all the more embarrassed.

The initiation had signaled the beginning of a very earthy training program. My innocent ears had taken in about every variation of vulgarity, and I had been exposed at the age of ten to many tales of sexual prowess and vivid descriptions of the sexual act, discussions on the use of prophylactics, usually known as "safes," and debates among the older caddies about who had achieved the greatest number of sexual conquests which were described as "pieces of ass."

"Don't ya like dirty jokes?" asked Dave.

"It's stupid to talk dirty."

"I bet you're scared 'cause you think it's a sin."

"Well, isn't it?"

Dave grinned, revealing his straight white teeth. "You been makin' too damn many Holy Hours."

"If I want to make Holy Hours I'll make 'em. It's my own business, nobody else's. Anyway, I sort of like bein' in the church all alone."

During the previous Lenten season, I had gone to Mass and received Holy Communion daily and I had made a series of Holy Hours after Lent had ended. During a Holy Hour I would say my Rosary and I would kneel at each of the Stations of the Cross, and at times the handsome dark-haired Father Williams would accompany me along the Way of the Cross. At such times I wondered if I too might have a vocation in me to become a priest some day.

In St. Catherine's when I was all alone beneath the high, awe-inspiring vaulted ceiling, kneeling before the ornate altars flanked by banks of flickering blue and red votive candles, I felt at peace with the world and, more particularly, I had the unusual feeling of being at peace with myself. As a young lone wolf, in that beautiful church, I knew deep down in my heart that I was not really alone. The God of my limited understanding was there too, as well as Jesus, and the Blessed Virgin Mary.

As we entered the old cemetery Dave laughed and asked, "What do ya want to do? Become a saint or somethin'? I'd never want to be a saint. It'd be no fun. A saint can't do a single damn thing. He can't even break a Commandment or else then he's not a saint anymore."

"But we aren't supposed to break Commandments anyhow, so why's it so hard to be a saint?"

"Listen," said Dave, "I don't want to be bad but I don't want to be a saint either. I just want to have some fun. So to hell with bein' a saint." He laughed and I went into a very familiar place, my silence. That was my cave, my retreat from the world, my wolf lair.

"Let's go over behind the big tomb," he said after we had ducked under the chain barring traffic from the old cemetery. "It's a good smokin' place."

"It's your funeral if ya get caught."

"Don't talk about funerals in this creepy place, Tommy."

We crouched behind a hillock formed by the underground section of the large tomb, and Dave revealed his pack of Chesterfields. "These butts are great." He opened the pack, carefully removed the first cigarette, struck a match, lit the cigarette, and as he was taking in his first drag he said, "Come on, Tommy, have a butt."

"Nah, I don't think so." I shook my head.

"It's up to you. Hey, did ya hear those guys in the caddie shack talkin' about the girl they saw gettin' it in the woods near the second hole? I wonder what it looked like. When I saw the picture of that couple doing it in that horny book the guys were passin' around last week it looked pretty weird." Dave puffed on his cigarette.

"Yuh, it did."

"I thought you didn't look at that book."

I blushed. "I didn't really . . . I sort of . . . when they gave it to me I couldn't help seein' it."

"You're a hot shit, Tommy. You couldn't help it? That's pretty good. Hah!"

"Aw, come on. Get off my back."

"Sometimes I think you sling it about wantin' to be a saint and all that baloney. Come on and have a cigarette, for Christ's sake. You mean you've never smoked yet? Not even once?"

"Never."

Dave shoved a Chesterfield into my hand. "Well, I dunno . . . maybe . . ."

"I'm not gonna force you. What the hell do I care if you smoke or not?"

I wondered if smoking could be a sin, and told myself it couldn't. Nope. It's only puffin' smoke. And how could puffin' smoke break any Commandment? "What the heck. Gimme a light."

For a long time I had not broken Mom White's taboo. I hadn't even been interested in smoking. But I had seen others doing it, and I had watched them apparently relishing each drag they took.

Since I had trouble lighting the cigarette, Dave reached over and took it. "Here, let me show ya."

When the cigarette end was glowing red, Dave returned it to me and said, "You gotta breathe in through your mouth."

I put the cigarette to my lips and a wisp of smoke entered my right nostril. I gasped, my eyes watered, and I removed the cigarette with a tremulous hand. "The damn smoke went up my nose, Dave."

"Shit. That's nothin'. You get used to it. Come on. Try swallowin' the smoke this time." Once again I tried, followed the instructions carefully, breathed the smoke in through my mouth, and swallowed. Then I doubled up coughing and threw the cigarette to the ground.

"Try it again," urged Dave. "You'll get used to it. Breathe in real slow. Ya don't have to swallow the damn smoke if you don't want to."

Again I tried and again I coughed. Then I shook my head and said, "I'm gettin' sort of dizzy."

Dave laughed. "When you get to be a vet'ran smoker like me you won't get dizzy at all."

As I grinned a sickly grin, Dave said, "Holy shit, your face is turnin' all green. You better not smoke anymore or else you'll get sick."

I stopped puffing but it was too late. Shouting "Oh . . . I feel . . .," I dove behind a gravestone where I tossed up from my queasy stomach, among other things, the cream-filled Devil Dog cake I had eaten on the way back to Norwood from the Golf Course.

When I recovered my composure, Dave said, "I got sick first time I smoked too. Don't worry. It's nothin' after you get used to it. It's a lot of fun, smokin' butts."

"Doesn't seem like fun to me."

"When you get to know what you're doin' it's different. You'll see."

"Yuh, I guess I'll see," I said unenthusiastically as we left the old cemetery and headed for Mrs. White's house. When we were about to enter the house, I asked Dave, "Do I look like I been sick?"

"Nope. Not with your tan and all those freckles. Hell, you look okay now, but you sure looked green around the gills up there in the old cemetery."

Even though I felt awful, I grinned at Dave and a knowing grin came back at me as we went into the house. We had shared a forbidden pleasure that day when I was initiated into the ranks of men who smoked. Yes, the pursuit of pleasure had brought more pain than fun. But there was an excitement in it for me. And now Dave and I had a special secret bond between us.

11

It was the spring of 1943, and I was walking with the Rothwell Brothers near the Tannery, heading toward 42 Mountain Avenue. Each of us had a one-pound bag of sugar in a plain brown wrapper. We had stood in the sugar rationing line at the A&P for a long time that Saturday morning.

"I think this is hoardin'," I said.

"So what if it is?" said Joe. "Hoardin's nothin'."

"I don't think it's hoardin'," said Dave, "but I wonder if they're in the black market up at the C&W. Mom gets a lot more butter and stuff than you're supposed to get."

"I wonder if it'd be a sin for us to eat black market stuff," I mused.

Joe retorted, "How the hell could eatin' be a sin?"

"Yuh, I suppose." I took a deep whiff of freshly tanned leather as we passed an open Tannery window where blue-overalled workers could be seen working inside. "I sort of like that smell," I said. "I don't think I'll ever get sick of it."

"I sort of like it too," said Dave.

Joe held his nose. "It smells like shit."

Ignoring his remark, I said, "I bet she'll have us stampin' tin cans again this after. There's a whole pile of 'em in the cellar. But at least it's better than workin' in the damn Victory Garden."

"Yuh, I hate that garden crap," Dave agreed. "You know what I feel like right now? A smoke."

"Don't ya remember what happened last week?" I asked.

"Yuh, I remember okay. I can still taste the damn soap in my mouth."

Dave and I had been strolling along a back street in Norwood, near the Post Office, smoking to our heart's delight, when Mom White had come walking toward us from the opposite direction as if directed by an ill wind. We had cupped the cigarettes in our hands and shoved them into our pockets, but we were too late. Smoking pockets and all, she had lifted the two of us by our ears and cracked our heads together. And later, in the cellar, she had stood us at the set tubs where we had gagged on mouthful after mouthful of a mixture of brown Kirkman's soap and warm water that she had forced into us.

As we recalled the episode, Joe laughed. "It was funny as hell hearin' her yelling at you guys and shovin' the soapy water down your throats. I could hear you gurglin' all the way up in the kitchen."

"It wasn't funny for us," I said, "so I don't think I'll smoke again around Norwood, that's for damn sure. Except maybe up the cemetery."

"Who cares what she says?" said Dave. "I'm gonna smoke when I feel like it."

"I dare ya to smoke now," said Joe.

I grinned. "I double dare ya."

"Triple dare me if you want to." Dave shook his head. "We're too close to the house now. I'll have me a smoke later, somewhere else."

"You're a yellow belly," taunted Joe.

"I'm not yellow," said Dave. "I'm just smart. And you better take it back about my belly bein' yellow."

"What if I don't feel like takin' it back?"

"Then I'll squeal about the Hershey bars you clipped up the Five-and-Ten yesterday."

Joe wasted no time saying, "I take it back. You're not yellow."

Peace was restored as we crossed the railroad tracks and walked toward the rocky path leading to Mountain Avenue. Then

Joe asked, "Hey, Tommy, did you finish that book you was readin'?"

"Yup."

"You've always got your nose in a book."

"So what? That's my business." This had become one of my favorite expressions.

"Yuh, I guess it is."

Joe sent a wad of spit flying at a nearby fence post. "Ya know who I think is the world's biggest pain in the ass? That President Roosevelt. I wish to hell he wouldn't be on the radio so much. He screws us out of the best programs. And ya know what else is a pain? Those stupid air raid drills."

Dave said, "The war could come here, ya know, so we gotta be ready."

"Well, if it came here I'd fight in it," said Joe. "I wouldn't be a draft dodger like that guy across the street. I'd help kill the enemy soldiers. And if they invaded us we could hide in the woods down the street and shoot those wicked lookin' Japs and Nazis."

I asked, "Shoot 'em with what? Sling shots?"

"We'd get some twenty-twos."

"Sure."

Dave said, "I wonder if Tom White's killed any Japs yet."

I said, "I don't think he's where the big battles are."

At Liggett's Drug Store, for twenty-five cents, I had bought a Hammond's Map of the World and with this map I was doggedly attempting to follow the progress of World War II, especially in the West Pacific's Marshall Islands where Mrs. White's son Tom was as an officer with the U.S. Marines. I still recall the names Kwajalein and Eniwetok, two of the islands where he spent some time.

On the face of the map I had written in block letters, "Tommy O'Connell." The same legend had also been inscribed on the inner page of my Webster's Collegiate Dictionary, on the inside cover of each of my other books, and under the seat of my Columbia bicycle.

"The dirty Japs stuck a knife in us at Pearl Harbor," said Joe, "so now we gotta go there and kill 'em all."

"Yuh, but a lot of our guys are gettin' killed too," said Dave. "Did ya see all the gold stars on the Honor Roll up the Square?"

I nodded. "It sure is hard to think of a guy you used to see walkin' up the street, and know he's never comin' back here again."

Dave agreed. "It's hard to think of, okay. I guess a lot of good guys get killed, but we gotta win, so I guess that's the way it goes." Death was very vague for us. We assumed we were a long distance from it.

In the center of Norwood's downtown shopping area was the perfectly manicured public park that was usually just called "the Square," and sometimes described by the Irish as "the Million Dollar Square," a subtle criticism of the town fathers' expenditure. That square was where we checked the Honor Roll that publicly listed names of Norwood military personnel serving during World War II.

When we saw gold stars next to some names, we found it hard to believe young men a few years older than us were gone forever from Norwood. "Gold star mothers" had special flags in their windows in those days too. It was a patriotic time when "draft dodgers" were viewed with contempt, and our enemies were evil incarnate. The Germans and the Japanese were depicted as monsters in comic books and films, and in posters at school.

Across the street from the Honor Roll, at the intersection of Nahatan Street and Washington, near St. Catherine's Church, was the scene of one of my bicycle accidents. I had been chasing a pal on my bike, and he had run a red light at Nahatan Street with no problem. When I foolishly followed him, a car coming from my left on his green light lifted me and my bicycle into the air and deposited both me and the bike on the sidewalk near the church.

I can still recall looking up groggily into a crowd of people who probably were wondering if I was still alive. Obviously, I was. Like heroes I had seen in the movies, after I had given the driver my name and address, I said casually, "There's nothin' wrong with me, I'm okay," and I limped away from the scene with my damaged bike, rubbing my aching head and hip. I was amazed at my lack of caution, and after that accident I became more careful with the new bike provided by the driver's insurance company.

Just up the street, the driveway next to Dreyfus & White's vegetable market was the scene of a later bike accident, which proved that I didn't always learn lessons effectively. Racing with another boy along the sidewalk where we were not supposed to ride, I saw a truck exiting from a driveway, carefully judged the distance, and began to pass its tailgate. Then an unexpected object appeared in front of my face as a length of pipe jutting from the rear of the truck collided with my front teeth, sent me flying, and left me with a chipped tooth that I carried through a number of decades before having it smoothed out by a skilled dentist.

It turned out to be a day for many memories. Then, just as we were entering Mountain Avenue, Dave asked, "Did we tell ya what our Pop told us?"

"What?"

"He's gonna take us back home right after school's out."

"Yuh." Joe grinned. "We're goin' back home to Hyde Park, so pretty soon we won't have to take any more crap from Mom White."

Dave said, "Yup, we'll be gettin' out of here."

I felt as if the wind had been knocked out of me. "Brother, it won't be the same without you guys."

"Maybe you ought to ask your Pop if you can go back and live with him and your Granny," said Dave. "If you went back to Dedham you wouldn't be far from us guys in Hyde Park. But even if you stay here, our Pop'll let ya come see us. He knows we've been just like brothers."

"Yuh, we'll ask Pop," said Joe, "and he'll let ya come see us."

"Yuh." I grunted, and in frustration I kicked a small pebble toward the edge of the pavement. Then I became quiet as we walked along. My mind was filled with memories of my six years with the Rothwell brothers. Measuring heights back to back. Doing chores together. Caddying at Norfolk Golf Course. Racing each other. Bike riding. Competing. Eating. Sleeping. Everything. Now they would be gone, and I couldn't quite picture their absence.

I muttered, "Nope, it's just not gonna be the same without you guys."

"We had lots of fun," said Joe, "even though she was a real pain in the ass. How about when we were clippin' apples and the Forbes Estate dogs almost chewed our asses?"

I laughed. "I never ran so fast in my life. And I dropped half my apples."

Dave said, "I thought we'd get an ass full o' buckshot."

"What about swimmin' in Ballicky Pond?" Joe recalled. "Every time I dove in that cruddy mudhole I thought a snappin' turtle was gonna get my pecker and every time I came out of the water I had to check and see if it was still there."

We all laughed, and Dave said, "Yuh Joe, you became a real pecker checker."

We also recalled the most delicious location in the community, after Furlong's candy and ice cream store. It was the Neponset Valley Farm, a farm that had its own herd of cows. There was no ice cream stand anywhere that could ever match the quality there, or equal the excitement of reaching up to that high counter with the right change, giving it to an older boy, and asking for butter crunch, with a sugar cone, and hoping he'd put a little extra ice cream in the scoop. If he happened to know you, he would do that. If he knew you really well, he might take your quarter and give you two dimes and a nickel back, along with the ice cream cone.

On a sizzling hot day, that luscious butter crunch ice cream from that oasis of delicacies would drip all over our fingers, glue them together with its creamy thick goodness, and soil our clothes. "Mom White's gonna kill ya, Tommy. Look at the mess you're makin' on your white pants!" But every slurp had been worth the long hot walk to get there, and the unkempt results.

As we talked on about the good times, we recalled those very special occasions when we had been able to buy sundaes and banana splits. And the conversation got us licking our lips. "Help! I need an ice cream! Now!"

"Remember the time we were at O'Toole's sand pits pickin' blueberries and Joe took a leak on a bush and . . ." I started laughing so hard I couldn't finish the sentence, so Dave finished it.

". . . and Joe almost got stung to death. Remember the big lump he got from the bee sting on his pecker? He could hardly walk!"

Joe said, "How was I supposed to know there was a hornet's nest in the bush I was pissin' on? I'll tell ya somethin'. I don't piss in bushes no more, that's for sure."

We were within view of the White house as the three of us walked along with our arms on each other's shoulders, reminiscing about our six years together. I mentioned all the huts we had built down the woods. "Yuh," said Joe, "we'd always work like hell gettin' old hunks of linoleum and makin' a hut and some pain in the ass'd come along and wreck it."

"Anyway, it was fun makin' 'em," said Dave. "Everything wasn't lousy here."

Joe laughed and said, "Right, everything wasn't shit for the birds, just almost everything."

In Mom White's defense, I said, "At least she cooks some good stuff, like bread puddin'."

Dave agreed, but Joe just grunted and said, "Shit on her cookin'. I'd sooner live with Pop. She can take her cookin' and shove it."

I thought about Joe's attitude and said, "I guess cookin' doesn't make much difference, huh? It's who ya live with that counts."

As we neared 42 Mountain Avenue, Dave said, "Right. It's who ya live with, and I can't wait to get out of here and go live with Pop."

That evening as we prepared for bed, Dave and Joe and I continued our reflections on the years we had spent together. We talked of hitching rides on freight trains and sneaking cigarettes. Petty thievery at the Five-and-Ten. Bloody rock fights in the woods at the end of the street. The umbrella man with his long beard. The rag man with his horse and wagon. Our attempts to get rid of warts with mumbo jumbo techniques.

We remembered all kinds of details, important and trivial. Kneeling on the hard seats of wooden kitchen chairs to say Rosaries that had been ordered by Mom White during lightning storms. The annual trips on the paddle wheel boat to Nantasket Beach from Boston harbor. The forced naps on the parlor rug. Paddling around in leaky boats at New Pond. Selling chances for St. Catherine's carnival. Having teeth pulled by the school dentist Dr. Curtin, otherwise known as "The Horse Doctor."

We recalled that special stone wall across the street from our St. Catherine's church, in front of the United Church of Christ. It had been just about perfect for sitting on and relaxing, but it seemed as if every time we sat there the police would move us along. The idea of more than two boys congregating meant potential trouble.

Dave and Joe laughed as they remembered the episode across the street from St. Catherine's at the magnificent Norwood Memorial Municipal Building, a gothic creation erected in 1928. It had a high bell tower where we thought our local version of the hunchback of Notre Dame lived. And sometimes we would try to sneak up those steep steps to the top, but were always stopped by a locked door.

However, that wasn't my great adventure there. It had happened while we were playing hide-and-seek, and I had impulsively jumped into a deep pit there which was designed to give light to a basement window. Not only were Dave and Joe unable to find me, but I also couldn't climb back up again. Finally, I had to yell for help, and a kind policeman responded, gave me a hand, and asked, "What is it you were doin' down there?" "Playin' hide-and-seek, officer." "Sure and ye hid yourself too well, did ye? Get on with ye now, it's gettin' dark."

Through laughter and wistful reminiscences we talked and talked, in a flood of nostalgia. All the memories surfaced. Coasting down the steep hill of the old cemetery and keeping our heads down as we flew under the driveway's chain. Collecting silver cigarette wrappers and saving them in a ball until the ball was big enough to sell to the junk man for a nickel . . . for "the war effort." Hot cross buns every week and Mass every morning during Lent. "Cheese it, the bulls." "On your mark, get set, go."

There was the memory of the plane crash too. One of the fighter planes at the small training field off Neponset Street, a Grumman Avenger, had made a spectacular crash landing on a heavily populated street near the high school, but the pilot hadn't been injured, and had miraculously avoided houses, yards, and people. The crashed plane was a sight we would long remember. Before the fire department had come we had all scrambled onto the plane, like scavengers, taking souvenirs. After getting caught up in the fever of the moment, I took a few bullets I had no use for. The bullets were several inches long, and their size astounded me. I hid them in the cellar, never told anybody about them, and purposely forgot where they were.

We also talked about Norwood's air ace, Colonel Lee, who had been known for his daredevil flying stunts before he had joined the Army Air Force. It was said that he had flown a small plane under the granite Nahatan Street bridge when a train was going by up above. It's still hard to imagine that he carried it off, but Lee continued to be a local legend during the war and was unscathed after flying many fighter missions in combat over Europe.

The only daredevil thing we could recall about Norwood's railroad bridges was following the tracks over them, sometimes balancing on the rails as we walked. We avoided looking through the frightening spaces between the ties, and tried to conquer our fear that we might trip and go plummeting down to the street below if we missed our footing. Once in a while, to increase our danger, we would hop onto a slowly moving train and ride a half-mile to the next stop. In Norwood, and in other towns with railroad tracks in those days, there was always someone who had been crippled in a railroad accident by pressing his luck the way we did. We were lucky.

Eventually, we were all talked out and said good night, but moments later as I pondered the imminent departure of the Rothwell brothers, there in the late evening quiet of the third floor finished room next to the attic, the sloped ceilings seemed to press down on me, the echoes of our conversation faded, and a black mood descended on my whole being.

The blackness of my mood was accentuated by another bit of bad news. My priestly idol, Father Williams, was being transferred to another parish. And as I lay there trying to rest my eyes, which refused to close even though I wanted them to, I pondered my dismal future.

If there was any security left in me at that moment in time it was shaken by the bitter prospects which would soon be realities. I could not picture my life at Mrs. White's group foster home without the Rothwell brothers and Father Williams to give me encouragement and emotional support. It was as if the wolves were leaving the wolf child behind and unconnected as they departed from the cave.

Being "different" was one thing; being abandoned again was quite another. In my eyes, these friends and that priest were as important to me as my heart and lungs. They were vital aspects of my life. And they were being ripped away from me in a very unfair twist of fate. I was both angry and frustrated. Why? Why? Why? Why this? Why now?

Reaching for my beads, I decided to pray the sorrowful mysteries. I certainly wasn't going to pray either the joyful mysteries or the glorious. I didn't feel joyful, and there was nothing glorious about my pals leaving and Father Williams getting sent away from Saint Catherine's.

As I prayed the sorrowful mysteries of the Rosary, tears filled my eyes and continued to pour down as I went through decade after decade of Our Father's and Hail Mary's. And when I had completed the Rosary I kissed the small crucifix at the end of the beads and I hung the beads over the post on the chair that stood next to the bed.

Then I wiped some of the tears from my face with the top edge of the bed sheet and I took the Miraculous Medal of the Virgin Mary, which I wore on a silver chain around my neck, and I kissed it and continued praying.

Please let me go live with Granny. That's where I ought to be, Blessed Mother. If I was back there I could still see the Rothwells a lot and I'd like it there much better than here. I especially want to go there now 'cause Dave and Joe will be gone pretty soon. And Dave has been prackly like my twin brother and Joe's been like my brother too. And it'll be wicked here without 'em. Anyhow, I'm awful sick o' this place, Blessed Virgin. I've been here long enough. Please answer my prayer. I really wish you would. I'm really sick o' bein' here. Haven't I been here long enough? Can't I go back home now?

Even as I prayed I felt that the odds were heavily against me. Negative experiences had shaped my attitudes. After all, I had repeatedly wished for my mother's return to full mental and physical health, and that certainly had not come about.

I now believe that in my early years my disgust with reality had opened a gate through which fantasizing had entered my psyche and become a habitual part of my character. After all, I usually wanted to be somewhere other than where I was. The only exception was when I could spend time at Granny O'Connell's house in East Dedham. I felt comfortable there.

On reflection, it's obvious that there was very little in my life that I was satisfied with, including my skinny body, the ears that were too obvious, the crooked teeth, the numerous freckles, and the head that I thought stuck out in the back like a Neanderthal man's.

Could fantasizing give me a rugged constitution, ears flat to my head, straight teeth, an absence of freckles, and a head shaped like a movie star's?

However, somewhat undaunted in the face of reality, I persistently engaged in impossible wishing, very unlikely wishing, and idle wishing. Yet every so often I concentrated on wishing for the possible. Even though the odds were slim, I knew there was a possibility that I might be allowed to return to East Dedham to live again with my father and Granny. So I wished, fantasized, and obsessively worried about that idea.

As I closed my eyes to try to sleep, more tears trickled down my cheeks, and even as I prayed I really doubted that my prayers would be answered. When it came to matters involving my father, I was all too aware of his many broken promises and my infuriating disappointment when he failed to deliver. So let's face it; I just didn't trust him. His behavior and its effect on me had left me with a very strong tendency toward pessimism based on unfulfilled past wishes.

Although I was not familiar at that time with the terms "outsider" or "lone wolf" and all their implications, I was feeling that way as I lay there in the third floor finished room at 42 Mountain Avenue in Norwood. But finally, emotionally exhausted and feeling very much alone and abandoned, I slept.

12

Lean and freckled, dressed in a blue short-sleeved shirt and denims, I was standing at the brink of the hill opposite the main entrance to Norfolk Golf Course, hitchhiking. Puffing on a cigarette, I waited for another car to come along.

There had been a dull ache in my spirit since the Rothwell brothers had gone home to their family early in the summer. Also, Father Williams' transfer had been hard to take. In the White house, I didn't feel close to either Bob Resker or young Frankie Salmon. Nor did I have any desire to associate with the two young new boys who, within a week of the Rothwell brothers' departure, had arrived at Mrs. White's as replacements. After all, they were in the early grades of elementary school, and I was soon to enter the seventh at Norwood Junior High. Any difference in age was a major item in the adolescent mind.

Carrying my sense of loss, and not knowing how to handle it, I felt very much alone in the busy White house. But I had my books to read; there was Norfolk Golf Course for caddying; and I was spending more time with my neighbor and classmate John. He had gone with me to the golf course that day. But he had decided not to caddy. Instead, he had hunted for golf balls in the woods and found enough to make an easy day's pay re-selling them to golfers. Earlier, he had hitchhiked home to beat the heat of the warm late-June day.

So there I was, on my own again, a situation that was becoming more and more familiar. Obviously, there was a touch of anxiety when I was on my own because I knew enough about the world to realize it could be a hazardous place for the unwary. But there was much about being on my own that I enjoyed, especially the sensation of freedom.

Whether my lone wolf independent tendencies were in me from conception, or had developed as a response to the early trauma in my life and my "incarceration" at Mrs. White's, I am not able to say for sure. Perhaps it was a combination of these factors. But one thing I do know is that the idea of having nobody to answer to but myself was a powerful one for me. I have always found authority of any kind irritating.

As an exercise in freedom of choice, after completing my eighteen holes I had gone to the clubhouse vending machine and gotten a new pack of Chesterfields for myself. I was going to hide them next to a gravestone in the old cemetery where I had experienced my first cigarette.

As I stood there hitchhiking, taking a deep drag, I sucked the smoke into my lungs. It burned on the way down but I avoided coughing, and I didn't feel nauseous because I had begun smoking more regularly. I was acting like a veteran smoker now. Like the big kids.

As I exhaled I sighed. "Ah, good." Then I took another drag on the Chesterfield and asked myself, what the hell's the difference if I smoke anyhow? Who cares? Mom White cares but why should I give a hoot about what she thinks? All I want to do now is get out of her house and go to East Dedham where I belong. And I'd sooner go to school in Dedham. I don't like the looks of Norwood Junior High.

When I go on vacation to Granny's pretty soon, I'll ask my father when I can go back there to live, but if he wanted me to he would have said something to Mrs. White or me about it. The Rothwell brothers are lucky. Their father wanted 'em back.

I'm sick of livin' with Mom White, and I'm sick of Norwood. And I think I'm even sick of school. I wish I could just read what I feel like reading and forget about school and tests and report cards and all that crap. I'm sick of caddying too.

I had caddied eighteen holes doubles the easy way that day, and the wide straps of the ladies' light canvas bags had been kind to my bony shoulders. "You've got it knocked, O'Connell," another caddie had yelled out when I had been assigned to the two women. The women had taken their time and my legs had grown tired from waiting on tees while they talked and allowed twosomes and even foursomes to pass through. At the end of the eighteen holes they had given me four fifty-cent pieces. The rate for eighteen holes was seventy-five cents per golfer.

I did okay with the two ladies. I got a half-a-buck tip. Better'n I did with that old tightwad Scotchman I had the last time. Imagine being so cheap you'd give a kid seventy-four cruddy cents and a stick of gum, and no tip. Someday when I'm a golfer I won't be a cheapskate like that. I'll give big tips.

A car came over the hill. I stuck out my arm and extended my thumb. The car whizzed past. And I wondered if I should have brought my bicycle.

I thought, Maybe I should have, but I don't think I'd feel like pedaling five miles to Norwood up huge hills after eighteen holes in the hot sun.

Another car came into view. Again I stuck out my thumb. Again the car whizzed past.

Cripes. Another stingy driver that won't stop to give a guy a lift. When I grow up and get a car I'll never pass a kid thumbing on the road. I'll pick up every kid I see. Even if there are six of 'em I'll pick 'em up. What's the big deal about picking up a kid when you're goin' someplace anyhow?

I jingled the four fifty-cent pieces in the pocket of my dungarees. During the spring the dungarees had shrunk a little and I had grown, so the pant legs stopped at my ankles and the pockets were tight.

I'll give her a buck-and-a-half to save for me. With the other half-a-buck I'll stop at the Waiting Room and get myself a Whoopie Pie, a Devil Dog, and maybe a lemon-and-lime, too. Boy, I could use a cold drink right now. It's as hot as . . . .

A gray Ford came over the brink of the hill with a lone woman at the wheel. I cupped the cigarette in my left hand, held out my thumb, and beamed a "How's-about-it" look toward the windshield of the car. The woman looked my way once, turned away, looked again, and braked to a stop. I flipped my cigarette into the gutter and hopped in.

"Where are you going, young man?" The gray haired, wrinkled woman had rimless eyeglasses and she seemed like a thin version of Mom White.

"To Norwood, ma'am." As I slid into the front seat I closed the right hand door.

"I see." She shifted into first speed and the Ford started moving. "I seldom pick up hitchhikers. You never can tell what type of person you might pick up and a woman can't be too careful, but you look like a nice boy. I'm an excellent judge of character. I can usually tell from a first impression what a person's really like. Evil shows up in a face, you know."

I nodded at her, said nothing, and looked out the window at the passing scenes. Houses in the distance moved slowly by. Trees in the fields moved briskly by. And the telephone poles zipped by, in a blur.

"Do you live in Norwood, young man?" "That's right." "What street do you live on?" "Mountain Avenue." "Where is that located?" "It's just beyond Hill Street near Railroad Avenue, one street away from the railroad tracks." "I see. Do you have any brothers and sisters?"

Uh-oh. Here she goes. What's she going to ask me next? What I had for breakfast?

"Nope, I don't have any brothers and sisters, but I live with some other boys."

"Oh? And they're not your brothers?"

"Nope, I live with Mrs. White." I assumed that the woman at the wheel would know Mrs. White. Everybody in Norwood seemed to know her.

"Who is she? I don't live in Norwood, you know. I live in Wrentham. That's where I'm going."

"Oh." I had not been to Wrentham but I knew it was beyond Walpole.

"Is Mrs. White your foster mother?"

"Not exactly." I wondered what made this woman so curious. "I'm not adopted. Mrs. White takes care of boys from Catholic Charities, that's all."

"Are you an orphan?"

"Sort of. Once I used to live with my father and my grandmother in East Dedham, and some day soon I'm gonna go back and live with 'em again."

"I see. You're just staying with Mrs. White until you're old enough to go back to your family."

We were approaching Norwood on Washington Street and had another mile to go. So far, so good. But she's so nosy. Next thing she'll be askin' about the last time I took a leak.

"You have no mother?"

My heart thumped rapidly because the subject of my mother was one I had consciously avoided for a long time. If someone asked about her I would just say, "I lost her when I was a baby." I would not say she was dead because that would have been a lie. On the other hand, I would certainly never say she was in an insane asylum because I knew people would not understand.

Instead of answering the woman, I shook my head and thought, I don't have to tell her anything. I don't even know this woman. Besides, it's none of her business.

"Do you have a mother?" The woman phrased her question a bit differently this time.

"No, I don't."

"What happened to her?"

I turned my head toward the woman, looked directly at her face, and said bluntly, "She's dead. She died when I was a little kid."

"Oh my goodness. You are an orphan after all." The woman was flustered. "That's too bad. How sad for you not to have known a mother's love, and to be an only child."

"I wasn't an only child. I had a brother."

"I thought you said you didn't have any brothers and sisters."

"I don't. My brother died when I was a baby."

She became even more flustered. "How sad to lose both your mother and your brother."

I looked out the window and said nothing. I had never lied about my mother before. I had evaded the truth and had couched my phrases in vagueness, but had never come right out and said she was dead. And I wondered why I had said it to the woman.

I guess it's easier to say she's dead. People understand that. They'd never understand if I said she's crazy in an insane asylum and I've never seen her. From now on if anyone asks me about her I'll just say she's dead. She might as well be. She doesn't even know me, and I don't know her.

"Can I get off at the next street?" I asked as we were approaching Railroad Avenue.

"Why, certainly." She braked and pulled over to the side of the street.

I said, "Thanks for the ride" as I stepped to the pavement. "You're welcome." As I was about to close the door on my side she leaned over and smiled at me. "I wish you good luck, young man." I blushed and stumbled away from the car self-consciously.

The Ford drove on and I crossed Washington Street. Cobblestones and old trolley tracks were still there on Norwood's main street, even though the trolleys had given way to bus lines. We had learned on our arrival at Mrs. White's house that those rails and that street were a distinct line of demarcation dividing the central portion of this heavily Irish community into two sections described as Dublin and Cork City.

Dublin was up the hill toward Westwood, and Cork City was below toward Canton. I lived in Cork City, which was the name of the city in Ireland near where Mrs. White had come from. Her pride was contagious, and we boys became fiercely territorial. We even thought Dublin boys had strange looking faces and "talked funny."

The bus to Boston that stopped at the Waiting Room had the words "Eastern Mass. St. Ry" written on its sides. And during my early years of reading I had thought the abbreviation meant "Saint Ry." I wondered who the holy person was, but later learned that it meant "Street Railway," and I was informed that the "Eastern Mass." did not mean a Byzantine religious service; it was the name of our part of Massachusetts.

When I arrived at the Waiting Room I breathed a sigh of nostalgic relief. For as long as anyone could remember, the Bonica family had operated it as a refuge from the elements, and a place for a snack while people waited for the Boston bus. This was where we bought pieces of black licorice candy that were about a foot long, chewy, and delicious. And on this day, after my ordeal in the car with the nosy woman, I decided to treat myself to a lemon-and-lime, a Whoopie Pie, and a Devil Dog.

As I sipped on the lemon-and-lime I reflected, that old bag was a real beaut. I never had anyone ask me so many questions. What the hell business is it of hers who I am and where I live and if my parents are dead or alive? Damn it. I'm sick of people askin' me questions.

When I was done I strolled along Washington Street toward Railroad Avenue, passing a couple of stores that were vacant. Since the Great Depression, vacant stores had been numerous, but sometimes there were temporary rentals. And there near the Waiting Room, about once a year for a few weeks, the itinerant gypsies would come to town, with their bandannas on their heads, earrings in their ears, and crystal balls. Renting one of the empty spaces, they would read palms, tell fortunes, and who knows what else happened behind their mysterious curtains.

As I was just about to pass Clark's Pharmacy on the corner, where I often ran errands for Mrs. White, my eyes were drawn to the inviting stairway entrance that led up several flights to the popular Bamboo Inn. Its tantalizing smell of Chinese food drifted out of kitchen windows far above the street, luring adventurous people up those awe-inspiring wide stairs to that elevated world of the Orient and its Asian delicacies. On rare occasions we would go there as a household, for chop suey.

When I turned the corner to head down Railroad Avenue, a sign in a tavern caught my eye: "Booths for Ladies." Actually, no self-respecting lady would have been caught dead there because even calling it a "dive" would have been far too great a compliment. It even smelled awful as we walked by there, and by habit we would walk around it in a wide arc.

A short walk along Railroad Avenue led me to the old cemetery, where I found a suitable gravestone that I wouldn't have a hard time locating later on. I pushed aside a clump of high grass at its base, inserted the package of Chesterfields, shoved the grass back into position, crossed the remainder of the graveyard, scaled a low wall, and half stumbled and half ran down the hill I had often used for coasting in the winter.

Memories came flooding back to me. Memories of exciting times with the Rothwell brothers, like when we went to the sprawling nearby tanning factory known as Winslow Brothers & Smith, where we would beg for pieces of scrap sheepskin to shine our shoes with. To this day I have never found anything as effective for buffing shoes as that sheepskin, and there was something special about the clean, pure woolly smell of those polishing cloths provided by nature, with a little help from the tannery.

The old cemetery also evoked clear memories. Often we did "I double dare you" stunts there. We could avoid an "I dare you" at times, but not a double dare. Afraid of being called "yellow," we would tease each other into entering an ancient abandoned tomb. Or we would taunt each other to mount a cemetery wall designed to contain erosion, and leap from there to the roof of one of the tannery's sheds several feet away. Sometimes we made it to the roof, but other times we fell to earth. The good news is that the fall was only a few feet, although it seemed very high to us at the time. We sprained a few ankles there, but our bones remained intact.

We also coasted down the steep cemetery hill on our Flexible Flyer sleds and just barely made it at high speeds under the heavy driveway chain that kept vehicles out of the area. If you lifted your head one inch you would be in the hospital, if you were lucky. We kept our heads down, and held on for dear life as we flew along the extension of Central Street, skidding to a stop before reaching busy Railroad Avenue.

While I was thinking about my years with Dave and Joe Rothwell there was a mist in my eyes. I really missed them. As I crossed the tracks, I shook my head and muttered to myself, "I'm so sick of everything here. Sick of it." After going up Hill Street a short distance, I entered the rocky path which went through the stony ledge-filled vacant lot at the end of Mountain Avenue, and I was still grumbling.

I wonder why I'm so sick of everything, I mused as I picked up a small stone, aimed it at a utility pole, heaved it, and scored a direct hit on my first try. Well, I ought to be glad I'm goin' to Junior High after this summer's over. I'll be wearing long pants finally, instead of knickers. And Mom White doesn't give ya the switch after you get into Junior High. But I'm still not that keen on going to Junior High here in Norwood. I'm not keen on anything any more. I'm sick of everything. Sick, sick, sick.

Well, at least I'll be going down to Granny's on vacation soon. I'll have some fun there with Billy and Margie in the neighborhood, and the other kids there. Before I come back here I'll ask my father when I'm gonna go back to East Dedham to live.

As I approached the brown and white colonial house at 42 Mountain Avenue I thought, it's funny how when you get sick of something you can't talk yourself out of it no matter how hard you try. I'm sort of used to this place now, and I only had my head shoved in the toilet once, and my mouth washed out with Kirkman's soap just once, and I haven't been switched lately, but I've been here six years and I want to go back to East Dedham with my father and Granny. People there just call me Tommy, not the O'Connell boy. If the Rothwells are old enough to go back to their family then I must be old enough too. I'm almost eleven-and-a-half. I can prackly take care of myself.

As I entered the driveway to White's, I smelled my favorite dessert baking and I thought, I'm even sick of bread pudding. I never in a million years thought I could get sick of bread pudding too. It's funny how you can even get sick of things you like. I can hardly get myself interested in reading even. I never thought I'd get sick of reading books. There's nothin' in the world I like more than books and now look at me. I'm getting sick o' them too. Yup, I guess I'm just plain sick of everything.

13

As the black '37 Plymouth clacked over the wood planking of the East Dedham railroad bridge, my eyes went to the gray tile roof of the dilapidated railroad station below. The roof was still in passable condition, but the rest of the structure was gradually sinking into the ground. I wondered why the familiar landmark was being allowed to deteriorate. Then the station was out of my line of vision, and the car turned left from Walnut Street into Walnut Place, where we jounced over the potholes of the old dead-end private way which was badly in need of repair.

"Well, here we are." My father pulled up in front of Granny O'Connell's old duplex with its familiar green octagonal asphalt siding and peeling cream-colored trim. On the left was Number 22, which housed my father and Granny, and at times my bachelor Uncle Joe. On the other side lived my Uncle Bill, Aunt Rita, and their three young boys.

We stepped onto the long roofless wooden porch which ran the width of the house. It was wobbly and squeaky, with missing rails in the railing, and rusty nail heads protruding from the deck. During my pre-Norwood years when I had lived with Granny I had dropped many a penny through the cracks in the floor boards to the inaccessible space below, and every so often I would dream of discovering an entrance there beneath the porch, and crawling under to retrieve the bonanza of lost coins.

My father was about to pull open the black screen door when I heard an old friendly voice. "Is that you, Tommy?" It was Mister Fairchild, the stooped-over widower who lived in the ramshackle

102

house next door. It was the only house on the street that looked worse than Granny's.

I saw the old man standing on his long side porch which had a framework even more rickety than Granny O'Connell's. "Hi, Mister Fairchild, I'm here on vacation."

"Eh?" The old man held his hand to his ear.

My father called out, "Tommy's on vacation with us."

"Oh." The old man brushed his wild gray hair from his eyes. "So he's on vacation. Well, that's just fine." My father put a hand on my shoulder and was about to lead me inside when Mister Fairchild said, "Hold up a sec."

The old man hobbled with his cane toward the O'Connell house, then leaned over the porch railing, held out a withered, wrinkled hand, and said, "Here's a little somethin' for you, young man." The old man's dark brown eyes twinkled as he spoke.

Smiling, I took the piece of red-and-white striped candy. "Thanks a lot, Mister Fairchild."

The old man chuckled. "Good to see you back here again, Tommy. Enjoy your vacation."

The old man shuffled back to his house, and my father and I entered my grandmother's house. In the dimly lit small hallway, my father removed his white straw skimmer with the red band, and placed it on the dark oak hat rack, a baroque monstrosity with a streaked mirror.

"Is that you, Freddy?" Granny O'Connell's loud clear voice emanated from the kitchen and echoed through the house.

"Yes, Mother. It's me and Tommy."

"Sure 'n' it'll be nice having Tommy with us a few days," her booming voice replied. After nearly a half century in America she had lost most of her Irish brogue, but certain Gaelic figures of speech and inflections would always remain.

As I passed through the downstairs rooms my large brown eyes surveyed the familiar small, dark, cluttered rooms. There was little that those eyes did not see. I was perpetually scanning. You become very observant and vigilant when you are raised with a potentially violent guardian like Mrs. White. Although

Granny's house was not large and airy like 42 Mountain Avenue, the organized disorder was neat enough for me, and comfortable in its basic lack of concern for aesthetics.

There in the mahogany bookcase in the parlor were the red bound Harvard Classics that Fred O'Connell had purchased in an explosion of literary enthusiasm. In the same bookcase was a partial set of blue-bound encyclopedias which ran from A-Art to Dib-For.

Before the living room window stood the black space heater with its small kerosene drum propped at its rear. In the far corner of the "parlor" was my favorite chair. Although the cushions were hard, the wide wooden arms made it ideal for reading and eating snacks at the same time.

I followed my father through the small dining room with its large mahogany buffet, the mahogany dining room table that was never used for dining, the prickly horsehair cushioned chairs that went with it, the old Morris chair, and the flat-springed cot where Granny slept.

As I stepped down the single step leading to the kitchen I saw an open pan boiling on the black iron kitchen stove which had been converted from coal to oil long after other people had converted theirs. The pan contained tea with some eggshells added. Asleep under the stove was Tony the cat, who did not enjoy being petted and wanted only to be left alone. He was one in a long line of cats named Tony. When one Tony died she would simply get a new one and give him or her the same name.

"You're just in time for a cup o' the tea, Freddy," said Granny, "and ye'll find some milk in the ice box for Tommy." In her squeaky rocking chair with the green paint half worn through to the undercoat of faded red, my grandmother rhythmically rocked back and forth, fingering her ever-present Rosary beads. Her long gray-black hair was tied behind her head in a bun, and her gaunt Irish face, with its large arched nose and prominent cheekbones, was a road map of small wrinkles. She was wearing a flannel bathrobe pinned at the neck with a miraculous medal of the Virgin Mary, and she reminded me of a picture I had recently seen of an old Indian squaw.

"Sure, I was just saying a prayer to the Good Lord to bring peace to the worruld. Let me see ye, Tommy. My eyes aren't good, ye know. Come over near me."

As I stepped over to her, she stretched out her bony hand with its wrinkled skin, took my hand, and squeezed it hard. Then she squinted at me through her large round steel-rimmed spectacles. "Sure, ye're not that little any more, Tommy."

She stood up, and my eyes were almost in line with hers. "Sure, he's big as me and still growing. Soon ye'll be looking down on me." She nodded her head and said, "I've always been small, ye know. My mother in the old country, God rest her soul, used to call me little Josie. I never was more than five foot but I'm getting smaller now the older I get."

My father returned from the pantry where the ice box and bread box were located, and put a quart of milk and a box of graham crackers on the table.

Look what she's got on the floor, I thought as I sat across from my father at the oblong kitchen table. She's gone and covered the linoleum with her old newspapers and burlap from old potato sacks. Granny's really somethin' with her potato sacks on the floor and the papers. Mrs. White would faint if she ever saw this place.

On the kitchen walls Granny had her own private photo and print gallery which included a print of the Last Supper, several rotogravure photos of leading local church figures, and a framed print of the Rock of Ages in which a woman was clinging to a large rock for dear life as the waves came pounding ominously at her little island.

"Drink up your milk, Tommy," ordered the old woman as she moved from the rocking chair to the kitchen table. "Sure an' I remember when ye'd knock the glass out o' my hand if I gave milk to ye."

"I used to hate it, Granny. I don't mind it now."

"Oh, 'tis good ye don't mind it. There's nothing as good for ye. Sure, I remember how we milked my father's cows in the old country and served it in a pitcher at the table. Now we get it at the store or they bring it to ye in a truck. Nothing's the same as it was anymore."

My father sipped his tea. "Nothing ever stays the way we want it to, Mother."

"Sure, 'tis best to put our trust in the good Lord." Granny slurped the tea in her tablespoon. "Only the good Lord above knows what's good for us."

I nodded my head and sipped my milk. Then with my tongue I maneuvered the soggy graham crackers stuck on the roof of my mouth. My father sipped on his tea for a few moments and then he stood up. "I've got some work to do at the office, Tommy. You can go out and play with the kids in the neighborhood. I'll see you later."

"Okay." It was no coincidence that I omitted the word "Dad" from my remark. Not since the day I had been left at Mrs. White's house six years before had I called my father "Dad." At first I had avoided the salutation because of frustration and anger and loneliness. Now the habit of omission was deeply entrenched.

When my father was gone and I was sitting there sipping milk and nibbling on graham crackers, and dunking some of them in the milk, Granny said, "He's always going off to his office. Sure, he thinks if he works day and night there they'll make him boss some day when the postmaster retires." She chuckled. "Well, a fat chance Freddy O'Connell has of being boss of anything. He's never been that good at managing himself, never mind the affairs of others."

I received no clear message from her comments about my father, and my father's employment at the Dedham Post Office held no immediate interest for me. This was also true of the rest of my father's world. Our lives had become totally separate.

The old woman took her cup of tea and carried it with her to her rocking chair. Then she began to propel herself back and forth. "Sure, he wasn't such a good manager when it came to Margaret either."

Margaret? That's my mother's name.

"He was off gallivanting more often than not." Granny rocked and fingered her beads. "Not a dime to his name did he have when you were born. She was the one that worruked steady, not Freddy. I liked Margaret. She was very decent. Yes, 'tis too bad . . ."

The words trailed off and she mumbled to herself as she fingered her beads almost in rhythm to the rocking of her chair. In rapt attention, I sat frozen in place with graham crackers before me on a chipped blue-and-white dish, and my glass of milk in hand.

I wonder why she's saying these things now. She never said a word about my mother before. It's funny how when I'm not even asking for it, the information comes.

"Her mother was a black Protestant, she was. Mrs. Henderson was a tough nut. Nobody hated Catholics more than her, but Margaret didn't think that way at all. She was Scotch and Protestant, but she was kind to one and all. She didn't care a tinker's damn if you were a Catholic or not. I liked Margaret. She was level headed.

"It wouldn't have surprised me in the least if Freddy got muddled, but I never thought Margaret would go that way. It's all in the past, it is, and there's no going back. Sure, the good Lord watches over us, and more we can't ask if we have a bit o' tea in the house and a bit o' bread.

"Faith, 'tis a bitter struggle, it is, every step of the way, Tommy, but you're young now and devil a care do ye have now with yere books and yere games. I wouldn't go back to do it over again though. No sirree. Life gives ye many a bitter pill to swallow."

She rocked and mumbled a few more prayers and as I sat there Granny's comments swirled in my mind and I thought, My mother was Scotch and her name was Henderson and she was Protestant. So I'm half Scotch and half Irish. I thought I was all

Irish and I thought I was all Catholic, but I'm half Protestant and half Catholic. Half and half. That's me, I guess.

During the remainder of my stay at the O'Connell house, I often joined the other boys and girls to play in the field up the street, and in the woods at the end of the street, and around the old railroad station to the rear of Granny's house. When I was not playing with my Walnut Place friends I was in the house operating as a lone wolf, entertaining myself with various books. My interest in reading had returned, and I could enjoy reading a book as much as playing outside with other children.

In the morning the rumbling and whistling of locomotives stopping at the East Dedham station would wake me up, and I would look out the window of my absent Uncle Joe's room which I was now occupying, and I would watch the people who took their train daily to Boston with their newspapers, bundles, briefcases, umbrellas and canes. I would romanticize the commuters' lives and then I would have breakfast and read for a while and rummage through the news clippings and papers beneath the dining room and kitchen tablecloths.

One day in the parlor bookcase I came across an old photograph album that contained a snapshot of a woman with an infant. I had never seen a photo of her before, but I knew that the woman was my mother. I took the photo album and looked first in the mirror, then at the baby picture, and nodded my head in confirmation as I noticed how the ears of the baby stuck out at the top. Yup, that's me and my mother. Just like Granny said, she looks like a nice person. She's got a nice smile and she's holding me like she loves me. But I don't remember her at all. Not a bit.

I took the album and went with it to a picture on the parlor wall which showed me when I was four years old, and I thoughtfully compared the photo album picture with the one on the wall.

My ears weren't so bad after I got some hair. I was a lot better looking when I was three or four years old. Better than now with these stupid crooked front teeth. My teeth were small and straight then. I wish they were now. I hate them being big and crooked. Maybe some day I'll have 'em pulled out and get some nice straight fake ones put in.

Day after day, I went back to the photo album and examined its pages closely. There were brown-hued snapshots of my father with me in an old convertible, several shots of me and Granny, some shots with my aunts and uncles, and a few of my grandfather holding me.

I wonder why Grandpa doesn't live with Granny. How come he's got his own old house on the other side of East Dedham and she has her old house over here near the railroad? She never says anything about him except after my father takes me to visit him. Then she asks, "How's the old gent?" He never says much about her either except maybe, "How's the old lady?" It's funny how they live in different houses. I wonder why.

There were many things I began to wonder about, but the answers remained mysteries because I was not apt to ask direct questions to my elders. I lived in a world where the slogan of adults was, "Children should be seen and not heard." However, as my vacation came to a close, my mind was obsessed with the question of whether or not my father would let me return to East Dedham to live with him at Granny's house. So it was a question I had to ask, no matter what.

Day and night during my two weeks of vacation I wondered about the possibility, but I didn't seem to be able to find the perfect time to ask the necessary question. My father was either going to his job or to the race track or to visit somebody. And the right time did not come until I found myself seated in the black Plymouth in front of Mrs. White's house in Norwood as I got ready to say goodbye to my father.

My heart pounded very rapidly, my throat felt parched, and my mouth was dry, but I finally turned to my father in a panic and blurted out, "Uh . . . can I ask you somethin'?"

"Sure, Tommy, go right ahead."

"When . . . uh . . . When do ya think I can come back and live with you and Granny?" I breathed a sigh of relief after asking the question. I had held back from asking it for such a long time that I had wondered if I would ever work up the courage.

"Well, I've been giving it some thought recently, Tommy." Fred O'Connell's blue eyes looked into space through the windshield of the Plymouth. "But I don't think you're quite old enough to live with your grandmother."

Not old enough? Dammit, how old does a kid have to be to live with his own father and grandmother?

"Your grandmother still doesn't feel well. She's not up to caring for a boy your age, and I'm working long hours at the Post Office, so I don't think it'd work out right now. I think it'll make more sense for you to go to junior high in Norwood and stay with Mrs. White till you finish the ninth grade. You'll be fourteen then, and able to watch after yourself pretty well. I think you'll be better off with Mrs. White for the next three years."

I remained dead silent and my lips were tightly pressed together as I struggled to hold back the tears.

"I'd like to have you come back to Dedham right now, Tommy. I wish I never had to bring you to Mrs. White's in the first place, but sometimes in this life we have to make difficult decisions and do unpleasant things. I know it's all very hard for you to understand now. But it's for your own good to stay with Mrs. White until you're finished junior high."

I worked up my courage and retorted, "But the Rothwell brothers went back home to live with their family." The tears were flowing down my cheeks. "And they're only my age."

I felt my father's hand on my shoulder. "They've got older brothers and sisters to help look after them. That's why they could go back to Hyde Park."

I knew he was right about that, and it was obvious that it was pointless to talk further about returning to Dedham. Actually, I had expected my father's negative answer even though I had fantasized about a positive response. But the reality was that I was unable to picture three more years at White's. So I felt like a prisoner expecting to be released and then having a six-year sentence extended to nine years.

"Will you promise you'll try to understand?"

I nodded my head but the nod was a lie. I did not understand, and I hadn't the least intention of trying to understand. My father gave me a handkerchief to wipe the tears from my eyes. "I love you, Tommy. I only want to do what's best for you."

I shrugged my shoulders and wiped my eyes. "I better go in now." I didn't want to talk with him.

My father reached out his hand and squeezed my shoulder. "I'll see you soon, son." Instantaneously, at his touch I felt nauseous. He reached in his pocket, took out his billfold, removed a five dollar bill, and gave it to me. "Here. Spend it on anything you want to."

"Thanks." I was grateful for the money, but I was furious at him for leaving me there for three more years. I stepped out of the car, walked slowly down the driveway toward the back door of Mrs. White's, and moved foggily along the driveway. The lone wolf who had hoped to be released from captivity was being driven back into his cage.

When I heard my father's Plymouth pulling away I thought, He says he loves me. That's a good one. He loves me and he just shoves me off to live in someone else's house for six years and when I want to go back home he says I'll have to stay three more years and he dumps me off at 42 Mountain Avenue and disappears. Yuh, he loves me okay. Shit.

14

It was a Saturday in the early spring of '44 and I was standing with my friend John on the outskirts of Norwood. "Whattayasay, Tommy? Are you gonna caddy today or go hunting for balls in the woods?"

I flicked the ashes from my cigarette. "It's no skin off my ass if I caddy or shag balls for a golfer or go hunting for balls. I just don't give a damn, John."

"I don't give a good goddam either."

John grinned, showing the two front teeth that jutted out enough to be classified as buck teeth. Yet John was not concerned, as I was, with the line-up of his teeth. He accepted them as they had been provided by nature. He was the one boy in the neighborhood whose teeth I would not have traded for. I would have traded for John's small ears and his stronger build, but not for the jutting teeth. He was the only boy I knew whose teeth were more prominent than mine.

John's parents were Irish immigrants like most people in the Mountain Avenue area, yet they managed to provide well for their son. His older sister worked, his father was a mill hand, and for extra income his mother cared for a young State ward named Loretta.

He had his own room, although it was small and had sloped ceilings. Also, he had a powerful short wave radio that received beams from Europe, which we would both listen to, and he had exercise equipment for muscle building. Any money that he earned for himself he kept for himself. He was not required to turn most of it in the way I had to, for clothing and other necessary expenditures.

"Here comes another car," said John. I stuck out my thumb but the car passed without slowing. The driver pointed his index finger to the right, meaning he would be taking the next right turn. It was a commonplace driver's pantomime apology, often a lie. After the car had passed, John turned, faced the rear of the departing car, clapped his left hand on his right bicep, swung his forearm upward, and then he extended the middle finger of his right hand skyward and yelled, "Take your fuckin' shit box of a car and shove it up your ass, buddy."

"What if he saw ya and came back after you, John? What would ya do?"

"I'd leap that railroad fence and run up the tracks like a rabbit with an ass full o' buckshot."

"Hah. Well, we better walk some more. Maybe we'll have a better chance for a ride at the next street." Traffic was sparse and we were nearly to the Norwood-Westwood Town Line before another car came into view.

"I'll give this one the thumb," said John. And when it appeared that the car was not going to slow down, he withdrew his thumb from its extended position, and slowly but surely extended his middle finger. The driver did not see it.

"Some day you're really gonna get it, John."

"I hope so." He laughed, pushed back the short sleeve of his sport shirt, and flexed his bicep. "Hell, I can take care of myself, Tommy. How's that for a right arm? Look at that muscle."

I examined it, felt it, and said, "That's funny. I think it shrunk, John. It sure doesn't look any bigger now than when you started that Joe Bonomo muscle buildin' course."

"You're just tryin' to kid me, Tommy. I know goddam well I've got bigger and harder muscles now than before."

"Whatever the hell you say, John."

"Sometimes you can be a wise bastard, ya know that? I used to think you were some kind of angel or somethin' 'cause you never used to even say shit before, or hell even."

"I say what I feel like now, John. Right?"

"Yuh, but I bet you won't say 'fuck'."

"So what if I won't? I don't feel like it."

"You don't dare, that's all."

"Bullshit."

"Then say it."

"Up yours, John."

"What the hell. It's up to you. You don't have to say it if you don't feel like it. At least you're a reg'lar guy now. I used to think you were a goddam saint."

"I used to think it too." I was no longer interested in becoming a saint. My belief in complete holiness and my faith in God had been shaken by the transfer of Father Williams, the departure of the Rothwell brothers, and the receipt of the news that I would be staying with Mrs. White for three more years.

Then, during the seventh grade, I had begun to pal around more with John, who was going through a very obvious "Who gives a shit" stage of his own early adolescence. And soon I had adopted a similar rebellious attitude.

"Here's the Town Line," said John. "How much you want to bet I can hawk a lunger from Norwood to Westwood?"

"I'll bet you a tenth of a cent. One mill. But no fair unless you stand back a couple of feet from the Town Line." I drew a line on the dirt with the toe of my sneaker. "Can you hawk a lunger to Westwood from there?"

John took the challenge. "Sure as shit I can, Tommy."

Taking in a deep breath, he coughed on purpose, worked a sizable ball of phlegm into the appropriate position on his tongue, and he blew. The greenish-yellow lunger sailed from his mouth and through the air in an arc, dropping to the ground just over the Westwood Town Line.

I laughed. "You're the champion spitter, John. Well, it looks like I owe you a tenth of a cent. I'll pay you back when I come across a one mill coin."

John chuckled. "I'll remember that. So who's the best damn lunger hawker in Norwood?"

"You're the king of the Norwood lunger hawkers, John."

"And you're the king of the hot shits. Hey, I just remembered somethin'. Ya know the other day when the little girl lifted up her dress to show us her underwear and she had nothin' on under her dress? Was that the first time you ever saw a bare broad?"

"That's my business." I blushed as red as I had blushed when the naive little girl had revealed her pubic area. My first clear view of the exposed female lower anatomy had embarrassed me, but not enough to refuse to look.

John laughed. "Brother, did your face get red."

"So what? Anyhow, what's the big deal about seein' a little girl?"

"It's a big enough deal." He grinned. "Every time I think about the look on your face when she lifted her dress, I think I'm gonna wet my pants from laughin'."

"You've got a weird sense of humor, John. Uh-oh, here comes another car." I extended my right thumb, and a squeal of tires signaled that we finally had a lift. At that point, we had walked nearly half way to the Norfolk Golf Course. Five minutes later we were at our destination.

"I'm gonna go lookin' for balls," said John.

"I guess I will, too. What the hell."

"I think I'll have myself a weed." George pulled a pack of Chesterfields from his shirt pocket. "Want one?"

"Thanks, John, but I've got my own." I took a pack from my shirt pocket.

"What are ya smokin'?" he asked.

"I've gone back to Kools again instead of Chesterfields because these are better for not gettin' caught by Mom White. The menthol conceals the tobacco smell."

"Hell, she prob'ly knows ya smoke. Lemme see your right hand." I held it out. "Holy Christ, no nicotine stains. How come?"

"I'm not a chain smoker like you, and when I start getting nicotine stains I scrub 'em like hell to get rid of 'em."

"Look at my fingers." John displayed what had the makings of a status symbol for a boy in the seventh grade. Both his index finger and the middle finger of his right hand were darkly stained. As we crossed a field near the second hole, he asked, "Hey, how come Mrs. White hates smokin' so much?"

"I dunno. Maybe she thinks it's a sin."

"Hell, smokin's no sin."

"I don't suppose it is."

Lighting up my Kool, I took a mentholated drag. I smoked about a pack a week and always hid them next to the same gravestone in the old cemetery. I knew better than to take a pack of cigarettes into the White house.

"I can smoke in the house anytime I feel like it," said John. "Pete doesn't give a damn what I do, and neither does my mother." John treated his father like an equal, both in using his first name and in the casual way he responded to his father's alcohol-oriented existence. In that house, authoritarian rule was not part of the child-rearing process.

"You're lucky, John. A guy can't do a thing in Mom White's house. She's a real pain in the ass." I viewed her as a puritanical nagging shrew. Resentful of her authority, I continued to question it inwardly, but I was not likely to openly question it. I knew I was still not too old to receive a wet face cloth or the palm of her hand across my mouth without warning.

Taking a stick, I pushed aside some leaves at the base of the stone wall bordering the second fairway, and a shiny surprise greeted me. "Hey, look John. I found a nice ball. No halves!"

"I wasn't even gonna say halves." I didn't know where the "halves" idea had originated, but around Mountain Avenue when anybody found anything, if a nearby boy yelled "Halves," the item had to be shared fifty-fifty unless the finder had immediately shouted "No halves!"

I examined the ball carefully, the way a diamond appraiser would examine a jewel, looking for flaws. "It's a nice Titleist. No cuts in it. I'll get six bits for it. That's equal to a round of caddyin'." I grinned. "No straps digging into my shoulders either."

John replied, "You said it, Tommy. Looking for balls sure beats caddyin'."

"Know what I dream sometimes, John? I'm walking along the wall at the second hole and I push aside a bunch of leaves with a stick and there under the leaves I find thousands of brand new balls. It's like discovering a gold mine. There are so many balls I can fill up all my pockets to overflowing and still have thousands more left. So I go sell the ones I've got. Then when I come back, guess what? The rest of the balls are all gone. It's a terrific dream except for the ending."

"Do you really have dreams like that?"

"That's nothing. My nightmares would scare you half to death, John. Wait till I tell ya . . ." From the direction of the second tee, we heard the echo of a club head striking a ball, and a moment later the ball thumped to the ground near us.

"I'm gonna get it," said John as we ran to the spot where the ball had landed. He scooped it up and called to me, "Let's blow this joint. I don't want to end up with an ass full o'golf clubs."

We ran to a thickly wooded area a hundred yards from where the ball had landed. Then, out of breath, we huddled down behind some bushes and waited. The golfers soon appeared in the distance, searched a while for the missing ball, and finally gave up. Then John said, "Let's head over the goddam hill toward the seventh. The coast is clear." Over the hill we went.

"What kind is it?" I asked as we strolled through the woods. He studied it and said, "It's a brand new Spalding. Maybe I can get a buck for it."

"You ought to," I agreed. Then I pondered the ethics of what he had just done. "Hey, do you think it's stealing when you take a ball a guy hits and don't give him a chance to look for it?"

"Shit, if I took a couple of balls out of a golfer's bag, now that's stealing, but not picking up a ball some duffer hits into the goddam woods."

"If the guy doesn't have a chance to look for it, I think it's stealing."

"For Christ's sake, Tommy, don't start talkin' like a saint again."

"Who's talkin' like a saint? I was just wondering about something. Can't a guy wonder?"

"I suppose so, but I don't think it's stealing."

"Ha! If you don't think it's stealing, then why did you run and hide?"

"'Cause the golfer might think a little different than me, that's why." John chuckled. "Anyhow, who cares if it's stealing?"

"You don't care about anything, John."

"Neither do you, you hot shit."

As the afternoon sun began to decline in the sky we walked toward the woods near the seventh hole. Making a wide arc around the seventh green so we would not be observed by the golfers there, we headed toward the portion of the seventh hole woods most likely to be the repository of lost balls. We were trudging over a ridge beneath an umbrella of pine trees when John grabbed my arm. "Listen."

"I don't hear anything."

"Wait." John put his finger to his lips. "Sh."

I stood silently, waiting, and then heard a muffled grunt coming from the other side of the ridge. Then another, and another.

John said softly, "Let's make like commandos and creep to the edge of the ridge and see what's cookin'." Along the blanket of pine needles we crawled until we could see down into a gully near where the dirt access road skirted the golf course. "Hey, Tommy, see what I see?"

Down below, stretched out on a car blanket in a group of bushes beneath the pines, we saw a couple in a position that left no question as to what they were doing. "Well I'll be . . . ." John held his finger to my mouth. "Sh . . ."

My heart pounded rapidly as I watched what was going on down below. All I could see of the woman, except for her mass of strawberry blonde hair, was a pair of white legs spread far apart, with toes pointing upward. The man was astride with his shirt on and his pants down to his knees. We watched with total fascination, and soon the man let out a groan, the woman sighed "Oh," and the two slumped together, motionless.

John whispered, "Let's shag our asses out of here. If that guy ever looks up and sees us, he'll kill us for watchin'." I nodded.

Then we crept along the mat of pine needless, and when we had cleared the pine grove John said, "I guess we can walk now."

"Yuh, I guess we can."

John said, "Christ, I heard about the woods near the seventh hole, but never thought I'd see somebody get laid there." I said nothing; I was deep in thought as I reflected on the event.

He asked, "Did you ever see anybody do it before?" I shook my head. "Me neither, but I knew it'd be like that." He laughed. "I saw enough horny pictures in the caddie shack."

In the caddie shack the older caddies were always circulating publications with lurid illustrations of sexual acts. And a reading could usually be had for a quarter. I had never requested a reading because I had drawn certain moral lines for myself. I would swear, but tried not to say "goddam," and I would not say "fuck." I would look at dirty pictures if someone handed them to me though. Yet I would not go out of my way to see one or acquire one.

"What a day this has been," said John. "Imagine seein' a guy lay a real live broad near the seventh hole. Now we really know what sex is all about, huh Tommy?"

"Yuh, I guess we do."

"We've seen the real thing. In the flesh."

"Yuh."

15

It was hotter than usual for late April, and we were trying to make ourselves comfortable as we sat on one of the unpadded green wooden benches of the Boston Elevated Railway train. When the train was pulling out of Winter Station, John said, "Taking the El's great. We ought to do it more. There's nothing like a good movie and then the penny arcade in Scollay Square for a 'peep show' and then eating at the Waldorf afterward." The Waldorf was not a ritzy hotel; it was a self-service cafeteria. "That apple pie 'n ice cream was great." John licked the corner of his mouth.

"The peep show wasn't bad either," I responded. The nude stripper in the hand-cranked film viewer had left an imprint on my mind but I had no desire to discuss it with John. That was subject matter that was better kept to myself, in my imagination.

Soon I was distracted by my own reflection in the window opposite me as the train rocked through the dark tunnel in the direction of Forest Hills. I wonder if I've got a long face like John said I had that time. It doesn't look too long in the window. From the way John talked, he had me thinking I looked like that guy in the horror movies. John Carradine.

As I stared at my reflection I tried to hold my jaw forward with clenched teeth in order to maintain a square-jawed look. I mistakenly believed that my jaw receded drastically, and I despised receding jaws as much as I disliked heads that jutted out in the back like my own did.

I don't look too skinny in the window, but that's prob'ly because I always look a little heavier when I wear a jacket. I really wish to hell I could gain some weight. I'm sick of being so skinny that my ribs stick out. Everything I have sticks out, including my ears. But I don't think they're as bad as they used to be. Maybe I'm growing into 'em.

"Ya know what we ought to do?" said John as the train left the tunnel and came to the open-air portion of the elevated railway. "We ought to go see the burley some day."

"How come you always think about goin' to the burley? Isn't the peep show enough?"

"A peep show's nothing compared to the burley. I'd give my right arm to see a burley show. Some day I'm gonna go to the Old Howard and feast my eyes on some real live strippers. Those broads take it all off sometimes, ya know. Can you imagine that?"

I shook my head because I found it very hard to imagine it. And that year, in the eighth grade, I had often thought about what it would be like to see a burlesque show because I was keenly interested in the female anatomy. Yet I was not as open about my sexual interests as my pal John. After entertaining any sex-oriented thought, I would be plagued with guilt until I finally decided to confess my indiscretion on Saturday afternoon in the chapel at St. Catherine's.

Swearing and dirty jokes no longer filled me with such guilt, but to me the mere thought of being intimate with a girl was as serious a sin as the actual act would be. I had been taught that the dividing line between sins of thought and sins of deed was perilously thin, and that both were equally frowned on by the Almighty. It had been impressed on me that the most serious of all sins were those involving sex. So I knew I would have to confess taking in the peep shows, but I was trying to avoid thinking of the necessary church visit.

"How about it?" John prodded me with his elbow. "Want to go in to Scollay Square again some day and go see the burley with me?"

"Maybe some day when we're a little older, John. After we start shavin'."

"Okay, it's a deal. I guess they'd never sell us a ticket with only this peach fuzz on our faces. We prob'ly don't look much older than that kid that's gonna leave Mrs. White's."

"Right." I paused and thought about the boy's departure. "He's a lucky stiff. He's gonna go live with his uncle and aunt after school's out. Then some other kid's gonna come. Ah, who cares who comes and who goes? I don't have much to do with the young kids at White's."

"Well, what the hell do they know about anything anyhow? They're wet behind their ears."

"Right, John. Write . . . with a pencil."

When the train stopped at Dover Street, I looked down below and saw two derelicts fighting over a bottle of wine in an alley below. "Hey, look at the stew bums fighting, John."

"Yuh, they're killing each other over that bottle. Seems like all the bums in the world live around Dover Street."

The train moved out of the station and when it passed Holy Cross Cathedral I automatically crossed myself, and John followed suit. Then we were silent for a minute.

I prob'ly ought to go to Confession more often, I reflected. I don't go much lately. I sort of save up my sins instead of running to Confession all the time. But after today I'll have to go again soon, dammit. Well, I'm still getting A's in Sunday School, and I'm still a pretty good Catholic, but I just say an Act of Contrition sometimes instead of going to Confession. And I don't bother doing Holy Hours anymore. I used to feel great after making a Holy Hour, but it just wasn't the same anymore after Father Williams left St. Catherine's.

"What are ya doing?" asked John. "Prayin'?"

"Yuh, John, I was prayin' you'd get to see the burley some day."

He slapped me on the back. "Now, that's something worth prayin' for."

"Save my back, John, I might need it some day."

"Hell, you'd never strain your back, Tommy."

"Yuh, I guess I'm sort of lazy."

"Lazy ain't the word for it. No wonder Connors calls you Old Man O'Connell in gym."

"Who cares?" I shrugged. Being in a period of rapid physical growth, I lacked energy most of the time. And due to my obvious slowness, the gym instructor was indeed calling me Old Man O'Connell. But my slowness was more than the result of my growth. I resented it when other people prodded me to move faster, so the more I was prodded the slower I moved.

"That was some joke when you got Athlete's Foot."

"It was no joke, John. I could hardly walk. You don't have to be an athlete to get it."

"You ought to know."

"Look who's talking. You're not a big athlete either. You're more of an athletic supporter." We both laughed and as the train entered Dudley Station, I told him, "I wish I could stay a little longer in Boston instead of going back to White's. I'm really sick of that place. I've never been so sick of anything. I'm getting so I hate to have her tell me to do anything. I just wonder who the hell she thinks she is. She lets me come and go without asking too many questions, and I don't have to ask permission to go places like up the liberry or to the show or over your house, but I'm sick of all her rules and it gets on my ass how she criticizes people. Nobody in the whole world knows anything but her, John. Know what I mean?"

"Yup. I know what ya mean." As the train was pulling into Green Street in the Jamaica Plain area, John nudged me. "Check that." A tight-skirted young woman left the train and went down the stairway while we both watched every movement of her departure. Then she was gone.

When the train pulled out of the Green Street station, I noticed a warning sign. "Look at that sign, John. 'Spitting Forbidden.' Isn't that a bitch? A guy can't even hawk a lunger. He has to swallow the damn thing instead."

John laughed and said, "Yuh, and they call this a free country."

We stared across the aisle through the windows of the elevated train as it passed above the Arborway "El" Terminal. "Well, John, soon we'll be out of the eighth grade and back thumbing rides to the golf course again. I think I'll mostly go hunting balls this year. I'm sick of caddying."

"I can't wait till school's over," said John. The mere thought of school's end brought a sparkle to his blue eyes.

"School doesn't bother me too much this year. I just screw off most of the time. Joining the Astronomy Club's the best one yet. I already knew what the Big Dipper was."

We left the train at Forest Hills station and as we went down the long steps, John took out a pack of cigarettes and lit up. I followed his example. "Ya know what, John? This summer I'm just gonna take it easy and I'm gonna read every book Jack London ever wrote."

"How come you always read every book a guy writes?"

"Hey, if you really like apple pie and ice cream, don't you keep eating it?"

"Yah, I guess so."

Along the route through Roslindale and Dedham to Norwood, in intermittent flashes, I concentrated on recapturing vivid fragments of the nude peep show we had seen at Boston's infamous Scollay Square, and each time I entertained the images I would get stimulated sexually.

That evening, as I lay in the cot Joe Rothwell had once occupied in the third floor finished room, while the two younger boys slept in the double bed, I closed my eyes and retrieved the picture of the peep show stripper, and my hand drifted down and I began to manipulate myself.

Then I stopped abruptly. I had never completely performed the act, although I had often felt the urge to do it, and had gone halfway at times, but I had always prayed to the Blessed Virgin to help me avoid the temptation of masturbating, and so far I had been successful. Also helping me to control myself had been a number of stories about people getting heart attacks from doing it, going insane or blind from doing it, and growing huge penises from doing it.

Also, I considered masturbation one of the most serious sins. Even when I had confessed the sin of impure thoughts in the confessional, the priest had given me twenty Our Fathers and twenty Hail Mary's and had lectured me on the need to pray to the Virgin Mary in order to avoid temptation. I did not want to knowingly offend the Blessed Virgin and did not want to willingly offend Jesus Christ and did not want to perform an act which would be a certain mortal sin.

But on that spring night in 1944, as I lay there alone in my cot in the finished room next to the attic on the third floor of Mom White's house, neither did I pray to the Virgin Mary nor did I remove my hand from down below. In a moment I was immersed in the act, and my heart pounded so fast I thought it would push through my ribs and explode. I felt as though I were revolving in space, and I was aware of nothing other than the excitement that engulfed my body.

"Ugh," I grunted involuntarily as I reached a climax. Then my whole body went limp and I lay on my back panting. The fleeting moment of ecstasy was over, and I felt weak and tired and depressed. Also, I remembered with vivid clarity all the fears that had filled my mind before. The possibility of having heart trouble. The growth of a monstrous penis. And the chance of going insane or blind. So there I was. Heart beating rapidly. Head aching. Self-image shrunken.

I thought of Jesus Christ on The Cross dying for my sins, and I thought of the Blessed Virgin Mary's astounding purity, and I was beset with a frustration which came close to suffocating me. I was enveloped in guilt as I said my Act of Contrition.

"Oh, my God, I am heartily sorry for having offended Thee . . . ." Lying there full of remorse, I vowed to attend Confession as soon as possible to bring a degree of peace back into my soul. But I had difficulty erasing the idea that by my action I had forfeited my claim to inner peace. I saw myself as the original Adam in the garden, with the fruit digested, and no regurgitation possible. And I wanted to hide from myself but there was no place to hide. So I went to sleep.

16

During the eighth grade the hormones got even more active, and provided a constant challenge. The girls were amazingly beautiful, and the urge to masturbate was powerful, yet the guilt I felt after doing it made the act seem like the most base depravity. It was my own private sexual conflict, and I shared its frustration with nobody, including my best pal.

I didn't even tell John about my embarrassing experience at the Golf Course one unseasonably cold day when I was there by myself. I had been over there looking for lost golf balls in the woods near the fifth hole, and the leaves from the previous fall had left a covering over the floor of the woods. I was browsing around, kicking aside leaves in search of balls, when I heard some giggling and heavy breathing a short distance away. I knew it must have been two lovers, and I was curious. So I began to tiptoe toward where they were.

Suddenly the floor of the woods gave way under me. I had tiptoed right into a small waterhole in the woods that had been perfectly camouflaged by the leaves. I was thoroughly drenched and I had to take my shivering body to Nick the groundskeeper's shack to warm up in front of his potbellied stove. When he asked me what had happened, I had said, "Brr. Lookin' for balls. Fell in some water." I kept very quiet about how my sexual curiosity had gotten me into trouble. In those days we made many wisecracks about sex, but we were very careful not to share the most explicit details about personal sexual events.

As John and I left Norwood Junior High on the last day of the eighth grade, John symbolized my inner feelings toward that school year when he turned toward the building, worked up a lunger, and spat on the white Corinthian column at the front entrance to the school building. "That's what I think of this place, Tommy. I'm sure as shit glad we're finally out for the summer, and I wish to hell I never had to come back here again. I can't stand the idea of one more year in this crap heap."

"Hey, the eighth grade wasn't so bad. I sort of liked English with Miss Byrne. What a dish she is. Funny how she never got married, huh?"

"Maybe she's saving herself for you."

"Very funny, John."

"How'd ya do on your card?"

"Same as the rest of the year." I shrugged my shoulders. "I got all B's, and an A in Art."

"I broke my hump and all I got was C's and a couple of B's. I can't figure out how you hardly study and you get all B's and even some A's. Hey, you know what, Tommy? I've been out of school more than a minute and I haven't even lit a weed yet."

"Me neither." I took out my pack of Kools.

"Are you still smoking those sickening things?"

"Sure, why not?" I lit my Kool and cupped it in the palm of my hand as I looked around to see if any of Mom White's acquaintances were in sight. "What the hell. They're cigarettes."

"Not in my book. I know I'm having a real smoke when I take a drag on a Chesterfield, but those weeds you smoke taste like damn Smith Brothers Cough Drops, for Christ's sake."

"So what, John?" I took in a large drag of the mentholated smoke and the two of us walked along for a few moments without talking. We were puffing on our cigarettes as we passed Norwood Hospital and strolled on toward the center of town.

John observed, "I saw you mentally undressing Olga on the front steps of the school, ya know. Hey, what the hell are you blushing for? Some days when I look at her I prackly pass out from the excitement. She's built like a brick shithouse."

"Yuh, she sure is. Do you think she puts out like all the guys say she does?"

John laughed. "Only for star athletes. But I don't think she charges. I think she just does it for the horny fun of it. I wonder if LaPierre ever made out with her. But she's not that hard up. With her build, she has her pick of the athletes, and LaPierre's no athlete."

"Do you think she wears falsies?"

"Shit, no. I saw her bending over up at New Pond one day and you never saw such a pair in your life. Oh yuh, I just remembered something. Did ya hear how they caught LaPierre in the boiler room playing with himself the other day?" said John matter-of-factly.

"You're kidding."

"Nope. Corcoran walked in and caught him in the act and LaPierre ended up getting the rattan from Eddie Nee while Corcoran held him down. Or maybe Nee held him and Corcoran swatted him. They were so pissed off at him they prackly killed him. That Nee is one tough jockstrap. He was a bigtime football player, ya know. But I think that goddam Corcoran's a fairy. Hey, ya know what LaPierre did? When Corcoran told him how crazy hacking off was, LaPierre told Corcoran to go shove his rattan up his horse's ass."

As we neared the Washington Street shopping area, we began laughing so hard we had to duck into a doorway and lean against a solid wall to support ourselves in our off-color hysteria. Then we plunked ourselves down on the steps leading to apartments up above, and we held our sides so we wouldn't burst.

When we were about to get up and move on, I saw, scrawled in red ink on the wall next to me, the words, "Fuck you." So I took my stub of a pencil and changed the first word to B-o-o-k by adding a few strokes to the first three letters.

"What the hell are you doin' that for? It's only a word."

"I don't like seeing it on walls."

"I never saw anyone else go around changing fuck to book. Sometimes I think you still want to be a saint."

"Do you really think that? Well, your ass is sucking wind, John."

John grinned. "And your ass is sucking bent carpet tacks." We both laughed as we walked along Washington Street toward our homes. "Guess what? When Corcoran and Nee gave it to LaPierre with the rattan, he didn't even flinch."

"Joe Rothwell used to do that when Mom White switched him. Some kids can take a beating better than others, or maybe they're more stubborn."

As a classmate hurried by, John said, "Hey, Jack, if you see Kay, tell her I want her."

"You're a real wise guy, John," I said.

John kept a very straight face. "What's so wise about saying if a guy sees Kay to tell her I want her?"

"You know and I know that if you listen close, 'if you see Kay' spells f-u-c-k."

"Come on, Tommy. Say fuck."

"If you ever hear me say it I'll kiss your ass."

"Is that a bet?"

I held out my hand and showed crossed fingers. "Not if I can help it." I took a drag on another Kool cigarette which I then deftly palmed so no passerby could see it.

As we passed the Five-and-Ten, John said, "Let's snag some gum." I nodded, and into the store we went. The Beech Nut and Doublemint were stacked on top of the counter, and we each flashed what looked like one pack of gum at the salesgirl, flipped our nickels onto the counter, and left the store.

Outside, John asked, "How many did ya get?"

"What do you mean, how many? I got one pack."

John laughed. "Look." He showed two packs of gum that he had palmed in such a way that when his hand moved fast it looked as though he had picked up only one pack.

"Wouldn't be worth it if you got caught, John."

"Shit, who's gonna get caught?"

"You."

"Ha."

As we walked by St. Catherine's, I automatically crossed myself. John did a double-take at first, and then he followed my example. That was his cue for launching a commentary on our recent Confirmation ceremony.

"And who'd that Bishop think he was, slapping us guys around?" John exaggerated the symbolic tap on our cheeks that we got from the Bishop. "I was gonna tell him I could flatten him easy if he didn't watch his step."

The ceremony was still vivid in my mind. "May the Holy Spirit descend upon you, and may the power of the Most High preserve you from sin," said the Bishop. "I sign you with the Sign of the Cross, and I confirm you with the chrism of salvation, in the name of the Father, and of the Son, and of the Holy Spirit." He had then lightly touched our cheeks and said, "Peace be to you," and told us that from then on we were "to live as witnesses of Christ, to work with Him for the salvation of souls, to unite with Him in the worship of the Father."

Before attending the Confirmation service, I had received both Confession and Holy Communion, and I had felt cleansed and pure. I had promised to try not to swear so much and to avoid having so many unclean thoughts and not to be so resentful of Mom White's authority. Within a week after Confirmation, I was once again swearing constantly, thinking many unclean thoughts, and was increasingly resentful of Mrs. White's authority.

As we walked along, John laughed, "Did ya get any converts yet?" I shook my head and he said, "I tried to convert Ray, but his folks are atheists. So I told him he ought to get the hell into the Catholic Church, and he told me I could shove the Catholic Church up my ass. Hey, how come you don't try to convert somebody?"

"I couldn't care less about converting people."

"That's funny," mused John. "You used to be prackly a saint and now you just don't give a damn about religion, huh?"

I shrugged. "I don't completely not give a damn, I just don't care as much as I used to, that's all. Can't a guy change?"

"Yuh, I guess so."

We stopped at Bonica's Waiting Room for two Devil Dogs, and then we headed for Mountain Avenue where I knew Mom White would comment on my failure to do my best in school, and John's parents would probably not even ask to examine his report card.

I correctly predicted Mom White's attitude. She closely scrutinized my card, analyzed the marks I'd received during the four terms of the eighth grade, and lectured me. "Ye ought to do your best, Thomas. It's only for yere own good to study, ye know. Sure and the good Lord helps them that helps themselves and don't ye forget it. I hope ye'll try harder next year. Ye should go to college some day 'cause ye've got the stuff upstairs for it."

My only reply was a shrug of my shoulders. I had found that silence and a facade of indifference in the face of criticism were extraordinary weapons of self-defense. I had also found that with peers, sarcasm was an equally good defense. But I carefully avoided using sarcasm with Mrs. White. I knew better.

17

It was near the end of the summer of 1945, and on August 15 the Japanese had surrendered. World War II was over, and there were great celebrations, but the overall effect on our young lives was minimal. Season by season, we went on with our same basic rituals. Now it was a sweltering hot Thursday, and I had just arrived at Norfolk Golf Course with John. "Let's check the caddie shack first," he said. "If too many guys are waiting, let's go hunting balls."

"What the hell, that'd be better than waiting all day around the damn shack and roasting my ass off."

We walked up the road a short distance, scaled a small banking, crossed the hill on the fourth fairway, passed along the stone wall behind the clubhouse, and entered the rear door of the dirt-floored, lattice-walled caddie shack with the flat tarpapered roof and the pervasive smell of urine, especially in the corner near the clubhouse.

"Hey look who's here," a voice called out as we entered. "The Norwood knuckleheads." The voice belonged to Red, our own Mountain Avenue bully, who, after achieving only "a draw" in a fist fight with John, had from then on treated him with a modicum of respect. I had never run afoul of Red because around him I had always kept a safe distance and watched my words.

"You're a hot shit, Red," said John. "Hey, you're from Norwood too, and you call us knuckleheads. Know what you are? The Norwood peckerhead."

"You better watch your ass," warned Red, his face flushing to a color matching his hair. "I still can take ya even if we fought to a draw first time."

"You're a lot o' talk, Red," grunted John.

Red leaped from the wooden bench where he was sitting, and John crouched into a fighting stance. Red laughed. "What the hell you getting all excited for, John? I'm just gonna get myself a Coke, that's all." He headed toward the pro shop.

I breathed a sigh of relief. Violence just wasn't my cup of tea. "Why don't you leave well enough alone, John?"

"I'd like to beat him to a pulp."

"Hell, your draw with him last time was just as good as a win."

"I know, but I hate that redheaded bastard's guts. Hey, you want to flip jackknives?"

"First, I want to carve my initials up there," I said, pointing to the thick beam at the top of the latticework where carved initials of former caddies were still there years later. It was like a caddies' Hall of Fame for all to see. "A hundred years from now someone's gonna see my initials there and wonder who TO'C was."

Standing on the bench, I carved TO'C '42 and when I stepped down to the floor I said, "Okay, John, let's flip knives."

"How come you carved forty-two up there? This is forty-five, ya know." He gave me a quizzical look.

"Forty-two's the year I started caddying."

"Oh."

We found an unoccupied corner of the caddie shack, drew a circle on the hard-packed dirt floor, and began attempting to flip our jacknives into the circle. There were several others waiting to caddy, including the two Cogan brothers from Dedham.

As we flipped our jackknives, the Cogans played blackjack, a favorite card game at the shack. Some of the Dedham caddies were tossing pennies against the wall. Each toss was worth a nickel for the one whose penny slid closest to the wall.

In the midst of the penny tossers was a new caddie from South Norwood who was known only by his last name. It was the same LaPierre who was always getting in trouble at the Junior High. "Shit," exclaimed Lapierre. "You guys cleaned me out. I ain't got a goddam cent left."

"No skin off my ass, LaPierre," said one of the gamblers. "I won fair and square."

"It pisses me off," said the short dark LaPierre, with the black curly hair and muscular build. "There ain't nothin' gets my ass so much as bein' broke."

The winner shrugged his shoulders, and muttered "T.S." This meant "tough shit," and I thought it might lead to a fight but just then the winner was called to caddy doubles.

This seemed to get LaPierre even more irritated, and he said, "If I don't get to caddy I won't have a red cent."

As LaPierre bemoaned his penniless state, Joe Cogan, the elder statesman of the caddie shack, looked up from the blackjack game and said "Ya know what I think, LaPierre?"

"Nope. What do ya think, Cogan?"

"I think you play with yourself." I knew the remark was meant to provoke LaPierre into a fight. But LaPierre looked at Joe, laughed, and said, "Sure I do. So what?"

Joe laughed. "Want to do it now? Right here? In front of us?"

"You think I'm yellow?"

Joe looked at his brother and counted the money on the bench next to their deck of cards. Then he said to LaPierre, "I bet ya two bucks you won't pound off right here in front of all us guys till ya come off." Joe pointed to the money on the bench.

LaPierre looked at Joe and laughed. "I'll take the bet, but first gimme a snapshot of a built broad."

"Here." Joe took out his wallet and removed a badly wrinkled snapshot of a naked girl lying on a rumpled bed with her legs spread. "Try this for size."

"Hey, who's this?" LaPierre stared at the photo. "She's built like a brick shithouse."

"Never mind who she is," said Joe. "You said you wanted a broad to drool over. Now ya got one. Let's see some action. One more thing, LaPierre."

Lapierre's round dark eyes looked up from the snapshot and focused on Joe Cogan.

"What?"

"Ya don't have any dough, huh?"

LaPierre shrugged. "Nope. I got cleaned out."

"How you gonna pay up if ya lose? If ya lose you gotta pay through the nose, pal."

"How can I lose? You bet I wouldn't pound off and I'm gonna do it."

"If I don't see the white stuff shoot out of your pecker, ya lose, get it?"

LaPierre shrugged. "I ain't gonna lose."

"Well, if ya lose, LaPierre, you'll kiss my ass." LaPierre's thick lips hung open. "If ya lose, you gotta kiss my bare ass, get it, LaPierre? But it's up to you. You don't have to bet."

LaPierre scratched his head. He wanted to win the two dollars. And he obviously didn't see how he might lose the bet. At this point, I looked at John, who returned my glance and winked. Then LaPierre said, "Shit, Joe, it's a bet."

LaPierre then stood near "piss corner" with his back to the solid wall which joined the clubhouse and pro shop to the caddie shack. Then he unzipped the fly of his dungarees and prepared to win the bet.

"Holy shit," exclaimed Joe. "The horny bastard's hung like a moose." Laughter rang throughout the caddie shack and mine was included.

LaPierre stood before the group on the hard-packed dirt floor with his oversized penis protruding upward from his open fly. He stared at the snapshot for a moment and then with his right hand he began to manipulate himself, while staring lasciviously at the snapshot.

"Beat it," yelled Joe. "Come on, LaPierre, let's see some cum juice."

"Come on," yelled John, catching the fever of the historical moment. "Masturbate, you sonovabitch."

LaPierre stood in "piss corner" with his legs spread far apart, and as he masturbated he rotated his head as if he were delirious, then stared at the snapshot, closed his eyes, and grunted.

"Is this for real?" I asked John. "Maybe I'm dreaming."

John laughed. "Hell, it's LaPierre who's doing the dreaming. He's havin' a wet dream in the daytime."

When the Cogan brothers heard John they both doubled up laughing. They were getting more than their two dollars worth. "Don't forget, LaPierre," yelled Joe, "if I don't see cream you'll kiss my ass."

LaPierre, without a break in the feverish intensity of his masturbation rhythm, glanced first at Joe, then at his sex organ, and he shouted angrily at himself, "Cream, goddam you, cream!"

This was when Red came back to the shack. "Holy shit, I thought I seen everythin'."

"Masturbate, you horny bastard," yelled John. Then Red began to clap his hands in rhythm to LaPierre's stroking action and soon the entire caddie assemblage was clapping.

LaPierre's head was rotating and his eyes were bulging, and finally the off-white viscous fluid erupted, shot about two feet from where he was standing, and after part of the substance landed on the snapshot of the unclad female, the balance fell to the dirt floor of the caddie shack where it seemed to gather some of the dust and dirt around itself and became almost spherical. Lapierre slumped against the wall and panted.

"I'll be damned," said Joe as he got up and gave the two dollars to LaPierre. "I didn't think you was gonna come off. I thought I was gonna make an ass-kisser out of ya." The other caddies laughed. "Here's the two bucks, LaPierre. You won the bet."

"Shit, that was easy. I knew I'd come off, for Christ's sake. What the hell's so hard about that, huh?" A roar of laughter ricocheted from the walls of the small caddie shack, but LaPierre wasn't embarrassed.

Joining in the laughter himself, he thought he was being accepted as one of the boys. To LaPierre, the sexual display was just an easy second phase of his initiation ceremony. The first phase was when the older boys removed all his clothes and forced him to climb the rough-barked elm tree at the rear of the caddie shack to retrieve them at the very time when a foursome was coming up the fairway. Then, after he had retrieved them, while the foursome was playing opposite the caddie shack, they had added to the initiation by throwing his clothes up on the flat roof of the caddie shack, and LaPierre, in his nudity, had to climb up the lattice work sides of the shack to get them, and finally clothe himself while golfers and an audience of his peers watched.

LaPierre zipped his fly and returned the snapshot to Joe, who took one look at the semen-coated photo and shoved it back at LaPierre. "Hey, what makes you think I want that crusty thing now? Not me, pal. Not with your cum all over it. Keep it."

LaPierre smiled. "Thanks a lot, Joe."

At that moment a loud shout came from the door of the pro shop. "Cogan brothers to the first tee." In about three seconds they were gone.

John leaned over to me and asked, "Are you gonna stay here and caddy or go looking for balls with me?"

"What the hell, I might as well go with you."

The picture of LaPierre's public masturbation was vivid in my mind as we crossed the fourth fairway. "I still don't believe what I saw, John."

He replied, "I never saw anybody pound off in public before. He's one crazy oversexed bastard."

"He sure is."

"Some people will do anything for a buck."

"You said it," I replied as we headed along the street toward the second hole where we would begin our search for lost balls.

As we walked John observed, "That LaPierre's about as horny as they come, right?"

"Yup, he's horny all right."

"No doubt about it. Horny and stupid."

"Right, John. He's about as horny and stupid as a guy could get."

18

It was the middle of June, 1946, and school was out for the summer. Finally it had come. It was the day I had looked forward to for nine years, and I was about to depart from 42 Mountain Avenue in Norwood. I could not quite believe it was really happening and I was in a kind of trance as I waited for my father to come.

I was across the street at my pal John's house, in my home away from home, sitting on the edge of his bed, with one of my long thin legs crossed over the other, drumming my fingers on my bony knees. Suddenly I threw myself back on the bed, with both elbows propping me up, and I said, "We've had some great times. Really great!"

"That's for sure." John tilted his ladder-backed chair until it touched the wall. "It's gonna seem real screwy walking by White's now. You've been there ever since I can remember."

"Well, I've been thinking about taking off from White's for so long it's hard to believe I'm finally gonna do it. I sort of wish I could be at Norwood High with ya, but you know how I feel about living with my father and my grandmother."

"Yuh, I know. Hell, if I lived with someone like Mrs. White for nine years, I'd want to take off like a bird, too."

"Anyhow, Dedham's only a couple of towns away. I'm not gonna disappear off the face of the earth."

"Yuh." John leaned back on his hard chair with his feet pressing on the brown tubular metal of his bed frame. "But it's gonna be different with you at Dedham High and me at Norwood."

"Yuh, it is." I took a quick look out the window. "I guess he still hasn't showed up." Distrust of my father's promises was at the heart of my relationship with him. Actually, it always amazed me when he kept a promise.

"He'll come," said John. "Anyhow, the people across the street know where to find ya. The last three years you've spent more time here than there."

"Mm."

"Know what I think? You're a regular religious sneak. You make like you don't study for Sunday School, and you get all A's, perfect attendance, and all those goddam graduation awards."

"So what, John? What's the big deal?"

"You gonna be a priest or somethin'?"

"Nope."

"I remember you makin' all those holy hours and novenas and stuff before you started hanging around with me. I thought you were gonna be a priest."

"Oh, is that what you thought, John?" I laughed.

"Yup. You were a religious pain in the ass. How come you turned into a reg'lar guy?"

With a grin, I said, "Maybe I just got fed up with being a religious pain in the ass." I shrugged my slightly rounded, bony shoulders. "Anyhow, who knows why a guy changes his mind about things, huh? It's a free country, isn't it?"

"But you changed from one kind of a guy to a different one, you hot shit."

I nodded my head thoughtfully. "You mean like before you took that Joe Bonomo muscle building course, how you were a skinny weakling, and now you're a he-man with bulging biceps?"

John laughed. "You sonovabitch. I don't think I'll ever figure you out a hundred percent."

"What's there to figure out? I'm just Tommy O'Connell, that's all."

"I know your name, for Christ's sake. What I mean is how you can be like a saint sometimes and other times you act as horny as me."

"I'm just human, John."

"Oh? Then when are you gonna get your first piece of ass?"

"Look who's talking. You're still cherry."

"But I'm gonna get some in high school," said John. "You can bet your ass on that."

"You mean you're not gonna save yourself for the virgin you're gonna marry?"

"By the time I get married I bet there won't be any such thing as a virgin. Hey, you know what I still wonder about, Tommy?"

"What?"

"How come you'll never say fuck."

"F-u-c-k is one word I don't feel like using."

"I bet you think it sometimes though."

"That's for me to know and you to wonder about, John. It's my business, nobody else's."

"I wish you'd say it, 'cause a long time ago you said if I ever caught you saying it you'd kiss my ass."

"You know damn well I wouldn't kiss your ass or anybody's."

"You mean you'd welsh on a bet?"

"Sure, if it was a crazy bet."

There was a brief silence, during which I thought about my father's plan to take me to South Station later in the day to get the train to Albany. From there I'd get a train to the Adirondacks and be at Saranac Inn for a summer of caddying with Dave and Joe Rothwell, who were already there. They had gotten out of school the previous week.

John's voice interrupted my reverie. "You look like you're far away, pal."

"Huh? Yuh, I was thinking about Saranac. Later on I'll be getting the train, and it looks like I'll be doing some reading for myself on the way. The gang at White's gave me *Pitcairn's Island* as a going away present. And when I get sick of reading I can always look out the window. I've never seen the state of New York before."

"Shit, it's a wonder you don't turn into a book. Hey, maybe some day you'll just be standing around looking like a person one minute and the next minute you'll have a cover and pages and they'll call you Tommy O'Connell, the book." We both laughed.

"Uh-oh!" As I looked through the window toward the White house across the way, I could now see my father's car pulling up in front of number 42. The once shiny black Plymouth that had transported me to Norwood at the age of five was now affected by nine years of weather and road grime. The finish had become very dull. "There's my father's car, John. Guess I better get over there. I have to say goodbye to the gang and put my stuff in the old Plymouth."

John led the way from his room along the small hallway, and down the narrow stairway. At the front door he put out his hand. "Take care, Tommy old kid." My hand met his and we both squeezed hard. Then John gave a last squeeze and a mist filtered over his eyes. "I'll miss ya."

"Same here. But I'll be seein' you. Don't worry, John."

"Sure."

His mother's Irish voice boomed out of the kitchen. "Ye'd better come back 'n see us when ye get settled, Tommy. Sure and we're goin' to miss ye."

"I'll be back," I shouted. "Don't worry."

I felt John's hand on my back. "Let's get together when you get back in September."

"It's a deal, John." I stepped out of John's house and squinted in the brightness of the June sun while I walked toward Mrs. White's house. As I crossed the street I took a quick look over my shoulder at John's enclosed porch, where he was now leaning against the window sill. He waved and shrugged his shoulders and disappeared, and my eyes became misty. I knew I would miss him, but I also knew I had to move on with my life.

While I had been over at his house, a small departure ceremony had been forming at White's. When I came in the back door and went into the kitchen I found it filled with familiar faces. After I had said individual goodbyes to all of them, it was time to approach Mom White who was standing with my father. Suddenly,

I became very nervous and my lips were dry as I walked up to her and said, "I'll be up to see ya once in a while, Mom."

"Sure and ye better. If ye don't I'll be down there after ye with the switch." She reached out her heavy right arm and with her still strong hand she gave my ear a symbolic twist. "Don't ye forget what I've been drumming into your head all those years, Thomas."

Her round ruddy face was about three inches from mine and her blue eyes were riveted to my brown ones as she said, "The good Lord helps them that helps themselves and don't ye ever forget it. Think for yourself and ye'll do good. Ye've got a good head and ye ought to go to the college after High School." She turned to my father. "Ye should see that this one goes to college when the time comes 'cause he's got the stuff upstairs for it."

"We'll do what we can." My father placed his left hand on my right shoulder and I had to control an urge to push the hand away. I didn't think of my father as my friend. Any trust I once had in him had greatly shrunk when he had left me at 42 Mountain Avenue nine years earlier. And my distrust had been seriously deepened when he had extended my stay for three additional years after the sixth grade.

When it came to Fred O'Connell, if something was supposed to happen, I had learned to believe it only when I could see it. And that was true of my departure from Mrs. White's. Only when I saw him could I believe it was actually happening, and even then there was some doubt.

When we had taken my clothes and my relatively few possessions out to the Plymouth, and my father and I were about to drive away, the farewell group assembled on the front porch of White's house and waved me away with shouts of good luck.

"Take care of yourself, Tommy," called out Mom White, standing with her blue-white hair blowing in the summer breeze. "Stop by when ye get a chance. And don't ye forget, it's every man for himself."

I nodded out the car window at her and waved goodbye, but my goodbye to Mrs. White did not turn out as I had thought it would. I was unable to shout something lighthearted or flippant because I was choked up and teary-eyed.

Nine years earlier I had entered Mom White's with tear-filled eyes, and now I was leaving it with my eyes in a similar condition. But the tears nine years earlier had been prompted by loneliness, fear, and abandonment. The tears in my eyes now were caused by other more mysterious emotions which gripped me unexpectedly.

For as long as I could remember, I had wanted to break away from the White house, and I had always pictured myself leaving triumphantly, with a broad happy grin on my face and a free spirit in my soul. I had predicted that on the day of my bold leap into freedom I would be the world's foremost role model for the word "confidence." So I was not prepared for an emergence of deeper, more confusing feelings.

As my father's old Plymouth rolled away from 42 Mountain Avenue in Norwood, I certainly wasn't feeling triumphant, had no grin on my face, and although I had a free spirit in my soul there was also a question mark in my mind.

19

As the train clacked through the heartland of Massachusetts toward Albany, New York, I was truly in my lone wolf mode. I had both seats to myself and I was deep in contemplation. It's funny how I don't even feel like I thought I would. I'm glad I'm free, but for nine years I kept thinking how rotten it was to be in a place like Mom White's, and I hated her bossing me around, and I was sick of all her damn rules and regulations, and I thought the day I got the hell out of there I'd be laughing my ass off.

But the whole gang was there on her front porch waving and wishing me good luck, and I thought about all the good times and forgot about the bad ones and I felt funny as hell with all those tears in my eyes, and I didn't feel like laughing my ass off. It's weird how sometimes you want something so bad you can't think about one other thing and then when you get what you want it doesn't feel as great as you thought it would.

My eyes went from the outside scenery to my own reflection in the sooty plate glass train window. Then I thought, This window makes my head look just the way I've always been afraid it looks, just like a football. Brother, I wish I had an ordinary round head instead, but nobody makes wisecracks about it. So maybe it isn't as bad as I think.

My mouth is the worst thing, I guess. I wish my damn teeth weren't so big and crooked. When I have some extra money some day, I'll get 'em yanked out and I'll get some nice straight false ones. Then I'll get rid of that stupid shadow right under my mouth where my teeth press against the skin. I'll be able to smile with my mouth closed without looking funny.

My attention went from my own reflection to the outside landscape, and my thoughts went back to life at White's house. I recalled how I had hated that place, yet it had gotten better when I was in Junior High, even though I always wanted to be elsewhere. After elementary school I didn't get switched with whip-like branches from bushes, and I never got my head shoved down the toilet again after that memorable incident. But as I thought about that shameful punishment I knew in my heart that I could not forgive her for abusing me that way. Once was too often.

I shook my head as the train rumbled along, and I thought, It sure was crazy the way she punished us like that. Maybe she's the one who should have been in the nuthouse instead of my mother. God, did she punish us for things. Good thing I was pals with John. He was one hell of a buddy. We did some great goofing off together at the golf course. Seems like it was a long time ago when I first started caddying. I was going into the sixth grade then.

Boy, did I hate dirty talk, and I was a real pain in the ass about it. If anyone talked dirty I said a prayer for him. Now I swear like a trooper and I talk dirty a lot and what's the big deal? Hell, it's only talk, that's all. But I try to watch my language in front of girls. Girls are really something. I only wish I didn't get so bashful with 'em.

I drove myself half crazy getting up the nerve to ask Jeannie to the dance. Then when I finally asked her she said she was already going with that football player idiot. Brother, you get yourself all worked up and do what you're afraid to do and you end up getting screwed anyhow. It's sort of a dirty trick but maybe the idea is I should do things when I first think of them instead of waiting too long.

Looking down at my wrist, I examined what had once been a cheap Westclox wrist watch. After it had stopped running I had removed the works, and in the empty case I had carefully placed a tiny picture of Jeannie Pieczonka that I had found in the files of our school magazine, the Junior Narrator, where I had served as feature editor.

Some day when I'm living in Dedham and I've got a few bucks, I'll call up Jeannie and ask her out. I've been nuts about her since I first saw her in the seventh grade. If I wasn't so bashful with girls I would have asked her out a long time ago, but all I did was dance with her once in a while at dances, and carry her books a couple of times. When I think about her I don't even think dirty. She's like a holy beautiful saint to me. She's so nice.

I wish to hell all girls were pure and nice. Then maybe I wouldn't think dirty so much and feel so horny. But nobody's as horny as LaPierre. I wonder if he'll waste away from being oversexed, and someday get so skinny he'll fall right through one of those little holes in a manhole cover and go down the drain and disappear forever. He's a real winner. If he keeps staying back he'll never get out of junior high.

I wonder what it's gonna be like up at Saranac Inn. It ought to be a ball with Dave and Joe Rothwell there, and there'll be horseback riding and canoeing and terrific swimming. I wonder what it'll be like at Dedham High. Prob'ly it'll be like Norwood Junior High. There'll be homework up to my ears, and tests all the time, and they'll prob'ly put me in the second college division. Yuh, with all the B's I got on purpose in junior high they won't put me in the top one. Hell, I think the second division's the best place anyhow. They really work your ass off in the top one. Who needs his ass worked off?

I'll really take it easy next year in school. Hey, why shouldn't I lay off a little? What's the big sweat anyhow? I wonder if they've got a liberry up at Saranac Lake. Hell, every place has a liberry. I'll be able to read what I feel like reading and I'll get dough from caddying, and maybe I'll have time to play a little golf with those old wooden-shafted clubs my father dug up for me.

Everything's gonna be new for me now. Saranac. The caddie camp. Leaving Norwood for good. Living back on Walnut Place with Granny and my father. Going to Dedham High. And I'll prob'ly visit Mom White once in a while. Now that I'm out of there I won't mind the way she is. Maybe I'll go see her on Saturdays when the bread's baking and the bread pudding's cooking. There won't be bread pudding at Granny's, that's for sure. I'll be living on tea and toast like her, and vegetables from cans. Granny's no cook. Not like Mom White. When I go back and see her I'll drop in on John, too. We'll still be buddies.

I nodded my head as I contemplated my past and my future, and as the train rocked along toward Albany where I would change for Saranac Lake, I thought, What the hell, I'm fourteen years old now and I'll be in High School in September and I'm old enough to be my own boss. I can do what I feel like and now I don't have to take any bullshit from anyone. It's up to me what I do from now on.

20

What did I do at Saranac Inn? I did exactly what I felt like doing! After nine years of strict discipline and rigid rules of conduct at Mrs. White's, I now began to experience an amazing freedom of movement, and I loved every moment of it. Even though I was just fourteen, I had the delusion that I was very mature.

With the Rothwell Brothers I had the time of my life playing the role of vacationer during the hours we weren't caddying. And sometimes we had little adventures. In the Adirondack Mountains, when we ventured into the forest we faced the unknown, and experienced real danger. There were bears and bobcats in the neighborhood, and I can still recall being confronted by startled copperheads and coral snakes.

It was a much less dangerous adventure to go swimming in the large lake near Saranac Inn, and it was not a high risk adventure to explore the lake in hired rowboats and canoes. Also, there was no risk at all when we sat around an evening campfire singing appropriately off-color songs. I have to admit that I preferred to avoid life-threatening situations.

However, I did have one misadventure I will never forget. That summer I was introduced to horseback riding, and was a bit terrified doing it, especially the first few times. Then, just when I was getting used to it, I rented a horse that had been described as "a gentle mare." Instead, it was a temperamental and very independent stallion. Once he learned that I was intimidated by his free spirit, he took off with me at a fast gallop in the forest bordering Saranac Lake.

He ran with me for a long time, and there was nothing I or anyone else could do about it. I am sure he was trying to toss me, but I hung on for dear life, and I can still recall crashing through narrow forest paths, with leaves of trees smacking against my body. Many times I had to duck to avoid large branches overhead, and I would crouch down and put my head next to his like I had seen cowboys do in movies. But none of my shouted instructions reached this horse's psyche, so he ran until he was as exhausted as I was. And never again, at Saranac or elsewhere, did I go horseback riding. That last ride was enough for me.

At the caddie camp barracks, I was one of the younger boys, and was surrounded by worldly rugged individualists from New York City, Syracuse, and other places where toughness was the standard, and boys in their late teens didn't play children's games. They gambled for dollars instead of the pennies we had used at Mrs. White's when we played cards. And when these boys won they often won big.

However, I wasn't good at poker. Instead, I tried blackjack and became pretty skilled at it. But I had a problem. I deeply detested losing, and losing was inevitable. So I began to bet on the side while other boys gambled. And this seemed to work well for me. But one fateful night my winnings did me in.

After I had won several dollars, which in those days really amounted to something, one of the older caddies talked me into buying two quarts of beer from him. Although I had never touched alcohol, I pretended it was the most natural thing in the world for me to drink, and I "casually" bought the beer.

Then I acted like an old hand at drinking, and I did not sip it slowly. I swilled it down, gulping and burping, and filling my stomach with the substance which soon began to take me into an altered state of consciousness that I had never felt before.

It felt exciting, and mature, and daring. And if I had any troubles, they certainly disappeared. But I drank too much too fast, got dangerously drunk, and became very ill before passing out on my bunk.

For days to come, I was so hung over that the supervisors of the caddie camp were very concerned about my health. They had no idea that the "illness" I had experienced was intoxication. As I recovered from the hangover I vowed not to drink again, and not just because I had gotten so drunk and sick. I also had an overwhelming sense of remorse over my behavior, and was very embarrassed that I could not "hold my booze" the way the older caddies could.

So my drinking episode was not very romantic. Instead, it was just another misguided adventure. But we also had a different kind of adventure. Sometimes we would leave the Saranac Lake area and with left hands on left hips, and right thumbs extended, we would hitchhike several miles to Lake Placid. Did we go there to skate? No. We were in pursuit of pretty young girls, and Lake Placid had an abundant supply.

I was half asleep, sprawled out on the wood slat bench in front of the Sunoco Gas Station on the outskirts of Lake Placid, and a soft female voice yelled "Boo!" Then two tickling hands jabbed at my armpits. I leaped to my feet.

"Well, I'll be damned. You might know it'd be you, Chris. How can a guy get any rest with a pest like you around?"

Christine put her hands on her hips. "Who's a pest?"

I said, "You are," as I picked straw out of the pockets of my all-purpose combination sport coat and jacket, and I wished that it had been pretty Jo tickling me instead of Chris. I wondered where Jo was now.

"Been sleepin' in haystacks, Tommy?"

"If you can't find a bed, you sleep in a haystack, right? So I slept in that old barn up the street last night. All the caddies went on strike, and they told us if we didn't come back to work we were fired, so I decided I'd take off like a bird. I'm sick of caddying anyhow. I'm not even going back to the Inn again."

She said, "And that's all there is to it?"

"Yup, that's all there is to it. It hasn't been the same since my pals got racked up in the accident. They're back in Boston now. Lucky they weren't killed. The car turned end-over-end fifteen times. I almost went for the ride, but I was betting on the side in a big crap game and I was ahead, so I stayed at the barracks instead of going with them. I was pretty lucky that night."

"How much did ya win?"

"Seven bucks."

"Lucky for me. You can take me out with it."

"Yeah, when Palm Sunday falls on a Monday."

"You're a stinker! Maybe that's why you like Jo. She's a stinker too."

"With you for a pal she doesn't need enemies."

There was a quiet pause. Then Chris grinned. "Who were you in the barn with, Tommy?"

"Just the cows, Chris. Who'd you think I'd be in there with? Haven't I been hanging around here long enough for you to know what kind of guy I am?"

"Nope, I don't know for sure yet." She grinned and then tickled me under the chin. "You're blushin', Tommy. Oh, that's so cute. Did ya have any breakfast yet?" I shook my head. "Come on up my house. Mom's gone up the street visiting, and Dad and my brother are already off to work, so we'll be alone and I can fix you bacon and eggs."

"I don't know . . ."

"Don't worry about what Jo's gonna think. You're hungry, aren't ya?"

"I'm starved."

"Well, let's go then." She tugged my arm and led me toward her house. Then when we reached a swing tied to an overhanging tree limb, she hopped onto it. "Come on, Tommy. Gimme a big push." I got behind her and grabbed the ends of the wooden swing seat with my two hands.

Methodically, she took my two hands and placed them on her hips and my skin tingled as my hands felt the softness of her body under her dungarees. She was taller than my girl Jo, and she had long black hair tied in braids, and she had large hips for a girl of fourteen. "Now push hard and run right under the seat. I want a nice big push, Tommy."

She stiffened her legs, stood on her tiptoes, and went limp. Then I pushed hard and as I ran under the swing, I tripped on a root and fell flat on the ground. "Damn." Getting up slowly, I wiped the dirt from the knees of my dungarees.

Chris was swinging in a wide arc. "Stop me from swingin' so I can see if you're okay!"

"I'm okay." I shook my head.

"I said stop me. I want to get off this swing." I reached up and stopped the motion of the swing, and she slid off and stumbled into my arms with her thighs against mine, and her soft breasts against my hard bony chest. She began to touch me with her hands, feeling my ribs and arms. "Are you sure you didn't break anything?" As she rubbed her hands over my chest and neck, my whole body tingled.

"I'm okay, Chris."

Blushing, I pushed her hands away, and she laughed. "I won't bite you, Tommy."

"Is that a promise?"

"Maybe." We both laughed as we headed for Chris's house and breakfast.

"Jo and her folks went visiting relations, and they won't be back till tomorrow," she said as we stepped onto her porch. "But you and me can have some fun, Tommy. I don't have any place special to go. Why not stay in our spare room tonight? I'll call Mom and ask her soon as we eat breakfast. I bet she says it's okay. She likes you 'cause she knows you're nice. You're blushin' again. You blush easy, huh?"

"Sometimes."

"Well, I think blushin's nice." She smiled, then nudged me with her elbow and whispered, "I think you're nice, too." Once again my face flushed. Then, as she began to fix me some breakfast, she asked, "Are you sure you're not goin' back to the caddie camp today?"

I shook my head. "They can have their stupid barracks. Some of those guys are real idiots. You never know when you're gonna find a dead snake under your pillow."

"But what'll you do for money? They paid pretty good there, didn't they?"

"Yuh. Two-and-a-half bucks for eighteen holes doubles. But you'd never get rich on it. The guys wanted three-and-a-half, so we went on strike. Then the Inn told us they wouldn't pay more than the two-and-a-half, and they said they'd get scab caddies if we weren't gonna come back off strike. But when the strike's over I'm not gonna go back. I've already sent my clothes and other stuff home. The paymaster still owes me some dough, but he'll send it to me in Dedham."

She shook her head. "You do exactly what you feel like doin', huh?"

"It's a free country, isn't it? Everyone can shift for himself, I always say."

"You're so fresh. Do you like plenty of bacon?" I nodded. "I'll give ya six hunks."

"You know something, Chris? Sometimes you're not such a pest after all."

She grinned. "You got upset when I woke you up, huh? I'm sorry for yelling in your ear like that. I just wanted to see if I could rattle you, Tommy. You always act as if nothing bothers you. Well, look at that. You're blushin' again."

"So what the hell's the big deal about it?"

"I wonder why you blush so much when I talk to ya." Chris taunted me. "I'm not gonna attack you or anything."

"Well, that's a big break for me."

"It all depends."

That was how the banter went during breakfast. And when we had eaten the bacon and eggs she called her mother to ask if I could stay the night, and she came back from the phone smiling. "Mom says you can stay as many nights as you want."

"Good deal."

As we walked toward the swing in the wooded lot, Chris said, "I knew Mom was gonna let you stay. When does school start in Dedham?"

"In two weeks."

"Well, you can stay for two weeks then." Chris laughed as she took her place on the swing seat. "It'll be terrific."

"Are you sure your Mom won't mind?"

"I bet she'd let you live here for good if you felt like it. But I suppose you want to go back and live in that rotten old place near Boston."

"It's not rotten there, Chris." I gave the swing a hard push and sent her swinging high.

"But it can't be as beautiful as it is here at Lake Placid. Do you think you'll be comin' back here again to see Jo and me?"

"Brother, do you ask questions."

"I think askin' questions is fun. I'm gonna keep askin' 'em till I drive you nuts."

"I wish you didn't say that." My mind filled with a picture of my mother in the insane asylum, where she had been since my infancy. Her condition made me feel especially sensitive to prying questions of any kind.

"I was only kiddin', Tommy."

"Yuh, I know."

"Do ya think I could really drive you nuts?" She hopped off the swing and placed the warm palms of her hands on my cheeks. "Don't worry, I won't. I'm sorry for teasin' you so much. Will you forgive me?" I nodded. "Want to kiss and make up?"

For an instant, I was tempted to do it. But then I remembered Jo. "Not now, Chris. Maybe some other time, like Easter Sunday when it falls on a Friday."

"It's a once-in-a-lifetime offer. Now or never."

"I guess it'll be never."

"You're a stinker, Tommy." She hopped back on the swing and I gave it a hard push.

"And you're a wicked tease, Chris."

"You don't think Jo is?" When she saw me shake my head she leaped off the swing, stood in front of me where I was leaning against a tree, and planted her hands on her ample hips. "Well, you should see her when she's with . . . Never mind, I'm not gonna say anything. Come on, you take a turn on the swing."

When I was seated on the swing, she came up behind me and slowly placed her hands around my waist. "You're tickling me, Chris. No horsin' around, okay? How come you didn't tease any of the other guys when we used to come see you and Jo?"

"They didn't have to be teased. They had a one track mind with no railroad train on it."

"You come right to the point, don't you, Chris?"

"Sometimes. You act like you're going steady with Jo, but you're really not, ya know."

"What's the difference? I'll be leaving here pretty soon to go back home anyhow."

"I wish . . . Never mind. No sense tellin' you what I wish."

She gave me a hard push on the swing and I yelled, "Hey! I don't want to crack my head on that branch up there."

"It might put some sense in it."

That was how we spent the day. I thought of Jo, anxiously awaiting her return, and Chris teased me relentlessly about girls, and about Jo. We had our meals together in her house, and late that night she took me to the cot reserved for me in the spare room. "You can sleep in this cot, Tommy. Isn't it nice?"

"It beats the hay that kept sticking into me last night."

"Want to show me where you slept in the hay?"

"Not tonight, Chris. I'm sort of tired. I hardly slept last night in that stupid barn and all I want to do now is go to bed. And if it's okay by you I'd like to get my 'jamas on."

"I won't look." She turned around. "I promise."

"Come on, give a guy a little privacy."

"What's there to see? Baggy shorts and bony legs? Anyhow, I won't look." She turned her back to me. "Go ahead and change."

"Okay then." I took off my dungarees, quickly pulled on my pajamas, and hopped into the cot. Then Chris turned around and looked down at me, smiled, and leaned over and adjusted the covers under my chin. "I'll tuck you in, honey bunny." She smoothed the covers with her hands, and I blushed. Then she leaned over and planted a soft kiss on my cheek, and my skin tingled.

Her blouse was hanging down loosely at the neck, and when she bent over I saw the soft curves of her budding breasts, and the excitement began to rise in me. But I thought, No, dammit, I'm not gonna let her get me all excited. She's cute, and she's nice, and I think she likes me, but I'm going with Jo, and that's all there is to it. Why the hell does she have to keep teasing me the way she does? Did she think I was gonna kiss her right back? I've never even kissed a girl, and the only one I want to kiss is Jo.

Chris, still standing near the cot, gave me a soft look, then turned and walked slowly toward the door, where she turned and dramatically whispered, "Good night, sweet Tommy." Then she blew me a kiss and said, "If you want anything, just call me. I'll be right across the hall in my room."

I began blushing. "Yeah, right, Chris. 'Night." The door closed and I was alone in the spare room, with the hall light sparkling through the cracks of the closed door, and the moonlight and starlight seeping in through the room's solitary window. For a while I lay on my back and stared at the sloped ceiling of the room, letting my thoughts roam.

Seems like every room I ever sleep in has a slope. The upstairs ceilings at Granny's are sloped, and the ceiling in our third floor room at White's was sloped too. It's a wonder I don't have a sloped head from smashing it against all the sloped ceilings. God, I remember when I first saw the sloped ceiling at White's. I was only five years old and boy, did I cry my eyes out. I guess I figured my world was gonna end when he left me there. In a way it did. It's never been the same with me and him since. Shit, if he was the kid and I was the father I sure as hell wouldn't have dumped him some place for nine years. But what's the use of thinking about it? It's all over, and in a couple of weeks I'll be with him and Granny.

Brother, I wish that damn Chris didn't tease me so much. God, is she built nice. Even when we've been swimming and I could see her whole shape in the bathing suit I never thought she'd look so sexy underneath. She's got bigger ones than Jo. But she's a good kid, and even though she teases a lot I bet she's never been touched. I shouldn't have let her kiss me on the cheek. I could tell she was gonna do it but I didn't stop her 'cause I sort of wanted her to. I better stop thinking about her 'cause then I'll get all excited. I think maybe I better say a prayer.

Hail Mary full of Grace the Lord is with thee. Blessed art thou among women and blessed is the fruit of thy womb . . .

21

As the Trailways Bus glided down one of the Adirondacks' steep mountain grades, I shook my head and wondered why I hadn't hugged and kissed Jo more the night before I left. We were all alone where she was baby sitting, and the children were sound asleep, but I was nervous alone with her. Then the people had come home and I still had not kissed her, so I had walked her home and at her door I finally put my hands on her soft cheeks and leaned over and kissed her on the lips. Then I had been so dizzy I'd almost fallen off the porch as I stammered, "I'll see ya tomorrow, Jo."

It was my first real kiss. It was warm and soft, and I wanted more but I was afraid she'd think I was getting carried away. Actually, I had the feeling that she wanted me to kiss her again, but I was terrified about where it would lead me. Finally, at the bus depot when she kissed me goodbye her kiss was even warmer and softer than the first one, and on the bus I was careful not to wipe her lipstick off.

As the bus bounced along I touched the palm of my right hand to my lips, pressed hard, examined the faint trace of lipstick on my hand, and at the same time I noticed the Westclox watch case on my left wrist, where Jo's photo had replaced Jeannie Pieczonka's weeks before.

You're beautiful, I thought as I looked closely at her image. Soft brown hair. Shiny brown eyes. Fair skin. Small warm hands. I'll write my letter to you now, Jo.

I took my writing pad and wrote, "Dear Jo." Then I added the letters "e," "s," and "t" to the word "Dear," squeezing the extra letters in. I continued writing, "As I sit on this bus heading toward Albany I can think only about you, Jo. I still have your kiss on my lips and I have your picture in what used to be my watch. I wish I could have told you what I wanted to tell you before I left for home. But when it comes to talking I sometimes don't say what I want to say. I can tell you now though, Jo. I can write it down in this letter so you'll know exactly what I wanted to tell you and how I feel about you . . ."

I wonder when I'll see her again, I thought. I wonder if next summer I'll be able to hold her and kiss her. But the caddie camp won't take me back after the way I went on strike and disappeared. Well, maybe I can find another job next summer at Lake Placid instead of Saranac.

"I will always remember our fun times together," I wrote. "We laughed at the same things. We joked and talked about everything. We held hands in the movies and we took walks together under the stars. We did everything together, Jo." I stopped writing as a mist came into my eyes.

I can't believe I'm leaving the mountains. I was just getting to know her. Maybe I shouldn't even be going back to Dedham and Granny. But where could I stay at Lake Placid? Jo was jealous as hell 'cause I stayed at Chris's house every night, but there was no room at her place, and her folks were so strict they never would have let me sleep there anyhow.

I never saw such a tease as that Chris. I sort of liked it actually, but it made me nervous so I guess I didn't like it too much after all. Chris didn't seem to catch on that I was going with Jo. I guess she didn't care. Ah, what the hell difference does it make? She's probably teasing some other guy right now while I'm heading for Albany. But Jo's no tease. She's nice and strict about how she acts. I like that.

I returned to my writing. "As I head for Albany on this bus, it seems like some sort of a dream, Jo. I wish you were here on the bus beside me. Then there would be no lonely feelings coming over me. I can't picture going to Dedham and living with Granny and my father and going to Dedham High and not seeing you."

As the bus climbed a long grade I thought, It's funny how I met Jo way up in the Adirondacks, so far from Norwood and Dedham. It's strange.

"How strange it is," I wrote, "that I met you during my summer at Saranac Lake. Just think how strange it is that . . ."

It was getting dark when the bus pulled into the depot at Albany, New York. And the first thing I did was mail the long letter to Jo MacDonald. Then, with my brown canvas bag in hand, I set out on foot toward the outskirts of Albany. On the bus I hadn't felt too solitary. In fact, I felt like a very mature traveler. But now, as I wandered through Albany, I felt like a lone wolf again.

Too bad I only had bus fare to Albany, I thought. Oh well, I can hitch the rest of the way to Boston. But it's almost dark, damn it. People aren't much for picking up hitchhikers after the sun goes down.

I was very slow getting out of Albany, and it was nearly midnight when I left the friendly truck driver who had brought me to Pittsfield, Massachusetts.

"Good luck, kid," said the heavy-set driver as I leaped to the pavement. I thanked him and waved as I slammed the door shut.

Then I walked along the deserted parkway near the center of the city. An hour later, at one o'clock in the morning, I was still walking. I figured if I kept moving it was better than standing in one spot and shivering. It was cold for early fall. And there was a bit of an anxious edge about me being alone so late at night.

Beneath a street light I saw what seemed to be a human figure, and I wondered, Is that a person or am I seeing things? Yup, it's a person. A bum.

I reached into my jacket and felt the hunting knife I had bought for my protection before I left Lake Placid. The blade was almost two inches wide and about four inches long.

"Hello Sonny." A deep voice came at me from the figure beneath the light. "Where are you heading?"

"Boston."

"You don't say, Sonny." The man extended his trembling hand and I shook it and thought, he must be a stew bum. That beat-up gray hat looks like it's been through a couple of wars.

When he didn't release my hand, I asked, "Hey, can I have my hand back?"

"Sure, Sonny." The grip loosened and he pulled his hand away. "What's your name?"

"I'm Dan Lake." I had decided to use an alias with people who were too curious.

The gray-bearded old man said, "Your name is almost as interesting as mine."

"What's yours?"

"Christopher Marlowe Smithers is my name, but I always say what's in a name."

"Oh, is that what you always say?" I grinned.

The older man glared at me. "You should learn to show respect to your elders, Dan Lake, if that is your name."

"I respect my elders if they respect me."

The old man scratched the curly, unclipped gray hair at the nape of his neck. "You have a point, young Lake. How old are you, Sonny?"

"My name isn't Sonny and I'm seventeen years old." I wondered if I might be taken for seventeen.

"Seventeen," muttered the other. "I see."

When I asked him where he was heading, he said, "I may be heading east and I may be heading west. I'm a Knight of the Road, you see. I go where the rails and the highways take me. I am alone in the world, and the world is my home, Dan Lake."

I grinned, thinking that the old man did not see my amused look, but then the old-timer scowled at me. "Never smirk when you are in the presence of a Knight of the Road. I have seen much of life, young man. I have acted, and I have danced, and I have phrased poems for small sums of money. Yes, and you might even say that on occasion I have sung for my supper. But as for a living, it is catch as catch can. I have no profession and I have no trade. But a man is himself, you know, not what he does. Not what he wears. Not how he looks. A man is what is in here." The old man thumped his own chest and pointed to his head. "A man is heart and head. Not what he does to earn his bread. Do you understand this old Knight of the Road?"

"Yuh, sure I do."

"Good. If you understand what I'm saying at age seventeen, you are on your way to being educated. Have you a high school certificate?"

"Not yet. I'll be a senior this year," I lied.

"There is more to an education than certificates, young Lake. Will you go to college one day?"

"I plan to."

"That is good," replied the old man, "but do not go for a certificate. Go to college to fill your mind and to understand the vastness of life. Do not go to college just for a diploma. Go for an education. Do you read?"

I chuckled and I pointed to my canvas bag. "I even have a couple of books in here. I read so much my pals think I'm gonna turn into a book some day."

The old man said, "There are worse things than turning into a book. You should read what there is to read. I walk with the words of Shakespeare, Byron, Keats, and Shelley swirling in a beauteous whirlpool within me, but few would say that I am educated. You see, I have no diplomas and no degrees."

"My Uncle Bill has no diplomas or degrees and he reads Shakespeare in the boiler room at the school where he's a janitor. He educates himself. So I'd say you're prob'ly more educated than lots of people with diplomas and degrees."

The old man smiled for the first time, revealing badly mottled teeth, with several missing. "That pleases me, young Dan Lake, more than I can find the words to express. You certainly . . ."

In mid-sentence the old man reached out and he squeezed my shoulder, shaking me lightly. Then he said, "I must go."

"But where . . ." The old man stepped out of sight behind a hedge at the edge of the parkway. Then I heard a motor in the distance, and saw a police cruiser heading my way. "Now I know why the old guy took off so quick." My heart pounded rapidly as I stood beneath the street light with my canvas bag in my hand. When the cruiser stopped, the burly officer leaped out. "Come here, kid."

"Yes, Officer." I hope he doesn't decide I'm a vagrant. I've only got four bucks on me. Maybe I'll end up in the clink if he doesn't like the way I part my hair or something.

The policeman put his hands on my chest and said, "Just a quick frisk, kid." The officer's large right hand stopped as it felt the bulk of the hunting knife within its leather case. "Well, what the hell have we got here?"

"It's a hunting knife," I stammered. "I . . . uh . . . I had it up at Saranac Lake . . . for fishing and stuff. I was a caddie up there this summer. I'm going home now to Dedham. That's right next to Boston."

The officer examined the knife. "What's your name, kid?"

I was going to say Dan Lake, but I chose the truth instead. "Tommy O'Connell."

"Well, it's a fellow Irishman, is it? The name's Heffernan." The officer stuck out his hand. "Put 'er there." We shook hands. "How old are ya, kid?"

"Fourteen."

"You ought not to be out so late thumbin' rides."

"The bus got me into Albany later than I planned and I was slow hitching a ride."

He looked at me understandingly, "Lad, did I see somebody with ya when I was comin'?"

"Yuh, there was an old guy telling me how he was a Knight of the Road and everything."

Heffernan laughed. "Did he quote Shakespeare?"

"He mentioned him."

"Well, he's queer as a three dollar bill, but he's harmless. He's been talking about Shakespeare most of his life."

"He said he was Christopher Marlowe Smithers."

"Sure, is that what he's callin' himself now, is it? Last year he was Charles Dickens Smithers." He handed back my hunting knife. "Guess you won't do any harm with this. Hop in and I'll bring ya to a spot where it'll be easier hitchin' a ride for yourself."

Five minutes later I got out of the police cruiser and thanked the policeman for the lift. "It's nothin', kid. All us Irish gotta stick together, ya know." He waved and I waved, and then the cruiser moved into the distance and blended with the night.

"Whew!" I exclaimed as I caught my breath. "For a while I thought I was gonna end up in jail. All I can say is I had the luck of the Irish tonight."

As I took my thumbing position under a street light and waited for another ride, I thought about how Christopher Marlowe Smithers had disappeared at the approach of the police cruiser.

I wonder if he's really such an oddball. A lot of what he said made sense. Like about certificates just being pieces of paper. That's all they are. Hey, next year I'm gonna just take it easy in school. Why work my ass off for a piece of paper? Nobody's gonna be on my back at Granny's house about report cards. Oops, here comes a car. I hope it stops.

The car did stop, and about an hour and a half later, after a dizzying ride through the steep hills of the Berkshires he let me out at a corner on Route Nine in Worcester.

What a crazy drunk, I reflected as I stuck out my thumb. The idiot almost went off the road when we went through all those curves in Jacob's Ladder. I can still hear him laughing like a madman every time we screeched around a curve. I'm lucky I'm still in one piece.

I touched my hands to my legs and chest. "Yup, I'm still here. It's a good thing I said my prayers. That madman was going almost a hundred."

Hey, look at me talking to myself. I wonder if I inherited some of what my mother has. Some day will I go loony like her? Imagine spending the rest of your life in a nut house. I wonder if she's got missing teeth and wild hair and a weird look in her eyes.

Who knows? I don't know anything about her. I'm fourteen-and-a-half and I've never even seen her as long as I can remember. If she got out of that asylum and I met her in the street I wouldn't know her, and she wouldn't know me either.

I wonder what it's like inside that place where she's been all these years. It's prob'ly dark and dingy with bars on the windows and people all dressed in rags like the ones you see in those nut houses they show in the movies sometimes. From what Granny said and other stuff I've heard, I guess she's in the asylum for good. Some day she'll probably die there and I won't even know my own mother's dead.

In a way, she's already dead. I think crazy's sort of like being dead. Maybe worse. Anyhow, whenever anyone asks about her I just say she's dead. What the hell, if I told people she was crazy they'd prob'ly look at me funny and think if they didn't watch out I'd have a fit or something. I wonder If I ever will have a fit and flip my lid like she did. Sometimes I wish I never found out what happened to her.

I shivered in the chilly dampness of the night as I waited for a ride toward Boston, and as I pondered my mother's fate I deeply feared a similar one for myself and thought how strange it was that I had never seen any of my relatives on my mother's side of the family. All I knew from the O'Connell side of things was that my mother's name was Margaret Henderson, her heritage was Scotch Protestant, and her mother hated Catholics, including my father.

Standing there, I tossed that reality around in my mind and thought, My other grandmother must have hated me too. Or else she would have come to visit me at White's. Imagine her hating a kid 'cause he's Catholic. I guess there are some pretty screwy people in the world. Yup, if they counted all the screwballs there prob'ly wouldn't be many others left.

Shaking my head, I mused, Why am I thinking about this stuff now? Sometimes I don't even think about my mother for months and then all of a sudden she comes into my head and I can't get her out. But I just can't help wondering what she looks like, and how it is to be crazy like her, and I wonder about those relatives I've never seen.

I just can't help thinking about it sometimes, and I can't help wondering if some day maybe I'm gonna go crazy too. They say some kinds of insanity are inherited and they . . . Good, here comes a truck now. Maybe he'll stop and pick me up. Truck drivers are usually pretty good guys. Yup. It looks like he's slowing down. Terrific. Here I go again. On my way home to Dedham.

22

The truck took me to the Boston suburbs, and two rides later, as the sun rose above the horizon, I was almost home, lugging my brown canvas bag and slowly walking the partially rusted railroad tracks leading from Dedham Square to East Dedham and Granny O'Connell's house.

After hitchhiking from Albany all night long, I felt as if I might be part of a dream. Was the whole summer a dream? Saranac Inn? The Caddie Camp? The strike? Jo MacDonald? Lake Placid? Sleeping in Chris's house? Maybe it was a dream, I thought.

I walked the train tracks with an elongated stride, skipping every other railroad tie. But every other tie was a little too long for my legs, and stepping on every tie was too short. There was no happy medium. So I tried walking the rail itself for a little while.

Stepping up, I balanced myself, and was placing one foot before another when I heard the sound of a locomotive. "Uh-oh. The early train's coming. Better get the hell off my high wire." I leaped to the cinder path next to the tracks, stood well over to the side as the black train rumbled past, and I wondered about being sucked in if I stood too close to it. No. Not the slow Dedham-to-Boston. It couldn't go fast enough to make a vacuum. The train was good at producing soot and noise, but not high speed.

As I proceeded along the tracks I blew several flakes of black soot from the lapels of my all-purpose tan jacket with the plaid back and the patch pockets. I knew from past experience that if I tried to flick the soot off with my fingers it would streak.

I walked along the base of the high granite wall bordering the Dedham High football field, and by the rock ledges near the railroad tracks, and when I had passed the rear of Margie Lunsman's house, with the East Dedham Railroad Station in view up ahead, I angled by the rear of old Mister Fairchild's house, turned to the left, kicked aside some high grass, and found the wide hole in the board fence separating Granny's house from the railroad property.

Ducking through the opening, I stepped into the old back yard and under the remnants of a grapevine which had not borne fruit for many years. I lowered my head to avoid the splintery weather-worn slats and rusty chicken wire, and didn't straighten up again until I reached the end of the vine.

Here I am, I reflected. I'm back at Granny's after waiting a long time, but now that I'm here it's just another Saturday. No brass band. No parade. No big welcome. No big deal. But I'm glad to be here.

I unhooked the latch on the back porch door, swung it open, went inside, and walked past the cot where I had frequently slept on hot nights during summer vacations. When I tried the door leading to the kitchen I muttered, "Damn, she's got it locked. Is she worried about thieves? As if there's anything worth stealing here."

I decided to go to the front door instead, and on my way I noticed that the small plot next to the house was thick with the irises that thrived there. Next I saw that my father's car wasn't parked out front, and I wondered where he was. Then I thought, What the hell's the difference? Who cares?

Those two words had become a basic part of my vocabulary, providing me with a defense against unmet needs and expectations. Yet there was a part of me that always expected my father to act like a parent instead of a missing person.

The next thing that struck me was that the old front porch was gone. Instead of the dilapidated porch I had loved, there was a set of bare cement steps. The sight of them irritated my sensibility. That porch had been one of the few stable entities in my life. I figured Uncle Bill must have done the work, and I wondered how many pennies had been found under there when he ripped the old floorboards out. I knew the house looked neater now, but I had liked the beat-up porch exactly the way it was.

At the front entrance, I opened the black screen door that led into Granny's side of her duplex. But when I turned the knob on the inside door and tried giving it a shove it would not budge. Dammit. What a character Granny is. Even in the summer when it's roasting hot she puts her rocks against the door.

I banged on the door with my fist, and waited. In a little while the yellowed curtain inside the cracked window of the black front door was pushed aside by a bony wrinkled hand, and I saw Granny standing there, squinting out at me. "Who is it?"

"It's me," I shouted. "Tommy!"

"Oh, 'tis you is it, Tommy? Wait till I move my rocks out o' the way." The curtain fell back into place and I knew she was bending over to remove both the scatter rug and the rocks that she carefully jammed against the lower portion of the front door to prevent drafts and frustrate intruders.

When the door opened and the old woman stood before me, her chin was about in line with my chest. "Well, it's the devil himself, is it? 'Tis good to see you, Tommy. I was just lying in my bed saying my Rosary and praying for yere safe return. 'Twas good of ye to send the note about yere coming. How was the ride on the bus?"

"Great, Granny." As I stepped into the small dark hallway I thought, There's no need to tell her about my hitchhiking. She wouldn't get it.

"Sure, ye're bigger than I am now." She stood beside me. "Ye're getting older and taller and I'm getting older and smaller. Faith, I was never more than five foot in the first place."

She talked as I hung my jacket on the oak coat rack. I had reached five-feet-seven that summer and I was tall and thin next to Granny who, in her late sixties, looked more like eighty as she stood stooped over and dwarfish in her brown plaid flannel robe.

"I have a pot o' tea on in the kitchen." She peered through steel-rimmed spectacles and as she talked she fingered her black beads. Her long hair, tied at the back with recycled gift ribbon, fell in a gray mass on the rounded contour of her back. Recently, she had developed a pronounced stoop, caused partly by what she called "the rheumatism."

She's really getting hunched over, I thought as I followed her into the small parlor. I threw my brown canvas bag on the hard cushion of the aged love seat. Then I did a double-take at the brown-hued portrait photo of Granny in its oval frame on the wall, and found it difficult to visualize her with a smooth face like the one I saw in the portrait photo. Currently, her face was very wrinkled, with large purple veins, a sallow complexion, sunken cheeks, and a wrinkled mouth devoid of teeth.

I followed her through the small dining room that doubled as her sleeping quarters. It was jammed full of familiar old furniture. The dark hulk of a buffet with its split and peeling veneer. The round dining room table I had never once seen used for dining. The dining room chairs with their prickly horsehair seats and backrests. The ancient Morris chair where she would sit at night, fingering her Rosary beads and listening to the cathedral-shaped radio. Her surplus army cot bed with the black and gold lion tapestry on the wall above it. On either side of the tapestry there were the two black silhouetted nudes that had been hung there by my itinerant bachelor Uncle Frank. They seemed very out of place in Granny's house, but there they were regardless.

The old woman carefully descended the single step to the kitchen floor, holding the doorway for balance. "The tea's boiling." She pointed a bony finger toward the portable oil stove mounted on one end of the bulky black iron Magee stove which was used just in the winter. The large stove heated the hot water that was only available at cold times of year. From the spring through the fall there was no hot tap water in Granny's house. The only hot water was what we boiled on the portable stove.

The tea had eggshells added, and it was rapidly boiling in the dented open pot. There beneath the stove, sound asleep in his own private haven, was the fluffy gray cat, Tony. He was the fourth cat named Tony who had occupied the spot under the stove, and all of them had rejected affection. I think they must have been Buddhists and very prone to detachment.

"Pour yereself some tea." She seated herself in the old rocker in the center of the kitchen floor. "Did ye have breakfast?"

"Not yet."

"Get yereself an egg in the icebox in the pantry, and boil it on the stove. I think there's corn flakes and evaporated milk in there too ye can have. There's a little pot at the sink for yere egg. Forage for yourself. Sure, I did enough waiting on others in my day."

In the pantry I found three eggs, a half-used can of White House evaporated milk, and a nearly empty box of stale Kellogg's Corn Flakes.

You'd think she'd have gotten rid of this icebox by now, I thought. Hardly anybody uses ice anymore. They all have refrigerators.

Placing the evaporated milk and the Kellogg's on the kitchen table, I went to the rust-stained kitchen sink where I put two eggs in a battered pan, which I partially filled with slowly running cold water that trickled from corrosion-filled pipes.

Now I was tall enough to look directly into my father's cracked shaving mirror as I stood at the sink. The face that looked back at me was boyish, straight nosed, freckled, and tanned from the summer sun at Saranac Inn. Beneath my mouth I focused on the shadow caused by the pressure of my large crowded front teeth. I despised that shadow, and I also disliked the way my ears seemed to tilt outward from my head at the top while hugging my head closely at their bottoms. The only thing about myself that came close to pleasing me was my mass of brown, curly hair, but at times even my hair got on my nerves.

This mirror's weird. If you move up or down or sideways you look different. You can't even tell what you really look like. I wonder where the hell my father is. All his crap is still here, that's for sure.

A long shelf over the sink held Fred O'Connell's Lavoris mouthwash, Bayer aspirins, shaving tools, and enough patent medicines to start a pharmacy.

I took the egg pan to the stove, touched a match to the kerosene-saturated wicks in the burner, and a small cloud of smoke puffed and blackened the pan. I put the burner elements back in place, adjusted the flame, and got myself one of Granny's least chipped cups. Then I poured out some of her strong hot tea.

"I have my own tea here," she said as she rocked in her rocker. "It's still hot from a while ago. 'Tis good to have a cup o' tea, thanks be to God."

"Yup, 'tis good. Where's my father?" As I sat there near the sink I poured some stale corn flakes into a bowl, sprinkled sugar on the flakes, and added undiluted evaporated milk.

Granny rocked and fingered her rosary beads. "Sure, who ever knows where Freddy O'Connell is? He's always gallivanting. He went off last night and prob'ly won't be back till Monday. Sure, he's not a homebody. No sooner does he get a bite to eat than he's in his high-powered car with a lady friend. I think he said he was off to the Cape." The car she had called "high-powered" was the '37 Plymouth that was now nine years old.

I made no reply as I went to get my eggs, and without prompting, the old woman talked on as I ate breakfast. "Ye'd think he'd have had his fill of the drinking and carousing after all these years, but it's off in the high-powered car he goes to the races with his lady friends. If he's not at the office he's at the track. Devil a bit he tells me about his business. Freddy just goes his way. It used to get under Margaret's skin sometimes the way he kept on the go. Off again, on again, gone again, Finnegan."

I laughed at her last remark, and I wondered if I was about to hear one of her famous monologues. I was right. "I liked Margaret, I did. She was a good sort. 'Twas too bad she had to go off the way she did." She pointed at her head. "I say a prayer for Margaret when I think of it. While she worked he gallivanted. Freddy was never one for the worruk. I think he took after the old gent.

"It wasn't because he liked the worruk that your grandfather became a barber. Dan just wanted to be his own boss, that was all. He'd never lift a hand to do a tap in the house. But he'd stay in the shop till all hours with his bottle and his friends. Sure his friends aren't helping him now that he's living over there in the old house on nothing but the Old Age money. But they drank his liquor with him, they did, and he'd cut their hair for nothing too the damn fool.

"Him and his booze and his playing the horses. Sure, that's why we moved here from Connecticut. Dan was always on the move. First we were in New York, then Connecticut, and we moved here so's he could be near to the Brockton Fair Grounds and the race track. If it wasn't for me saving the money from when I was a maid for the high muckamucks, and the money I took from his pockets when he was stone drunk in his chair, we'd have had nothing to eat and he'd have never got his own barber shop.

"But never a word o' thanks from Dan O'Connell. Sure it's all water over the dam now. 'Tis a bitter struggle it is. Ye don't know the half of it." She paused. "Oh, 'twas too bad about Mister Fairchild. He was dead two days before they found him."

"Mister Fairchild? Dead?"

"Sure he's six foot under now," she answered matter-of-factly, with a nod of her head. "God rest his immortal soul. He's in the care of the good Lord now. Sure that's where I want to be. I've had enough of this mixed up worruld, and all the fighting and quarreling and bickering. There's no end to the wars and the famines and the troubles. It won't be long before I'm seventy. 'Tis a long time to be around. Ye wouldn't know about that. Ye're only twelve."

I shouted, "I'm fourteen!" I was insulted by being viewed as two years younger.

"Sure, if ye're twelve or fourteen, what difference does it make?" She fingered her Rosary beads. "Sure ye've been well taken care of by that White woman. She made a bundle on the lot of ye. She lives in her grand house with the son all college educated."

I said nothing, but I could not picture how Mrs. White had "made a bundle" on the money she got from Catholic Charities for her work. Years before, I had come to know that the truth as my grandmother saw it did not necessarily coincide with the truth as others saw it, and that in her own vocal way she was a living example of the relativity of truth.

Her previous comment returned to my mind. Old Mister Fairchild. Dead. I could not imagine the old neighbor next door unable to hold out a withered hand with a piece of candy in it and say, "It's good to see you, Tommy."

The house began to shake. Dishes rattled. The pictures on the walls vibrated. But it was definitely not an earthquake. The eight-fifteen to Boston was pulling into the East Dedham Railroad Station to the rear of the house. So I moved the curtain on the window next to me, giving me a clear view through the screened porch and out toward the station. I loved to watch the commuters file onto the train with their newspapers and briefcases. I wondered about the world they lived in. Would I be doing the same thing some day? And would I be living on the better side of the tracks instead of "the other side" in East Dedham?

As the locomotive trembled, belched steam, and rumbled out of the station, Granny launched into another subject. "William works his head off in the boiler room over at the Quincy School, and Rita throws away his money faster than what it comes in." I knew my Aunt Rita was probably next door in her adjoining kitchen on the other side of the duplex hearing every word.

Granny raised her voice. "She throws away more after a meal than the gang of them eat. William goes off to stoking boilers and working like a dog while she flops around living the life of Riley. He's too good a provider, and devil a bit does she appreciate it. She just runs off with her lady friends to theaters and spends his money faster than what he makes it.

"Sure, she's always got something new for her back. Nothing but the best for Rita. She fills her face with candy and cakes and paints her face with the damnable lipsticks. The damn fool William had to marry her. Not a choice did he have." She rocked and fingered her beads. "'Tis a bitter struggle it is."

I knew that Rita did the best she could on Uncle Bill's modest salary as a janitor, and simply kept house and fed the kids and went to the movies once a week. But Granny thought Rita was living it up. As I took in Granny's monologue I wondered how Rita could stand living next door in the duplex, within earshot of Granny's ranting and raving.

"A squanderer is what she is," continued Granny as loud as before. "And a wastrel!"

I chuckled. "What did you say?"

"She's a wastrel is what I said. She squanders William's hard-earned money with her lights blazing all the day and half the night. Helping the Edison get rich is what she's doing while William slaves like a dog so she can live like a grand lady. She ought to be in on Commonwealth Avenue married to some rich Yankee banker the way she prances around with her fine clothes and putting on airs like she does with her tea parties and all her lady friends."

I laughed. "Sure."

"'Tis not a laughing matter, Tommy O'Connell. A penny saved is a penny earned, ye know. Take care of the pennies and the dollars will take care of themselves. That one'll drive William to an early grave, she will. 'Tis no laughing matter at all when a man's married to a squanderer and she spends his money faster than what he makes it. Rita doesn't know what the word conserve means, and the more he gives her the more she connives to see what else she can get. If it isn't a toaster it's new dishes. There's no end to it. When I first saw her I knew in a minute she'd be a curse to him. Not one thing upstairs did she have. She knew how to swing her bottom was all."

I laughed again and reflected on my basic belief that she should have been a stage actress. They would have heard every word up in the balcony, with that booming voice of hers. Actually, she was always on stage, even for an audience of one. And I knew she made up many things as she went along, yet believed every word of her own fiction.

Responding to my outburst of laughter, she said, "Ye don't know what I'm saying." She pointed a bony finger at me. "Little do ye know now. It's a valley of tears, Tommy O'Connell, and ye better know it. Nosiree, life is no . . . whatchacallit. It's no picnic."

I rose from the table, still grinning at her, and placed my dirty dishes in the sink, rinsed my hands, and then wiped myself dry with the soiled dish towel which I picked up from the moldy water-logged wooden countertop next to the sink. Thinking about how perfect Mrs. White's house had been, I shook my head in dismay at my grandmother's primitive level of housekeeping. Then I placed the mildewed towel back on the counter and headed toward the front of the house.

As I climbed the narrow stairs I noticed that their rubber treads had been worn smooth with the passage of time and the friction of many feet. At the top of the stairs I knocked on the door of the bathroom that served both sides of the duplex, and since I heard no outcry I went into the familiar cubicle.

Daylight filtered in a gray haze into the bathroom through a jammed-shut skylight which was coated with locomotive soot. The toilet reminded me of the one in Mom White's cellar. This flush box was also suspended from an overhead beam and activated by a pull-chain. The toilet was far from its original white condition, unlike the spotless toilets at Mrs. White's. And there was no washbowl. If you wanted to wash your hands you had to use the water from the bathtub's faucets.

The ancient porcelain bathtub had claw legs resembling lions' feet, and its rust stains were indelible. Underneath lay large balls of dust. I had never had seen that kind of dust at Mrs. White's. Dust was Mrs. White's enemy, and she always defeated her enemies with her Electrolux. But Granny didn't even own a vacuum cleaner. A carpet sweeper and a broom, that was it.

In the warm months at Granny's house only cold water came from the water faucets feeding the tub. In the cold weather the limited supply of hot water was supplied by circular tubing that was heated by the kerosene burners in the kitchen stove, channeled into a storage boiler next to the stove, and piped upstairs. But the bathroom itself was unheated. So comfort while bathing was never available in Granny's house.

After I had urinated I stepped into the upstairs hallway and peeked into the larger of the two small bedrooms. My father's room was sparsely furnished with a large metal-framed double bed, a cluttered oak dresser, and a straight-backed oak chair with a miscellany-covered seat. As I looked at the belongings on his dresser, I thought, This room is still as sloppy as ever.

On one side of my father's room was a door with a small padlock on it, and on visits throughout my childhood I had wondered what was behind the looked door. On more than one occasion I had dreamed that my insane mother was confined in there, in chains, with a gag in her mouth to keep her silent. I avoided looking at the padlocked door as I left my father's room and went into the room that would be mine, at least until Uncle Joe returned from Europe where he was working as a civilian for the U.S. Army, helping to locate the graves of military personnel killed during World War II.

On visits to Granny's house I had always enjoyed Joe's company because of his wry wit, but whenever he came around I would have to move in with my father. This was a problem because I no longer felt comfortable sleeping in a bed with another person. I treasured my privacy, in bathrooms and bedrooms, and even though I had been surrounded by people at Mrs. White's I was basically a lone wolf emotionally there too. Solitude was my friend, not my enemy.

As I entered Joe's room I realized how small and dark it was, even in the daytime. There was only one window and that was shaded by a towering oak tree located between Granny's house and the monstrous duplex next door. The owner was Jordan, and his tenants lived on the side facing Granny's. With the oak tree in full leaf above, and a row of high lilac trees in leaf below, there was little of the next house or the sky visible from the window of my new room.

I yanked the string attached to the ceiling light fixture, and watched the bare bulb swing back and forth at the end of its rusty chain, projecting eerie shadows about the room. Then I dropped to a sitting position on the very thin mattress supported by its sagging flat spring.

The brown enamel of the tubular steel bed frame was chipped in spots, and the makeshift bedspread was a patchwork of recycled bed sheet sections sewn together with bits of colored yarn and black thread.

Under the bedspread I knew there was a rough blanket, one ragged bottom sheet, and no top sheet. This was not Mrs. White's house. This was another world. And I was in for a surprise when my eyes lit on the window curtains, also pieced together from old bed sheets. She had taken a large number of red-and-white shamrock shoulder patches that Uncle Joe had brought home from the Army, and she had sewn them along the edges of each curtain for a border that added a dash of color.

Very creative, I thought as I threw myself on my back on the bed. Brother, am I bushed. I haven't slept since the night before last. Hitchhiking isn't the greatest way to spend a night. Some people act real funny when they pick you up, and lots of 'em talk your ear right off, and ask you about everything including what you had for your damn breakfast.

My sleepy gaze fell on the tarnished silver-and-black crucifix on the wall next to the bed. Jammed between the crucifix and the wall was a frond of dried Easter palm leaves, and I wondered how old the palms were. I decided they were "old as hell."

I can't really picture Uncle Joe being that young, I thought as my eyes went to his Dedham High School graduation photo which had aged to a dark brown in its frame on the closet wall facing the bed.

Staring at the long crack in the plaster of the sloped ceiling above me, I wondered if all my life I'd be sleeping in small rooms with slanted ceilings that I kept bumping my head against if I didn't watch out.

Well, I mused, I'm back in Dedham at Granny O'Connell's finally, and who the hell cares about the sloped ceilings anyhow? My father's room has one, and this room does, and even the bathroom does. But the main thing is I'll be pretty much on my own here. Granny talks a lot but I can let most of it go in one ear and out the other.

I prob'ly won't see that much of my father. He's always off some place with some woman. I wonder if he's still married to my mother. It must be weird being married to somebody who's in an insane asylum. But if he's still married to her, how come he goes out with all kinds of women? I guess that's his business. Why the hell should I care? What he does is his problem, not mine.

Like Mom White always used to say, "Take care of yourself, Tommy O'Connell. If ye don't, nobody else will." She was right. When you get right down to it, who really gives a good shit about me anyhow? My father's mainly interested in his own life. But Granny must care because she's letting me stay here. And back at Lake Placid, Jo cares about me. At least I think she does. But now I wonder if I'll ever see her again. Last summer seems so unreal now.

Brother, I can hardly keep my eyes open. Oh well. It's only Saturday morning. I don't have a thing to do till school starts Tuesday. I guess I'll take a little nap. Then maybe this afternoon I'll see some of the kids in the neighborhood. Then tonight I'll go down East Dedham Square and hang around the drugstore. I can do whatever I feel like doing now, like I did this summer. That's a break. It isn't too fancy here, but after nine long years at Mrs. White's I'm really free now. Free as a bird. And I can do exactly . . . what I . . . feel . . . like . . .

23

The year 1946 was drawing to a close, and at twilight on the day after Christmas I decided to go down the steps leading to Granny's dirt-floored cellar. Earlier that day, I had taken the remnants of a small ham, protected by waxed paper, to the other side of East Dedham to my grandfather's house, and Dan O'Connell had asked, "How's the old lady?" I had told him she was okay, and when he had asked me, "How's she using you?" my answer was, "I'll survive . . . if I'm lucky." Food was in short supply at Granny's house, and I had a large appetite.

As I stood near the kerosene barrel, I shivered. "Brother, it's cold down here." I took an unopened letter from my shirt pocket, examined the envelope, and then shook my head. No sense opening it, I thought. She'll be asking if I plan to go to Saranac next summer and I'm not gonna go back. I couldn't care less about Saranac now, and I'm not interested in Jo anymore either.

I lit a match, touched it to the unopened letter, and as the flames began to curl upward I dropped the letter to the hard-packed dirt floor of the cellar and watched it burn to black-and-gray ashes.

That's that, I thought. I've tossed the watch case with Jo's picture into the Mill Pond, and now I've burned her letter. Marie's the only one I care about now. She's the most beautiful girl that ever lived, and I think she likes me. Boy, it was terrific when she let me walk down Whiting Avenue with her the week before Christmas vacation, and she . . .

My thoughts were interrupted as a train rumbled into East Dedham Station. Then from up above in Uncle Bill's side of the duplex I heard the sound of my cousins banging around and the mangy part-Dachshund howling. Bill was proud that the whining dog had royal canine blood, and was "sired by My Brucie." But I wasn't impressed by the partially pedigreed canine. I also wasn't impressed by the way my cousins were acting up next door. Outbursts of noise and craziness like theirs just had not been allowed at Mrs. White's house. At 42 Mountain Avenue in Norwood it had always been quiet enough to read a book. But this was not Mrs. White's.

As I stood there wondering how the old house could withstand the torture those kids inflicted on it, I conjured up the thought that it might literally cave in some day soon. Then I kicked the letter's ashes so they would be inconspicuous. Next I tiptoed up the squeaky cellar steps and quietly opened the door at the head of the stairs. Granny was rocking and praying in her chair in the kitchen, and when I saw her I decided to wait a second to see if I could sneak upstairs without her noticing me. I didn't want to set myself up for any of her nagging.

After a few moments the old woman rose from her rocker and shuffled toward the kitchen sink, out of my line of vision. I heard her open the door to the cabinet beneath the sink where she kept old rags and empty tin cans. Then I heard the sound of rushing water filling a can, and realized she was urinating that way instead of going upstairs to the bathroom.

At this point I slipped through the doorway and into the dining room, and started whistling the song, "I Can't Begin to Tell you."

As I entered the kitchen, Granny was hurriedly closing the sink cabinet door. "Is that you, Tommy?" She squinted at me through her round steel-rimmed eyeglasses.

"Yup, it's me."

"There's some peas in the pot on the stove and some hot water for tea. The ham's gone but I think there's some boloney in the ice box. Get yereself some supper. Ye can forage for yereself."

After she had shuffled past me and entered the dining room, I opened the door beneath the sink and saw a LaTouraine Coffee can partially filled with her urine. "Holy Shit," I muttered. "She's living in the Dark Ages. But at least she doesn't piss outdoors. I bet she pours her piss down the sink. Hm. I suppose in an emergency I could do the same thing."

I took a gray rag and began to wipe a dish before placing it at my spot at the table. Then I heard her voice boom out: "Sure, ye're worse than yere Uncle Joseph when he comes here. He's always wiping the dust off things. But if it's good enough for the likes o' me it's good enough for the likes of you. Do ye think this is the Waldorf Astoria?"

"Nope, it's the Ritz Carlton." I laughed as I continued wiping dust and lint from the plate.

"Nothing's good enough for the brats o' today," she muttered as she left the kitchen again. Then I heard her heavy footsteps on the cellar stairs.

I assumed she was going down to get some oil for the space heater in the living room. And I had a burst of conscience about not getting it for her. But she was used to taking care of things herself, so I let go of the idea of taking on any new traditions. Then I wondered if she would smell the fire I had lit down there. No. It wasn't likely. Her nose and other senses weren't that keenly attuned anymore.

Taking the dented pot from the top of the black iron stove, I went to the sink, drained off the water from the warmed peas, heaped some on my plate, and returned the pot to the stove. At the refrigerator, I leaped right back in frustration after opening the door. "Yuck! She's pulled the damn plug out again so the Edison won't get rich. Look at this cruddy warm gray boloney. I'll be damned if I'll eat crap like this." I threw the dried up, scum-coated luncheon meat into the tin garbage can near the kitchen sink.

When Granny returned to the kitchen, she poured herself a cup of tea, and flopped down into the old rocker with the paint half rubbed off. "What did the old gent say when ye brought him the ham?"

"He said he was glad to get it, and he also asked how you were doing."

"Sure, it's little he cares how I'm doing. All he ever cared about was himself and his bottle." She gave a little chuckle. "Was he in his cups?"

"Not that I know of," I lied.

There had been a strong rum smell in his place that afternoon, as on some other occasions. Old Dan O'Connell's apartment in the old house that he and Granny and their children had once occupied smelled of pipe tobacco, chewing tobacco, grime on the floor, and an overflowing spittoon. The aromatic blend that my grandfather's living habits created was similar to the blend of aromas in the smoke-filled den of gambling iniquity known as Humpty's Pool Room, where I had become a regular visitor.

That afternoon Grandpa had sent me to do some errands, as usual, to Rosie's Variety Store which was next to her son Leo's auto repair shop. One product Grandpa ordered was Sylpho-Naphthol disinfectant to sprinkle on the caked grime covering the linoleum kitchen floor. Each item was dutifully recorded in Rosie's little book where she kept track of customers' purchases which were paid in full when their Old Age check or some other check arrived.

For a while my grandfather had reminisced about his days in his barber shop "before the legs went." He had talked about having pool tables as well as barber chairs, and endless streams of people who had used the shop across from East Dedham's Mill Pond as a gathering place. He said crowds had gathered to listen to the world championship boxing matches like the Dempsey-Firpo fight when he had installed the first crystal set in the area to pick up radio signals from Boston, and had added loudspeakers to get the sound to hundreds of people outdoors.

As he had talked about the old days he chewed tobacco and pinched snuff and smoked cigars. Old Dan, once known as

Friendly Danno, had been in a good frame of mind that day. However, a few weeks earlier, in a foul mood, he had accused me of the evils of conniving and greed, and had tried to get me to admit to him that I only came over to visit him because of the money he gave me for doing errands. I made no such admission.

"In his day he could drink the Mill Pond dry," Granny said. "Sure and he could pour it into himself just like he had no bottom." I chuckled, took another tablespoon of peas, and nodded at the old woman. "It's a devil of a habit, the drink." She stopped fingering the Rosary beads and put her cup of tea on the black stove's ledge. "Well, a Merry Christmas to the laddie buck. I always send him over a plate of ham the day after Christmas. He likes that."

But you never see him, I thought. You haven't seen him since I can remember. It's like you were never even married to him except for sending some food over on holidays.

As if she had read my mind, she said, "'Twas no picnic when I was living with the old gent. 'Twas a bitter struggle. Sure, life is a valley of tears, ye know, but I don't cry any more, I just sit and rock and pray for the sins of the worruld."

You sure do, I thought. By now the sins of the world should definitely be all taken care of by your praying.

As I sipped my tea and swallowed my peas, and chewed my stale bread coated with her uncolored margarine, Granny talked of the awful flu epidemic of 1918 and other catastrophic times, and recalled people "passing out in the middle of the night" and being "carted off in pine boxes." She talked about "famines" and "pestilence" and "accidental deaths." She talked about people "going berserk and getting carried off in the wee hours of the morning with their hands and feet tied so's they wouldn't run amuck."

Then she set off on one of her favorite tangents. "That one over there, she's no damn good." She shouted toward the other side of the duplex, hoping she would be heard by Aunt Rita. "She throws out garbage enough to feed the poor in India. She's nothing but a wanton trollop. 'Twas a bad day for William when he married the likes o' little Rita. All he saw in her was her bottom . . . ."

I laughed as I finished my meatless meal. It was not a vegetarian household by choice; it was just that there was seldom enough money to buy meat, fresh vegetables, or fruit.

Since there was such a gap in age between me and Granny, I could usually be fairly detached from her sermons, and I was a continuing audience for her. An audience of one listener.

When her diatribes weren't aimed at me I thought they were very funny. However, her own children, my father and uncles and aunts, didn't think she was funny at all. But I had enough distance from her to be objective, and I wasn't kidding when, thinking she couldn't hear me, I would say, "You're a fabulous character, Granny."

"Sure I'm a lot o' things. I suppose I'm a character too. I've been around too long though, and all I want now is to meet my Maker and . . . ."

She was about to start another monologue when I rose from the table, satisfied with her performance, and as I stepped into the dining room I could hear snatches of her loud commentaries on "gallivanting," "rumholes," and "drinking and carousing."

My next words were "Holy shit!" And the words weren't about Granny's monologue. I saw the part of the rug next to the living room space heater going up in flames. "Dammit, she'll burn this house down one of these days!" I flipped the end of the rug over and stamped it flat to extinguish the blaze. It was the third time that winter I had found the rug on fire. Granny habitually turned the space heater's oil flow too high.

Oh well, I reflected, if it isn't the space heater going up in flames it's the kitchen stove exploding. This old place is one big booby trap. No central heating here, like at White's.

I slumped into the chair with the wide arms and began to browse through a copy of my father's Columbia magazine, and I found myself wondering where he was that evening. Then, an instant later, I closed the magazine and flipped it onto the table next to the chair. Ah, what the hell do I care where he is? He's in his own screwy world and I'm in mine.

I went to the bookcase, took down Darwin's *The Voyage of the Beagle* from the incomplete set of Harvard Classics, and I was about to begin reading when Granny stormed into the room. "Sure and all ye want to do is make the rotten Edison rich. It isn't even dark yet and ye've already got all the lights in the house blazing away."

She reached over and put out the light I was using, and I responded, "I can't believe this! Damn it, I give up. A guy can't even put a light on around here without you having a fit."

"Ye can use all the lights ye want when ye're paying the bills," she retorted, and went back to her kitchen muttering about "the brats o' today," which meant me and my whole age group.

She could be very irritating when she set her mind to it, as she had done on another recent evening. I was listening to Archie's Tavern on the radio and she started yelling about Archie being "no good" and "making the Irish out to be nothing but drunkards." When I had told her it was all in fun, she had said I knew nothing and insisted, "Some Yankee writes Archie's Tavern to make fun of the Irish."

At any rate, after having the lights shut off while I was trying to read, I decided to go upstairs to change from my gabardine slacks into my corduroys. As I was about to climb the stairs I heard the radio blaring in the dining room. "Our Father who art in heaven, hallowed be thy name . . . ."

Oh no, she's got Archbishop Cushing on again. If it isn't the Rosary it's the Catholic Hour or the Irish Hour or it's those news broadcasts she listens to with the same news over and over.

The radio, I had learned, was at once her friend and her enemy. She loudly responded to the remarks of newsmen and announcers, criticized them eagerly, answered their rhetorical questions, and debated with them. In addition, she would call the newscasters "dirty blackguards" if they said anything favorable about England or Winston Churchill.

"Winnie is no damn good," she would shout. "He's a Black Protestant is what he is. He'd like to hang all the Catholics, ye know. The devil take the English anyways. They're a bad lot. John Bull can go rot in hell, God forgive me for saying it."

She's really something, I thought as I climbed the stairs to my room. What a character! She's always upset with somebody. "Little Rita" or the neighbor "Jordan" or "John Bull" or "sheenies" or "Eyetalians" or "Franklin Delano" or "non-Catholics."

As I entered my room and pulled the light chain, my eyes fell on the Christmas cards standing in a row on top of my bureau. They were mostly from people I'd known during my years with Mrs. White in Norwood. As I noticed them I thought, Christmas is almost nothing here. Yesterday was just like any other day except for a few decorations, the small ham, and the five dollar bill my father gave me on Christmas morning along with his note wishing me a Merry Christmas.

From my own meager savings I had bought a tie for my father and a jar of hard candy for Granny. Now, a day later, I was thinking about how things were so different at Granny's. Brother, she owns this old duplex, but the way we live we might as well be on welfare. Ah, what the hell. I suppose this place is better than nothing. At least nobody's on my back and I don't pay any attention to most of her nagging.

I had developed my own method of coping with her nagging, which at times could be incessant. On occasions when her nagging could not easily go in one ear and out the other, and I found it hard to see some humor in her actions, I would shout a sarcastic reply at her and make a quick exit from the house, slamming the front door behind me as I left. I could never have shown such anger at Mrs. White's. Anger was Margaret White's own royal prerogative, and punishment would have been the consequence if anyone else dared to be upset.

As I put on my chino pants with the frayed pockets, and slipped into my yellow short-sleeved sport shirt, I was thinking, I hate to break that five bucks he gave me, but I need bus fare. It's too cold to walk all the way up to Dedham to meet Mike at the liberry. Oh yuh. Maybe there's some change in that mess on my father's little bureau.

I went into my father's cluttered room and there on the dusty bureau top, among countless other items, I found a scattering of pennies and nickels. As I took enough to pay my bus fare, I considered the ethics of pocketing his coins without permission. "Well, what's his is mine, and he's never around the house enough to give me a chance to ask him for permission." I was satisfied with my rationalization.

Downstairs in the small front hallway I put on the old army field jacket Uncle Joe had left behind him, and I yelled toward the kitchen, "I'm going up the liberry, Granny." Just before leaving the house I reached into the jacket pocket, took out a pack of Pall Malls, lit one, and dramatically swung the front door open, puffing smoke as I stepped out into the cold late December night.

As the storm door was closing, I growled, "Damn, I would go bang that wart against the edge of the door. If it isn't one thing, it's another. It's either a wart or a rash or athlete's foot or something else."

Walking along Walnut Place I thought, She's a beaut shutting off the light on me like that. Mom White was a nagger sometimes but Granny takes the prize. What a screwy way to live, because of no dough. It must be nice to have a buck. The five I got from my father for Christmas will be gone pretty soon and then I'll be broke again. Broke Tommy O'Connell, that's me.

Well, at least I've got the five bucks. I prob'ly ought to get some new underwear with it, but I think I'll use it to shoot pool, and bowl, and maybe have me a soda at the drug store. I can get the underwear some other time.

I took a drag of the cigarette. Then, as I exhaled, the smoke combined with the steam of my hot breath against the cold night air and formed a cloud before my face. As I waved it away I thought, She flips her lid when she sees me smoking. She should have seen me drinking beer last summer at Saranac. And if she saw me taking a mouthful of that old Martini and Rossi bottle in the pantry a few weeks back she'd have thrown a conniption fit. I should have known it was gas to prime my father's car. Boy, did I spit that lousy stuff out fast.

To hell with drinking from strange bottles from now on. Guess I'll stick to smoking. Seems like I've been smoking forever. That was really something the day Dave talked me into smoking my first cigarette. I got sick as a dog.

It's funny how I can remember some things like they were yesterday, I thought as I reached the corner of Walnut Street and walked toward East Dedham Square. And sometimes I can't remember a thing from a day ago. But now I remember the crazy dream I had last night.

God, it was more like a nightmare than a dream. My mother was in this huge cage surrounded by all kinds of crazy people and she was looking out at me and yelling and leaping around. It's screwy. I haven't even thought about her lately, then I go and have a dream about her that scares the hell out of me.

I shivered, both from the cold and from recalling the nightmare. Quite often my nights would include nightmares, and sometimes sleepwalking. If I had a nightmare when my father was around he would apply cold wet towels to my forehead to pacify me. After having an extremely vivid nightmare, I would wonder if I might lose my mind as my mother had. Then, to reduce my level of anxiety, I would try to stop thinking about her. But periodic reminders of my mother's condition were inevitable.

"Crazy" was a common word, and even though I used it myself as though it meant nothing to me, each time I said that word or "nuts" or "screwy" there was an image in my mind of my incurably mad mother. The mother I couldn't remember.

As I dwelled on the subject that haunted me most in life, I reflected, My father never mentions her but Granny was talking about her again a few weeks ago, saying it was too bad she "went in the head" and how it was so "hard to imagine Margaret being in that asylum in Boston all these years."

It's hard for me to imagine it too. It's also hard to imagine nobody ever going to visit her. I wonder if I ought to go see her some day. Nah, there's no sense thinking about that. Besides, the Henderson relatives prob'ly go see her. Or do they? They never came to see me during the nine years I spent at Mrs. White's. Well, my mother's never seen me since I was a baby, so she wouldn't even know me. Nah, there's no sense thinking about my mother at all. It's like she's dead. And it'd probably be better if she was dead. Then I wouldn't have to lie about her.

As usual, I wished that the problem of her insanity could disappear. And in my conscious mind, for brief periods, I could avoid thoughts of her, but at night when I slept I was no longer in control and I would often find myself surrounded by swirling scenes that showed my mother's photo-album face, the only image of her that I knew, popping up and then disappearing.

Then I would find myself running and falling and sinking and sweating and suffering. At night I could not escape the insecurities and fears I always carried deep inside. Yet despite my inner insecurity, I had somehow managed to develop an outward air of casual confidence. And it was with that attitude that I walked along Walnut Street smoking my Pall Mall and heading toward the bus that would bring me to Dedham Square to meet my pal Mike at the library.

Even though the inner Tommy was extremely sensitive and vulnerable, and I carried around with me an undercurrent of deep anxiety, I usually acted like a self-assured human being, and played the part of the calm one, the one Mrs. White had called "the quiet one." And when I played that part I did it so convincingly that I could almost believe it myself.

Yes, I could have won an award for playing the role of "the lone wolf."

24

The June air was hot and humid on the last day of school, and in unison Mike and I heaved a sigh as we left the side entrance of Dedham High and began the summer of '47. I was tall and lean and my friend Mike was a bit shorter, but much broader in the shoulders, and very rugged.

In "B Division" of the College Preparatory Course in our sophomore year, Mike had earned himself the unofficial title of Class Clown. There was never a dull moment with Mike around, and I was one of his best audiences. He was an expert mime, and I appreciated his offbeat sense of humor, except when it was aimed at me with too much of a critical tone. At times Mike would even make fun of the way I held a sandwich so that nothing would fall out of it.

"Did you get any D's on your card?" asked Mike.

"Never had a D. I don't believe in getting D's. But I managed to get C minuses in French and Algebra."

"Are you shitting me about never getting a D?"

I made a sign over my chest. "Cross my heart and hope to fart."

"Hell, almost everybody's had some D's. Not even one? Never?"

"I wouldn't bullshit you, Mike. In Junior High I got mostly all B's, and a few A's in the seventh and eighth grades, and just a few C's in the ninth. Back in elementary I got all A's."

"That's really weird. So you were a real egghead once, huh? Hey, if you got such good marks before, how come you're not doing that now?"

"I'm sort of on vacation from studying too much. I'm taking it easy and having fun."

"What does your father say when he sees your cards?"

"I don't think he cares much about my marks."

"Jesus, my Mom and Pop are always on my back. They never graduated from high school in Italy, and they want me to get good marks so I won't have any trouble getting into college."

"No sweat, Mike. You'll make it. Hey, college is a long way off."

"Yup, two more years cooped up in old Dedham High. Well, I'm sure as hell glad we're out for the summer. What are ya gonna do? Work?"

"Not if I can help it. W-o-r-k is a four letter word that I try to avoid. What do I need money for? All I spend it on is shooting pool and playing the pinball machine down at Humpty's pool room."

"Is Humpty's that cruddy place up over the First National store in East Dedham Square?"

"Yup, it's a real raunchy place, Mike. Lots of stew bums around, and tough guys too. Some of them are right out of prison. But usually they don't bother anybody, and I sort of like playing pool. It's fun once you get the hang of it."

"Some day I'll have to go down there with ya. The only thing is, I'm gonna be busy helping my father this summer, building chimneys and stuff. I hope I'll see ya this summer once in a while. We had a lot o' laughs this year."

"Going up the liberry every night beats hanging around the house. Whenever I spend too much time at home, it can really get to me. Granny can get on a guy's nerves something awful. Boy, sometimes she's like one of those toys you wind up with a key, and she keeps on yacking as loud as she can, and just won't stop."

"Yuh, I heard her nag you a few times when we were on the phone." Mike recalled that Granny had been yelling at me about shutting off the lights. "She was really giving it to ya, right?"

"Yuh. She thinks if I put one of her damn lights on I'm making the Edison rich, and if I use too much water when I'm washing my hands I'm making the Dedham Water Company rich. One thing's for sure, nobody's gonna get rich on Granny O'Connell."

"Well, at least it's better than that place you used to live, right?"

"In some ways it is, and in others it isn't. But I'd sooner live with my own relatives even if they can be pains in the ass sometimes. Granny always says 'The devil ye know is better than the devil ye don't know' and I think she's got a point."

Mike laughed and then we were both silent for a while as we walked along. During that bit of silence I found myself comparing Mike to my former Norwood pal John. The first difference that came to mind was that John had never asked me questions about my past. And I still preferred to avoid discussing it. It was my own business, and that was that.

While I was concentrating on my reflections we reached the railroad bridge that marked the end of our walk together. At this point, I always followed the railroad tracks toward Granny's house on Walnut Place, and Mike would go in the opposite direction to his home near Brookdale Cemetery.

Mike said, "I been wondering how come I always hear you talking about your father and grandmother and you never say anything about your mother."

"I just don't feel like talking about her, that's all. She died when I was a little kid, so what's there to talk about?" I thought that would stop his questions.

"Oh." Mike nodded, leaving the subject dormant. Then, after an uncomfortable pause, he asked, "How come you don't have to go to Christian Doctrine classes at Saint Mary's?"

Would there ever be an end to his questions? But I knew it wasn't Mike's fault that I was so allergic to questions. I tried to give him an answer without showing him my irritation. "I think I learned enough religion at Saint Catherine's in Norwood."

"That's what I think about all the years in Saint Mary's Sunday School too, but those damn priests always call up if I try to skip."

"Hah. They don't call me because nobody knows I'm living here in Dedham again."

"You're lucky."

"I suppose so. But I'm still a soldier of Christ, Mike. I go to church every Sunday and Confession once a month." I was making light of it, but being part of the Roman Catholic Church was about as necessary to me as life itself.

"Does your grandmother still go to church?"

"Yuh, she always gets a bus down at East Dedham Square, and she'll keep going till she can't stand up anymore. She's gotta atone for the sins of the world. It's her job." I chuckled.

"How come I never see you in Church with her?"

"She goes to early Mass." It was true that she usually went to early Mass, but even when she went to a later Mass, I made it a point not to go with her. I thought someone might mistake the wrinkled old woman for my mother, and in my adolescent self-centeredness I did not want anyone to think I might have a mother so old. At times, when she happened to be attending the same Mass, I would watch her as she shuffled down the aisle with her hunched over shoulders, her lint-covered black wool coat, and her wrinkled skin, and I would say to myself, "Boy, is she a relic of the Dark Ages."

Mike shook his head. "You wouldn't think an old lady like that'd want to get up so early for Mass."

"She's just a character, Mike. She's got her own ideas and doesn't give a damn what anyone else thinks. Well, I guess I'll head for Walnut Place." We shook hands.

"Take care, Tommy. Keep it in your pants."

"Yup. Stay loose, Mike. Loose as a three fingered goose."

Mike walked away grinning. Then he suddenly turned and shouted, "If you find it hard getting up in the morning, throw some ice water on it."

A group of girls walking a short distance behind us tittered, I blushed, and Mike burst out laughing and danced up and down while holding his sides.

He's a hot ticket, I thought as I waved goodbye. Then, as I went down the open wooden steps leading from Mount Vernon

Street to the cinder railroad bed, I recalled how Mike had our class laughing all year long with his antics.

Yuh, B Division's great. In A Division they make the kids work their asses off and nobody gets any laughs. I'll prob'ly stay in B. My card's not too good and not too bad, the way I like it.

I was strolling along the tracks heading toward the East Dedham Railroad Station when I heard a high pitched call. "Oakie ... key ... key ... key ..." The call was followed by derisive laughter.

My face flushed as I turned to see redheaded Louie hustling along a shortcut path to my right with my friends Fran and Johnny. Louie was a year ahead of us, and he had recently started his own unique misuse of the nickname some of my classmates had given me. He would scream "Oakie ... key ... key ... key ..." always with the same shout and ringing laughter. I waited for the group, and when I was a few feet away from the small squinty-eyed redhead, I said, "Hey, Louie, why don'tcha go pound sand up your ass? Or maybe some rock salt!"

Louie's face reddened as the others laughed. Fran said, "Don't mind Louie, Tommy. He's always been a pain in the ass, right, Louie?"

Laughing nervously, Louie replied, "You ought to know. It takes one to know one."

Johnny joined in the attack. "You're all mouth, Louie, and no action."

"Whattaya mean, I'm all mouth!" retorted Louie. "You're all nose, Johnny, and this guy here is the one who's all mouth." He pointed at me. "Look at those huge teeth!"

Feeling the blood rush to my face, I retaliated, "Your redheaded ass is suckin' broken bleach bottles, Louie." Fran and Johnny joined me in a gale of laughter at Louie's expense.

"You're all full o' cat shit," snapped the redhead. "You're all pinheaded sophomores."

"You never give up, Louie." said Fran. "You're always needling everybody. Know what you are? A real ass wipe."

"What do you know, Franny? You're always in a hopper wiping your fanny."

Fran's face flushed as he grabbed Louie by the shirt collar. "You know what I told you about that crap, you asshole? One o' these days I'm gonna really cream ya, Louie, and you're gonna be spitting out your goddam yellow teeth."

"Lemme go, for Christ's sake." Louie tried to squirm from Fran's firm grip on his shirt collar. "You know I didn't mean nothin'. I was just screwin' around. Can't you take a joke?"

"You're the joke." Fran relaxed his grip on Louie's collar. "You're a joke on the human race." I grinned, self-consciously cupping my hand over my mouth to cover my prominent teeth.

A moment later Louie parted from the group and went his way without another word. In his silence he was admitting temporary defeat. As my friends Fran and Johnny proceeded along the tracks, Fran asked, "What say, want to go shoot pool?"

"Well . . . I'm down to my last quarter."

"Come on," he urged. "We can each pay for a game, win or lose. Even if I win both games I'll pay for one of 'em."

"You think you can beat me two games?"

"Sure. I beat ya two out o' three last time."

"You had a run of shit luck."

"That's easy for you to say. You lost."

"We'll see who loses today."

"You guys and your pool," said Johnny. "How come you take it so serious?"

"You don't get it, Johnny," said Fran. "Pool's only a game with us. A game to the death. Hey, I'll tell you what. When I beat Tommy two games you can play the winner."

I laughed. "That'll be the day."

"I wouldn't waste any of my money on pool," said Johnny with a grin. "I'm too cheap."

"What makes you so cheap anyhow?" asked Fran.

Johnny shrugged his muscular shoulders. "Maybe 'cause my folks aren't always throwing money my way like yours do."

"My mother doesn't want her poor little boy getting broke," said Fran with a chuckle.

I joined the discussion. "My grandmother throws nickels around like manhole covers. She's still got her christening money from when she was a kid in Ireland. Two pence!"

We all laughed as we walked past the Boston Envelope Company where we could hear the clatter of machines producing envelopes downstairs and paper drinking cups up above.

"Hey, ya know that little Italian broad in there?" asked Fran. "The babe with the tight white T-shirts? Do you guys think she wears falsies?"

"I bet she does," said Johnny. "How could they stick out so straight if they were real?"

I added my contribution to the analysis. "I saw her running through the Square the other day, and they bounced like the real thing."

"I know one way to find out if they're real," said Fran with a grin. "Just grab a nice handful."

"If you frig around with her, you're crazy," said Johnny. "You'll get the creepin' crud."

"But I'm hot to get my first piece," said Fran. "Do ya know any virgins that put out, Johnny? So's I won't catch the crud?"

We all laughed as we approached the shadowy doorway leading to the Pool Room above the First National grocery store. Right before stepping into the entrance I looked across the Square to see if any of my Walnut Place neighbors were around, because I didn't want to be known as a "regular" at Humpty's. I saw no familiar faces.

As we began climbing the long flight of wide creaky stairs leading to the second level of the blighted two-story building, Johnny said, "I'll just come in and watch you guys."

Halfway up I was panting. "They ought to get an elevator in this place. These stairs are ridiculous." Strenuous exercise was never my favorite thing.

Fran laughed. "An elevator? Hah. It's a wonder Humpty's even got a pisserie."

In Humpty's there were four very well maintained tables. Three were for pocket billiards, which we simply called "pool." The other one was reserved exclusively for straight billiards. The tables were the only items in the Pool Room that could be viewed with respect. Most of the cues were warped. There were missing numbers in the sets of scoring tabs strung on wire over each table. The embossed metal sheeting of the ceiling, designed in a bygone era, shed flakes of ancient caked, cream-colored paint that had to be picked gently from the tables by fastidious pool players.

It was not what you might call a sanitary setting. The wooden floor was coated with layers of grime, smelly overflow from spittoons, stamped out cigar stubs, and flattened cigarette butts. The benches lining the walls had wooden slat seats, and in between the slats was a similar grime from decades of unwashed use.

As we entered the pool room laughing, the old man known to us as Humpty thumped toward us. He did not have a wooden leg, but one stiff-jointed leg gave the same effect. "Want a table, boys?" He peered at us over his small rimless spectacles with his right eye, which was the only good one. The left eye was made of glass, and sometimes he would matter-of-factly remove it and wipe it with his linty handkerchief, then return it to its socket. It was similar to Granny's ritual of taking out her false teeth and soaking them in a jar of water next to the sink.

"Yuh," said Fran, "we want a table."

The proprietor pointed to the only unoccupied pocket billiards table. Then Fran looked at me. "It's the table near the pisserie, Tommy. I hope the hell nobody has to use it for a dump 'cause I dunno if my stomach can take it."

I responded, "When we shoot near that end, we'll just hold our breath."

The old man, who seemed deaf to our comments, focused his good eye on us and asked, "Eight ball?" We nodded. "Two bits." I handed over a quarter and said, "I'll pay for this one." All the while I was thinking, It's my last quarter, and I bet Humpty has a million last quarters from guys like me tucked away under his mattress. What the hell. It's only money. What's money but a weird substitute for barter?

"Want to break?" asked Fran.

"Okay. You can break next game." I eyed up several warped cues before making a choice, and then made a fairly good, but unproductive, break. I muttered, "Didn't sink a damn thing."

"Turned out to be a good break for me," said Fran, who pocketed four low balls in succession.

I was not pleased. I had never been a very good loser. "I bet you've been sneaking up here to practice."

"Aw, come on, Tommy, admit it. I'm just good at this game, that's all. You know I haven't been up this place since last time I was here with you."

"At least you could let me have a damn turn."

"What the hell for? Maybe I can shut you out without giving you a shot. That'd be great after you sayin' I used shit luck to win two out of three games last time."

"Go ahead and shoot," I urged as I chalked my cue, ". . . if you can get it up."

Fran laughed, took aim, drew his cue back, and tapped the cue ball toward the six. The six nicked the corner of the side pocket and rebounded to the center of the table. The cue ball scratched in the far corner. I reached into the corner pocket and retrieved the cue ball, grateful that I was getting a turn. After all, Fran might be on the verge of skunking me.

"Let's see you knock off four in a row," he said.

"Sink 'em all, Tommy," urged Johnny.

I shrugged and lined up the cue ball for position to drop the thirteen ball into the right side pocket. Then I tapped the cue briskly, and the thirteen did drop into the side pocket, which set me up nicely for the eleven.

"Shit luck," said Fran, trying to disturb me.

I grinned nonchalantly, leaned over to make my next shot, and drew back the cue, but the backward motion of my right hand was stopped by a body to my rear. "Christ's sake," growled

Jock, a very muscular epileptic who had occasionally gone wild and torn apart Humpty's pool room. "Whatcha tryin' to do, O'Connell? Goose me with your goddam cue stick? I missed my shot 'cause of you bumpin' me, you skinny bastard. Ya lookin' for trouble?" Jock stood before me with his hands on his hips.

"I never go lookin' for trouble, Jock, especially with you," I replied, worrying that he might have one of his fits and tear me apart.

"Well . . . ." His glare softened. "I ain't pissed off at ya. I just wanted to see if I could getcha all shook up." He laughed a deep laugh.

I grinned broadly. "I sure as hell wouldn't want you pissed off at me, Jock."

"Forget it, kid. I know you didn't bump me on purpose, right? It wasn't nothin'."

"Thanks, Jock." I did not quite know why I was thanking him, but I did nevertheless. And as I bent over again for my next shot, I breathed a sigh of relief. For one vivid moment I had pictured myself as the raging Jock's bloody victim. Although my teeth were not lined up perfectly, I preferred my imperfect ones to none at all.

I tapped the cue ball, drove the eleven into the corner pocket, and Fran said, "Pure unadulterated shit luck."

I grinned as I eyed up the fourteen ball, which I knew could be easily tapped into the side pocket. "Three to one Oakie don't make it." It was a familiar but unwelcome voice coming from the long bench to my rear where onlookers sat. My nemesis, the damned pest Louie, had come into Humpty's without me seeing him enter. I tried to ignore him.

All I need now is that idiot needling me, I thought as I snapped the button on the powder dispenser and rubbed the white powder on the skin between my left thumb and index finger to reduce friction. Then I leaned over, drew back my cue, adjusted my aim, and shot. Great, I thought as the fourteen dropped into the side pocket and the cue ball rolled to the bank in direct line with the fifteen ball.

I asked Fran, "How do ya like that for position?"

"Nothing but shit luck."

"Shit luck, Oakie . . . key . . . key . . . key . . ." shouted Louie.

"Pound sand, Louie," I retorted.

"I thought it was good shooting," said Johnny.

"Well, at least someone appreciates my finesse."

"Finesse your ass." Fran laughed. "It's shit luck."

As I dropped the fifteen into the corner pocket I asked, "Was that shit luck too?"

Fran took a long drag on his Chesterfield, and spewed out the smoke. "If I was shooting it would have been skill. But with you shooting it was absolutely nothing but shit luck."

"Hah! You're just trying to rattle me."

"Bet your ass I am."

I said nothing as I lined up the ten, which looked like a good clean shot. I had sunk four in a row, and if I got my fifth it would put me out in front. I was about to tap the cue ball when the door to the pool room swung open and in walked the little hunchback Eddie Cooney, swinging a battered black briefcase that was almost as large as he was. Puffing on a cigar clenched between his yellowed teeth, Eddie grunted and headed toward the toilet.

After the hunchback, known for his diarrhea, had entered the toilet cubicle and only half closed the door, Fran said, "I think we're gonna have to take time out. Eddie's prob'ly got the beer shits."

I laughed, turned toward Fran, took in a lung full of air, held my breath, then took a quick shot at the ten ball. I missed my shot. "Shit!" Frustrated, I went toward a bench far from where Eddie was relieving himself.

Fran then said, "Now I'll polish you off." He took aim at a low ball and as he drew his arm back to make the shot I said, "I see liquid shit running under the hopper door. Yup, that's what it is. Don't slip on it, Fran."

Fran laughed at the precise moment his cue contacted the cue ball and missed his shot. He said, "Now we're even. Hey, what say we wait till the little hunchback gets done in the pisserie before we finish the game. Christ's sake, he's about the only one in town that uses that rotten hopper to shit in. He's got no pride. Some day when he pulls the chain I hope he goes down the drain. I'm sick of his grunting and wheezing. They thought he was gonna die two years ago when he got hit by that car out in front of the Fire Station, but no such luck for us. He's still running around with his cruddy briefcase and his stories. I wonder if he ever sells any those cheese cloth shirts of his to the stores. All I see him doing is spreading gossip like a goddam old bag."

The door to the toilet opened, and out of the foul-smelling chamber came diminutive Eddie, belatedly zipping his fly.

"That uncouth little bastard," muttered Fran. "It's a wonder he doesn't walk the street with his pecker hanging out." We all laughed. There was nothing in the world as funny to us as talk about genitalia and the waste products of the human body.

While Eddie made his exit from Humpty's pool room, having played no pool and spent no money, but having accomplished his personal mission, I sniffed the air. "I guess the coast is clear now." On my way to the table I hunched my shoulders and shuffled like Eddie, and the others laughed.

"You're a hot shit," said Fran.

"But my hot shit smells like perfume compared to Eddie's. Mine's got a special essence. I think I'm gonna bottle it and call it Canal Number Five."

Fran said, "Why not call it Essence of a Raunchy Locker Room, and add a few sprinkles of diarrhetic aroma for a real special blend?"

We laughed at each other's earthy remarks until tears filled our eyes, and Johnny, who was not as amused as we were by references to fecal matter, shook his head. "Don't you guys ever get sick of that shit talk?"

"Never," I replied. "Hey, where there's life, there's shit. Ours is not to reason why, ours is but to shit or die. Show me a man with soul so dead who never to himself has said, I've gotta take a shit. Fran and I are gonna make shit popular again, Johnny. It's been underground too long. We're gonna start a new movement. A bowel movement!"

Fran held his sides laughing and Johnny grinned. Then Fran gasped. "Know what? You're turnin' into a shit philosopher . . . that's what . . ." Then he fell into hysterical coughing laughter and I broke down and joined him.

"I gotta go now," said Johnny, shaking his head.

"Where ya goin'?" asked Fran. "Home to take a shit?"

I held my now aching sides, threw myself on the bench along the wall, and pleaded, "No more shit talk, Fran."

Fran laughed. "What a shitty idea."

I blurted, "At this point I think it's an excrement suggestion!"

We left the pool room a while later, each having won a game, and I said, "Keep loose, Fran, but not too loose, okay?"

"I'll try."

"One more thing before I forget it, Fran. Thanks for a real shitty time at the pool room."

"I just remembered something," replied Fran. "I stuck up for ya the other day. Johnny was saying how you eat shit like a dog and bark at the moon, so I told him you do like hell bark at the moon."

"Thanks a lot."

"Think nothing of it. Hey, look, I'd stick up for a shit philosopher any day."

"Well, I think we've run the subject of shit right into the ground today."

Fran responded with a laugh. "That's where shit belongs."

"It makes the grass grow browner," I said with a grin as I stepped out into the street. "Take it easy, Fran, and always remember that it's a brown world. Not dark brown though."

Fran finished the routine we had performed many times. "Right, just sort of off-brown."

"I'll be dipped in shit if I ever forget," I shouted as I crossed East Dedham Square, the centerpiece of Dedham's blighted section.

In a pantomime response, Fran pretended that he had to take a shit, and then he disappeared around the corner as he headed along Bussey Street toward the Mill Pond and his own neighborhood.

Fran's street was just a short walk from the Boston-Dedham Line, and once you stepped over that line you could always tell you were out of the suburbs and in Boston. There would be huge potholes in the streets, and the West Roxbury stores had a definite city look.

I was not a country boy, and neither was I a city boy. I was strictly a suburban type who enjoyed living near Boston but never had a desire to live there. They could have their city, and they could have their cows and ducks and chickens out in the country. Dedham was my kind of place. I felt comfortable there, despite the discomfort that went with living in Granny's house.

25

To adapt myself to life in East Dedham I had created rituals that were a continuation of activities I had pursued in Norwood. I visited either the Dedham Public Library or its East Dedham Branch daily, to do homework, read, or borrow books. Also, I made regular visits to Gates Pharmacy, which had a soda fountain and tolerated my age group. We were not called teenagers then. You were simply a "kid" until you had a full-time job to prove you were an adult.

If I wanted a change of scene and my pals were not around, I often went to Humpty's pool room in my lone wolf mode. Sometimes I would play pool by myself, but since money was in short supply most of the time, I would usually content myself with watching the older men play, and I would quietly listen to them expound their views on life.

You might say I was operating like a fascinated observer from another planet. Since the pool room was not a nonprofit public service enterprise, I would legitimize my presence there by playing a few solitary games on Humpty's pinball machine, wasting a few nickels.

It hadn't taken me long to adjust to East Dedham because in its declining state it posed no challenges. At that time of my life, East Dedham suited me well because I had lost interest in challenges. My East Dedham was the section of town many solid citizens preferred to believe non-existent, and it was the ideal location for a noncompetitive lifestyle.

Instead, it was a starkly visible collage of rundown stores, dilapidated tenements, and taverns doing a booming business. There were more taverns per block of stores than in any neighboring community. The Square was also, at times, a place of muscle men doing handstands on car fenders, drunks looking for fights, whores plying their trade, and young men-on-the-make whistling at tight-sweatered factory girls.

At Granny's house, in the shadow of the East Dedham Railroad Station a few blocks out of East Dedham Square, I was an official resident of "the other side of the tracks." But I was not ashamed of it, and when asked where I lived I would say without hesitation, "In East Dedham next to the railroad station." I was content to float along in the basically stagnant pool of East Dedham apathy. I was happy to be out of the world of competition and advancement. And I often told my friends, "I'm sick of studying hard, so I'm sort of taking a vacation."

My off-beat vacation resort was East Dedham Square, and in Doc Gates' pharmacy, a place that had not been designed to be a school, I gained a practical education. I saw Doc Gates turning away alcoholics attempting to buy rubbing alcohol. And I watched as self-styled sales representative Eddie Cooney stole expensive cigars and shoved them into his briefcase. I looked on with fascination as another Eddie named Grafton, who had one large grayish-yellow tooth in the center of his upper palate, drooled over girlie magazines and loudly slurped Coca-Cola and other products he had purchased with his welfare money.

In the security of Doc Gates' pharmacy I had an excellent and fairly safe vantage point for observing the varieties of human nature, but sometimes I would get cornered by our local religious fanatic Henry Martin, and I would find myself overexposed to his unrequested sermons on the evils of the day.

Henry attended every Mass and funeral at St. Mary's Church. He had a very loud voice and poor hearing, and he had a habit of responding at length to the parts of the Mass where the parishioners answered the priest. I'm sure he tested the patience of every priest.

Legend had it that he had attempted to become a brother in a monastic order but had been repeatedly refused because of his very poor eyesight. However, Henry's legal blindness did not prevent him from crossing the five-way intersection in East Dedham Square unaided. He would shuffle across the street with no look to right or left, raise his hand in the Sign-of-the-Cross, wave his blessing at the passing traffic, and because of many miracles of nonverbal communication the cars would stop and Henry would get to the other side unscathed.

I recall one time at the pharmacy when I allowed the beady-eyed, sallow-complexioned Martin several minutes of my undivided attention during which I had listened to an impassioned lecture on the evils of smoking, playing pool, and imbibing alcohol. Well, I hadn't had a drink since the episode at Saranac Inn, but I was guilty of the first two on a regular basis. However, I was not about to make a Catholic confession to Henry no matter how holy he thought he was. And just listening to Henry was penance enough for all of my sins.

By the time he finished his sermon I had a splitting headache that could have passed for a bad hangover. But the experience provided a good lesson for me. It was the last time I lent him my ear. From then on, when he would address me I would exclaim, "Gotta go now, Henry! Good to see ya."

As a result of my very practical education in East Dedham, I developed an understanding of and a deep resistance to moochers, ear-benders, and other kinds of extremists. In the ongoing drama of East Dedham, extremists played most of the parts. East Dedham, for me, provided a distillation of some of the best and a bit of the worst of humanity. It was a place where the twists and turns of the human condition were displayed openly as both good and evil did their ongoing dance. Yet on the plus side, hypocrisy was just about unknown in our blighted part of town.

During the summer between my sophomore and junior years at Dedham High, I was presented with an unexpected period of rest and contemplation. It was early August as I rested on the surplus Army cot in the screened porch, thinking about how I had ended up flat on my back. My Jack London book, *Call of the Wild*, was on the window sill, my eyes were closed, and I was recreating the chain of events leading to my bed-ridden status.

It had seemed like a pretty good idea, trying to make a boat out of two surplus fiberglass airplane gas tanks. To obtain the tanks, I had chipped in six dollars with my neighbor Billy O'Neil instead of buying the underwear and socks I needed so badly. As we pursued our Huckleberry Finn fantasy, our teen egos had become a bit inflated by the time the pontoon style boat was ready for launching. We borrowed two of my cousins' red wagons and very proudly dragged our invention through the Square and down to the Mill Pond. Then when we tried to christen it with a Coke bottle, the bottle wouldn't even break. Instead, it just kept bouncing off.

I thought I was terrific when I won the toss for who was going to be the first skipper, but I didn't think I was so terrific when the thing sunk and I scraped my feet on something very sharp in that polluted water. Never give up the ship though. Not us. We finally fixed the alleged craft so it could float, but it could only go in one direction, with the current. Well, at least it floated for a few minutes. Didn't the Wright Brothers only fly for a couple of seconds on their first try? I guess we weren't total failures.

So there I was, laid up on the cot in the middle of the summer with my feet all infected and looking like trench foot. Lying there, I did a lot of thinking, thinking, and more thinking. Brother, I don't have any dough, so I can't get any new underwear. And I'll prob'ly end up with no part-time job when I go back to the A&P. I only worked three days before I called in sick, so they won't want me back. Ah, who cares? Who wants to be a bundle boy anyhow? That job's for the birds. For all I know that's what messed up my feet. They got really swollen after carrying bundles that rainy day, even before I scraped them in the polluted water. Besides, there's a good side to this. At least now I've got plenty of time to read. That's a break.

It's swell that Billy's been getting me books out of the East Dedham Branch. Pretty soon there won't be a book down there I haven't read. I've read all the Zane Grey's, the Fu Manchu's, the Sherlock Holmes series, and most of the Nordhoff and Hall adventure books. I guess there's nothing I really like better than reading and just plain thinking about things.

I had done a great deal of "just plain thinking about things" in the first weeks of convalescence. It was one of the few times after leaving Mrs. White's that I had thought at length about my past and wondered to a degree about my future. One result of my reflections was the reaffirmation of my desire to attend Boston College. Because of that, I decided to improve my grades in the coming Junior Year at Dedham High.

During unrealistic mental meanderings I had also considered the possibility of going out for the cross-country track team, and I saw myself easily winning medals. The science teacher, "Pete" Peterson, had been after me to go out for track. He thought my thin, streamlined body made me a natural track performer. But this concept was in direct contradiction to my slow moving nature. More in keeping with my nature was the thought of using my ancient wooden shafted golf clubs to try out for the Golf Team.

While I was lying there on the cot thinking about the books I had read, my untimely ailment, and my future plans, I heard the first evening train pulling into East Dedham Station. Raising myself up on one elbow, I gazed through the patched screening of the enclosed back porch, and I thought, here they come. Look at them. All the commuters are coming back to God's country again. Back to good old East Dedham. Crusty paradise on earth. Crappy place of everlasting beauty. Ideal worst location for . . . .

"How are the feet doing, Tommy?" My father's voice interrupted my critical thoughts.

"They're getting better, I guess, but the Absorbine Junior that the doctor told me to put on them stings like anything."

"A little pain never killed anybody," he said as he sat on the edge of the cot.

"I suppose that's true, but I could live without it."

"In a few years you won't even remember being laid up like this," he said, unconsciously smoothing the graying strands of hair that he combed from left to right across his head to cover the growing bald area. "It's just as well not to remember some things. At least your feet are healing. Time heals everything. Your lungs healed, too."

"My lungs?"

"I thought I told you about that." His light blue eyes fixed on my face. "It was touch and go with you about six months after you were born. You lost your appetite first, and then you lost weight instead of gaining. Actually, you lost about half your body weight, and when we took you to Children's Hospital in Boston they said your left lung was almost totally collapsed. We carted you in there for quite a few months before the heat treatments brought it around. It's strange how some things heal and others don't."

Fred O'Connell's pale blue eyes turned from me and gazed off into space, and I knew it was one of those reflective times that he had every so often. One of those times when I learned things about his past and mine that I wouldn't have dared to ask about.

"Margaret . . . your mother . . . her mind never healed after you were born, and things got even worse when she went into a deeper depression after your brother was born. We boarded you and Jackie out so she could get some rest, but she still didn't come around. God, how I remember the night we lost little Jackie. Getting word about his illness from the family that was taking care of him. Racing over there to get him. Seeing him turn blue from pneumonia. Feeling him dying in my arms on the way to the hospital.

"Margaret just got worse and worse. So I began drinking heavily to try to forget my troubles, but there was no way to escape from the way things were. I left you with one of Margaret's relatives near Dover Street for a while. It's all slums there now and it wasn't much better then, so I didn't leave you there long. You stayed with other people too. Finally, we brought you back here to your grandmother's and we did the best we could. But Mother wasn't feeling well herself, so I had to bring you to Mrs. White's. Nothing seemed to go right for us in those days. They were rough times."

He paused and heaved a sigh. "But much of it was my own fault, Tommy. I was weak and ignorant. I should have fought the Hendersons, but after your mother acted like she wanted no part of me anymore I made the mistake of letting them take full charge of her. They wouldn't consider a psychiatrist. They said she wasn't insane, just a bit under the weather. Well, I had no money, and we were in the middle of the Depression, and I didn't even have a steady job. So I thought I had to rely on her people. But they penned her in like an animal up in their attic with the door locked and the windows barred, and I didn't know what to do, but finally I faced up to them and took her to one of the best psychiatrists in Boston.

"It was too late to bring her back though. He said she had dementia praecox and schizophrenia and paranoia. Also, he said she was incurable, so she had to be committed." He wiped his bony brow with his large-veined hand as his blue eyes stared through the patched screening and gazed sorrowfully toward the lilac trees along the lot line.

Why is he telling me this now, I wondered. When I wanted to know before, he never said a word. How come I'm getting the dramatic routine now all of a sudden?

"After she went to the hospital I went to visit her at first. But she either acted like she didn't know me or she cursed me. She only wanted to see her mother. Nobody else. Not you. Not me." He shook his head. "She'd always been such a very calm person. Patient. Easygoing. Like nothing ever bothered her. Then . . ." He snapped his fingers. "Just like that, she would be suspicious and violent.

"At first when the doctors said she was incurable, I didn't believe them. But she got worse and worse and hated me more and more. Then they said it was hopeless. She became so hysterical it did neither her nor me any good to make the visits. On our last visit she took you and heaved you across the lobby of the asylum and tried to kill you, but you landed in one of the potted plants. So we never went back there again. In the beginning I prayed for her recovery, but I stopped praying after a while.

"Then I started the heavy drinking, and I gambled a lot, and nothing seemed to help. One night I went to Boston Harbor and stood at the edge of the pier and wondered what the point in living was. I hated everyone who was happy and I hated myself for being so miserable. My wife's insanity took her from me. My son Jackie was dead. And you cried so much I could hardly stand the sound of it or the sight of you. I hated everybody."

He stopped and looked at me. "God, how you cried. When you were living in other people's houses you cried. When I brought you back to Walnut Place to your grandmother's house you cried. Seemed like you never stopped crying."

He looked out the window again, and then I felt like saying, "What the hell did you expect me to do?" But I held onto my silence.

"I couldn't muster up enough courage to drown myself. Maybe I still had a glimmer of hope she'd recover. Maybe I believed Margaret and I and you could live a normal life again. It just wasn't in the cards though. It seems like yesterday, but it's all in the past now. 'This too shall pass away' it says in the Bible. Like your foot trouble. In a few days it'll be a thing of the past."

Not one word did I say as my father concluded his reflections. Frozen in position, I had listened with unflagging interest while displaying no outer emotion, and without asking questions. There was something in me that stopped me from displaying emotion in his presence, and it had been that way since the day he had left me at 42 Mountain Avenue in Norwood when I was five years old. I didn't trust him with thoughts or ideas that were dear to me, just as I didn't trust him to make decisions affecting my life. After all, I had learned from past experience that his involvement in my life was summed up in one word: "unpredictable."

When he reached over and softly touched my knee, my leg stiffened automatically. Then he stood up and said, "I'll be gone for the next few days. I'm going to Maine for a little breather."

You're a great one for your breathers, I thought. I don't know where the hell you get the money for 'em. We never see much dough around here.

When my father had gone, I remained on the cot thinking, I suppose he's going with that woman from his office. I wonder what the hell they do in Maine together. She doesn't look romantic. She's more like a frontier woman. Hardly even looks like a woman. She's not like Suzie with the red hair. Boy, she was so pretty and very sweet and friendly. I wish he could have married her, but the fact is he's still married to my mother, even though he hasn't seen her since I was a baby. So he prob'ly won't marry that character he goes to Maine with either. Ah, what the hell do I care anyhow? I never see him that much. Who gives a good shit what he does?

While I reached out for my book on the window sill, my father's remarks filled my mind. And when I went back to reading it was difficult to concentrate. With a whispered apology to author Jack London, I put the book down, dropped my head back on the lumpy pillow, closed my eyes, and thought of the mother I had never seen since my infancy.

I had two pictures of her in my head. The first was the smooth-faced, dark-haired, friendly, smiling woman whose picture I had seen in the old photo album. The second picture was a raving, wild-eyed madwoman. The picture of her as a violently insane person frightened me intensely and I often worried that I too might be destined for madness. Especially did I harbor such fears after having one of my wild, swirling, engulfing nightmares. After each of those awful nightmares I would wake up thinking I had experienced a bit of madness that might grow into a continued madness like my mother's.

While I was lying there on the cot thinking about my mother, I could hear the potatoes boiling on the kitchen stove. Then Granny shouted, "There'll be some potatoes for ye in a few minutes, Tommy."

"Okay," I yelled back.

"Sure, your father's gone again already, isn't he? Off again on again gone again Finnegan."

I laughed. "She's incredible." I didn't think my voice would carry to the kitchen.

"Sure and aren't we all," she replied. Then she went back to her rocking and praying, and I returned to my thinking.

Being crazy must be like a long nightmare, I thought. Imagine my mother cooped up in that insane asylum year after year. Just being cooped up in this porch a few weeks has me half nuts. Imagine her with all those crazy people. If you weren't crazy when you went in a place like that, I bet you'd get that way quick. It's hard to imagine her in a nuthouse, but that's where she is.

Let's see. I'm fifteen now, so she's been there about thirteen years. I must have been about two when she got sick. Maybe a little older. Mm. When my brother died I was two and he was only one. Then she was sick for a while before they put her away. I guess that's when I lived in Boston near Dover Street, in the Boston slums. I must have been almost three when she got put away for good. But I don't remember her. I hardly remember anything before I was five years old. What did he say she had? Oh, yuh. Dementia praecox. I'll have to look that up.

I reached over to the window sill where my books were lined up in a neat row, took my Webster's Collegiate Dictionary, and soon found "dementia."

It was "Any condition of deteriorated mentality. Dementia praecox: A form of insanity developing usually in late adolescence and characterized by loss of interest in people and things and incoherence of thought and action."

I laughed. Hell, losing interest doesn't sound too crazy. The incoherence is prob'ly the crazy part of it. I flipped the pages. Loose. Disconnected. Hell, that's how Granny talks. Does she have dementia praecox, too? But my mother's must be worse than Granny's. It's prob'ly when words jumble up and make no sense, with plenty of screaming and yelling. What were those other words my father mentioned? Oh yuh. Paranoia and schizophrenia. I wonder how you spell 'em.

Para-noy-yah, I sounded the word in my mind. Oh, here it is. It has an "i" instead of a "y" like I thought. "A chronic mental disorder characterized by systematized delusions of persecution and of one's own greatness, sometimes with hallucinations."

Hallucinations. Those are prob'ly like my worst nightmares, but more real. Having paranoia must be a bitch. It sounds like I have some paranoia myself. At Mom White's I always thought I was persecuted, and I thought I was great too. I still do. Is it only a delusion? What the hell. If I feel like getting all A's I get 'em. Or if I feel like getting all B's, I get 'em. But I don't feel so great when I get oversexed and horny. Most of the time I think I'm great though. So maybe I've got paranoia, too. Hell, I bet everybody has a little paranoia. It's prob'ly when you have too much of it that you get dangerous and they call you insane.

What was that other word, I wondered. Oh yuh, schizophrenia. This is gonna test my spelling ability. Let's see. S-c-h-i-t- . . . Nope. Nothing here. I don't see the word "shit" either. Hey, here it is. Schizophrenia. "A type of psychosis characterized by loss of contact with environment and disintegration of personality." Wow. That sounds rough. Imagine her having all three of those things and her personality falling right apart like my father said. It must have been wicked for her. Like those horrible nightmares I have when everything's swirling and I can't quite make things out and I think things are coming at me and tearing me apart and chasing me and smothering me. It's no wonder she didn't even know him after a while, or me either, like he said. But it's funny how she still knew her own mother.

I wonder why her mother didn't want to put her in a hospital so they could help her. God, she went and locked her up in their attic like an animal in a cage instead. Her damn mother prob'ly helped drive her crazy. I wonder if that other grandmother's still alive. She'd be old like Granny now. I prob'ly have a whole batch of cousins, too, and aunts and uncles I've never seen. But none of 'em ever came to see me in Norwood or here in Dedham.

Maybe they all hate me 'cause I'm a Catholic. It's funny how my mother didn't hate Catholics and even married one. But I wonder if he's still a Catholic. He talks like one, but how can he be one if he doesn't go to Church? I wonder if my mother ever has times when she's not crazy and remembers my father and me.

Maybe she remembers things like when they took that picture in the photograph album with me on her lap. But she was hopeless, they said, and she had dementia praecox, paranoia and schizophrenia. So she prob'ly doesn't remember a thing. Brother, in that book I read, some of the doctors said that stuff can be inherited. I hope I don't inherit it and crack up and go into an insane asylum some day like her.

Boy, imagine my father planning suicide. If he'd done it I'd have been a real orphan. Then I would have been a State kid instead of a Catholic Charities kid. That prob'ly would have been even worse than White's. Did he say he hated everybody? Even me?

Imagine hating a little kid. It wasn't my fault my mother went crazy. But I guess he hated the way I cried a lot. And he got sick of hearing me, and he didn't want to live anymore. It's hard to picture that. But I suppose if your wife cracked up and your baby died and your little boy cried all the time maybe you'd get pretty fed up.

It's funny how he told me all about it today. It was like he was on a stage reciting Shakespeare. After all these years I guess he suddenly figured I was old enough to hear some of it. Hell, I already knew a lot even though they tried to hide it from me. I pieced most of it together from what I heard when nobody thought I was listening, and what Granny said sometimes when she was rocking and talking and not thinking about me being around.

I think my mother would be better off dead than in that weird asylum. I went by that place I think she's in when I saw the Rothwells in Hyde Park and we went to Mattapan to that deli. What a dark, dingy, ugly place. It must be wicked there. I wonder how long she'll have to live in that cruddy place. I wonder if she'll still be there when I'm all grown up. I wonder . . . .

"Yere potatoes are on the table," shouted Granny, "and there's some canned peas and carrots for ye. Ye can fill up on vegetables." She pronounced it "vedge-etta-bulls."

"Some day I'll prob'ly turn into a vedge-etta-bull," I said as I shuffled into the kitchen in the old pair of moccasins with the toes cut out so my swollen feet could stick out into the open air. "I wonder which vedge-etta-bull I'll turn into. A turnip? An onion? A pea?"

"Ye could do worse." She nodded and fingered her beads.

"Yup, I s'pose I could. I guess that almost goes without saying, doesn't it? No matter how bad things are they can always be worse. And they can always go without saying."

26

Mike and I were avoiding the frigid late January air by huddling inside the Dedham High side exit while we waited for Fran and Johnny. We stood quietly for a while and then Mike suddenly asked, "Hey, how come you quit the track team?"

"How come you quit football last year?"

"I got tired of sitting on the bench."

"Well, I quit track 'cause I got tired of running my ass off, Mike. Besides, I had a really bad ingrown toenail that was killing me." I did not tell him that I had also felt sharp chest pains and was afraid they might be heart trouble.

"I thought you'd be a speed demon with that lean build of yours," said Mike.

I ignored his reference to my lack of weight. I hated being so thin. "Well, Mike, I guess instead of being an athlete I'll just be a big sport. But I might go out for the Golf Team in the spring though. That's my speed. You get to sit down on the tees. I guess I was giving myself a snow job with the runner bit. I signed up mainly because old Pete Peterson kept nagging me about it on the way out of Chemistry class. He said I had a perfect build for track. Hah. I'm just not the type. I wouldn't even run if my house was on fire."

He laughed. "Then how come you have the pep for washing dishes at the soda fountain?"

"I sneak ice cream for energy every chance I get. Anyhow, I only work a couple of afternoons, and Harry's no slave driver. Guess what? I'm getting a big promotion next week. I'm gonna jerk sodas. You guys'll have ice cream coming out your ears when I wait on you."

"Good deal. Look, here's Fran and Johnny. Hey, you guys, we're gonna have it knocked. Next week Tommy's gonna be a soda jerk at the Four Hundred."

Fran echoed Mike. "Hey, we'll really have it knocked." And Johnny said, "Sounds good."

The food situation in Granny's house always had a close relationship to the money situation. And money, which had never been very plentiful in my environment, had come into even shorter supply in the O'Connell household during my Junior Year at Dedham High. Expense hand-outs from my father had virtually disappeared, and I had heard my father complain to Granny about "trouble at the Post Office." Then he had begun to spend increasingly less time around the house, and the food situation had rapidly deteriorated.

When neither my Uncle Joe nor my father were living at Granny's it was malnutrition time. Granny had no personal interest in her stomach, and I wondered if she had learned fasting from reading about Gandhi. When my father was missing she would automatically cut back to bare essentials, and as she said, "Fill up on potatoes," she would hand me a meatless plate. If I was lucky she would supplement the potatoes with canned vegetables. "Fill up on the carrots and peas," she would say as she heaped them in a cereal bowl for another all vegetable meal.

When my father did one of his frequent disappearing acts, he would go to the local A&P first, to get a case of canned vegetables to tide me over and keep me from starvation. The typical repetitive diet was either peas, string beans, or carrots-and-peas. On rare occasions I remember how he would buy a whole case of Dinty Moore's beef stew to appease my ferocious appetite.

Also, there was a bottled cheese spread that he would buy in bulk. I would spread it on toast and imagine I was eating a grilled cheese sandwich. On the plus side, we usually had a good supply of peanut butter in the pantry. It was an item that never seemed to go bad or get moldy.

Of course, finding fresh bread to put the peanut butter on was another problem. Granny got her bread at the Happy Home bread outlet in East Dedham Square, and much of it was more than one day old. When the mold was obvious I would have to cut it out like a surgeon would remove a lesion. And when we had meat in the refrigerator, usually in the form of bologna, I developed the habit of sniffing it before eating it.

Granny had a habit of removing the electric plug from its socket because the electricity that was used to run the old Kelvinator was "making the Edison rich." If the bologna had a coating of gray matter on it I didn't have to sniff it. I would simply shove it into the garbage can at the sink, and I would attempt to compensate by eating as many ice creams and hamburgers as I could during my shift at the Four Hundred in Dedham Square.

I never spoke about my ongoing hunger to others because I lived by Mom White's clearly stated words on survival. "The good Lord helps them that helps themselves." I expected no help from friends or relatives, but sometimes Uncle Bill and Aunt Rita would invite me to share a meal with them next door on the other side of the duplex, and the way that family ate each day always seemed like a wonderful feast to me. They had balanced meals, a rarity for Granny.

So I was basically cold and hungry as our quartet of High School juniors faced the frigid January wind and walked along Mount Vernon Street toward the railroad bridge. I was the long and skinny one in the group. Fran was about my height but weighed more. Mike was a bit shorter, muscular, and had a heavy bone structure. Johnny, a lifter of weights, was about as tall as Mike but leaner and more muscular.

We laughed as Mike, who refused to take life seriously, reviewed his antics of that day. But my attention was diverted by my discomfort in the extreme cold. The lightweight unlined green plaid mackinaw jacket I had bought on sale at Sears for $7.95 was not enough protection. The others were dressed more comfortably. Mike had his fleece-lined leather aviator's jacket with a fur collar and a fur-lined cap. Fran was snug in a fur-collared fingertip jacket with a heavy lining. And Johnny had a tight-fitting, sheepskin-lined, black leather jacket like motorcycle riders wore.

"Hey, are you guys going down the tracks or down High Street?" I asked as we approached the Railroad Bridge.

"There's still a lot of snow there," said Fran, pointing to the tracks. "Let's take High Street. Maybe if we go by the Envelope Company we'll see the broad with the pointed knockers."

Mike laughed. "I ought to walk home with you guys. All I see are the gravestones at Brookdale Cemetery on the way to my house. No broads."

At the intersection of Mount Vernon and High Streets, where Mike would go left and the rest of us would go right, Mike asked, "You guys want to go to the show tonight?"

"What's up there?" I asked.

"I forget the name of it, but there's an actress in it with a forty-inch bust." He paused. "And that's only her left one."

Fran laughed. "Okay, I'm going."

I grinned. "Seeing as how you twisted my arm I guess I can scrape up half a buck."

"Guess I'll go too," said Johnny with no obvious enthusiasm.

"If the movie gets dead," said Mike, "we'll have a burping contest, and maybe tonight I'll bring my screwdriver so we can take some more seats apart."

We all laughed as Mike went his own way. In a few minutes we were right near the Boston Envelope Company, and I was still shivering in the cold wind when we caught a glimpse of the Italian girl with the provocative anatomy. Suddenly my mind was no longer on my body temperature. She was operating one of the machines that folded the flat envelope cutouts into completed envelopes. The three of us stopped and stared at her through the chain link fence.

"She's built like a brick shithouse," said Fran.

"You said it," I agreed as I stared through the large window in which the Italian girl was framed. Her tight white sweater accented her upper anatomy and her skin-tight jeans left no question about the shape of her lower body.

Fran laughed a dirty laugh. "Holy shit, wouldn't that warm a guy up on a cold day?"

"You're all talk and no action," said Johnny.

"How do you know?" asked Fran.

"You're still a virgin."

"How much you want to bet?"

Johnny shrugged. "I'm no gambler."

At this moment the Italian girl turned sideways, displaying the fullness of her breasts within her tight white sweater, and I said, "Wow, look at the size of them."

As Fran muttered, "What a pair," she moved out of our line of vision. "Shit! And I was just ready to come off in my pants."

"Jeez," said Johnny, "she sure does wear tight sweaters."

"She puts out," said Fran confidently.

"You're sure?" I asked.

"Sure I'm sure. You know Joe Walsh? He says he's given it to her at least ten times."

"No kiddin'."

"Why would I kid ya?"

When we reached the Square where we would take different streets to reach our homes, Fran asked, "How's about a game of eight ball before you go home, Tommy?"

"I've had enough pool for this week."

"Me too, I guess. What the hell. Might as well go home and let my mother nag me till it's time for us to go to the movie. You want to meet down the drugstore later?" We all agreed. "Six-thirty?" We nodded and then went our separate ways.

While walking up the Walnut Street hill toward Granny's house, I thought of the Italian girl at the envelope company with her prominent breasts, and as I began to get stimulated sexually I said to myself, This is one of those horny days, I guess. All I had to do was see her showing off her amazing knockers in that tight sweater. Brother, is she built!

A few minutes later I was in the ancient duplex at 22 Walnut Place, and the first thing I heard was the old cathedral-shaped radio blaring and Granny commenting loudly on the news of the day. With that distraction, I temporarily restrained my sex drive.

But later that evening I saw the movie starring a woman with breasts of vast dimension, and her larger than life shapeliness restored my primitive urges. When I arrived home from the movie, Granny was asleep in her cot in the dining room and my father was asleep in his own bedroom, and I softly closed my bedroom door and pulled the chain that activated the unshaded low-watt incandescent bulb.

"Incredible," I whispered to myself as I began to undress. "What an amazing build she had." I was obsessed with thoughts about the actress as I took off my rough wool tweed trousers that my father had bought for me on sale at Raymond's department store in Boston. The store "where u bot that hat," the ads said. And I hung the pants neatly on a hanger. Then I took off my wide brown-and-yellow tie and the white dress shirt that was displaying a deteriorating collar.

I look like the rag man, I thought as I examined my T-shirt, which was sloppily patched under the arms with red and black yarn. My baggy shorts were patched at the crotch with remnants of old grayish yellow bed sheets sewn on with heavy black thread by Granny. And the heels of my socks she had patched with bits of material from old underwear. "Waste not, want not," she would say.

Reflecting on her art work, I thought, it isn't exactly invisible mending. It's a far cry from Mom White's. I never had to wear patches there, and at school in Norwood during gym class I never had to sneak in and out of my clothes, using my locker door as a screen so nobody would see my raggedy underwear. Yup, things are different here. Granny's a throwback to the Dark Ages. She's got that wringer washer but instead she uses brown soap and a washboard at the kitchen sink. And she's afraid she'll get the

Edison Company rich if she runs the damn washer, but shit, there's no fear of anybody getting rich on Granny.

What the hell though. At least I've been free since I've lived here. My father's not around that much, and the stuff she says goes in one ear and out the other. Poor but free, that's me. Well, better get some sleep now. Out with the light. Holy shit. This linoleum floor's cold. Look at all the ice inside the windows. Boy, is it freezing in here. No furnace in this old house, just the kitchen stove and the old space heater downstairs. Up here it's just like being outdoors.

I shut off the light and then dove into the bed and as I pulled the heavy "comforter" up around my neck I thought how nice it would be to have a warm bedroom with a warm floor. And I imagined how it would be to walk across a bedroom floor barefoot in the winter without freezing my feet off.

As I lay flat on my back, which was my habit, I watched the tree shadows cast on the sloped ceiling by the street light in front of the house next door. Then I mentally reviewed that evening's movie and I recalled the partially exposed mountainous breasts of the star. And as I lay there dwelling on various portions of female anatomy, the excitement began to expand within me.

However, just as I was about to dissolve into the emotion of the moment I said to myself, I better not. When I do it I feel like a horny sinful bastard whose heading straight down into the fires of hell. Sure, plenty of guys do it and don't give a good shit about doing it, but it makes me feel so damn guilty, and I guess I'm afraid of going crazy, like they say, or getting a heart attack.

All I need is a heart attack. I wonder if those chest pains I get are heart trouble. They're prob'ly just my nerves. I've always got some kind of ache or pain. But there's no sense screwing up my nerves from playing with myself, is there? It wouldn't be worth it.

As I lay there worrying I steadfastly maintained control. Then I grinned as I remembered the joke about the boy who was rhythmically masturbating and all the while yelling with each stroke, "I don't care if I do die. I don't care if I do die."

How come I get so horny sometimes, I wondered. Right now I feel so horny I can't believe it. But I won't do it. Dammit. I'll say a prayer. Yuh, I'll say a Hail Mary. Maybe that'll help me. Hail Mary full of Grace, the Lord is with Thee, blessed art thou among women, and blessed is . . . .

As I prayed I tried to get my mind off horny women and just focus on the pure ones, and I prayed, Hail Mary full of Grace the Lord is with Thee. Help me to be pure and holy, blessed Virgin. Help me not to get so excited. I don't want to, but sometimes I feel like I just can't help it. I wish I never learned how to play with myself. Hail Mary full of Grace the Lord is with Thee. Blessed art thou amongst women and blessed is the fruit of thy womb, Jesus. Holy Mary, Mother of God, pray for us sinners, now and at the hour of our death. Amen.

I was on my second decade of Rosary beads when I saw a bright new patch of light on the far wall of my bedroom, and I recalled several weeks earlier when I had seen that same patch of light, and I had looked from my window, and across the way in the room directly opposite mine I had obtained a glimpse of one of the teenage girls who lived there.

She had been very well proportioned and as I had stared across into her lighted bedroom, looking between the branches of the trees which had shed their leaves, I had seen the silhouette of her large breasts for an instant before her light had gone out.

The patch of light I was now seeing on my bedroom wall was interrupted by a blur of shadow. Then the patch of light was the same again, and I thought, that must have been her. I bet she was moving across the room. The patch of light's real bright so her shade must be up. Maybe she's gonna undress. Maybe I'll see her if I go to the window. Son of a bitch. I know I should just say more prayers and wait till the light over there goes off, and I ought to go to sleep. But I want to see if she takes all her clothes off. To hell with it. I'm gonna look.

I threw off the bed covers and crept to the edge of the window. Then I knelt shivering on the cold linoleum floor of my unheated bedroom, and I gently moved the curtain so that I could see across the way into that bedroom, without myself being seen.

God, is this floor cold. Br-r-r. I must be screwy to be doing this. Oh-oh. There she is.

One of the girls was standing there, framed in her lighted window, with her shade up as high as it could go. Standing before her dresser, right in line with the window, she took off one item of clothing after another, like a stripper. And by the time she got down to her underwear, my heart was just about pounding out of my chest. I was awestruck as I saw her turn from her mirror and face the window with its undrawn shade. Then, in the full light, she slowly took off her bra and flung it over her bedpost.

Holy shit, I gasped. I never saw a girl that was that well built. Unbelievable.

As she took off her panties I could make out the dark shadow of her pubic hair, and I was just about overwhelmed by the sexual urges that rose up in me. A moment later she put her pajamas on, turned off her light, and left me standing there with my sexual urges undiminished.

Throwing myself on my bed, I reflected on the need for self-control. Then I told myself that self-control had its limits, and that the need for relief from frustration had merit too. And finally I said, "To hell with it," and I masturbated as fast as I could, to get it over and done with.

A few minutes later, exhausted, I lay on my bed shaking my head and muttering, "Dammit." Then I sighed and went slowly to the bathroom, where I took some toilet tissue and wiped myself off. Then I went back into my bed and lay staring at the shadows on the ceiling.

Shit, why did I do it? Why don't I have any willpower? What's wrong with me? Am I some kind of a nut? A peeping Tom? Why do I let a girl's body excite me like that? I better say a prayer.

I said an Act of Contrition and thought, I'll go to Confession tomorrow afternoon, and then I'll feel better about myself. I've really been doing fine for a long time now, too. I've been disciplined and feeling good about myself and my willpower. Then I have to go and screw it up, just when I think I couldn't care less about sex. God, do I hate myself when I do something like that. It makes me feel hopeless. Like a real jerk.

I can't respect myself when I do things like that. I really hate getting carried away like that because my standards don't allow that stuff. Even if I swear a lot, and talk dirty, there's a certain line I can't step over when it comes to sex or I lose respect for myself. Respecting myself means more to me than anything else in the world. So why do I do things that lower my respect for myself? Why? Why? Why?

Well, tomorrow after I go to Confession I'll have more respect for myself again, and I'll feel like God doesn't think I'm as hopeless as I think I am. But I wonder sometimes why he made it so complicated. He gave us all these urges, and then when we use them we shaft ourselves. I guess it all goes back to Adam and Eve. They muffed it, and the rest of us are still paying the piper. Screwy world.

I began to pray, I believe in God, the Father Almighty, Creator of heaven and earth, and in Jesus Christ, His only Son, our Lord, who was conceived by the Holy Spirit, born of the Virgin Mary, suffered under Pontius Pilate, was crucified, died, and was buried. He descended into hell and on the third day He arose again . . . .

My eyes grew heavy in my head and then they closed as I drifted off to sleep, and I thought I would be at peace with my body and with my God.

"No . . . no!" I cried out. "No . . . no!"

"It's okay, Tommy." My father's voice was somewhere in the distance, but the tidal wave was coming and was going to engulf me in its enormity. It was filling the horizon, with its frothy swirling mass relentlessly pushing onward. And there I was, alone on the shore, standing frozen in one spot as it approached. I couldn't move, but I could shout. "No . . . no . . . no!"

"It's okay, Tommy." I could hear my father's voice somewhere in the distance, coming in hazily. But the wave was also coming, and it was going to smother me, drown me. "No . . . no . . . no!"

"Tommy." Something cool touched my forehead, and I thought it was the water of the tidal wave instead of the wet end of a towel.

The huge wave was coming over me, smothering me. "Noooooooooo . . ."

"Tommy, it's okay." My father's voice seemed to echo from within the wave. "It's okay."

It's not okay. There's the wave, coming at me, and he says it's okay but it's still coming. It's gonna drown me. I'll be gone forever. I'll be wiped out.

The damp cool sensation covered my forehead again, and I began to make out my father's face, which seemed to blend with the wave. "It's only a nightmare, Tommy." My father's face became clearer but the wave was still there. "Never mind, Tommy."

Finally the wave was gone, and I was there trembling in my bed with no wave bearing down on me, and my father holding a cold towel against my forehead. "A nightmare," he said. "That's all it was." And then my father returned to his own bedroom and I was alone with my memory of the tidal wave.

It was so real, I thought. I was definitely gonna drown. And my heart's still pounding so hard it feels like it's gonna push its way out of my chest. Well, I guess I better say some prayers. Hail Mary, full of Grace, the Lord is with Thee; Blessed art thou . . . .

27

It was a cold and windy March day, and I was shivering as I walked along the tracks toward the East Dedham Railroad Station. I had just parted company with Mike after we had walked as far as the Mount Vernon Street railroad bridge. Johnny had stayed after school for Photography Club. And Fran had gone to St. Mary's School Hall for Fife and Drum Corps practice. As I walked along I tried to picture Fran playing the fife, but couldn't, and I recalled with a chuckle how angry he got when Mike called his instrument the "skin flute."

I strolled along the railroad bed until I reached the spot where a ledge rose to my left and a high granite wall formed a cliff to my right. There was no one in sight up ahead, and when I looked to my rear I saw no one there. Since the coast was clear, I then reached into my pocket and took a small scrap of paper from my wallet, read the words once, and as I walked along I sang, "I had you . . . I held you . . . you gave me all. Your love dear . . . I shattered . . . beyond recall. Now that I've lost you, please understand . . . I'm here forever, at your command."

As I sang the song, my soft throaty voice warbled as Bing Crosby had warbled in the thirties, and I saw myself as Bing had been at that younger age when he had recorded "At Your Command."

"Foolish conceit . . . in my heart it would beat . . . and to think that my heart would obey . . . ." As I sang I envisioned myself on a stage with a microphone in hand, receiving the adulation of a large audience. "Now that I've lost you . . . please understand . . . I'm here forever . . . at your command."

As I folded the slip of paper and returned it to my wallet, I congratulated myself on having it almost completely memorized. Currently, I had committed about twenty of Bing's older songs to memory. Songs like "Prisoner of Love," "Yours is My Heart Alone," and "Just One More Chance." My favorite was "I Surrender, Dear."

I burst out in song again. "We played the game of stay away . . . but it cost more than I can pay . . . Without you I can't make my way . . . I surrender dear . . ." I sang with the Crosby warble until I was within sight of the East Dedham Railroad Station. Then I rapidly concluded the number. ". . . to you, my life, my love, my all . . . I surrender, dear."

Looking around to be certain nobody had been listening to my performance, I breathed a sigh. I was very self-conscious about my singing although I believed I had an excellent voice and knew I could carry a tune well. But I did not want to sing in front of others. Not one or two or three others. I dreamed big dreams, and pictured singing on the radio and in the movies and on stages of crowded amphitheatres. I sincerely believed I had a voice that could please millions, and I was convinced that someday when Bing Crosby was old I would fill the Groaner's shoes.

As I took a shortcut through the railroad fence and passed the rear of the abandoned Fairchild house my mind was filled with the melody and the words of "I Surrender, Dear." Especially the words. They were romantic, somewhat tragic, and poetic, as were most of the Crosby songs of days gone by.

"Is that you, Tommy?" Granny's resonant voice met me as I entered the front hallway.

"Yup . . . it's me."

"Is it you, Tommy?" Her voice rang out again.

"No, it's President Truman just dropping in to pass the time of day." I laughed at my own sarcasm.

"What did ye say?" Her voice echoed through the small rooms as I walked out to the kitchen where she sat rocking, as usual.

I shouted, "I said it's me."

"Oh it's the devil himself, is it?"

"'Tis that, the devil himself." I propped my report card against the wall next to my father's spot opposite me at the supper table.

"There's some fresh milk left in the ice box." She pointed her wrinkled right hand toward the second-hand Coldspot refrigerator that had replaced the old Kelvinator. I opened the door of the refrigerator and reached for a half-filled quart of milk. Then I took the cap off the warm bottle and sniffed it. "Shit. It's sour."

"'Tis only three days old," she said. "'Twill do ye no harm to drink it. Ye remind me of your Uncle Joseph. Always smelling things to make sure they're fit for ye. Sure and ye'll eat a peck o' dirt before ye die, ye know."

"Granny, if you'd let the refrigerator run instead of pulling out the plug the stuff wouldn't go bad." I took the cord and inserted the electrical plug into the wall socket.

"The Edison has money enough without taking all of mine," retorted the old woman as she rocked in her rocker and fingered her rosary beads. Then, noticing that I had put the plug in, she got up and went and pulled it right out again.

My voice grew loud as I poured the sour milk down the sink drain. "We'd be better off with the old ice box than a refrigerator you keep shutting off all the time."

"Ye've a quick tongue, ye have," she muttered.

"If you don't have a quick tongue around here, you're sunk."

"What was it ye said?" She cupped her hand to her ear.

"Nothing!" I shouted.

"Sure ye don't have to holler."

"I give up." I shrugged, opened a can of White House evaporated milk, filled my glass half full, added water, mixed it, and gulped it while standing at the kitchen sink. Then I looked into the cracked and distorted shaving mirror and began to comb my thick curly brown hair.

"Ye'll comb it right out of yere head. Ye spend enough time in front of the mirror, ye do. A lot of good it'll do ye dolling yereself up. Sure it won't earn a nickel for ye."

"I earn a few nickels up at the Four Hundred." I stroked the comb through the curly snarls of hair.

"Sure I don't know what ye do with yere nickels. I never see a one."

I laughed. "I go to the race track and place bets."

"It wouldn't surprise me in the least. Freddy has left many a week's pay at the two-dollar window."

I chuckled. "Where'd you get that expression?"

"Sure, I wasn't born yesterday." She rose and shuffled to the side window to look out through the enclosed porch toward the house next door. Then she shouted, "The dirty blackguard Jordan was out there again today. He's building his outhouse on my land. He's no good, that one."

"It's a garage he's building, and it's on his own land."

"Little do ye know, Tommy." She returned to her rocker. "He was out there tearing up my lilacs to make room for his outhouse. I'm not all blind yet. I saw the dirty blackguard with his snippers. If I turned my back on him he'd snip the hair right off o' my head. He's a bad lot."

"Can you name one thing he's ever done to us?" I was still standing at the mirror, examining my face and combing my hair.

"He's been trying to take my land for years." She nodded her head in emphasis. "He moves my bushes every chance he gets, so's he can have another inch o' land."

If she keeps saying that, I thought, some day I'm gonna believe her. Then I'll be just as screwy as she is. What an imagination she has.

I put my comb in my pocket, took a small bottle of clear liquid from the cluttered shelf above the sink, laid the palm of my left hand flat on the counter, and with a cotton swab I dabbed acid on a large wart, while mumbling "the damn thing" as the strong solution burned the tender skin surrounding the foreign growth. Because I was self-conscious about it, I had taken to keeping my left hand out of sight whenever possible.

"The dirty damn blackguard!" She leaped from the rocker, waved her bony fist, stamped her right foot hard on the floor, and shouted, "Him and his damnable outhouse on my land! I've a good mind to burn it down when he finishes with it. It'd serve the devil right."

"I'll write to you when you're in prison, Granny."

She shouted toward the house next door, "Yere no good, Jordan. A dirty blackguard is what ye are."

I muttered, "She's going into her famous actress routine again."

"Jordan, may your soul rot in hell forever, God forgive me for saying it!" she shouted.

"Granny, who was that famous old-time actress you mention sometimes?"

"Bernardt. Sarah Bernhardt. They knew her all over the worruld, they did."

"Well, they'll know you too, Granny. One of these days you'll definitely get an Academy Award. You're the best actress of the year."

"What did ye say?"

"Never mind." I put the bottle of acid back on the shelf. "You wouldn't get it."

"Ye think ye're pretty su-ave, ye do." She always emphasized both syllables in the word "suave." Waving her bony hand at me, she said, "But ye don't know what's in store for ye. Devil a care do ye have now."

If that old woman says that to me one more time, I thought, I'm gonna flip my lid. She thinks my life's been a picnic.

"The brats o' today don't know what hard times are. They don't know what it is to go without."

Well I sure as hell know what it's like, I thought. I haven't had a good meal in this house since I moved here from Norwood.

"They don't know what the word famine means. Not a lick do they know about life."

I'm getting the hell out of here, I thought. I've had all I can take of her yacking. "I'll be back later for supper," I said as I strode toward the front door.

She shouted after me, "Yere stomach is all that matters to ye, and all yere fancy clothes, and yere slicked-down hair."

I slammed the front door behind me and thought, she thinks I dress like Clark Gable because I have more than one shirt. If I buy a new pair of socks she thinks I'm a big spender. Shit, the war's been over a long time now, but she still operates like rationing never stopped.

As I walked along Walnut Place away from the O'Connell house, I pushed my pants down on my hips so the cuffs would meet the top of my shoes and at least partially conceal the obvious patches that she had applied to my socks. Then, as I turned the corner into Walnut Street and began walking toward East Dedham Square, I told myself I was lucky to be living at her place.

I smiled to myself as I recalled the night a few weeks earlier when I had reached my limit with her monologues, and Fran had been frustrated by his mother's constant nagging.

"Let's get away from all this horse shit," we had agreed, and over a game of pool we had decided to hitchhike as far as we could go, with no single destination in mind. We had thumbed down Route One from our homes in the Boston area as far as Pawtucket, Rhode Island. Then the skies had opened and drenched us with torrential rain that motivated us to head back toward Boston again. And home began to look pretty good to us. Late that evening, after returning to good old East Dedham soaking wet, Fran and I had agreed that although our homes left much to be desired, no home at all would have been worse.

It's funny, I thought as I recalled the episode, how your ideas change when you're shivering and soaked to the skin. Nothing ever looked so good as Granny O'Connell's duplex that night. Things can always be worse, I guess. But I can only take so much of her damn nagging.

As I passed Gates Pharmacy, I glanced through the display window, and inside I saw the little hunchback, Eddie Cooney, puffing on a stogie and blowing a combination of stogie smoke and foul breath into good-natured Doc Gates' face.

That Eddie's a real character, I thought as I crossed the square toward Humpty's pool room. East Dedham is full of odd characters, but Eddie takes the cake. Oops, I spoke too soon. There's Henry

Martin crossing the street and making the Sign-of-the-Cross to the passing traffic. I better get the hell into the doorway and upstairs to the pool room before he gives me a sermon.

I went up the long flight of stairs to the pool room where Jock, the epileptic, was playing pool with Joe Walsh, the bartender in the club car on the Boston-to-New York railroad run.

Joe talked to me between shots. "Hey, Tommy, like you should have seen the pussy I got in New York this week. Like she was so old I think she was a waitress at the Last Supper. But she was built like wow, man!" I laughed. "You think I'm shitting ya?" Joe ran a comb through his thick black Vaselined hair. Then he smoothed it down with the palm of his hand. "Like I don't deal in snow jobs, man."

"I believe you, Joe."

He grinned, showing some gold fillings. "Some night you ought to come along with me and like dip your wick, man."

I laughed. "I don't need the syph."

"Hey, man, I don't shack up with anything but clean stuff. I had the crab course once, man. Like my balls itched so bad I was like that book, *The Tiger's Revenge* by Claude Balls."

I grinned. "You're a character, Joe." Joe returned to the game when Jock missed a shot, and having no great inclination toward spectator sports, at least on that occasion, I went back to the pinball machine.

A while later as I descended the steps of the pool room I thought, why the hell did I spend my last two nickels on that damn pinball machine? If I still had 'em I could get an ice cream at the pharmacy. Ah, what the hell, I can get all the ice cream I want when I work at the Four Hundred tomorrow. Then I'll have a couple of bucks in my pocket again too. But now my shoes need soles. Seems there's always something to keep me broke. I need underwear and socks bad too, but I guess I'll have to get the damn shoes fixed first.

I wonder if the Holy Rollers will roll tonight, I thought as I passed the Bethel Tabernacle Faith Home with its imitation brick shingles. They'll all be leaping up and yelling, "Hallelujah, Christ has risen, for I have seen the Lord!" I wonder if they actually roll on the floor. Through the window, all I've seen 'em do is leap up and down and sing a lot.

I kept walking up the Walnut Street hill toward Granny O'Connell's house, and on Walnut Place, just as I was about to pass the very large duplex owned by the Jordans, my neighbor Betty stepped out her front door, smiled, and said, "Hi Tommy."

"Hi Betty." I waved at her and kept moving as my face turned scarlet at the memory of seeing either her or her sister completely naked on one occasion and almost naked on others.

I wish I never saw what I saw, I thought as I skirted my father's faded black Plymouth and entered the house. I wonder if they know I was watching them. Hey, maybe they wanted me to. They sure didn't pull their shade down. Brother, what a show.

Entering the old duplex, I made my way to the kitchen where my father was seated at the supper table examining my report card. "Hi Tommy."

"Hi." Avoiding the word "Dad," I seated himself across from him at the table, and observed him as he swallowed a mouthful of canned peas. Then he said, "I was just looking at your card. It's good except for that mark in conduct."

"The red C? That's just for cracking a joke once in a while."

"You're there to learn, not make jokes." His pale blue eyes were aimed at my face.

"I know what I'm there for." My bluntness with him was a habit.

He looked at me, said nothing, signed the card, and passed it to me. "Your marks have improved."

"You need a good average to get accepted at Boston College," I replied as Granny served me a bowl of canned peas topped by a slice of hard, gray, week-old bologna.

"Ye can fill up on peas," she muttered as she shuffled back to her rocking chair, "and there's some evaporated milk there for ye."

My father asked, "You're definitely planning to go to B.C.?"

"Yup. When you get a degree from B.C. it really means something."

"Yes, it does." He ran his hand across his own scalp, which was now nearly bare except for the strands of gray-brown hair which he combed straight across his head from one side to the other in an unsuccessful attempt to cover the large bald area. "I hope we can swing it for you."

"I thought Granny saved up some money in my name to help me in case I wanted to go to college."

"She did but I don't think you can count on it."

"Oh." I frowned.

"Don't worry. If you get accepted, we'll get you the money. But we'll just have to cross that bridge when we come to it."

My father rose from the table, went to the sink behind me, rinsed out his mouth with Lavoris, spat it into the sink, and put his hand on my right shoulder. "I'll see you later, son."

Then, a few minutes later, I heard the sound of the Plymouth heading up the street, and he was gone for the evening. I would soon be gone too. The two of us spent only the bare minimum of our time in Granny's house. We ate our sparse diet there and we slept there, that was about all.

I finished my peas and gulped down some diluted evaporated milk mixed with water. As for the week-old bologna, I had already grunted "Shit," and then placed it in the rusty tin can on the counter to my rear. I knew she would curse when she saw it, but I was determined not to eat rancid bologna.

Granny was slurping a large cup of over-steeped tea as I sipped on the evaporated milk. "That wastrel over there . . ." Her voice boomed out as she pointed toward the nailed-shut door separating my uncle and aunt's kitchen from ours. "She throws out enough good food in a month to feed all the hungry little ones in China. Poor William worruks his fingers to the bone and she ups and spends his hard-earned money faster than what he brings it home."

"A wastrel!" she shouted, vehemently waving a wrinkled bony hand toward Rita's kitchen. "That's exactly what ye are, little Rita, you're nothing but a damnable wastrel. Ye only knew how to wiggle your little bottom, that was all, and poor William knew no better. Sure, he had an eye for the ladies."

She'll run that subject right into the ground, I thought as I rose from the table, gave my mouth a quick water rinse at the sink, and said, "I'm going up the liberry."

"What is it ye said?"

I shouted, "I'm gonna go see the Pope in Rome. I've got a special audience lined up."

"Oh, 'tis not nice for ye to talk that way, Tommy O'Connell." She shook her head and fingered her Rosary beads. "May the Lord forgive ye for saying what ye did about His Holiness the Pope."

"I give up," I mumbled as I combed my hair.

"What is it ye said?"

"Nothing."

"I may not hear lots o' things with my ears so hard of hearing, but I know ye said something, Tommy."

I shouted impatiently, "All I said was I'm going up to the liberry!"

"Sure, don't I know it." She chuckled "Aren't ye running off to the liberry every night after ye pack in your supper? A devil a lot o' studying ye do at the liberry all right."

I shook my head in frustration, and as I viewed her image in the distorted shaving mirror, I asked myself, why do I try to talk to her? She's too old to get anything I say.

Giving my hair a few more strokes, I muttered, "Damn that cowlick in the back. It won't lie flat."

"'Tis not nice to swear," she said as I headed for the front door.

"Nope. 'Tis not nice." I left the house, shaking my head, and I thought, Sometimes she really gets to me, but I definitely shouldn't let it bother me. Half the time she doesn't know what the hell she's talking about. The catch is that I'm lucky she's giving me a roof over my head. Still a guy can only take so much yacking, and she's getting worse every day. Sometimes I have a hard time letting it go in one ear and out the other. I wonder why some people have to do so much yacking? Why can't they just be quiet sometimes instead of always acting like they're delivering a State of the Union address before a Joint Session of Congress? Oh well, I guess it takes all kinds to make a world . . .

28

Granny's nagging seemed to reach a crescendo that year. Unfortunately, the crescendo had a life of its own, and the situation became so intolerable that both my father and I agreed that we had to leave her house and move across town to my grandfather's place for a respite. However, that old house had its drawbacks too.

We learned that there was some truth in two old expressions: "The grass is always greener in the other fellow's yard" and "Absence makes the heart grow fonder." After a while at Dan O'Connell's house, with its view of the Mill Pond and Big Blue Hill in the distance, Granny's place right next to the East Dedham Railroad Station began to look better and better. So back we went, with gratitude.

It was the night before the Fourth of July, in the summer of '48, and I was standing with Fran on the street corner in front of Doc Gates' Pharmacy in East Dedham Square.

"Are you back at Walnut Place for good?"

"Yuh, I guess so. My father was about as fed up with Granny's yacking as I was, but it didn't work out over at my grandfather's. That old place is in worse shape than Granny's. It was gettin' so I hated to go to bed because I might get bombed by falling ceiling plaster." Fran laughed. "No shit, Fran, it was wicked up there on the top floor right under the leaky roof. It leaked right on my bed. Besides, there was nobody to make any meals. Not that Granny's a cook, but she boils water once in a while."

"What about your aunt Mary? Doesn't she live over there next to your grandfather?"

"Yuh. But she stays locked inside her own little apartment and nobody ever sees her. She cooked a couple of meals for us and sent them upstairs, but that was all. And my grandfather's as hard to live with as Granny. He's always grouching and turning the radio up loud so you can't even hear yourself think. No wonder him and Granny couldn't live together."

Fran said, "You're a hot shit talking about the two of them like that."

"What the hell, it's the truth."

"You're a great one for the truth, right?"

"Is that a crime?"

Fran laughed and lit up a Chesterfield. "Not yet."

I puffed on my Lucky Strike. "You never get sick o' Chesterfields, right, Fran?" He just shrugged his shoulders and inhaled. Then I recited, "She was only a farmer's daughter but oh what a Chest-ter-feel."

He pointed at my cigarette. "Lucky Strike means fine tobacco. L.S.M.F.T. Loose sweaters mean flat tits." We had a double meaning for just about everything in life.

Mike arrived. "What's the big joke?"

"Same old sex jokes," I replied. "I think we're in for one of our famous Dirty Hours."

Fran shouted, "Speaking of sex, there's Johnny."

"You might know you three would be talking about sex," he said as he approached us.

Mike said, "Tell us a better subject."

"You've got me."

The four of us set out across East Dedham Square toward the Fourth of July carnival which was set up on a gravel plot across from the Mill Pond, a few blocks out of the Square. And as we neared the busy carnival grounds, Mike shouted, "Help me."

"Whatsamatter?" asked Fran.

Mike laughed. "I just saw that broad that works at the Envelope Company. The one with the big pointed knockers." He began walking in a stooped-over position, holding his hands over his genitals. "She's crippling me."

Fran responded. "For Christ's sake, Mike, why don't you proposition her? Maybe she'll let ya take her on the merry-go-round or the Ferris wheel, and you could plank her when nobody's looking."

We kept wisecracking and laughing as we went through the carnival grounds observing the rides and booths and eyeing the females. Then Mike said, "Watch this." He squinted his eyes and mumbled, "The Lord is my shepherd." Then he made the Sign of the Cross and shuffled along as only one other person in East Dedham shuffled.

At that moment, coming the opposite way, I saw Henry Martin, the near blind religious fanatic who was the brunt of Mike's imitation. I laughed so hard I had to hold the edge of a tent to steady myself. Then when the others saw Henry and got the full impact of Mike's take-off they joined me in my comically altered state.

Mike, with a very straight face, went on with his imitation. He had totally absorbed himself into the role. Then, when he was done with Henry Martin, as we all strolled through the carnival grounds he imitated one after another of the "characters" who abounded in East Dedham.

It seemed that for everyone who was on or below the margin of normalcy, the carnival was an event not to be missed. And never before did Mike have such a handy array of subjects for his mimicry. He imitated Humpty's limp, Cooney's wheeze, Grafton's wild-eyed stare, MacLeish's muscle flexing, and Hart's nasal monologues.

"Sometimes you're a cruel bastard with your imitations," I said after we all had laughed until our sides were aching.

"You mean when I do something like this?" Mike screwed up his whole face to resemble the desiccated "Bromo twins." The two withered women had the reputation of being addicted to Bromo Seltzer.

Wheezing through my laughter, I blurted, "That's exactly what I meant, Mike, but you're a hot shit."

"Uh-oh," said Fran, "here she comes, the old whore." He was talking about an old Italian woman whose public image had eroded many years before.

"They should call her Marconi because I think she puts out by wireless," said Mike. "I wonder if she knows algebra. Do you think she could add up 2Q and 2Q and get 4Q?" More laughter followed.

"Mike, some day you'll get yourself in big trouble with your imitations," warned Johnny. "You'll make fun of the wrong person and you'll get something ya don't expect."

"I hope so," said Mike, "'cause I've been waiting a long time to get something I don't expect." We all laughed, including Johnny.

Then Mike yelled, "Hey, Rosie!" as the buxom old redhead passed by. Rosie, who was widely known for her casual approach to sexuality, turned a tight-lipped, over-powdered face to Mike. When he asked, "How's business?" her hand wiped the air and missed his nose by about an inch. But Mike only laughed.

"Fresh little bastard," she muttered as she left us.

"Just like I told ya, you almost got it that time," said Johnny.

"Do you think she wanted to give it to me?" Mike grinned. Nothing could stop his antics.

For a while longer we stayed at the carnival, tried the penny toss, and then attempted unsuccessfully to knock lead-bottomed imitation milk bottles off small stools to which they were probably magnetized.

Next we headed toward the fireworks. "Hey, look over there in the bushes," said Mike. "How much ya want to bet it's Joe making the broad with the pointed knockers. He didn't waste any time, did he?"

"If it's him," I said, "you better not give him any lip or you'll end up at the dentist real soon."

Mike chuckled. "Maybe you're right. Instead I'll just go over and ask him how his Lackanookie is comin' along. Do you know what I mean? That rare Hawaiian disease? Hey, I can't believe my eyes." Mike clapped his hands. "I've gotta be seeing things. Look over there next to the big tent. Isn't that Eddie the queer?

And a little kid with him?" It seemed that most of the Eddies who hung around East Dedham were odd characters. But this one was not a native. He was a visitor from a more affluent section of town.

In the shadows near the big tent we could see the outline of the huge form that could only belong to this other Eddie who, in his early twenties, was well over six feet tall and weighed more than two hundred. He was handsome, masculine looking, had no known occupation, and spent much of his time hanging around Dedham High School taking young boys for rides on his little red motor scooter. When I had first moved to Dedham I had been warned to watch out for him in the movies. He had a way of quietly sliding into seats next to young boys, and the next move was always sharing some candy with them, followed by a hand on the knee.

"Hey, Eddie, how much are you paying tonight?" shouted Mike toward the figures in the shadows.

Fran yelled, "Hey, Eddie, how's about me? I've got a real craving."

We all laughed hard as we walked away from the carnival toward East Dedham Square. Then Johnny groaned. "If he comes after us I'll see you guys later."

Then the large figure we had seen, and the small one, disappeared into the shadows.

"We scared the shit out of 'em," said Mike. "I wonder who his new recruit is."

"Who cares?" said Johnny. "I believe in minding my own business."

"Me too," I joined in. "I'm with you, Johnny."

Johnny continued to rub it in, at Mike's expense. "Don't ya have anything else to think about but sex, Mike? Why don't you get a hobby or something?"

"Sex is my hobby." Mike laughed hard. "Hey, Johnny, it's not my fault that East Dedham is full of horny bastards and perverts. What's the big deal if we crack some jokes about it? Look, it isn't just East Dedham people either. Eddie the queer comes from across the tracks, and his folks have lots of dough."

"Speaking of sex," said Fran, "I'm really upset about that New Look the girls are wearing. It's a leg man's nightmare. I'm a thigh man myself, and it's killing me when they wear those dresses that go right to the ground. Why are they hiding? What's their problem?"

Mike said, "It's no problem for me. I'm a knocker man myself. The catch is I haven't seen any good plunging necklines except on TV. Do you know that TV set they have in the store window in Dedham Square? The other night Faye Emerson was on, and you should have seen her. Is she built!"

"My mother's gonna get us a TV pretty soon," said Fran, "so I'll be seeing all the good shows. I bet we're gonna be the first on our block with a set."

"Mine's gonna be the last," I said. "We've still got a crystal set instead of a radio." I was only kidding, but in another era my grandfather had actually been the first person in his neighborhood with a crystal set.

"Hey, I'm still wondering about the New Look," said Mike. "Know what I think? The dresses have gone down as far as they can go, right? Some day I bet they go all the way up, and I bet the broads'll be walking around prackly bare-ass."

"I hope it happens in my lifetime," said Fran. "But I wouldn't be able to walk. I'd be a sex cripple, and I'd be lugging my pecker in a wheel barrow."

We were all laughing hard as we turned the corner into East Dedham Square, and as we passed some drunks sitting on the wide wooden step on the corner in front of the barroom an angry voice came in our direction like a projectile. "Ah, whassogoddam funny?" It was Stow, an alcoholic who spent a large chunk of his days in the Bridgewater lock-up taking the rest cure, at the invitation of the police. Public drunkenness was a crime in those days.

Mike took his bait. "The world's funny, Stow."

"No shit." Stow stumbled to his feet and held himself up with one hand on the wall. "I dunno if I shink ish funny."

Mike laughed. "Everything's funny."

Fran jabbed Mike with his elbow and whispered, "Lay off him."

"Wouldn't be funny if I flattened ya. You're Eyetalian, ain'tcha? I flattened lots o' Eyetalians."

Mike's face reddened. Then, with me on one side and Fran on the other, we led him up the sidewalk, away from Stow. "Whassamatter?" Stow's voice followed us along the sidewalk.

"Nothing, Stow," said Fran. "We've just gotta go to an appointment, that's all"

"Shit," growled the red-faced Stow, "I gotta fuckin' appoint . . . appoy . . . Shit, I got a . . . ."

The four of us quickened our steps and left him mumbling to himself. "Some day, Mike, you're really gonna get it," said Johnny. "That guy's as strong as an ox even when he's pie-eyed."

I chimed in, "Why the hell do you screw around with drunks all the time, Mike?"

Mike shrugged. "I can't help it. I like to take 'em off, just like this. 'Ah, whassogoddam funny?'" He did a perfect imitation of Stow, including the drunk's way of holding up a building so it would not fall on him. Because the mimicry was so effective, and the laughter from us was so extreme, Fran almost choked on the smoke from his Chesterfield and I had to slap him on the back to stop the reflex.

"I'll be okay," blurted Fran. "Goddam Mike . . . he's such a hot shit!"

"That was nothing," said Mike without a trace of modesty, "Wait'll you see my imitation of old Jake Ryan, our favorite English teacher. The only thing is I can't do it unless I get a sport coat with a hole in the elbow and a blackboard covered with chalk. Hey, you know what? Jake gets a kick out of my comedy routines. He laughs the whole time he's kicking me out of class! I'm gonna miss old Jake. I hope I get him in study hall next year. Did I tell you he gave me back my Jew's harp, my kazoo, and all the other stuff he took off me this year? He's a good egg."

"I can't picture you guys in college," said Fran.

I responded, "We'll be there because we want to be, and paying tuition, so we won't screw around."

Mike said, "Right. If you want to make something out of yourself these days you need a college degree. It's a ticket."

Fran laughed. "The only ticket I want is a ticket to the Old Howard or the Crawford House so I can relieve my lover's nuts."

We laughed our way along High Street, reflecting on the characters we had seen at the carnival, and as we approached East Dedham Square, Johnny, the least sex-oriented in our group, reacted to our loud antics this way: "Just in case anybody asks, I don't know you guys."

29

On a crisp Saturday afternoon late in the month of October, my pals and I were en route to observe one of the legendary burlesque shows at Boston's Old Howard. As we climbed the grimy steps leading from the MTA's underground rapid transit station near Scollay Square, I thought how amazing it was that, finally, after so many years of thinking about it, I was actually going to the burley with my friends.

"This is gonna be my first time, guys. When I lived in Norwood my pal John was always talking about going but we never went."

"It's the first time for me, too," said Johnny.

"My first too," said Mike.

Like a veteran of some kind of foreign war, Fran said, "I went last year with my cousin, and I ended up with lover's nuts for about a month after." As we stepped out into Scollay Square, Fran pointed to a saloon across the street from the MTA station. "See that place over there? The Crawford House? That's where lots of horny broads hang out. Some day I'm gonna go in there and get me some action."

"You're all talk," said Johnny.

Fran laughed, "Shit, Johnny, if you knew what was good for ya you'd keep your mouth shut. I think you're neuter gender, for Christ's sake."

Everyone except Johnny laughed as we crossed the wide portion of Scollay Square and entered the Saturday afternoon crowd near a cluster of penny arcades. "Look at the queer bastards staring at the peep shows," said Mike. "Hey, let's go in this creep joint and watch the freaks. Come on!"

"We'd be late for the show," said Fran. "There's no sense missing any. They say this babe Peaches really knows how to throw herself around. So make up your mind, Mike. Are we gonna watch oddballs in penny arcades or bare broads?"

"You call that a choice?" said Mike, and we all laughed as we went up the alley leading to the Old Howard Burlesque Theater.

"Can youse guys spare a quarter for a slug of gin?" Our laughter was interrupted by a voice from a dark doorway, and we saw a ragged bum huddled there. "I'm not givin' yez any bullshit about wantin' a cup o' coffee. All's I want's a goddam slug o' gin."

Mike stopped. "You're an honest rummy. Well, maybe I got two bits."

"Come on." Fran grabbed his arm. "Let's go."

Mike resisted. "I just want to help the poor bastard out."

"Yuh," said the bum, "let him help a poor bastard."

Mike laughed. "What a hot shit you are, calling yourself a poor bastard."

The bum snickered. "What the hell. That's what I am, ain't I?"

Mike fished out a quarter. "Here, buddy."

As the bum reached out a trembling hand, Mike placed the quarter in his palm. "Thanks for helpin' out a poor goddam bastard."

Mike grinned. "It's nothing."

The bum got up, limped down the alley in the direction of the Square, and disappeared around a corner. Then Mike performed a take-off on the bum's limp, held out a trembling hand, and made the plea, "Whatayasay, ole buddy? Can youse guys help out a poor goddam bastard?" The rest of us laughed as Mike walked with the bum's limp all the way to the ticket booth in front of the Old Howard.

As we stood in the litter-strewn and bum-filled alley, awaiting our turn at the ticket window, I needled Mike. "I bet you gave that bum two bits just so he'd talk to ya and you could take him off later."

"So what? It was worth it. He was a hot shit."

"You never get sick of making fun of people, do ya?" Johnny joined the attack.

"That's 'cause people are funny." Mike kept a straight face. "Want me to take you off?"

"Aw, come on, Mike."

It was our turn at the window, and we opted for the balcony. It was all we could afford. Fran didn't seem pleased with our chosen location, but the majority ruled. As we climbed the squeaky, narrow steps leading to the balcony, Fran said, "I hope you guys don't have to use the pisserie. It's cruddier than the one in Humpty's poolroom."

"We'll just have to hold it till later," I responded.

Mike chuckled. "I'm gonna hold it till Peaches starts taking it off. Maybe I'll keep holding it until . . . Hey, it sounds like the show's already on."

The audience was laughing as we took our seats. In the courtroom scene that was already in progress, the large-breasted blonde defendant was in the witness chair, with her tight skirt up near her hips and a camera in her hand.

"Yes, your whoreship, I'll tell the truth . . ." She stood up, with a quick shimmy. "the whole truth . . ." Another shimmy. "and nothin' but the truth . . ." A swing of her breasts. "so help me . . ." A forward thrust of her pelvis. "God!" The audience roared.

"Order in the court!" shouted the judge, leaping up with cloak extended, his wild eyes gleaming, and his white hair flying in all directions. "Order in the court!" He pulled out a large bologna-shaped yellow balloon and slapped his bench with it several times. "You may proceed, prosecutor."

The frock-coated prosecution attorney spoke. "And just where were you on the night of March sixteenth?"

The large-breasted defendant adjusted her skirt even higher, and then spread her legs. "Now lemme think, your lawyership. Now I remember what I was doin'. I was usin' my camera."

"You were what?"

"I was focusin'." The audience howled.

"Order in the court!" shouted the judge. "We will have no focusing talk in these chambers . . . with all due respect for the ladies of the jury." He pointed his balloon toward the jury of scantily clad chorus girls.

"I object, your whoreship!" shouted the plaintiff's attorney, a pot-bellied, red-faced giant of a man. "If my client says she was focusing she's telling the truth . . . and nothing but the truth."

"Objection overruled. Truth or no truth, I'll have no talk of focusing in my courtroom." The audience broke into laughter after each line.

Mike jabbed me in the ribs. "Holy shit, what a show! It's the best focusin' show ever!"

The large-breasted defendant rose from her seat and slithered to the judge's bench. "I hope you don't think I was just playin' around when I said I was focusin'. I always focus after supper. Would your whoreship want to focus with me sometime? I'd just love to show yez how I focus." She swung her hips in sync with a clang of cymbals.

"I strenuously object," shouted the prosecuting attorney with a flourish. "The defendant is trying to sway the judge."

"Oh no I ain't," retorted the blonde defendant. "I never swayed a judge in my life. I was just askin' him if he wanted to focus with me."

"That's all she was doing!" shouted the judge. "This cute little lass only wants to show me how she focuses." The audience dissolved in laughter.

"I'm finished my questioning," announced the prosecutor, "and I'm tempted to kiss off this farce."

"Order in the court!" The judge leaped up and bashed his long balloon on the bench. "I'll have no talk of kissing farces in my court. Order in the court! Order in the court!"

"But . . ."

"The court will hold you in contempt if you try to kiss a farce in these chambers." He paused. "What's this I see?" Swinging her way toward the side of the stage went the extremely large-breasted defendant. "One moment, cute little lass." The judge waved his hands at her.

"Yes, your whoreship." She rotated her hips and lifted her dress as the drummer did a loud series of rolls.

The judge smirked. "I'll have to see you in my private chamber later so you can demonstrate for me how you focus." He licked his lips lasciviously and the audience laughed and applauded. "Now you just go shift for yourself, cute little lass," shouted the judge as the blonde defendant left the stage with an exaggerated swing of her hips.

When the laughter had subsided, the judge called out, "Next witness." Then, onto the stage, shuffling along with greatly exaggerated slowness, came a tall, extremely thin, redheaded man who was dressed in nothing but long gray underwear. Swinging back and forth in front of him there was a cardboard padlock that was attached to his fly.

With gusto, he tilted the large padlock toward the hysterical female jurors, who immediately threw themselves into a giggling fit.

"And who are you, sir?" asked the prosecutor.

"I'm the defendant's boy friend, your lawyership."

"And what is the reason for that padlock?"

"I told my girl friend I was finding it hard getting up and out in the morning and she told me to wear a padlock on my fly." Laughter filled the Old Howard.

"How long have you had this condition?"

"You mean findin' it hard? Or the padlock?"

"Both," said the prosecutor.

"Since the first time I focused with her."

"Order in the court!" shouted the judge at the laughing audience while slapping his balloon down hard on the bench. "I can understand your finding it hard getting up in the morning, sir. Especially with such a cute little lass for a girl friend, but I object to this talk of focusing."

"But it's the truth, your whoreship, sir. So help me, your whoreship. It's the truth, the whole truth, and nothin' but the focusin' truth."

Mike nudged me and blurted, "This is the . . . high point of . . . my life."

"Yuh. It's fabulous."

Fran yelled, "This is nothing. Wait till you guys see Peaches take it all off!"

When the comedy skits ended with the judge's dismissal of the cases under consideration, fifty-cent grab bags holding a nickel's worth of merchandise were sold during intermission. Later, the band went into a brassy fanfare, the briefly clad chorus girls attempted a high-stepping dance, and then came the moment we had waited for.

"And now, ladies and gentlemen, our featured attraction. The one and only . . . Peaches!"

There she was, with a long pink gown covering her tall frame from neck to ankles, and flaming red hair cascading down her back like a blazing trail of fire as she slid slowly and demurely across the blue-lit stage. Moving provocatively to the tune of "A Pretty Girl is Like a Melody," she rhythmically swayed her hips to the primitive beat of the drums, and as she moved she unhooked snap after snap, dropping one piece of clothing after another to the stage floor.

"Holy jumping shit!" said Mike. "She's down to her goddam bra and those little panties. Is she gonna take it all off?"

Fran replied, "If there's nobody here from the Mayor's office she'll peel it all."

I sat entranced by the undulating form of Peaches the stripper, who without doubt possessed the largest pair of breasts I had either seen or dreamed of seeing. With her red hair flowing in the misty blue of the stage lights she moved her pelvis up and down against the edge of the stage curtain while holding onto it and squealing with delight. As the tempo of the music increased, Peaches kept up the pace. Then suddenly she left the stage curtain dangling, and slid to the floor in a prone position. Flat on her back, with legs spread and buttocks bouncing against the stage floor, she moved to the frenzied, savage beat of the drums.

Her hands then found their way to the snap of her lace bra, and with a sweep of one hand it was off, revealing the total view of massive breasts and a cherry glued to each nipple. Then she leaped to her feet, with her breasts rotating to the rhythm of the loud brassy band music, and her pelvic area began to thrust forward steadily as the tempo of the music intensified.

While swinging her breasts in arcs to the beat of the band, she pursed her lips, blew kisses, and tossed her red mane for emphasis while asking the audience in pantomime, "More?"

"More!" they yelled. "Take it all off!"

"Yuh," yelled Mike, leaping up in his place and waving his arms. "Take it all off, Peaches!"

"Take it all off!" the crowd roared again.

"For Christ's sake, take it off!" shouted Fran.

I said nothing as I sat there silently awestruck by the scene unfolding before my eager eyes which were fixed intently on the unclad body of the stripper.

"More?" Peaches' lips pursed in a kiss.

Again the excited audience shouted, "Take it all off!"

The band played on as she took off her panties, keeping only a G-string to pretend to cover her pelvis, and as she ceaselessly undulated her body with its exaggerated anatomy, I found myself tingling all over.

Then came a loud drum roll as Peaches peeled off the one remaining item of underwear, throwing the G-string to a baldheaded man in the first row, who feverishly attempted to jump onto the stage but was held back by a husky usher.

"I don't blame him for trying," yelled Mike.

Fran said, "Did ya ever see such tits in your life?"

"Shit, no," said Mike.

"Never," said Johnny.

"Nope," I said.

"What's she gonna do now?" Mike asked Fran.

"You'll see."

Peaches' body was moving in the steady sexual intercourse rhythm she had been developing for several minutes. Then she reached up and untied a red ribbon from her hair and dropped it to the floor, and with a brassy blare of trumpets enhancing her movements, she spread her legs to reveal a clean shaven pelvis, and inch by inch, she lowered her body toward the floor.

"Look," said Mike. "She's gonna try and pick up the ribbon with her pussy. Holy shit, I don't believe this is happening."

"You better believe it." Fran laughed. "Hey, she's got it! She picked up the ribbon! And now here comes the finale."

The orchestra began slowly, and Peaches stepped gingerly to the side of the stage. Then, with her head erect and without a stitch of clothing on her body, she slid toward center stage with her hips swinging and her massive busts swaying from side to side.

The spotlights went from blue to red to pink, and Peaches, shimmying all the while, slumped to her knees, stretched her arms outward toward the transfixed audience, and as her huge breasts rotated to the rhythm of the band she thrust forward her shaven pelvis, all the while sighing as if in the final stages of intercourse.

Then Peaches threw her last orgiastic bump to a primitive roar of drums, and the crowd gave her a standing ovation. As for me, I heaved a deep sigh as a burst of semen came streaming out of my engorged penis which I had surreptitiously pointed upward inside my shorts a few minutes earlier.

"I wish to hell we could stay for the next show," said Mike as we got up to leave.

"Yuh, me too," said Fran, "but they clean out the place after each show. It's not like the movies where you can hang out all day."

"All I can say is it was worth coming to Boston for this show," said Mike, laughing. "I'll have this hard-on for a month."

"Me, too," said Fran.

Johnny said nothing, and I walked along quietly, feeling the wet semen beginning to dry to a crust inside my shorts, and wishing there had been a way to deal with it.

"Sonovabitch," said Mike, "we'll have to go to the burley again sometime, right, you guys? That stage show was funny as hell too. Your whoreship . . . you better stop that focusing talk . . ." Mike laughed and the rest of us did too, and soon we were repeating all the lines from the courtroom scene.

However, beneath my casual surface I was very guilty. Shit, I thought, I let myself get more excited by that damn Peaches than I thought I would. I figured if I had enough willpower I wouldn't even care if she stood there bare-ass, but sometimes my mind can be thinking one way and my body another. Maybe it'd be good for me to stay away from places like the Old Howard.

30

In April of 1949 I felt that my future looked very optimistic, and I had a good reason for this outlook. The long-awaited acceptance letter had arrived from Boston College. My eyes were misty as I stood next to the parlor window, scanning the letter. Then I gave a nod, muttered "Good," folded the letter, and put it carefully into my shirt pocket.

Going into the front hall, I took off the brown corduroy sport jacket I had bought for nine dollars several weeks earlier at Filene's basement in Boston, and I hung it on the rack. To help raise the money for the jacket, I had sold my old Columbia bicycle for four dollars to a young opportunist who bought used goods cheap and sold them at a profit.

"Is that you, Tommy?" Granny's voice came at me from the dining room.

"Nope, it's Archbishop Cushing."

"Is it you, Tommy?" she repeated.

"Yup, it's me," I shouted.

"'Tis good to have someone in the house. It's lonesome with Freddy gone to Maine or wherever it is he went, and your Uncle Joseph come and gone so quick too."

I reflected, At least when Joe was here for his visit we had decent meals to eat. When I'm the only one around I have to eat like she does. Just tea and toast and vegetables. If I see another bowl of Ann Page's canned diced carrots and peas, I think I'll vomit.

As I passed through the dining room, which had not been used for dining since becoming Granny's bedroom many years before, I saw her on her army surplus bunk bed, raising herself up on one elbow.

"'Tis painful, whatever was thrown out of kilter. Sure I'd be better off dead. I'm no good to anyone. 'Tis a bitter struggle. Get a cup of tea for yereself. I think the water's hot. Ye can forage for yereself."

"Like a lone wolf in one of Jack London's books?"

"What is it ye said?"

"I said I'll forage for myself."

"'Tis good."

I stepped down the single step from the dining room to the kitchen, where I began preparing a cup of tea for myself. Then I went to the pantry to get some bread, and the first word that came out of me was "Shit." It was my response to seeing that the remaining bread was covered with green mold. "Yuck. And double yuck. Unadulterated putrefied shit!"

"'Tis not nice to swear."

"'Tis not nice to starve either," I responded when I found nothing edible in the refrigerator.

"If ye look hard ye'll find a bite of something. 'Tis no easy matter to buy food with little or no money coming in. Sure, Freddy took most of my savings with him to Maine to open his hotel or whatever it is he's doing up there."

"It's a motel, Granny. It's a little smaller than a hotel. And if there's no money coming in, how come you don't apply for some old age assistance? You're entitled to it."

Her voice roared from the next room. "They give ye nothing unless ye're destitute. Before you go on the dole they make ye sell the house and every last thing in it. Anyways, I don't want to be no ward of the government. With the little I've saved and the few dollars your Uncle Bill gives me for rent, I'll manage." I knew it was futile to argue with her when her mind was made up.

Draped in her brown plaid flannel robe, with Rosary beads in her hands, she shuffled into the kitchen and stood next to me near the portable oil stove that was now on top of the large cast iron stove that had been disconnected from the oil supply to save money in the warmer weather.

"You're not supposed to be up, Granny. Doctor Moran told you to stay off your feet."

"Shush now. Is Doctor Moran going to feed me, is he? Faith, I'm on the mend now, and it wasn't a bad break, he said. It was a whatchamacallit, a simple something or other of the pelvis."

"A simple fracture."

"Yes, that's what it was." She nodded her head and turned up the heat in the portable oil stove. "I never saw the like o' those dogs that knocked me over." She recalled the day she was walking home from East Dedham Square and had found herself in the middle of a dog fight. As she added some tea to the pot on the black stove, she said, "They were big as you." She looked up at me. "Sure, ye're getting taller and I'm getting smaller."

A spurt of growth had pushed my height to six feet, and I was thinner than ever, with my teeth and cheekbones even more prominent due to the lack of covering flesh, and I was self-conscious about that.

I grinned down at her. "I guess a dog wouldn't have to be too big to be bigger than you."

"They were big enough, the blackguards, and before I knew it they had me on the ground, ye know. Sure I don't recollect how I got myself home after it. I was there in the chair a devil of a long time before ye came home that day."

"You had me scared," I said as I took a box of graham crackers from a shelf in the pantry. I clearly remembered my feeling of dismay as I came into the kitchen that day and found her sitting motionless in the rocking chair, still wearing her black woolen coat and stiff black hat. Suffering from shock, she was sitting so still I had thought she was dead.

Then I had called out "Granny" and finally her unblinking eyes had moved, but she had not been able to speak. I had called Doctor Moran first, then Uncle Bill at the Quincy School boiler room. The shock symptoms had faded and hospitalization had not been necessary, but the doctor had ordered, "Keep her off her feet for at least a month."

In less than two weeks Granny had been walking from her cot in the dining room to the window in the parlor to look outside. She was not concerned with the dictates of doctors or anyone else, for that matter. She followed only her own rules.

"You better get back in your bed and rest," I said as I dipped a graham cracker into the boiling hot tea to soften it.

"Don't start dictating to me," she warned. "I took enough of that from your Uncle Joseph when he was home. He likes to be boss, he does. 'Tis little wonder he never married. Nobody would put up with him. He came well by it, ye know. The old gent was a great tyrant in his day, but he has no one over there at the old house to boss but himself. Your Uncle Joseph and the old gent never like to leave things the way they are. They always like to change the setup of things."

I reflected, So do I. But that's not easy to do around here. Brother, did she get upset when I turned up the clean side of the old braided rug in the parlor after Joe left for Washington. I didn't think she'd notice it, but when I got home from school the next day she had it back the way it was before. She was tearing at me for a week, muttering about how some people "like to change the setup of things." Her and her saving the other side for some future special occasion like her own wake! Big deal. The damn rug's mostly made out of her old stockings anyhow.

"I'm just going to sit and rock now and say my Rosary." Granny lowered herself gingerly into the rocker in front of the large black kitchen stove.

She does enough praying to blot out the sins of the world, I thought as I sipped on the hot tea. She ought to get together with that fanatic Henry Martin and form a new religious order.

"I'm tired of it all," she said as she slowly rocked. "I'm seventy and I've had my fill of it. All over the worruld they're fighting and quarreling. Sure and it's a pity. Every time I turn on the radio there's a news flash about a murder or a rape. But I like to hear the Irish Hour and tap my toe to the jigs and reels. The Irish like their music, ye know. In the old country we danced and sang till all hours. But 'twas a long time ago." She paused and rocked and then started up again. "Oh, 'tis no fun at all after ye get married. There's lots of dirty diapers and mess to clean up, and it's no easy job to raise the little ones."

As she talked I dipped graham crackers into my hot tea, trying to pop them into my mouth before they crumbled. I only half-listened to her monologue.

"Are ye going to the Howard Johnson's to worruk today?" she asked.

"Nope, I go in tomorrow afternoon."

"Well, 'tis good for ye to work. It never killed a man, ye know."

I laughed. "It almost kills me."

"What is it ye said?"

"I said there's nothing like work."

"'Tis no good to be idle." She nodded as she rocked and fingered her beads. Then there was a rattling noise outside the back door, and I saw the rotund outline of Mrs. Newton heaving its portly way across the back porch.

I better get out of here, I thought, if I don't want that pain in the ass bending my ear. I leaped up from the table, grabbed my cup of tea and a handful of graham crackers, moved rapidly through Granny's room, and softly tiptoed up the stairs to the room that was mine now that Uncle Joe had left town.

Stretching myself out on the bed, I propped a pillow behind myself and picked up Hemingway's *The Sun Also Rises* from the chair next to the bed. Turning to the page I had dog-eared, I began to read. Then I abruptly closed the book and reflected on my state of mind.

Hey, I'm just not in the mood for reading right this minute. I'm in one of those moods where I feel like thinking about me and my destiny. I guess I'll just flake out and think about next fall when I'll be a freshman at Boston College. I hope I make out okay there. It's the only college I've ever wanted to go to.

The guys from B.C. High will be one jump ahead of me in Latin and Theology because they've had that stuff up to their ears. But they'll prob'ly be bored. I won't be. The Liberal Arts. That's my idea of education. Language, history, and philosophy with the Jesuits. Yup, I'll be training my mind. Well, right now I better hang up my school clothes before I wreck them.

I carefully removed my shoes and placed them under the chair next to the bed. Then I took off my trousers, arranged them neatly on a hanger, put my shirt over them on the same hanger, and hung them in the closet. I then placed my tie on the tie rack next to the closet, and in my mind I turned over this phrase: "A place for everything and everything in its place." It had been one of Mrs. White's favorites.

Sitting on the edge of the bed, I looked down at my white socks and considered their deterioration. That's what I get for buying cheap socks. They've got holes in them already. Pretty soon they'll look like this beat-up T-shirt that Granny went and patched with yellowed pieces of old bed sheets and shreds of old underwear and black-and-blue thread.

I really screwed up wearing this old underwear today. I forgot we were gonna have gym. I had to prackly hide inside my locker when I changed so nobody could see my underclothes. The poorest kids in East Dedham have better underwear than me.

I'll have to get myself another T-shirt when I get paid this week, but by the time I get my pay there's hardly anything left. I better not shop at Brody's. They screwed me on that flannel shirt last winter. The damn thing shrunk to the size of a handkerchief when Granny washed it in the machine. I always get screwed when I buy stuff in East Dedham Square.

That bandit Leo DeLapa really shafted me when I bought those used so-called waterproof army combat boots. The first time I wore them in snow my feet got soaked. What a clip artist. That's the way it goes when you've got no dough. They see you coming. It's a lot different than it was at Mrs. White's. We had clothes for best and school clothes, and old clothes too.

With my shoulders on my knees and my chin cradled in the upturned palms of my hands, my eyes went out of focus as I gazed deeply into the past and conjured up a mental picture of a younger Tommy O'Connell totally outfitted in new clothing.

Then I shook my head as I sat in my small dark bedroom at Granny O'Connell's with my head held up by my hands, and I thought, At least I don't have to worry about messing up my clothes. Hah. They're messed up all the time anyhow. "Clothes make the man," Mom White used to say. Well, if that's true, then I'm a bum. But Granny doesn't see it that way. She says, "The good Lord on high doesn't give a hoot what ye have on yere back. It's what's inside ye that counts." So maybe I'm not so bad off after all.

I took out the letter from Boston College, studied it again, and thought, I'm gonna need twenty-five bucks for the acceptance fee. I guess I'll have to save up because Freddy's short on dough. Well, I've got till the end of July to pay it. It's always something, isn't it? I see my way clear to get some underwear and socks, and then comes the request for the acceptance fee money.

"Hah, I think it's tough now? Wait till I have college tuition bills to pay." Oops, I'm starting to talk to myself out loud, just like Granny does. I've been listening to her too long. She doesn't give a shit if she has an audience. She's a weird character, but I guess I'm weird too. I don't have enough to eat or buy clothes and I think I'm gonna go to college. My father's up in Maine with that woman trying to start a motel business, and how do I know he'll even come across with the tuition? I hope he doesn't screw me up. Ah, what the hell, he said he'd dig up the dough when the time came. I guess I have to wait and see.

I reached over to the windowsill and took a piece of Doublemint gum, unwrapped it, and then began to chew it. The gum habit took the place of cigarettes. Increased smoking had brought me dizzy spells and coughing fits, and when I had begun to cough up blood, I decided to give up the weeds.

You can't win, I thought. I'm not coughing now because of cigarettes, but my teeth are aching from chewing gum. What the hell kind of a body am I stuck with? If it isn't a bitchy rash, it's a cold, or a toothache, or a coughing fit, or a headache, or pains in the chest. Seems like there's always some part of my body in an uproar. Well, I've got a good brain, but a challenging body. Can't have everything.

I wish I could just read and relax and not have to worry about money or work. I'm not much for work. If it wasn't for the free food there, I would have quit Howard Johnson's long ago. I get exhausted when I'm on my feet a long time. I should have been born rich. If I was born rich, I wouldn't be on this hard bed with a cruddy, cracked sloped ceiling over my head. I'd be eating like an ancient king. Sleeping on mattresses with inner springs. Traveling around the world. And just plain taking it easy. Imagine having enough to eat and plenty of clothes and plenty of dough to spend.

Wonder what I'd do if I had all kinds of dough. Sail in a yacht? Nope. I'm too lazy for that. The funny thing is, I'd prob'ly do what I'm doing right now. Only in a different room, with different clothes, and definitely a different mattress instead of this hard one. I'd flake out, read, listen to the radio and watch television, and sing songs. But I wouldn't work. To hell with work.

I stretched out on the bed, laid my head back on the lumpy pillow, and as I closed my eyes I saw myself in a large square room with a high flat ceiling and many windows, stretched out on a soft bed, with a good light shining down on the book I had chosen to read. There was a buzzer next to my bed to press when I desired my meal, and along with thick rugs on the floor, and colorful drapes on the windows, there was a view of the ocean.

What am I thinking about? A plush hotel? Yup. A place where I could have my privacy when I felt like it and be waited on when I wanted to be. Like at Saranac Inn, but that's on fresh water. I'd like it better near the ocean. It's funny how you think of all kinds of things when you're flaked out with your eyes closed. Boy, the people at Saranac Inn had it made. I wonder if money made them miserable. They didn't look it. Seemed like they were having a ball. Hell, I didn't have much money up there, and I had a ball, too. So I guess money isn't everything.

After we went on strike at the caddie camp I had a terrific time at Lake Placid with Jo and her friend Chris. I wonder what Jo thought when I didn't answer her letters. What if all of a sudden I showed up there some day, I wonder what she'd say to me. Shit, she's prob'ly married already. Those kids marry young up there in the mountains. Well, those Lake Placid days are all gone now. Over and done with.

Back to right now, brain. What's the deal right now? Well, I should have asked Audrey to the prom sooner. She said she would have gone with me if she hadn't already said okay to Jack. But I don't get it. If she doesn't like Jack that much, why is she going to the prom with him?

I'll never understand girls, and the way they think. I guess it's hard to live with them sometimes, but it's hard to live without them, too. Ah, what's the big deal about the prom anyhow? I'd end up broke trying to dig up the dough for the tuxedo and flowers and stuff. Hey, who cares about the prom? They can have their idiot prom, with the boys making believe they're Little Lord Fauntleroy, and the girls pretending they're Shirley Temple. It's one more expense I won't have to deal with. To hell with the prom. They can take it and stick it.

31

It was Graduation Day and I was sitting on the edge of my bed with my copy of *Reflections*, the Dedham High Class of '49 yearbook. I was in a very orderly mood. The book was on my lap as I sat in my very orderly room. My maroon cap and gown were hung carefully over the entrance to my very orderly closet. And I was about as orderly as I could be with what I was wearing. My choice of wardrobe was simple because it was the only set of clothes I owned. I was wearing my slightly frayed brown corduroy sport coat, a white shirt that was turning gray, a wide yellow tie with a jagged maroon streak running through it, and a pair of shiny dark brown gabardine pants that were too heavy for June. That was the best I could do, considering the nearly empty state of my bank account.

There was an hour to go before I had to be up at the school, and I was in a nostalgic mood as I gazed dreamily at my Dedham High yearbook.

"Best of luck to a swell actor . . . Ethel." An actor? Some actor. I had two lines in the class play and almost forgot one of 'em. "Best of luck to a swell friend and derelict. Pete." I got a lot of notoriety from playing the part of the drunk. "To the Mayor of East Dedham. Luck and success . . . Maggie." I guess she saw me hanging around the Square and going up to the poolroom all the time.

"To Tommy, one who has many remarks . . . Joan." Now what the hell does she mean by that? Does she think I'm a wise guy? I only tease her because she's so nice. "Good luck and lots of fish. Fran." What a character. He can't forget about the poolroom even when he signs my yearbook. "To Oakie. All the luck . . . Mike." He didn't even write anything funny! He horses around a lot, but basically I think he's pretty serious.

"To Tommy, my buddy . . . Joey." How will I ever forget her? What a sexy babe. "Good luck, Tommy. A swell kid with a sense of humor . . . Eino." What a character. He never stopped raising hell for a second. "To Oakie. Lots of luck . . . Johnny." We can all use plenty of that, pal.

I laughed as I read, "To Tommy, a superswell speller. Keep up the good work. Marie." Oh Marie, how amazingly beautiful you are! And thank you for the compliment. Spelling champ, huh?

Imagine me studying all those lists of words for weeks and weeks and then standing up there on that stage like a nervous wreck, and sweating and shaking and then becoming the winner of the Senior Class Spelling Championship. But what a terrible day it was when I lost on an easy word at the Boston Public Library. Ugh. Big wound in chest. Oh well, maybe I can wear my Boston Herald Traveler silver medal on my lapel like those stew bums in Scollay Square with their old Army medals.

"Best of luck to a cute fellow . . . Jeannie." God, what a beauty. My heart was in my throat every time I tried to talk to her. "Good luck to the Golf Team . . . Shorty." Hah. We lost more than we won. We mostly goofed off. A one-letter man, that's me.

To Tommy, who had the fate of sitting in front of me in Senior English . . . Audrey." I also had the fate of seeing more of you than I wanted to see when you were picking things up off the floor. I wonder if you dropped things on purpose, Auds. You were a real tease sometimes. I almost asked you out a few times, but the time never seemed right. Maybe I'll ask you to go to a Boston College dance with me. It's hard to believe I'll be at B.C. next fall, after this summer in Maine helping at my father's motor court.

"You were awfully funny in the Class Play . . . Carolyn." Well, I guess I made a pretty good drunk, but after the play Miss Grant said she wished she gave me a bigger part. What a character, telling me she gave me the drunk part because I was emaciated looking. And I was just beginning to think nobody noticed how skinny I was.

It's funny, I thought as I closed the yearbook, how much fun Dedham High was after I got into a few activities. When my marks got better I guess it didn't hurt either. Nobody likes a moron. Uh-oh. It's almost time to go.

I put on my cap and gown, and after a graham cracker and tea snack I met Fran and Johnny at the Square and we headed toward the Dedham High auditorium for the ceremony.

Our Class of '49 assembled, sat through a series of traditional speeches, and then we filed up onto the stage one by one, received our diplomas, turned in our caps and gowns, and joined those who had come to wish us well.

As I scanned the crowd to see if my father and any uncles and aunts were there, my retentive memory propelled me back to the day of my First Communion at St. Catherine's in Norwood. My father had been among the missing that day, and vestiges of the disappointment were still with me. So I scanned the crowd looking for him, and when I saw him I breathed a sigh of relief and thought, Well, he came this time, what do ya know about that? Amazing.

After the ceremony I joined my father and two pairs of aunts and uncles, and my father urged me to smile. "Let's see those nice white teeth."

I hated being told I had to smile, so I responded, "Like this?" I clenched my teeth and bared them, like an irritated wolf.

"You should be proud of your teeth." My father put an arm around my shoulder and hugged me, and I stiffened at his touch.

"Right." I hated my crowded teeth.

"Congratulations, Tommy." Uncle Joe Guiod gripped my hand and shook it. "Seems like not so long ago when Grace and I were driving you down to White Horse Beach in your diapers."

"He's still as cute as he was then." Aunt Grace kissed me on the cheek and I blushed.

Then I felt Uncle Bill's strong left arm around my shoulders, and he squeezed me very hard. "I'm proud of ya, Tommy. I wish I graduated from high school myself. You're still going to college, right?"

"Yuh, I'm gonna go to B.C."

"You'll be the first O'Connell to set foot in a college. I bet you'll get honors."

"All I want to do is graduate, Bill."

Aunt Rita, Bill's wife, kissed my cheek and said, "You got a good head on your shoulders, Tommy. You ought to go far. Anyway, the best of luck to you."

"Thanks, Rita. You'd think I was taking off for good or something. I'll still be right next door to you characters, you know."

Bill laughed. "If I come over there and catch you not doing your studies I'll give you a good wallop, and don't think I can't still take you on either, even if you're tall enough to look down at me."

"I know you can take me, Bill."

Bill grinned. He was very proud of his strong physique, obtained through many years of shoveling coal into Dedham's Quincy Elementary School boiler.

Then I heard my father talking to Joe and Grace. ". . . and it's been a long time since taking him to Children's Hospital to bake his lung. Never thought he'd pull through. He hasn't had it easy, losing his mother and boarding all those years at Mrs. White's in Norwood. It's been no picnic for him but he doesn't look too much the worse for it. Of course, he could use a little weight on his bones and . . ."

As they continued to analyze my life, I felt my face flushing from embarrassment, and I wondered if this was how a freak in a circus sideshow would feel when being scrutinized.

Joe shoved an envelope into my hand and said, "A little something for you, Tommy." Bill followed suit with another envelope.

My father reached into his pocket, withdrew his wallet, took out three bills, and shoved them into my pants pocket. "This should get you that watch you've been wanting."

"Hey, Tommy." It was my pal Mike's voice. "You ready? Everybody's taking off for Nantasket."

"Yuh, I'll be all set in a sec." I remembered that Mike had not met my aunts and uncles. "Uh . . . these are my aunts and uncles. This is my buddy, Mike. Uncle Joe Guiod, Aunt Grace, Uncle Bill, and Aunt Rita. You know my father."

Then it was time to head with the rest of the class to Nantasket Beach on the Atlantic Ocean where the last farewells of the graduates would be extended to one another in the noise and bustle of Paragon Park with its cotton candy, taffy apples, speedy roller coasters, tilt-a-whirls, bumper cars, and Fun House.

"Take care of yourself," said my father as I left with Mike to join Fran and Johnny.

"Yuh, I will. Don't worry."

My father gazed at me with his penetrating light blue eyes, and there seemed to be a bit of a haze over them. Then he squeezed my hand and said no more.

I blushed slightly, and as I turned to leave them I told my relatives, "See you later. Much later."

32

During the summer of 1949 I went to Maine to help my father and his partner Hazel with Brookland Motor Court, their enterprise just North of Wells, Maine, on Route One, near Drake's Island, an area known for its beautiful pristine beaches. I wasn't that much help due to my inherent physical laziness. But I did my part as an ad hoc carpenter's helper when my much more physical father put the finishing touches on the ten seasonal prefabricated cottages they had bought in Randolph, Massachusetts, and had erected on the field next to the highway.

The close quarters during that hot summer in the small shack on the large field had been confining, and trying to make conversation with my father, Hazel Berg, and her brother Russell had been a chore for me. The Bergs were definitely not communicators, and my father was a sporadic lecturer. Since he took the lead in intensity, I mainly listened when he talked. My impression of him, as with Granny, was that he was his own best audience.

During the summer I kept thinking about what it would be like to go to Boston College in the fall, and was very obsessed with that subject. Finally, a long-term goal was coming into being, and I had great enthusiasm about entering the next phase of my life. But fate does not always fit in with our plans as we pursue our goals, ambitions, and fantasies. And by the time the summer of 1949 came to a close, fate presented a quite different scenario than the one I had optimistically envisioned.

As the Greyhound bus rolled across the Maine-New Hampshire line en route to Boston, I was asking myself why I had believed my father's promise to have my tuition ready for me when I needed it.

Now the time has come and he says he's too deep in debt. So it's no college for me this year. Him and that so-called business! He could have stayed in his old job, but instead he quits and takes off to Maine with Hazel. I wonder what he sees in that woman. They don't have anything in common except the business. She's nothing like him. She likes to dive off rocks into freezing cold water and dig clams and crap like that. She doesn't know how to cook or anything, and she hardly even looks like a woman.

As the bus rolled along and I gazed blankly at the passing countryside, I thought of the redhead that he had spent time with years before. Yes, I thought, Suzie was a real woman. I wonder what happened to her. He doesn't talk about her anymore, but he calls Hazel "Suzie" sometimes and Hazel's so far out in left field she doesn't even seem to care. Hell, she's in her own screwy world.

I wonder if he'll marry her, but how can he? He'd have to divorce my mother, and I don't think he'd do that. Nope. He'll prob'ly wait till she gets old and dies before he gets married again. I can't imagine her being there in that insane asylum after all these years. I wonder if I ought to go see her. But she wouldn't know me and she prob'ly doesn't remember she ever even had me, so I don't know what the point would be in going to see her. But some day maybe I'll go anyhow.

Soon, as the Greyhound rolled its way through northeastern Massachusetts, I was reflecting on my return to East Dedham. I really looked forward to rejoining my friends where there would be an ease of association instead of the strained atmosphere at Brookland Motor Court. Both Fran and Johnny had taken jobs in Boston factories, and Mike had worked that summer with a small contractor as well as with his own father on masonry jobs.

Next summer I'll just stay in Dedham, I thought. I don't want to spend another summer with my father and the Bergs. They can have their motor court. That's pure bullshit when he gets me off to one side and tells me someday it'll be my place. The sign on the wall says "Proprietor Hazel Berg." It doesn't say a word about Fred O'Connell, even though he kicked in a lot of Granny's money, including the dough she was gonna give me to help with college.

I wonder where I'll work this year. Prob'ly in a factory where they pay you peanuts for working your ass off, but with all the unemployment who can be fussy? What choice is there except cruddy jobs?

I'll have to work and scrounge and save dough all year long. That's the only way I can be sure to get to Boston College next year. Too bad I screwed around as much as I did the sophomore year of high school. I could have had a scholarship. Well, at least I did what I felt like. I took it easy most of the time. Some people never do what they feel like.

B.C. will be harder than old Dedham High. They flunk plenty of freshmen. Well, I guess there's no sense worrying about that now. It's another year away. A year of working and getting books from the liberry, and hanging around. Maybe I'll get a car. I've got my license now. I wonder if that was just a snowjob my father gave me about turning Berg's old '34 Plymouth over to me next spring. He's the guy who said I could count on going to B.C. this fall. From now on I'll believe what he says when I see it.

I glanced down at the white line on the finger where my Dedham High ring used to be. The rest of my hand was well tanned. Hah. Goodbye, ring. I scrounged to buy you and even did without other things, and now all I've got is some white skin where you used to be. Then pretty soon the tan will be gone and the skin will be all white and that will be that.

Maybe I made too big a deal out of that ring. I've never had much luck with things I cared too much about. Maybe I shouldn't care about anything. Funny how I lost that ring in the ocean in that big wave. It was sort of like that dream I've been having where the tidal wave higher than the housetops comes at me and just when it's gonna drown me that's when I wake up screaming and yelling and leaping around. What a bitch of a dream. It's almost as bad as the one with the thousands of snakes all around me and after me. But they don't get me. They just scare the shit out of me, that's all. God, how I hate dreams like that. There were real snakes up there in Maine this summer too, all over the place. I wish there was no such thing as a snake or a tidal wave.

Well, no more Dedham High School. It's all over and done with now. Pretty soon Johnny will take off and join the Air Force. Then Fran will join the Navy. Mike will be studying at Boston University. And me? Hah. I'll be working at some flunky job saving up my tuition for next year. Seems like I graduated from Dedham High a long time ago, but it's only been a few weeks. Time really stops dead up in Maine. The natives don't even care what day it is.

As the bus rumbled along I thought of the days I had spent on the girl-filled beach, and my female-oriented reflections prompted me to speculate about my sexual future, and particularly my virginity. As the bus hit a pothole on Route One near Boston, I thought, It'd be screwy to wait forever, but it'd also be screwy to play around and then expect a nice girl for a wife. I just have to hold out. Then it'll be all the better when I finally get married. The only hitch is, I get so damn excited so much. I wonder if I'm more oversexed than most guys.

My thoughts continued to roam through a broad range of sexual and other speculations as I changed from the bus to the elevated railway, then from the MTA car to the Eastern Mass. Street Railway bus going to Dedham. When I arrived at Walnut Place I realized I could never get used to Granny's house without the beat-up porch out front. Those cement steps that Uncle Bill built were for the birds, as far as I was concerned. I liked the old wooden porch even though it had been very rickety.

It feels good being back here on Walnut Place again, I mused. There's Margie sitting on her front porch with her mother. She's a nice kid, and so are the other kids around here. But the touch football days in the field up the street are all over, and I'll soon be working full-time, and then I'm gonna be a freshman at Boston College. I'm no kid anymore, that's for sure.

"Hi, Margie," I waved to her as I opened the black wooden screen door leading to Granny O'Connell's side of the duplex. Margie returned my greeting, and as I stepped into the house Granny's voice rang out, "Is that you, Tommy?"

"Yup, it's me."

"Is it you, Tommy?" She called out again from the kitchen. "The ears aren't good today."

"No!" I shouted. "It isn't Tommy. It's Winston Churchill. The dirty blackguard Winnie is here." I laughed as I threw my little brown canvas bag of clothing onto the hard-cushioned love seat in the living room. Then I headed for the kitchen. "Yup, it's me, Granny. It's the devil himself."

She was seated in the old rocker, near the black iron Magee stove, dressed in her flannel bathrobe. Squinting up at me through her aged, steel-rimmed spectacles, she said, "Oh, 'tis you, is it? Well, 'tis good to have someone back in the house. Did you enjoy your time in Vermont or wherever it was?"

"I was up in Maine." I sat down at the kitchen table and looked out through the rear porch toward the East Dedham Railroad Station beyond.

"Sure, one place is the same as the next when ye get to be my age. Vermont or Maine, I wouldn't know the one from the other." She fingered her Rosary beads and rocked back and forth with her lips quivering as she thought of what she would say next.

She's really getting old and wrinkled now, I observed. Look at her, all wrapped up in that beat-up flannel bathrobe on a warm day like today.

"I just sit and pray is all I do. Sure 'tis good for someone to pray for the sins of the worruld, but I've had enough of it. There's no end to the fighting and quarreling, ye know. If they're not having it out with the Germans and the Eyetalians, they're at it with the Russians. 'Tis too bad men like to fight so much. I had my share of it with the old gent. He'd come in from the barbershop all soused up and light into me, but I was a fast runner those days, so out in the back yard I ran till he cooled off. I was never one to fight 'cause it does no good, ye know. 'Tis a waste."

"I guess it is."

"Sure it is," she affirmed, "and don't ye forget it." She waved her gnarled arthritic hand toward the stove. "Fix yereself a bit of tea and make some toast to tide ye over till supper. Ye can forage for yereself. Sure, I don't have much in the house but there's some vegetables in the cans, and ye can fill up on those. In a minute I'll put some potatoes on to boil. I wouldn't care if I never ate a morsel. Many's the time in the old country us little ones went to bed hungry, but we survived, most of us."

"I wonder if I will," I mumbled.

"What was that ye said?"

"I said it's a nice day. 'Tis grand."

"We can thank the good Lord for that now, can't we? If ye've got a roof over the head and a bite to eat, ye can thank the good Lord for that too." She crossed herself with her Rosary bead crucifix, then kissed it.

Shrugging my shoulders, I went to the portable kerosene stove and lit the burner. It belched a puff of black smoke as the wick ignited. "Time to give this monster to the junk man," I said as I leaped back. When the smoke had dissipated and only the flame remained, I took the open pot, filled it half full of water, and placed it on the burner to heat it up for tea.

I went back to the table and propped my chin in my hands, and sat thinking about how hot the stove would make the kitchen in a few minutes. Well, at least it's better here than in that shack in Maine. Like Granny says, this place is "a roof over the head."

"The fellas ye used to live with in Norwood at Mrs. White's house were here," Granny announced. "What's their names? There's two of them."

"The Rothwells. When were they here?"

"I forget now. Sure my mind goes berserk and I forget things that happen a minute ago, but still I remember what happened when I was a little one in the old country in Castle Cove. I think it was a couple of weeks ago they were here. The small one, what's his name?"

"Joe."

"Well, he was much cleaner than the last time he came here. I think he said he was going into the Marines. No, it was the Air Force. He said he'll write ye all about it."

"The Air Force? Well, he'll get to see the world. What about Dave?"

"The tall thin one? What did ye say his name was?" I repeated the name. "Yes, 'twas David. Now I recollect it." She rocked and fingered her Rosary beads and her lips quivered as she recalled the Rothwells' visit. "He's going to some college out in the West, I think he said. In Wisconsin or Michigan. Sure, I've never been past New York. I told him you said you were going to the college yereself."

"Not now. My father can't dig up the money."

"What did ye expect?" She chuckled. "Frederick never was one to hold onto a nickel. Money burns his fingers, it does, so he throws it away as fast as he gets it in his hand. He took every cent he could get from what little I had, and he went and put it in the whatchamacallit business. 'Tis too bad ye can't go to the college now, but ye have the high school behind ye. In the old country we only went to the sixth grade."

"I'm still gonna go to B.C. but I'll go next year instead. Pretty soon I'll get a full-time job and save my own tuition money."

The old woman nodded her head. "'Tis the only way. Ye can't depend on Freddy for it. Sure I won't ask anything of ye even though it costs a bundle to live these days. Ye can't buy a loaf of bread and a can of beans without handing over a dollar. 'Tis hard for them with big families. William has to work like a dog, and as fast as he makes it Rita spends it."

Uh-oh, I thought as I rose from the table. Here she goes on Rita.

"She throws more away each day than I eat in a week." Granny emphatically pointed a gnarled index finger toward the other side of the duplex. "She takes advantage 'cause she knows he's a good provider."

"Shit."

"The Lord forgive ye for what ye just said." She crossed herself.

"The toast just burned. I didn't swear at you."

"Oh, 'tis good ye didn't," she muttered. "'Tis not nice to swear."

"Right, Granny, 'Tis not nice." This is some toaster, I thought. You can't take your eyes off it for a second. Some day I'll save up and buy one that pops up when it's done.

I put the charred toast in the rusty tin can on the sink counter, and then I put another piece of nearly stale bread into the toaster. As I moved toward the stove to get my tea I wondered if I would have time to pour the tea without the toast burning. At the table, I poured the tea quickly, and as the first wisp of smoke curled up from the toaster, I flipped the toaster door open, yanked out the toast, and praised myself. "Good timing, Tommy."

"What was it ye said?" She cupped her hand to her ear.

"I was just talking to myself."

"Sure I do it all the time." She chuckled

I responded, "Where can you find a better audience, right?"

She nodded. "'Tis true. Ye don't have arguments when ye just talk to yereself." She rocked and said, "They're all dead, ye know. All the ones I knew over on Belknap Street. The only one left there now is the old gent. 'Tis a wonder he doesn't burn himself up with all his smoking and drinking. Sure, there was always a bottle in his barbershop for him to swig, but I never touched it. Bessie Foley gave us the pledge in the old country, ye know, and all us girls swore we'd never use it. It brings nothing but trouble, and there's enough o' that in the worruld without adding to it with the damnable drink." She chuckled. "When they bury the old gent, they'll have to put a bottle in his hand."

I laughed. "You're a fabulous character, Granny."

"I suppose I am, but all I want now is to go to my rest, and I pray every day for the good Lord to call me. A lot has changed today. When we were young in the old country we danced and we sang and 'twas nice, but after I got hooked up with the old gent here it was no bed of roses. He'd get soused up and many's the time I had to fish his pockets to buy some food for the little ones. Then we had all that trouble with your mother, God love her. 'Twas too bad they had to put her away. After they laid your brother out, God rest his immortal soul, I think that did her in.

"Sure and it's best to forget some things if ye can. Like the plagues killing our neighbors. It was always a bitter struggle to stay in one piece. If it wasn't one thing it was another. The old gent could drink the Mill Pond dry in his day, ye know, and the booze got him wild. When I wouldn't fight with him, that got him wild too. But 'tis all over now though, and I just want to meet my Maker and rest in peace."

"Hah! You'll prob'ly live to be a hundred."

Granny shook her head thoughtfully. "'Twould be a punishment. Sure, every bone in my body aches with the arthuritis and the rheumatism. I can just about hold my beads. Faith and I don't know what I'd do without them. When I say my Hail Mary's I'm at peace and I hold it in for nobody. Not a soul. Love thy neighbor as thyself, the good Lord said."

I smiled, recalling her tirades against my good-natured Aunt Rita, and I thought, You're a character right out of a novel, Granny. You give Rita the business every day, and at the same time you talk about loving your neighbor.

She continued her monologue as I finished my tea and toast. Then I stood up, looked at myself in the distorted shaving mirror over the sink, and began to comb my thick, curly hair.

"Ye'll comb it right out of yere head," chided the old woman. "Look at Freddy, he hasn't more than five hairs left now, and he was always in front of the mirror lathering it up with the pomades. He thought he was pretty su-ave," she said, emphasizing both syllables.

Shit, I thought. I can't comb my hair without a running commentary from her. I'm gonna get the hell out of here until suppertime. Maybe I'll go down the poolroom or the drugstore.

Later I can call the guys and see what's up for tonight. Maybe we'll get the bus up to Norwood and bowl a couple of strings. I've still got a few bucks left after paying my bus fare from Maine. Well, I can start saving for college after I get a job. I'll prob'ly end up in some cruddy factory like the Boston Envelope Company. But hell, if I'm gonna get to college, I'll have to take a cruddy job and save up. That's the way it goes.

As I left the house, I fantasized about the day when I would no longer have to take cruddy jobs. Yup, after I graduate from Boston College I'll get a job where I use my brain, not my back. Hell, anybody can use brute strength. Maybe that's why most jobs get on my nerves. I'm not the brute type. And do I hate being bossed! I even hated it this summer when my own father bossed me. I wondered who the hell he thought he was with his boss routine. I like to be asked to do things, not told. Some day I'll be my own boss.

33

The year was 1950, and the Friday night in the middle of May was a warm one. I was about to take my newly acquired very old car and launch it on its maiden voyage, and my pal Fran was on hand for the occasion.

"Is the motor any good?" he asked as he gave the 1934 Plymouth business coupe a close look.

"Russell Berg said he overhauled it a couple of years ago." I turned the key in the ignition. "He said it doesn't burn a drop of oil." The starter wheezed, but the engine would not start.

"Try pumping the gas," suggested Fran.

I gave the gas pedal three pushes, turned the key, and pressed against the starter button. This time the engine caught. "There she goes, Fran."

"Sounds pretty good."

"Not bad for a car that's almost as old as us, huh? It's like those ads you see in the paper, 'good trans.'"

"Hah! How's the clutch? Does it slip?"

"Seems okay. Whatayasay we take a little spin around town while we're waiting for Johnny. He got home late from the job, I guess."

"He's racking up the overtime, huh?" Fran dragged in a lung full of Chesterfield smoke, then blew it out slowly.

"Yuh, but he can have it. Forty hours is enough for me. I can't wait to punch that time clock at night. But it's better since I've been in the shipping room. I get more dough and I don't have to work so hard. I'm getting ninety-eight cents an hour now.

I started at eighty-seven. I'm coming up in the world. Some day I might hit a buck an hour. Hey, I could end up a millionaire, Fran. If I play my cards right there may be a great future for me at good old Boston Envelope Company. Some day I might be in charge of the whole shipping room." I laughed as I concluded my employment commentary.

"You're not much for work, right?"

"I think it's just a necessary evil." I turned the old Plymouth left from Walnut Place onto Walnut Street.

"You better get used to working because you're gonna be working all your life."

"Not dog work, Fran."

"Who are you supposed to be? King Shit? Are you better than the rest of us slobs?"

"I'm as good as I think I am, and I'm gonna start on my college education next fall, and someday I'll get a job where I get good pay for using my brain, not my back."

"You really go in big for that using the brain shit."

"Bet your ass I do." I pumped the brakes on the descent toward East Dedham Square. "These damn brakes aren't so hot. Look how I have to pump to make 'em work."

"At least they're hydraulics," said Fran.

"Yeah, but I'd be better off with mechanical ones that worked instead of hydraulics that don't. I hope I don't have to pay for a brake job right off the bat. You know something, Fran?"

"What?"

"I've got almost five hundred bucks saved now. Enough for my whole first year's tuition and books."

"How the hell did you do that and get this car on the road too?"

"It wasn't easy. And since I got the car I haven't saved much. Just to insure this car it costs more than the car's worth."

"Did you buy property damage?"

"Sure. With these lousy brakes I need it."

"Guess what?"

"What?"

"I'm thinking of getting a car myself. There's a guy my father knows that's got a nice thirty-seven Plymouth four-door and he's thinking of trading it. I might be able to get it for two bills." Two bills were two hundred dollars in local language.

"Hey, then we could ride in style. It'll be sort of hard jamming the four of us in this coupe. And with a four-door we'd have room for picking up babes, right? Speaking of babes, have you been over to see your new steady after work lately?"

"Yup. Can't ya see the way my ass is draggin'?"

"What if you get her pregnant?"

"I'm not gonna get her pregnant."

"You're sure of that, huh?"

"Sure enough."

"Mm-hmm." Fran and I had very different philosophies about our sexual behavior, so I decided not to waste my time pushing my ideas about waiting until marriage.

We were both quiet as we drove along High Street toward Dedham Square. When we passed the Boston Envelope Company at the bottom of the long hill near the Mill Pond, I pointed out the window, saluted, and shouted, "Three cheers for Bee-Co, the world's greatest employer."

"I'm surprised you haven't gotten some ass from one of the broads in there," said Fran. "Lots of 'em put out, don't they?"

"A lot of 'em do, I guess." I avoided a direct comment about my own activity and observed, "There's one who bends over so far I can see her big knockers every time I walk by her folding machine. You should hear the dirty jokes she cracks."

"We've got some women like that where I work too. The jokes babes tell each other can get pretty goddam raunchy."

"They know more than how to run a machine, right?"

"Right, they know how to tease guys. Do you know something? There's one thing that gets on my ass more than anything else in the whole world."

"What?"

"A girl that won't fuck."

I slammed down hard on the slowly reacting brakes of the old Plymouth, pulled the car to the side of the road near Saint Mary's, and then I fell on the steering wheel laughing at Fran's sexual candor. "Hah, that's what I call knowing your own mind."

Wiping the tears of laughter from my eyes, I started off again in first speed. Then, after shifting into second gear when we passed Saint Mary's, I made the Sign of the Cross automatically, as I had been doing since early childhood each time I had passed a Catholic Church.

"For Christ's sake, do you still go around blessing yourself?"

"Why the hell shouldn't I? Is it a political crime or something, Fran?"

"I think it's a lot of horseshit."

"Believe what you want to; it's a free country. But if you think Church is a lot of horseshit how come you still go to Mass on Sunday?"

"I don't go every Sunday, just when I damn well feel like it."

I shrugged. "Well, I always say let a guy do what he wants, as long as he doesn't screw anyone else up while he's doing it. Hell, I don't care if you lay every babe in Boston or if you become an atheist. Just don't expect me to do the same thing. I've got a mind of my own."

"That's for damn sure," said Fran as we passed through Dedham Square, drove around the traffic dummy, and headed back toward East Dedham. "But I don't get it how you can stay cherry. Nowadays if I don't tear off a piece once a week I think I'm gonna crack up. How the hell do you stand it?"

"Sometimes I wonder how long I can hold out. But I think if I want the girl I marry to be a virgin, what's fair for her is fair for me."

"When it comes to sex, pal, there's no such thing as fair."

"I'm not on your wave length."

"No shit."

"You said it, no shit."

We drove along in silence for a while, and after we had passed by the Boston Envelope Company again on our way back toward

East Dedham Square, I remembered a letter I had gotten from a former Norwood pal who was in the Air Force and stationed in Virginia. "My old neighbor Bob Haddad thinks he might be going to Japan near where his twin brother Ron is. He thinks plenty of guys are gonna be fighting in Korea pretty soon."

"Not me. Do you think I'm gonna get drafted into the infantry and have my ass shot off? When things start getting hot I'm gonna join the Navy. I'd sooner put in my four years and stay alive than get drafted for two and end up with my ass blown off in a goddam foxhole. In the Navy if a ship gets sunk at least you get a second chance when you hit the water. They can take the Army and stick it."

"Well, I guess I won't have to work up a sweat about the service. I'll be getting a deferment when I start Boston College next fall. You're prob'ly right about the Navy, Fran. My old Norwood pal John joined and he eats it right up. He's on the West Coast now making time with a babe in Frisco. The babe has a convertible and John wrote me he's almost as nuts about the car as he is about her. Just like you, after John got his first piece it went to his head like a fever."

"That's how it is. You'll see."

"Yup." I chose silence again, instead of speculating about my sexual future.

When we slowed down near Johnny's house, the old Plymouth started bucking, and Fran said, "These old shit boxes can't go very slow in high speed. You prob'ly need to hit the clutch."

I gave it the clutch and some more gas and the bucking stopped. "Well, it's good trans anyhow, Fran. Hah. I was over to Leo Lore's garage, and he asked if I'm collecting antique cars. He said if I need parts, he's gonna have to make them. He's looking for a voltage regulator for me now. This one's on the way out."

"Well, you got the car for nothing! Beggars can't be choosers."

"What an original expression, Fran. What about not looking a gift horse in the mouth? That's another original. Come to think of it, who'd want to look into a horse's mouth except another horse?" I stopped in front of Johnny's house, kept the motor running so it wouldn't stall, and sounded the horn. "How's that for a horn?"

"Real horny." He smiled.

"Yuh, Fran."

As Johnny pushed into the front seat, next to Fran, he asked, "What's the big joke?"

"That's what she said," replied Fran, "when the bed broke and the spring went up her ass."

"You guys never stop," said Johnny. "You'd think you'd have that dirty talk out of your systems by now."

"There's no hope for us," I said as I crunched the shift lever from neutral into first speed.

Commenting on my shifting, Johnny said, "Grind me another pound. Extra lean."

I said, "Never look a gift horse in the mouth, Johnny, unless you really like horses' mouths."

Fran said, "Don't ever bite a barking dog either, and don't throw glass if you live in a stone house."

"Especially if you're half stoned," I added.

As the Plymouth started bucking, I said, "Too slow in high speed, I guess."

Fran laughed. "Keep it bucking. I'm horny." He put his hand on Johnny's knee.

"Let me out of here!" yelled Johnny, only half in jest. "I mean it!"

"Don't worry," I said. "He's not after your ass, he's got something steady going now."

"You guys . . ." Johnny shook his head. "I wonder about you sometimes. How come you've got hot pants all the time, huh?"

"Don't ass me," I replied.

"Don't ass me either," added Fran, "but I think we're the normal ones. Speaking of hot pants, you won't believe what I saw today on the way home."

"What did ya see?" I asked. "Johnny getting laid?"

"Aw, come on," pleaded Johnny. "What is this? Another Dirty Hour?"

"You said it," replied Fran. "Let me tell ya what I saw. I was going by the Mill Pond and there on the banking I saw old Stow, crocked to the gills and . . . oh . . . ha—ha—ha—I can't believe it but I saw Stow . . . ooh . . . hah . . . hah . . ."

"Come on, Fran, spit it out!" At this point, Fran's infectious laugh caught hold of all of us and even though we didn't know what he would say next we had a group laughing fit.

Finally he blurted, "Old Stow, he was standing there . . . ah-hah-ha . . . oh . . . ho . . . ho . . . he was standing on the bank of the Mill Pond . . . ." Fran threw his head against his knees and his curly hair fell down onto his forehead as his laughter tore him apart.

"Spit it out!" I pleaded. "Come on."

Johnny looked out the window on the right side. "Maybe you ought to let me out so I can vomit."

"Stow was standing on the banking playing with his horse cock. God!" He folded up laughing again. And as I formed a mental picture of drunken Stow masturbating publicly on the bank of the Mill Stream I joined Fran in uncontrollable laughter.

"Hey, the car's gonna go off the road," warned Johnny, who was also laughing, in spite of himself.

"I'll pull over to the side . . ." I wheezed out the words through gusts of laughter. "You're shittin' us!"

"Nope." Fran crossed his heart. "Cross my heart and hope to get horny."

The laughter continued in random spurts until we reached Mike's house near the cemetery. We were still laughing as Mike squeezed into the single seat of the Plymouth business coupe, half on Fran's lap and half on Johnny's. He said, "I see the Dirty Hour's already started, you guys. Hey, this is a great car, Tommy."

"Get your hand off my leg," yelled Fran.

"That's no hand," said Mike, "that's my dick."

"Aw, come on," pleaded Johnny. "Jeez."

I said to Mike, "Wait till you hear what Fran saw on his way home from work."

Fran became convulsed in laughter again as he tried to tell his story, and I was no help. But finally Fran was able to tell the story for Mike's benefit, and when the new round of laughter had subsided Mike said, "I wish I could have seen it. I would have written a paper on it for my biology class and called it 'A Study in Public Masturbation.'"

We all dissolved in laughter as I maneuvered the old coupe into the center of town. Then I pulled over to the curb near a dilapidated building just outside of Dedham Square. "Speaking of public masturbation," I said as I shifted into neutral and kept the motor running fast in order to charge the low battery, "did I ever tell you guys about LaPierre up at Norfolk Golf Course and his great masturbation demonstration?"

"Come on," said Johnny, "isn't one masturbation story enough?"

"Hell, Johnny," said Mike, "the Dirty Hour's just begun. Come on, Tommy, tell us."

"Okay. You all know where Norfolk Golf Course is, right? I used to caddy there all the time when I lived in Norwood. At Norfolk they used to shout their own club cheer: 'We don't drink . . . we don't smoke . . . Norfolk . . .'"

As I recalled the caddie shack episode, Mike and Fran exploded with laughter, and Johnny overcame his own restraint and joined us in our chaos.

"And you mean . . ." Mike gulped as his chest heaved, "if LaPierre lost the bet and didn't come off in front of all you guys he was gonna have to actually kiss the other guy's ass?"

"Yup."

"You're really not . . . hah-hah . . . not shittin' us?" Fran's face was turning purple from laughing so hard.

"Nope." I laughed. "You know I wouldn't shit on you. I might drop some excrement on you though."

Mike interjected, "Or maybe some feces! But I don't like shitting on a friend. Piss on him maybe, but not shit. Hey, that's what friends are for!"

There were tears in my eyes by the time we all stopped laughing. "I laughed so hard I cried."

Mike said, "I laughed so hard I shit my pants!"

Johnny shouted, "Get off my lap then!"

"I'm only shitting on you!"

"That's what I'm afraid of."

Another roar of laughter filled the car, and when it had died down I noticed it was getting dark and I asked, "Now that we have this limousine, and the lights are working so far, where are we gonna go?"

Mike said, "We can go to see Fran's girl. Share the wealth, okay?"

Fran wasted no time saying, "Nothing doing. How about Roslindale? There's some wild babes there."

"I don't know how this car would be in that traffic on Washington street," I said.

"How about Norwood?" said Johnny. "We could go to the Sport Center."

"Sure," said Mike, "We're all sports! We can watch the babes bowl."

For about five minutes we debated the merits of going to Norwood, and finally, when it was obvious that no agreement would be reached, I said, "What the hell, this bus is going to Norwood. Are there any objections? Speak now or forever hold your ass."

"You're the driver," said Johnny.

"It's your covered wagon," said Mike.

"Let's roll," said Fran. "There's no sense just sitting here."

Soon we were moving along Washington Street toward Norwood, in high speed, and once again the old Plymouth was bucking. Mike shouted, "More! Keep it bucking, Tommy! I'm getting all excited!"

Johnny shouted, "Not while you're still sitting on my lap, you're not!"

"Just be glad you're not sitting on mine, Johnny!" shouted Mike.

Fran laughed. "Mike found it very hard getting up this morning."

"Yuh, he's getting old," I said. "That's why."

Mike said, "Right, guys, it's harder and harder getting up every day. Ay-yuh, ain't as young as I used to be. Ay-yuh."

I said, "Just a couple of visits to Maine and Mike already sounds like a native."

"Ay-yuh," replied Mike, who then went into a series of imitations of Maine Yankees.

Then it was back to the Dirty Hour, where one off-color remark followed another in almost endless succession. Mike would invent far-fetched stories. Fran would tell vividly detailed tales of his sexual escapades. And I would join in, up to a point. As for Johnny, he would just shake his head and look at us as if we came from another planet.

As we neared Norwood, the old Plymouth coupe continued to rock with laughter as our very off-color minds conjured up a can-you-top-this sequence of blue language that eventually motivated Johnny to say, "Why don't you guys lay off for a while, huh?"

"Right, Johnny," I said. "I guess we're not exactly setting a good example for a growing boy like you."

"Speaking of setting a good example, how's about getting some booze?" suggested Mike. "I hope you didn't shave, Johnny."

The legal drinking age was twenty-one, and none of us qualified, so the one with the darkest beard would be the courier. That was Johnny, who said, "I didn't have time to shave before you guys picked me up. But it isn't fair for me to buy you guys the booze. I don't even drink, and I could end up in the clink . . ."

Mike laughed. "That's what friends are for!"

"Brother, you guys . . ."

"Come on, Johnny, get us some beer," said Fran. "You don't have to chip in for it. Look at it this way, it costs you nothing and think of all the fun you'll have watching us make assholes out of ourselves."

"Well . . ."

"Aw, come on, Johnny!" we shouted together.

"Okay," he said reluctantly. "Give me the money."

Soon we were sitting at New Pond in the nearly empty parking area where lovers met, and the three of us consumed two quarts of beer while Johnny was looking on. This time I managed to avoid getting sick to my stomach from drinking too much too fast, but I got very dizzy. The next stop was the Sport Center snack bar, where we found a booth in a corner near the juke box, and ordered coffee.

"I'll have a whole wheat on rye with water on the side," said Mike to the fat waitress.

"What did ya say?"

"I want a little on the side." Mike laughed at his own innuendo. Like the rest of us, he lived in an off-color world where just about every statement had a sexual meaning.

"You tryin' to be a wise ass? You want me to report yez to the manager?"

"All I said was I wanted whole wheat on rye with a little water on the side," replied Mike.

"Ain't no such of a thing." The fat waitress shook her head.

"Never mind then. Just give me the coffee."

"I'll have coffee-half." I said. "Half coffee and half booze."

The fat waitress glared at me. "You tryin' to be a wise ass too?"

I blushed, "Nope, I'm trying to order coffee."

"How's about a reg'lar coffee?" asked Fran. "With a shot in it."

"Youse wise asses better watch out," said the fat waitress. "I kin have yez kicked out o' here, ya know. You ain't been drinkin', have yez? You could get run in for that. Anybody could see yez are minors."

"They don't have to drink to act that way," said Johnny. "They always act screwy. Can I have a reg'lar coffee, too?"

"Yeah," replied the waitress. "I'll get yez all your coffees." She headed toward the kitchen. Then Mike got up, shadowed her, and mimicked her waddling walk. When we all laughed, the waitress turned and then Mike spun toward the jukebox. "Let me see now. Freddie Hall. 'Talk about your Beau Brummel . . . talk about your city swells . . .' Yup. Assa one I want to play." The waitress moved on, shaking her head.

"What did you play?" I asked when Mike came back to the booth.

"Beau Brummel." Mike grinned. "I'm gonna play it five times."

"You're a nut," said Johnny.

". . . talk about your city swells," blared the jukebox. "We've got one right in our town. I mean Elmer Hashway Brown . . ." Mike joined Freddie Hall in song and soon we were all singing along with the jukebox. ". . . he's got a funny little pinch backed suit, a bamboo cane . . . takes an um-ba-rella when he thinks it's gonna shower . . ." Mike leaped up and went into a mock soft-shoe across the dirty asphalt tiled floor of the snack bar, pretending he had a cane in one hand and a straw hat in the other.

"You show 'em, Mike," I yelled.

"Strut your stuff," yelled Fran.

Johnny warned us, "You guys are gonna get us thrown out o' here."

The record was playing for the fifth time when the fat waitress came for our money. "Did youse guys play that there record all those times?"

"Of coursh not," said Mike, exaggerating the beer's effect. "I'd never do a shing like that."

"Ah . . ." The waitress grunted and raised her hand to Mike.

Mike did a pseudo-flinch. "Aw, come on now. You wouldn't hit a little kid, would ya?"

"Knock it off, Mike," warned Johnny.

The waitress scowled. "Yez all better knock it off or I'll get a hold o' the goddam cops."

"Aw, hey." Mike shrugged his broad shoulders. "What's wrong with playin' a little record? It'sh good clean fun, right?"

The waitress collected our coins, glared at all of us and said, "No sense talkin' to yez. You're crazy as hell, all of yez."

"Let's go, Mike." I said. "I think you're pressing your luck."

Mike reluctantly complied and we all single-filed from the snack bar and went up the narrow stairs to the bowling alleys.

It felt very hot upstairs, and the combination of heat and beer brought a glow to my cheeks. Then I said to myself, Uh-oh . . . there are the girls we were talking to a couple of weeks ago. Kay what's-her-name and her friends. Hey, I like that new girl with them tonight. Nice smile. Beautiful reddish hair. What a nice looking girl. But if we start talking to them now they'll know we've been drinking. "Hey, Whatayasay, you guys, let's take off out o' here."

"We just got here. What's the rush?"

"It's roasting in here." I loosened my shirt collar, but my pals paid no attention to me. There was no escape.

"Hey, look who's over there." Fran nudged me with his elbow.

"Who?" I feigned ignorance.

"It's those babes we were talking to last time we came here on the bus. Look at the new one with 'em tonight. Is she built!"

I looked and agreed that in addition to her pretty smiling face and long reddish hair, she was indeed "built." I said, "Oh yuh. Mm."

For a while we watched the girls bowl, and paid special attention to certain movements which were part of the bowling technique. Then, when the girls finished their bowling and were about to leave, Mike yelled, "Hey, girls, what's new?"

"Oh hi, Mike," said Kay, the tall heavy one with the sandy blonde hair. "Hello, Tommy." She knew me from my years with Mrs. White when I lived just a few streets away from her house.

"Hi, Kay."

"I guess you boys have already met Janie and Nancy. This is our friend Mary Killoren. She goes to Regis College."

Kay Lamminen introduced Mary to me. "This is Tommy O'Connell, Mary. He used to live here in Norwood with Mrs. White."

"Nice to know you. I used to see you when you visited the Monahans. They're my neighbors." As Mary smiled at me I felt myself melting inside.

"Nice to know you too." I shoved my hand out and clumsily shook hers while trying to aim my beer breath in another direction.

Kay introduced Mary around, and for a while our group of four boys and four girls stood in the lobby of the Sport Center, talking about Norwood and Dedham, bowling and high school. And as the time passed, the effect of the beer lessened.

The girls were talking about Norwood High and animatedly relating inside stories, when I said to Mary, "Hey, I thought Kay said you went to Regis."

She laughed. "Kay always says things like that. We're all seniors at Norwood High."

"Well, you could have fooled me. So you're not a college girl, after all, huh? What are you gonna do when you graduate from N.H.S.?" I found myself talking only to Mary.

"Work, I guess. I'd like to go to college but my folks can't afford it."

"I'm going to B.C. in the fall," I said proudly. My head was clearer now, and I was not blushing as much. "I've always wanted to go there. I've been working in a factory this year to save up my tuition."

She smiled. "You must really want to go."

"Yuh, I do," I said. Then we talked and joked together for a while, and after the girls said goodnight we piled into the old Plymouth coupe and headed toward Dedham.

On the way, Fran said, "I bet you those babes put out."

I defended them. "You're so horny you think every babe puts out."

"I hate girls that don't." He laughed.

"To each his own," I said. "Who wants a girl that's just an apprentice whore anyhow?"

"I do!" shouted Fran, laughing again.

"Aw, come on, you guys," said Johnny. "Don't start another Dirty Hour."

Mike defended us. "They're just having a sexual difference of opinion, Johnny. Speaking of sex, I had this dream last night that I was taking a leak out my bedroom window and all of a sudden I got all excited and then the window fell on my pecker. And you know what? When I got up this morning my pecker was sore as hell . . . and all bruised. I'll have to keep it in a sling till it feels better. I think it got fractured."

The air in the small Plymouth reverberated with laughter as we neared Dedham. Then, one by one, I deposited my pals at their houses, and when I pulled away from Johnny's I had no passengers left. As I maneuvered the faded old gray Plymouth through East Dedham Square, I thought of the girl with the pretty smile and the long auburn hair.

I think she likes me. I really like her. That's the kind of nice girl I want to marry some day. Great personality. Brains. Soft voice. Very friendly. Nice. Mary Killoren. I like that name.

"Yours is my heart alone," I began to sing softly, "and without you, life holds no charm. Yours every thought I own . . . our love the theme of every dream. All that makes life seem worthwhile . . . dwells in your eyes, and the spell of your smile . . ." As I vocalized in the old Crosby style, I thought of Mary and her sweet voice and her friendly smile, and I ended my love song as I turned into Walnut Place. ". . . half so sweet to me as your voice whispering I love you, dear."

After getting out of the Plymouth I slammed the door hard so it would close all the way, and as I walked toward Granny O'Connell's house I thought, Some day when I don't have to scrounge for tuition dough, maybe I'll ask her out and we'll go dancing or to a show or something. Funny. I've got dough saved up but I'm still hard up. There's always something the dough has to be spent on, like clothes or car insurance or tuition. Ah, what the hell, I've never had much dough. I ought to be used to it by now. But it'd be good to have a little extra.

34

I was walking toward the employee parking lot on the other side of High Street, across from the Boston Envelope Company. In my left hand I held a paper bag filled with envelopes, and with my right hand I was flipping my car keys high in the air and catching them. I was dressed in my faded blue denim dungarees and a light blue shirt with sleeves rolled up to my bony elbows.

When I reached the near-antique 1934 Plymouth that I had painted light blue with a quart of enamel and a brush, I looked at the car with pride. Then I slid behind the wheel and threw the bag of envelopes on the seat and thought, These cars get so hot during the day. It's only June but it's like an oven. Let's hope it starts. Good. What a relief. Leo Lore sure knows how to fix cars. He's got the starter working now, and the lights don't keep going off anymore when I'm driving along at night.

As I pulled out of the parking lot, I passed some tight-dungareed factory girls, waved at them, and whispered, "Will ya look at that hip action." Soon I took my right turn into High Street, but I had only driven a few yards in the direction of East Dedham Square when the car hit a pothole and the bag of envelopes began to slide off the seat.

Just as I leaned over to try and stop them, the car swerved and almost hit a utility pole, and I muttered, "Shit, I better let the damn things fall." I returned my right hand back to its position on the steering wheel as the envelopes fell to the floor. "That's the way it goes when I do something that's not exactly ethical. It never works out for me. I shouldn't have walked off with those envelopes. Everybody else brings them home but when I do it I get bad luck."

The old Plymouth hit another pothole near East Dedham Square, and the front end vibrated for a moment. Then I eased off on the gas pedal and the vibration stopped. As I rolled along with the coupe's windows wide open and the flat glass windshield cranked open about three inches at the bottom, I began to sing softy, "Summertime and the livin' is easy . . . Fish are jumpin' and the cotton is high . . . Your daddy's rich and your ma is good lookin' . . ."

I stopped singing and thought, Nope, I'm not too crazy about that one. "When I Fall in Love" is my favorite song now. I like the way Nat King Cole sings it. "When I fall in love it will be forever . . . or I'll never fall in love. In a restless world like this is, love is ended before it's begun . . . and too many moonlight kisses . . . seem to fade in the warmth of the sun . . ."

Passing through the Square, I self-consciously stopped singing. Then, as I was climbing the Walnut Street hill in second speed, I continued, "When I give my heart it will be completely . . . or I'll never give my heart . . . And the moment I can feel that you feel that way too . . . is when I'll fall in love with you." As I sang I had the Crosby warble, and in my mind I saw myself making records and having them played all over the world.

Turning into Walnut Place and coasting down the slight grade toward Granny's duplex, I repeated the song's last words: "And the moment I can feel that . . . you feel that way too . . . is when . . ." I stopped singing in mid-phrase as I pulled up to Granny's place, where I saw my father's car parked out front.

Inside, as I passed through the small dining room I saw my father stretched out, apparently asleep, on my grandmother's Army surplus cot. I decided to say nothing, and stepped down the single step leading to the kitchen.

"Is it you, Tommy?" asked Granny, rocking in her rocker and fingering her black Rosary beads.

"Yup, it's me."

"Sure I was just praying for peace to come to the worruld some day. 'Tis no good, all the fighting. Go get yereself a cup of tea. Forage for yereself. There's some potatoes boiling and yere father brought some hamburg. He's come down from New Hampshire or wherever it is."

"Maine, Granny."

While I fixed my tea, her commentary on world affairs continued. ". . . and now they're talking about fighting it out in Korea. Sure and I don't even know where it is. Somewhere near China, I think. There's no letup. 'Tis too bad."

"That's life, Granny."

"Sure, ye'd think the men would have their fill of the fighting. But yere grandfather never did. He was always ready to light into me. Devil a one he has to light into now over there in the old house."

"Yup." I sat down at the table. "All he does now is listen to ball games on that old radio and chew tobacco and pinch snuff and smoke his pipe."

"Don't let him fool ye," she said. "Ye'd never find Daniel O'Connell without his bottle handy."

"He never drinks in front of me."

"Ye aren't out the door when he puts it to his lips; don't ye think I know him? Sure I put up with all those years of his traipsing and gallivanting and boozing it up."

"Mm-hmm." I sipped my tea. Then I heard my father sighing and stretching, and a moment later he was in the kitchen, putting his hand on my shoulder. "Hi, Tommy."

"Hi." My whole body stiffened at his touch, and after all the years of habitual omission, I was still unable to say the word "Dad." The distrust was very deep.

"I had a few errands to do down this way, so I drove down from Maine this morning. How's the car running?"

"Pretty good. I had some trouble with the lights and the voltage regulator and the starter, but Leo Lore got it working for me."

My father's light blue eyes fixed on me. "Leo has a knack for diagnosing. He's like a good doctor." He paused. "Has it been a little easier for you to get around since we fixed you up with Russell Berg's old Plymouth?"

"Sure."

"How's the job?" He smoothed down the graying hair that he combed from left to right across his head to cover the bald spot.

"Not bad. They've got me in the shipping room now. It pays a little more than the floor boy job did, but nobody who works at the Boston Envelope Company gets rich."

"No, I suppose not."

Granny rocked back and forth in her rocker and went into a monologue about the state of the world, and on the local level she attacked Aunt Rita's habit of throwing too much food into her garbage pail. Then she went on to explore a variety of subjects, and it did not seem to offend her that her intended audience was not listening.

"Would you want to come to Maine again this summer?" my father asked.

"I think I'll be working at the Envelope right up to September."

"I see. Well, maybe you could come for a few days vacation." He got up and made a cup of tea for himself and asked Granny, "Mother, where's that hamburg I brought?"

"Sure and it's in the icebox. Ye can forage for yereself."

I smiled, knowing from past experience that the refrigerator, which the old woman insisted on calling an icebox, would not be plugged in.

A moment later, my father, seeing no light on when he opened the refrigerator door, scolded her. "Mother, how many times do I have to tell you that if you don't keep the refrigerator's electricity on everything will go bad?"

I laughed. "She doesn't believe in electricity."

Then Granny responded, "Keep it on? So's I can give all my money to the Edison? 'Tis easy for you to say. Ye don't have to pay all of my bills." My father remained silent.

I said, "Granny's got a mind of her own."

My father nodded. "There's no changing her, I guess. She lives in her own world."

"Yup," I said, and at the same time I thought, So do you, Fred O'Connell.

As the train from Boston rumbled into the East Dedham Station, my father said, "It certainly makes the whole house shake, doesn't it?"

"I hardly ever notice it. I suppose if there was an earthquake at the same time every day I'd get used to that too."

Granny's booming voice filled the whole kitchen. ". . . and Fulton Lewis Junior was saying we'd soon be sending American boys to fight over there." Granny was recalling the news of the previous evening about Korea. "He said we'd be conscripting lots of them." Neither of us answered her.

My father fried some fatty hamburgers and put two on my dish and two on his own. Then he put several unpeeled boiled potatoes on my plate and two small ones on his own. And at this point the old woman rose and shuffled to the table, squinting at our meal through her round steel-rimmed glasses "'Tis good ye can fill up on the potatoes and the hamburg. All I need is my cup o' tea and my piece o' toast. It's enough to keep me going. But it's about time I got the call. I've been around too long."

She fixed herself a large cracked white cup of tea and returned to her rocking chair. In a loud voice she reflected, "In the old country we thought it was bad there and we couldn't get over here fast enough, but I wonder sometimes now if some of us might have been better off staying at home. Yet there was no worruk. Sure, it's a far cry from those days to the worruld of today. The brats o' today all speed around in their high-powered cars . . ."

I knew she included me in those "brats o' today" because from her viewpoint the ancient Plymouth fell into the classification of a "high-powered car."

After finishing my hamburger, which I doused with ketchup, I then separated the white portions of the potatoes from the black parts that weren't edible, and when supper was done I stood before the distorted mirror over the sink and combed the snarls out of my thick, curly brown hair.

After that, I gave my teeth a quick brushing with bicarbonate of soda mixed with salt, and while my father remained at the table reading The Boston Globe, I headed for the parlor where I planned to continue the John Marquand book I had borrowed from the Dedham Public Library.

I started where I had left off and had completed only a few pages when my father came in and sat at the table near the kerosene space heater. Deciding not to acknowledge his presence in the room, I continued reading. Then he cleared his throat and took a deep drag on his cigarette. "I suppose you have your first year's tuition saved by now."

Closing the book after dog-earing the page, I replied, "Yup, I do."

"I imagine you're anxious to get started at B.C." He blew a perfect smoke ring.

"Yup, I guess I am." I don't have to depend on you coming across with the dough either, I thought as I stretched my legs straight out and clasped my hands behind my head against the backrest of the chair.

"Too bad we couldn't get you started last year."

"Yuh." Too damn bad all right. You said it.

"It takes a while to get a motor court rolling. They say it usually takes five years. I wish we could have gotten you started at B.C. last fall, but I don't think it's done you any real harm to work. You'll look back some day and be glad you worked a year."

"Maybe so." But if I started B.C. last year like I planned I'd be going into my sophomore year now, like Mike.

"You always appreciate the things you have to work hard for," he said. Well, that means I'll always appreciate everything I ever get because nobody seems to be handing things to me on a platter. "Take the motor court. It's hard getting started, and it's not making money now, but when it starts to pay, I'm sure I'll appreciate it more."

"I'm sure you will." My tone was partly sarcastic.

"Business hasn't been so good up there, Tommy, and the overhead's heavy for us, but it beats working for someone else. The thing is, the cash situation is tight at the beginning of the season. So I wonder if you could loan me some of the money you've saved. I could use five hundred if you have it. I'll pay you back in the fall before your tuition is due."

I stared up at the ceiling and said nothing as I thought, How the hell do I turn my own father down? Dammit, he would come around looking for a loan right now. I've got four hundred and ninety two bucks saved, and that's enough for my first year's tuition and books and a little left over. I'd be crazy to let him get his hands on all of it. Maybe I'll let him borrow three hundred. Then I'll have enough left for my first quarter's tuition, my books, and the sport coat I'm getting at Maurice's Men's Store. Yup, that's what I'll do.

"What do you think, Tommy?"

"Well, I guess you can borrow three hundred."

"Fine." My father smiled broadly. "That'll be a big help right now. I think I can get another couple of hundred from your grandmother. I'll make it up to you, Tommy. Don't worry, you'll get your money back Labor Day. And someday I want to turn my share of the motor court over to you. I'm not just up there in Maine for myself, you know."

"Mm." Hah. So you're gonna cut me in, huh? But the whole place is in Hazel's name, you hot shit, so how are you gonna give me a share of something you don't even own?

"Some day it'll be a going business and you'll benefit from it." His light blue eyes focused on me in a dreamy way, as if he were gazing beyond me at some distant horizon.

Oh boy, here he goes into his big philanthropist act. Next thing he'll be giving me a snow job about how crazy he is about me and he'll ramble on about my mother and the years of tragedy. Uh-oh, that reminds me. I guess I better tell him about that guy that came looking for him. "There was a guy here from the State, looking for you."

"Did he say what he wanted?" My father was getting very tense.

"He didn't exactly say. He just asked a lot of questions, like where were you living now and stuff. So I told him exactly what you told me to say if anyone came snooping around. I said I didn't know where you were. Then the guy looked at me sort of funny and said it seemed kind of strange I wouldn't know where my own father was." I chuckled. "I just told him a lot of things in life seem kind of strange. Then he wrote something down on his pad and took off."

"It was just a matter of time before the State came out and investigated. The State isn't quite as generous as you'd think."

"What do you mean?"

"Well, in a case like your mother's, with her in the State hospital all these years, you'd think there'd be no question about the State paying the bills, but if they think you can pay anything, they chase you. So that's why I have to put everything we own up there in Hazel's name and nothing in mine. That way, the State can't come after it. As for me, I have no assets, so they can't get blood out of a stone."

"Especially if the stone's in Maine, huh?" God, what an escape artist. No wonder he took off up there instead of going down to Plymouth or Cape Cod. When Freddy takes off, he crosses the border.

"They won't let you forget." He gazed out the parlor window. "In Maine I'm able to forget for long periods of time, but then one day when you least expect it you get a reminder and it all comes back. I can remember it like it was yesterday. The day they told me your mother's condition was incurable."

There had once been a time when his memories fascinated me, and each detail seemed precious, but for years there had been no new information. So I wondered how long the current lecture would last. From time to time, I was chosen to be his captive audience. And this was one of those times.

For approximately an hour I listened as he gazed out the window and recalled my mother's affliction with mental illness. ". . . and I don't suppose there was much I could have done, but I feel guilty when I think of how it began. All the guilt in the world won't change anything now though. It happened a long time ago . . . so long ago."

The early evening shadows cast hazy reflections from Walnut Place into his light blue eyes as he seemed to be nearing the close of his discourse, and I said "Yup" while thinking, She's still alive in that State mental hospital, for God's sake. You haven't seen her since I was a little kid and you'd think . . .

As if he had been reading my mind, he said, "We have to live our own lives, Tommy. We have to go on as best we can." The twilight filtered through the dusty windows and accented my father's bony face.

"Yup, I guess we do." I got out of my chair. "Well, I have to take off now. I told the guys I'd pick them up. We're gonna bowl a few strings up in Norwood. Are you staying here tonight?" He nodded. "I'll go to the bank tomorrow noon during my lunch break and I'll get the three hundred." I edged my way into the tiny front hallway. "See ya later."

"Okay, Tommy."

As I drove up Walnut Place toward Walnut Street in the old blue hand-painted Plymouth, I reflected on how frequently he had gotten into the subject of my mother lately.

Shit, when I was small and worrying my ass off about it all the time he never said a word. It was the secret of the 20th Century. Now when I don't even want to hear about it, he's ready to rattle on and on. What a character he is.

35

It was a quiet Monday night in August, and I had nothing else to do, so I went to Humpty's pool room in East Dedham Square, in its far from prestigious location above the First National Store.

"Like where's all your buddies, man?" Joe Walsh dropped the eight ball into the corner pocket.

"They're bushed from the weekend." I fished a quarter from my pocket to pay for the game I had lost to Joe. "None of them felt like coming out tonight. I didn't feel much like it myself, but it was hot as hell in my room and I figured I had enough rest. I didn't exactly work my little ass off today at the factory."

"Where'd you guys go this weekend? Hampton again?" Joe put his cue into the wall rack.

"Yuh, I'll say we did. We started with the beer the minute we hit there and didn't stop till we left. We almost got arrested for drinking on the beach. The Hampton Beach cops like to fill up their clink every weekend. Hampton's dry, you know. You go to Salisbury for booze and sneak it back to Hampton."

"What about quail, man? Did ya get any?"

"Well, we horsed around with some girls from Regis College, but it was strictly platonic."

"No tail?"

"No tail, Joe."

"Like it's all young stuff at Hampton, right?"

"Right." We headed for the exit from Humpty's blighted poolroom.

"Take it easy," I called out to the proprietor over my shoulder. We didn't call him Humpty to his face, and none of us knew his real name.

The old man was racking the balls at the table we had just left. He grunted and a droplet of moisture dripped from his stuffed-up nose onto one of the balls. "He really knows how to communicate," I said to Joe as I followed him down the long flight of wide, squeaky stairs leading to the street below.

"Hampton's full o' jail bait, right?" Joe held fast to the previous subject.

"Yuh, they're sort of young for you, but not for me. Hell, I'm only eighteen. Are you twenty-one?"

"Twenty-two." Joe straightened his bright red tie and tossed his head with the confidence of advanced maturity.

"Hey, you're an old man; I'm just a growing boy."

"Like you're old enough to want some fresh quail, man, right? Some fur."

"Some what?"

"Some pussy."

"I think I understand you now, Joe. Where do you get that language you speak?"

"New York, man. The metropolis. I made three different babes down there last weekend. Now I'm just about petered out."

"I think you're shitting me."

"Why would I shit ya? What's the percentage? Hey, you got treads, man?"

"You mean tires?"

"Like four wheels, man!"

"I'm parked over in front of the newsstand."

"Want some hair of the dog?"

"Hell, I'm just getting over my hangover now."

"Like that's when ya need it, man."

"Not me, Joe. I know when I've had enough."

"Like let's go to my place," he said. "My sister's out for the night, so we'll have the place to ourselves and there's beer in the freeze box, man. Like break down and relax, Tommy. Like live, man."

"Well . . ."

"Like I won't take no for an answer. Let's get in your chariot and rotate, man."

"Ah, what the hell." Yuh, I thought, what the hell's the difference anyhow? There's nothing else to do around here.

A few minutes later we were in the tiny second floor apartment in the two-story row house across from the Mill Pond, where Joe roomed with his sister in between Boston-to-New York train trips.

"This place was built for midgets." I ducked my head as I entered the living room. "God, it's hot in here." The place was sweltering from the extremely humid August heat.

Joe went right to the pantry, and I could hear the refrigerator opening and closing, followed by beer bottle caps popping. As he handed me a large mug of beer he said, "Like this'll fix what ails you, man."

"What ales me? Is that a pun, son?" I sucked the foam off the top. "Not bad." I wiped a layer of sweat from my forehead with my handkerchief.

After about half an hour, he asked, "Like you been gettin' much quail lately?"

"No problem for me, Joe." I was not apt to share such data, or lack of same, with anyone, least of all a casual acquaintance like Joe, who as far as I was concerned inhabited a world of values that was very remote from the one I lived in.

Joe whipped out his comb and started running it through his thick black Vaselined hair. "Like you're all set, huh? You're not hot to trot?"

"Right, Joe, all set." I knew that a discussion of my own philosophy of sexuality would be completely wasted on him.

"I need some scuzz, man." He was muttering as he refilled the beer mugs. "Need it bad, man." While he poured the beer, he told me more about his sexual conquests in New York City.

I cautiously kept to myself my experiences over the weekend at Hampton with the cute shapely girl I had been paired with on a quadruple date. The hot passion of her moist kisses still lingered in my mind.

"Like I need quail, man," Joe persisted.

"Why don't you just take a vow of abstinence, Joe? Hah!"

"Like no meat on Friday's one thing, man, but no quail's somethin' else, and there's this shape that's hot for me over in West Roxbury, and she'd come over if I called her."

"Oh? I'm supposed to sit around playing tick-tack-toe with myself while you shack up?"

Joe was very persistent, and pleaded that if I were a real friend, the least I could do was a favor for someone in desperate need of sex. With two more beers under my belt, I finally agreed.

After a quick phone call, he shouted, "She's hot to trot, man. Like she's built like the Empire State, man, looks like a movie star, and she can never get enough of me. She's twenty-two, man. No jail bait. An easy make. What the hell."

"She's no big challenge, huh?" I chuckled as we headed for the old Plymouth.

"Like I don't need a challenge, man. I need sex."

As we were driving toward West Roxbury, the Plymouth swerved and Joe asked, "Like man, you okay to drive?"

"Like sure, man. Hah." The beer was hitting me now. "Whassa . . . whassa big deal about driving, huh?"

"Like nothin', man, so's you don't wrap a tree around us."

"No sweat, Joe."

"Hook a right down past the cemetery."

"Like right, Joe, I'll . . . like . . . hook a right, like right?" I was having fun imitating his use of the word "like."

As we drove along, I told him about how I had been stopped by the State Police on my way back from a dance at Marshfield down on the South Shore because my bald tires had screeched as I took a curve coming off the highway at the Dedham exit on Route 128. ". . . and I was only going about twenty-five. Just gave me a warning. Good thing he didn't smell my breath. Had a few down the beach."

"Like he probl'y figured this for a hot rod, man."

I laughed. "Could be." I had painted the engine silver in a burst of enthusiasm for having an old car that truly looked different. I had also taken the side panels off the engine compartment and painted the wheels yellow, providing a vivid attraction for the police. "But this crate won't go over forty without the front end shimmying all over the road."

"It's transportation, man, right?"

"Sort of." After the warning from the State Police, I had put the hood panels back on the car, and painted the wheels the same blue as the rest of the car. "Got enough problems without cop trouble too, Joe. Can't afford fines. Got enough challenge paying my tuition and keeping this car on the road."

By the time we reached West Roxbury and the white colonial house where Cora lived, I was almost seeing double. But my eyes were able to focus on Cora, who was dressed in a tight pink wool turtle neck sweater, with still tighter dungarees. She was all that Joe had said about her. She was shapely, had a face like a magazine cover girl, and was obviously eager to make herself available to him.

She situated herself in the middle of the only seat of the coupe, between the two of us, and she took an instant liking to me. "He's cute," she said to Joe. Then she turned to me as we pulled away from her neighborhood and she said, "You're really cute, do you know that?"

"No comment." I laughed. "I'm just a growing boy who's minding his own business and trying to stay out of trouble."

She laughed. "Do you think I'm trouble? You guys have been drinking, haven't you? God, it smells like a barroom in here. Is this car an antique?"

"Right," I said. "I think it's French Colonial."

She laughed again. "You've got a sense of humor, Tommy. But you didn't answer me when I asked if you thought I was trouble."

"One way I stay out of trouble is not answering questions like that."

I shifted the floor shift into high gear, and found my hand pressing against the inside of her thigh. She whispered, "I like that" and pressed her thigh even harder against my fist, which I then moved back to the steering wheel where it belonged. "Oh, you don't like?"

I kept my eyes on the road, but I could see her face turning toward me. "No comment, Cora."

As we went around a curve I felt the softness of her large breast pressing against my elbow, and her thigh pressing against mine, and then I felt her hand rubbing slowly and methodically along my leg, and I thought, Old Joe wasn't kidding when he said she's hot to trot. I thought she had a craving for just him though, not the whole world.

While we were getting settled at the apartment, I managed to find out that she had just graduated from Clark University in Worcester, where she had been named queen of just about every major festival held during her college years. I told her I was going to B.C. in the fall, and then she said, "You're only a freshman? Just a kid? Well, I still think you're cute." She started running her fingers through my curly hair. "I could go for you, Tommy."

I looked over at Joe. "I think I'd better take off out of here. I just remembered an appointment . . ."

Cora started laughing. "Know what, Joe? I think we've got a virgin on our hands. A real live honest-to-goodness virgin. I thought they were extinct."

"Like he's no way a virgin, shapeliest one. You don't stay in East Dedham as long as he's been here and still call yourself a virgin. This kid's been around . . . like a doughnut."

She laughed. "Well, maybe I'll give him a turn with my doughnut tonight. Booze, Joe, where's the booze?"

To create a little space between myself and Cora, I volunteered to get the beer, poured some for each of them, and sat myself in a kitchen chair off to one side. We drank and talked, and a little while later, Cora shouted, "Let's do it, Joe!" My face turned as red as a ripe apple.

Joe did not delay in taking her up on her offer, and as the two of them headed toward the living room, she turned and said, "Don't go anywhere, kid. I've got enough for two."

My face now turned to a color close to purple, and when I heard "Dancing in the Dark" on the record player and the sound of the sofa squeaking, I thought, she learned more than liberal arts out there at Clark U. She's a regular nympho. She doesn't give a good shit who she does it with, and how many she does it with in one night.

"More, Joe, more! Uh . . . uh! Do it! Do it! Yes!" I could hear her shouting and squealing.

"Easy, baby." It was Joe now. "Nice and easy. Like nice, baby. Nice."

"Faster, you bastard! Do it again and then get that cute kid in here."

I took a swig of beer and shook my head and thought, what the hell am I doing here? Is this how I want my first piece to be? Huh? Shit, if I ended up in there I'd prob'ly give her a lecture on why she should stop putting out, and start praying for her, and she'd get so pissed off at me she'd throw a conniption fit.

"I'm gonna get the hell out of here," I muttered as I got up and took one more swig of beer. "So I'm the last o' the East Dedham virgins, huh? Hah! I guess I'm gonna stay that way a bit longer . . ."

As I tiptoed down the narrow dark hallway, the sofa was still squeaking in the background, Cora was demanding more, and Joe was moaning. "Well, Joe," I muttered, "when she sends you to get the kid, there's gonna be no kid to get. She's all yours. No sloppy seconds for me tonight, pal."

As I went down the stairs, I tried to avoid bumping my head on the lower-than-average ceiling, and I recalled that Joe had the problem of getting the girl back to her home in West Roxbury, but there was no way I could picture staying on the scene.

"Your problem, Joe," I muttered as I went out the front door, and stumbled down the steps toward my car. "You got what you wanted, Joe, and I guess you're gonna have to pay the piper, as

Granny would say. Call a cab, Joe. Shit. Only a short ride. Won't cost much. Gotta go, old buddy."

As I drove through East Dedham Square a few moments later, I rolled up the window so my voice would entertain nobody but myself, and I began singing one of my favorite lone wolf songs loudly, "We three, we're all alone, living in a memory. My echo, my shadow, and me. We three, we're not a crowd, we're not even company. My echo, my shadow, and me . . ."

When I got out of the old Plymouth in front of Granny's duplex, I gave the malfunctioning car door a hard slam so it would close all the way, and then, with the effect of the beer still very strong in me, I groped my way up the front steps and into the house.

In order not to wake up the old woman, a light sleeper, I left the hall light off and slowly felt my way up the familiar stairs to the second level. I had the number of stairs memorized and didn't even need a light. Then, lying flat on my back with my eyes open, I thought in fragments about my evening with Joe Walsh and Cora. Pretty girl, I reflected. Shapely. Sexy. She liked me. But shit . . . a nympho. Nope. No point to having sex that way, like animals. Animals don't have a conscience . . . they just follow their instincts. So they've got more integrity.

That Cora knew I was a virgin, huh? How'd she know? Written all over my face? Maybe she knew about me the same way I knew she was no nun. Screwy world. I'm gonna wait, dammit. Seems like everybody I know does it except me . . . and Johnny. But maybe he's a eunuch. Or neuter gender. I've got all the drives. But I'm gonna wait. There'll be a nice sweet girl who thinks like me. A girl like Mary. A girl with standards.

It'll be worth waiting for. But how long? Makes no difference. Gotta wait. Can't call myself a Christian and act just like Joe. But it seems like my kind of thinking is really going out of style. Like I'm from the Dark Ages. Ah, who cares? What I believe is what I believe. It makes no difference if the whole world doesn't believe what I believe, long as I believe it. I've got my standards, take them or leave them. And if I leave them I feel shitty. Gotta stick with my standards. Only way I can live with myself. And if I can't live with myself, then what?

Hey, Joe's Joe and Cora's Cora and I'm Tommy, and there's nobody I have to impress but myself. Nobody to answer to but God. I prob'ly should have been more honest with Joe about what I think. With her, too. I was sort of playing along with them. But it'd be like lecturing a rummy about demon rum. What's the point? We all know what right and wrong is. No need for lectures. No need. Hmm. Drank too much tonight. I've got to lay off. Gets me oversexed. Gets me thinking about doing things I don't even want to do right now. No point to that shit.

Gonna wait, that's all. I just have to. Some day I'll marry a nice girl. Pretty. Nice personality. Nice smile. Intelligent. Definitely no nymphomaniac. So what's good for her should be good for me, too, isn't that right? Yup. Gonna wait. Worth it.

My eyelids became heavy as I thought, Gotta watch who I hang out with. I remember how Mrs. White yacked at us about keeping good company. "Ye're judged by the company ye keep, sure as the Lord made apples." Mm. Yup. She was right about that.

I breathed a deep sigh, and began to pray with my eyes closed: "Angel of God, my guardian dear, to whom His love commits me here, ever this day be at my side, to light and guide . . . or is it light and guard? Nope. Light and guide. Let's see now. Ever this day be at my side, to light and guide. Or is it guard? Nope. To light and guide, to rule and guard. Amen."

As sleep came to me, it was the spinning-down-and-around and disappearing-into-the-bowels-of-the-earth kind of sleep that goes with very heavy alcohol consumption, and I was repeating over and over in my mind, "Ever this day be at my side. Ever this day. Ever this . . ."

36

September 1950 had finally come, and it was the big day. It was my first day of classes at Boston College and I was up in my bedroom, almost finished getting ready. I thought, I better get moving. I don't want to be late for my first class. I should have left earlier just in case the old car conks out on me.

I brushed some dandruff from the shoulders of the light blue double-breasted suit I had bought a week before at Gilchrist's basement store in Boston. It had been the cheapest suit in my size and had cost $14.88. My blue cotton shirt was fresh from Jimmy Soo Hoo's Laundry, where I had been having my shirts done for twenty-five cents each. My lavender tie, a knit one, I had gotten on sale when I bought the suit, and it seemed to go with the outfit.

I already knew the dress code at Boston College. They didn't allow casual clothing in those days, and required suits or sport coats, with ties. So students put together amazingly creative combinations to meet the code, without concern for how colors or patterns matched. It was not unusual to wear a plaid flannel shirt under the sport coat, with an outrageous tie.

I was about to pull the string and extinguish the ceiling light in my room when I thought, I better double-check my financial situation. I'd be off to a great start if I got all the way over to Chestnut Hill and found out I left half my tuition dough home.

Flipping open my wallet, I examined its contents and nodded my head. Yup, it's all here. Enough for my first quarter's tuition and books. But I was crazy as hell to lend my father that dough last spring. I worked like a dog saving that money. It's a good thing I didn't let him have the whole five hundred, like he wanted me to. I'd be out like Strout. All he sends me yesterday is a hundred and a big snowjob about sending the other two hundred later on.

He's a great note writer though. He doesn't pay all the dough back like he promised, but he tells me I have all the brains in the family and he wishes me luck at B.C. Shit, if I had any brains I wouldn't have given him the dough. I'll be lucky if I ever get the rest of it. I guess Granny's got him figured when she says he can't hold onto a nickel. Him and his damn motor court. And it isn't even really his. It's in that woman's name. Some day maybe you'll smarten up, Tommy, and you won't be such a damned pushover.

I yanked the light string, out went the unshaded light bulb, and I went down the dark narrow stairs singing softly, "When skies are cloudy and gray they're only gray for a day. So wrap your troubles in dreams, and dream your troubles away."

In the hallway below, I took a last look at myself in the distorted, silver-streaked mirror built into the monstrous baroque oak hat rack. Reasonably satisfied with my reflected appearance, I shouted, "See you later, Granny. I'm off to Boston College."

"What is it ye said?" She came shuffling into the living room.

"I said I'm taking off now for Boston College. I'll see you tonight."

She squinted at me and adjusted her round steel-rimmed eyeglasses. "Sure, it's the devil himself, all dolled up in the fancy clothes and going off with himself to the college in the high-powered car. Faith and ye don't have the price of a sandwich and ye look like you're living the life of Riley."

"Well, for your information, Granny, my clothes are from bargain basements and the old Plymouth's about the lowest-powered car in America. Hell, it's almost an antique."

"'Tis not nice to swear." She shook her head and put the crucifix of her beads to her lips. "The Lord have mercy on your immortal soul."

"Well, I have to get going now."

"When did ye say ye were coming back?"

"Tonight."

"Oh, it's not a place where ye stay there all week. Is it like the high school?"

"Not exactly, Granny. It's a college where some guys live in dormitories but most of us live at home. I'm what they call a commuter."

"Sure I only went to the sixth grade in the old country. Little do I know about the high schools and the colleges or anything else nowadays. It's all a conundrum is what it is."

"Yup, it's a conundrum. I have to get going. See you later." I went toward the door.

"Safe journey to ye then, and safe home." Her swollen-jointed fingers manipulated the rosary beads in her hands as she moved toward the front window of the parlor.

I went outside, and was about to go down the steps of the cement porch when the door on the other side of the duplex swung open. "Hey, Tommy." It was Uncle Bill.

"Whatayasay, Bill? How come you aren't over at your boiler room?"

He came outside and grabbed me by the shoulder, shook me a little, and pumped my hand. "I just wanted to give you a little send-off, Tommy. It isn't every day an O'Connell goes to college. You're the first one." His large rugged hand squeezed mine like a steel pliers.

"Save the hand, Bill, I might need it some day." A mist came into my eyes because my uncle's good will gesture had surprised me. Then, to make matters worse, the doorway of the other side of the duplex suddenly filled up with Aunt Rita and my cousins Billy, Bernie and Jimmy. My face grew very red and the mist in my eyes thickened. I was uncomfortable receiving displays of affection because I had been left to my own devices so much during my young life. It stunned me when it seemed that somebody cared about me, and I didn't know how to handle it.

"Good luck at college," said Rita. "I hope ya like it and do good there."

"Hooray for Tommy," yelled the three boys. "He's goin' to college."

I blushed. "I'm only a commuter. You'd think I was leaving forever or something. I'll be seeing all you characters tonight."

As I slid behind the wheel of the old Plymouth, Uncle Bill yelled, "Stick with the books and you're gonna be okay, kid."

I waved back at them and called out, "I just hope the old crate starts." When I pressed my foot down on the starter button, the engine coughed and turned over, and I breathed a sigh of relief. Shifting into first speed from neutral, I tried for a smooth motion so the gears wouldn't grind. But they ground anyhow.

Then I saw an almost imperceptible movement of the yellowed gauze parlor curtains. There she was, peering at me through her steel-rimmed spectacles, and waving her wrinkled arthritic hand. I could see Granny's shriveled lips quivering and forming the familiar words, "May the good Lord help ye on your way." I knew she probably could not see me clearly with her failing eyes, but I waved at her, and then I waved at Uncle Bill and his family, and as the old Plymouth began rolling along Walnut Place on my way to Boston College, my thoughts took on a life of their own.

Sometimes my relatives are really odd characters, but they mean well. It was sort of nice the way Bill came home and even kept the boys out of school so they could all wish me luck. I guess he thinks going to college is a pretty big deal. He's always been a little frustrated about not finishing high school. But he's a bright guy, and over at the Quincy School in his boiler room he even reads Shakespeare.

As I drove down the Walnut Street hill toward East Dedham Square, I recalled what Mom White had said to me when I visited 42 Mountain Avenue in Norwood a week earlier. "If ye want to get ahead in the world of today ye've gotta be college educated."

Yup. She really knows the score. No doubt about it. That's why she always kept drilling the need for education into our heads. "The good Lord helps them that helps themselves," she always used to say.

Well, I guess you can't really depend too much on anybody in this world except yourself. At least if you're in a screwy setup like mine. If I depended on my father to come across I'd be shit out of luck.

I hummed and sang for a while as I drove up High Street toward the VFW Parkway, and when I blended with the highway traffic, favoring the gas pedal so the car wouldn't buck, I wondered what it might have been like if my family had been more traditional; for example, having two parents and a fairly normal home situation. But I found it hard to picture, so I just shook my head.

Nope. I can't imagine what it'd be like if my mother wasn't over in the nut house like she's always been. I suppose if things were normal she'd be proud of me going to college. But what the hell's the use of thinking about something that can't happen? I don't have a normal family, so I'm a lone wolf, and that's all there is to it.

Brother, it sure is weird thinking about her being in that asylum all these years though. I wonder if I should go over and see her sometime. I've got my own car now, and I could go there any time, but it'd probably kill me to see her cooped up in that loony hatch. Anyhow, I guess there's no point in going to see her because she wouldn't even know me.

The Plymouth rolled onward and I turned my thoughts away from my mother's status. Then, in a little while I was in Newton, at Chestnut Hill. I was really touched by awe as I saw Boston College's Gothic spires.

Stopping for the red traffic light near the tree-shaded gate, I thought, Well, here I am. This is it. Seems like I've been thinking about coming here forever. Whenever I thought of going to college I always thought of Boston College, no other one.

I followed the arrows to the parking lot near the Chestnut Hill Reservoir, and I found a spot for the old Plymouth. Then I shifted the transmission lever into reverse so the car would not roll down the slight incline while I was gone.

Moving faster than usual, I mounted the long steps leading to the plateau where the buildings were clustered. Then I went to the Registrar's Office, and the Bursar's Office, and picked up my class schedule, a book list, and the receipt for my first quarter's tuition. After that, in the basement of the College of Business Administration, I found the bookstore and got all my required texts.

Then I left that building because I was not a business major. I was a liberal artist, not a business type. My first class, Theology, was in the Tower Building where most of the Arts and Sciences classes were held. A&S was the oldest curriculum, and it seemed fitting that it was held in the oldest Gothic building, which looked very much like a medieval church.

On my way across the open space between the buildings, I examined the new Philosophy Building that would soon complete the long awaited quadrangle. It was not quite finished, and my attention was drawn to an inscription over the archway I would be walking through in the years ahead. With my back to the Science Building and Business Administration, I read, "You will come to know the truth and the truth will set you free."

Yes, that's what education is all about. The truth. This is where I'll learn the truth about all kinds of things. It'll be worth all the waiting and all the scrounging for tuition money. Uh-oh. My receipt. Where is it? I'll need it to get admitted into class.

I leaned over, placed my new books gently on the grass, and began to fish my pockets. Then came a sigh of relief. The valuable yellow slip was safe in my inside suit coat pocket.

Guess I better put this slip in my wallet, I thought as I kneeled to retrieve my books. Without it I'll be shafted. One thing I don't want is a screwed-up first day at B.C. Oops, I better not kneel too hard on this grass. It'll be a long time before I can afford another suit, and I don't need grass stains on this one.

Soon I was seated in Theology, with no grass stains on the knees of the light blue suit, and my Bursar's receipt safe in my wallet. All else seemed to be in order.

"As sons of Boston College," the priest began his introductory lecture, "you should hold your heads erect and walk with confident steps. Jesuit colleges such as Boston College have produced countless scholars and poets, scientists and authors, jurists and generals, heads of states, Popes, and yes, canonized saints and blessed martyrs of God. My good young men, believe me, yours is a noble heritage."

A noble heritage, I thought. Yup, that's what it is. No doubt about it. The Scholastic tradition goes way the hell back in history.

"Open your minds now, young men," he urged. "Absorb what Boston College offers. You have at your own disposal a distillation of the wisdom of the ages. We are here to develop the whole man, and we want to expand your souls while we broaden your intellects. Our motto is 'Religioni et Boni Artibus,' meaning that we are dedicated to religion and the fine arts. We will offer you a truly liberal education. We will surround you with theology and philosophy and the classics, and we will immerse you in history and literature, language and science. In four years, when you leave these portals, those of you who stay on with us will be well-rounded and very well educated human beings. You will also be better Christians."

That's what I'm here for, I thought. That's why I've been scrounging and saving and working my ass off at the cruddy Boston Envelope Company.

After a brief lecture on the origins of the Catholic Faith, a review of the course syllabus, and a summary of the details of our first Theology assignment, the priest excused us and I soon found myself in a class on Humanistic Poetry.

After welcoming us to Boston College, Mister Folkard, one of the few lay professors, asked us to open our books to "Invictus." Then he took us on a tour of the words and lines of the poem. As he talked, I related much of the message to my own life.

He intoned, "I thank whatever Gods may be for my unconquerable soul." Yup, that's a good line. My unconquerable soul. Well, almost unconquerable. I can certainly screw things up sometimes.

"In the fell clutch of circumstance I have not winced nor cried aloud." Well, I guess I wince a little when I get shafted. I'm not exactly stoic.

"Under the bludgeonings of chance my head is bloody but unbowed." I've been bludgeoned a little but I'm still in one piece. I don't exactly have it made like lots of guys at B.C. with their folks paying their tuition, but I'll make out, and I'll probably appreciate my education more than they do.

". . . and yet the menace of the years finds and shall find me, unafraid." Seems like everybody runs a little scared. But as long as you don't give up the ship, that's all that counts.

"It matters not how strait the gate, how charged with punishments the scroll. I am the master of my fate; I am the captain of my soul." That's like what Mom White says. "It's every man for himself." If you get screwed up it's usually your own fault. Like me lending my father most of my savings. I was taking my chances and I knew it. So I've learned another lesson, I hope.

When the English class was over, I spotted a familiar face in the group that was crowding toward the hallway. "Hey, aren't you from Dedham?"

"Right. I'm Ozzie Curtin and I live right near the Dedham-Boston line."

"I thought so. I'm Tommy O'Connell."

We shook hands, exchanged a few ideas on our first Theology class, and then I asked him about his name. "My real name's John, but I was stuck with Ozzie in grammar school. I think they got it from the Wizard of Oz."

"Hah. That's show biz."

"Yup, that's show biz." Ozzie grinned.

"What's your next class, Ozzie?"

"History with Mister Daly."

"Me too. I guess we're in the same group."

He told me our Theology professor was infamous for his final grades. "He can be cruel."

I shrugged my shoulders. "The way I see it is if a guy studies, he should make out okay even with a hard marker."

Ozzie nodded. "That's the way I think too." We reached the main corridor and Ozzie said, "I have to see the Dean about a scholarship I won last year at B.C. High, so I'll be a few minutes late for class."

"Oh, you went to B.C. High? I went to Dedham High . . . class of '49."

"Mm. I was class of fifty. Where'd you go last year? To prep school?"

"Sure. I studied full-time at the Boston Envelope Company for a year. That was my prep school."

"You worked there? Really? Most of us came out of B.C. High or some other Catholic prep school."

"I think maybe I was born to be different."

Ozzie replied, "There's something to be said for being different. It makes life interesting. I better get going, Tommy. See you later. By the way, do you have a car?"

"It's more of a conversation piece than a car."

"Can you give me a lift back to Dedham later?"

"Sure, if you don't mind risking your life."

"Well, I'll take a chance." He laughed. "It'll be an exercise in faith. Besides, nothing ventured nothing gained . . . to coin a phrase. See you after our History class."

"Okay. Stay out of trouble, Oz."

"I'll try."

As I headed along the dimly lit corridor with its dark mahogany paneling, I thought about how good it was to make a new friend right away. Oh boy, what was his last name? Yup, Curtin. Ozzie Curtin.

Let me see now. I've got a few minutes to kill before History. Maybe I should make a visit to the chapel. What the hell, why not? Brother, I better lay off the swearing. It's not exactly a sign of culture.

The sky was clear and cloudless as I left the Tower Building and its Gothic architecture. While strolling along the sidewalk under the linden trees my mind was open and eager, and my soul was calm. I entered the small dark chapel in St. Mary's Hall, and genuflected. Since I was the only person there at that moment, I had my choice of seats. Then I placed my books down in a handy spot, and kneeled to pray.

I crossed myself and said three Our Father's, three Hail Mary's, and three Glory Be To The Father's. The banks of blue and red votive candles on each side of the altar flickered as I kneeled there, and prismatic rays of sunlight beamed on me through the stained-glass windows. Also, there was another kind of glow radiating from me at that moment. It was a glow of contentment, accompanied by a feeling of inner peace.

After finishing my prayer ritual, I sat silently in St. Mary's chapel thinking about the Latin mottoes that abounded at Boston College. Ad Majorem Dei Gloriam. A.M.D.G. "For the greater glory of God." Religioni et Boni Artibus. "Religion and the Fine Arts." I could relate to these messages at depth. I knew I was in the right place.

That's the ticket. Boy, that's the way to go. The development of the whole man. The body and the soul. That's what I'm after. I guess that's what I'm alive for. I'm on a quest to find answers to my own questions, and I'll find them. I know I will. "Ask and you shall receive, seek and you shall find, knock and it shall be opened to you."

I think the answer is in the motto on the arch at the Philosophy Building: "You will come to know the truth and the truth will set you free." I've only been here a while and already I feel like I've found something very special. I've been set free to explore what I want to explore. And I think I'm on the verge of solving a riddle. The riddle of my own life.

I crossed myself, took my books, genuflected at the end of the pew, and moved from the darkness of the chapel into the brilliant sunlight There was a bounce in my step and a hint of a grin on my face as I strode under the linden trees and into the shadows cast by the Gothic spires of the Tower Building.

The feeling of peace that permeated my whole being was a little bit at odds with the usual me. In my psyche, anxiety was the most common feeling, no matter how much I tried to appear calm and unruffled, no matter how much I played the role of the confident lone wolf.

Climbing the wide granite steps leading into the old building that resembled a cathedral, I reached for the large iron ring that would open the massive oak door leading into the dimly lit corridor. As my hand touched the metal ring I paused and recalled the times when I had feared I would never get to B.C., and I remembered the times I had acted as if getting there made no difference to me at all.

As I began to pull on the ring I thought, Here I am, Boston College. I'm here to absorb what you've got to offer, and I'm here to expand my mind. I'm a college man now, and not a kid anymore. But I've always felt like more than a kid, haven't I?

Well, kid or no kid, college or no college, when you add it all up I guess I'll always be basically the same Tommy O'Connell anyhow, right?

Or will I?

The End

Epilogue

A half-century has passed since 1950, and the lives of the cast of characters who helped shape my early life have either changed considerably or have ended.

My father, Fred O'Connell, remained in Wells, Maine, and continued in the motor court business with Hazel while raising his second family of five daughters and a son. Eventually, I forgave him for his deficiencies and their impact on my early years. I came to realize that his self-centered approach to life when I was a child was not a personal affront to me, because he was not intentionally harming me. It became clear to me that any child who happened to be around during that stressful period in my father's life would have experienced similar treatment. Fred died in 1988 in his early eighties, and Hazel died a few years later.

Margaret Henderson O'Connell, my mother, was destined to spend the rest of her days at Boston State Hospital. The only time I was in her presence after early childhood was at her memorial service. She died during the time around 1970 when I was living in Maine, and her relatives traced me to let me know about her demise. It was a strange reunion, and I have not seen any of the relatives on her side of the family since that time.

Mrs. White, whose various slogans still ring in my ears, died of heart failure at about the age of 60 while I was a student at Boston College. When I visited her at Norwood Hospital before she died, she vehemently emphasized the importance of my higher education. A very intense person, she was not casual about her strong convictions. And she had a powerful way of getting her messages across. Those messages remain deep in my memory bank.

My grandfather, Dan O'Connell, died in his early eighties, also when I was at Boston College. Granny O'Connell attended Grandpa's wake and funeral, and that was the closest she had come to him during more than twenty years of marital separation, even though their homes were only about one mile apart. They were never divorced. As for Granny, she lived to her nineties, and was telling vivid stories until the day she died.

Dave Rothwell went on to college and medical school, became a surgeon first, and later attained eminence as a pathologist in Minnesota and Wisconsin. His brother Joe moved to California and took up a career in long distance telecommunications.

As adults, the Rothwells and I drifted apart as friends, except for annual Christmas cards. But I met Joe many years later during his visit to a sister in Massachusetts. His view of life with Mrs. White was about as negative as an impression can get. Years later, when I lived in Maine, Dave visited, and his view was that living with Mrs. White had not been a problem for him. My own view falls somewhere in the middle.

I can see that I experienced mental and physical abuse from her fierce temper and cruel punishments, but I also know she helped motivate me toward healthy educational and spiritual growth. So each of the three of us boys ended up with quite different impressions about our lives at Mrs. White's house. We were much like three people witnessing the same accident from very different vantage points.

Bob Resker, who opted to live with Mrs. White instead of returning to his own relatives, graduated from Boston College, went on for a Master's Degree in Business Administration at Babson College, and then developed a career as a manufacturers' representative. When Jim Dervan returned from the U.S. Navy, instead of living with his aunt one street away, he moved in with Mrs. White and attended Boston University. I knew him better as an adult than during my time at Mrs. White's. In his late thirties he decided to go into teaching, but right after achieving the educational credentials he needed, he had a heart attack and died before reaching age 40.

Mrs. White's son Tom, a Boston College graduate who inspired me to aim for B.C., went on to graduate school for a Master's Degree, and became a teacher and guidance counselor in the Newton, Massachusetts school system. There his fundamental kindness and compassion provided a favorable influence on many young lives.

As for my pals, Fran went to Boston College after serving in the Navy, and then carved out a productive career with the federal government. Mike went to Boston University, and later had his own construction company. Johnny chose a career as school custodian.

Following Boston College, John "Ozzie" Curtin went to B.C. Law School and eventually rose to president of Boston Bar Association and then president of American Bar Association.

What about my life? Well, I didn't replace Bing Crosby as the superstar of the world of vocalists. My singing primarily takes place in the shower, and that's enough.

I graduated from Boston College *cum laude*, after interrupting my studies following my junior year to get married first and then to spend two years as a voluntary "draftee" in the U.S. Army. On discharge, the G.I. Bill of Rights helped me to complete my Bachelor of Arts Degree in History and Government. After Boston College, I chose to continue my liberal arts education at Boston University Graduate School where I earned my Master of Arts Degree in History.

During my marriage of nearly 30 years to Mary Killoren, we had three wonderful daughters and one wonderful son together. Currently, we have nine beautiful grandchildren and a great-granddaughter. We lived in Georgia while I served in the U.S. Army there, and except for a few years in Ogunquit, Maine, most of our family life was centered in Dedham. Eventually, I was motivated to run for political office, and won a seat on the Dedham School Committee. After two years I was elevated to the post of chairman, which seemed to me to be quite a distance from my origins on "the other side of the tracks" in East Dedham. It symbolized my own upward mobility.

In the world of work, I served for several years with Amica Insurance as an investigator of accidents on the highways and in the home. I went on to the accident prevention field and rose to the post of CEO of the Massachusetts Safety Council, was a member of the Governor's Highway Safety Committee, and also served as executive director of three other important organizations in the fields of public housing, the auto industry, and long-term health care.

In 1978, based on mystical urges, my lone wolf psyche motivated me to leave the world of executive leadership at age 46 to pursue a more independent path. I set out on a spiritual journey that led me into a very enlightening relationship with God. Some describe it as "cosmic consciousness." In an interesting twist of fate, I experienced a mystical "mountain" experience a few decades after living for nine years on "Mountain" Avenue as a child.

Along the way, I served as a freelance writer, mass media specialist, and communications consultant with health and human service agencies. In a professional affiliation, I rose to the post of president of American Medical Writers Association, New England Chapter. In addition, at Boston's Channel 25 I created and hosted my own weekly TV public affairs show, "It's Your Life." The show ran for three years and gave me the opportunity to interview spiritual leaders and many others in lives of service.

Working as a freelance journalist, I served for eight years as a national correspondent for The U.S. Journal of Drug and Alcohol Dependence. I covered the northeastern part of the United States, attending major conferences and seminars where the experts provided insights into addictive disease, which I consider the world's major public health problem.

From 1986 to 1998, I wrote a weekly freelance column, "On Addiction," for The Cape Cod Times. Then I did a weekly health & lifestyle column online for Cape Cod Journal (1999-2000). Recently, I have written freelance health columns for The Cape

Codder. Also, at Cape Cod Community Media Center, I created and hosted the TV series "Understanding Addiction."

For many years here on Cape Cod I have operated as an independent writer, lecturer, and educator. Serving as an adjunct faculty member in Language and Literature at Cape Cod Community College, I teach writing and act as a tutor/mentor and advisor. Being part of this educational community has been a very rewarding experience. I enjoy the freedom of working there part of the week and pursuing my own lone wolf activities during the balance of my time.

In recognition of various activities, I was listed in the 1995-1996 edition of *Who's Who in the East*. Considering my early years, I found this invitation quite interesting. Also, in its recent 25th Anniversary Collector's Edition, Cape Cod Life Magazine selected me as one of the "Top 100 Influential" people on Cape Cod, based on my journalism.

Recently, I have developed my own publishing enterprise, Sanctuary Unlimited. My Website address is www.sanctuary777.com, and my various books are listed there, with excerpts. Also found there is *Lifestyle Journal*, my online publication where about 200 of my essays on addiction and mental health are available as a public service resource for people who wish to further their knowledge of these subjects.

For twenty years I have been a member of the Secular Franciscan Order, which is also called the Third Order of Saint Francis. This spiritual affiliation helps inspire me to try to practice the kind of Christian principles that motivated Francis of Assisi, who was called "the mirror of Christ." In other words, I am trying to live a God-centered life "in the world," while not being caught up in the materialism of the world. My blessings are many, including a wonderful family, loving friends, caring colleagues, and a vast assortment of friendly acquaintances.

Also, I receive a continuing education in spiritual matters through a Unitarian Universalist fellowship. This helps me to broaden my spiritual perspective. To those who might wonder how I bridge the gap between Catholic and Unitarian approaches,

I can only say that I believe in a loving God whose Spirit has no limits and boundaries. The God of my understanding is the kindly parent of all people and loves them all unconditionally.

On reflection, I believe my lone wolf mentality has served me well in various occupations where I played either a leadership role or operated as a freelance journalist, editorial consultant, educator, and lecturer. More importantly, the lone wolf psyche has led me into a more comfortable relationship with my own spirit and a close relationship with the God of Love.

That's about it for now. The daily adventure of life goes on. Good luck. God bless you.

(You are invited to visit www.sanctuary777.com and either leave your comments about this book in our Guest Book or email us. The comments may be used in our advertising.)

Other Books by Tom O'Connell
Published by Sanctuary Unlimited

_____Improving Intimacy: 10 Powerful Strategies—*A Spiritual Approach.*

A look at spiritually based intimacy, addictive relating, control, listening, communication, conflict. *"Positive . . . powerful . . . very readable style."—Cape Cod Times "It's the finest example of anyone writing on this subject."—Don LaTulippe, WPLM, Plymouth.*

_____The Odd Duck: A Story for Odd People of All ages

A cheerful, inspiring fable for all "adult children." A lost duck raised in a chicken coop feels odd. After an identity crisis, she begins a quest for self-worth and healthy, lasting love. *"A cheerful, punning little allegory mostly for grownups." (Bostonia Magazine) "a parable for spiritual reawakening . . ." (Seniors Cape Cod Forum).*

_____Danny The Prophet: A Fantastic Adventure

An unforgettable novel about a man reluctant to be God's last prophet. A trip into another dimension with a politician, a sage, an angel, perilous adventures, and divine revelations. *Readers' comments: "Wow!" "Astounding!" "Funny!" "A wonderful book!" "A pleasure to read!" "Imaginative!"*

_____The Monadnock Revelations: A Spiritual Memoir

The true story of Tom's mystical journey. He reports on unusual experiences of other dimensions of reality, including what is often described as Cosmic Consciousness. *Readers' comments: "Encourages, energizes and inspires . . ." "It warmed my heart and inspired my soul." "A treasury of inspiration." "Extremely visionary, well written, inspiring . . . a great book." "I loved it!"*

_____Addicted? A Guide to Understanding Addiction

This is a useful, practical, educational guide that explains addiction's causes, effects, recovery process, relapse, prevention. It covers alcohol, nicotine, other drugs, food, gambling, sex ; discusses women's issues, co-dependency, and world outlook. *"provides a wealth of information . . . fills a long-standing void . . . is highly readable . . . should make an important contribution to any curriculum . . . You have done the job remarkably well. Congratulations!"—Blaise Gambino, Ph.D., Director of Research & Education, Gambling Program, Center for Addiction Studies, Harvard Medical School, The Cambridge Hospital.*

Read excerpts from Tom's books at
www.sanctuary777.com